Scatter

Terry Hayman

Fiero Publishing

Contents

Prologue

2006

THE FIRST THIRD-YEAR PRESENTER today was Aaron Aristide. His paper was on how your memory of a face is affected by whether the face is from your own race or a different one. Aaron was born in Haiti. It made sense.

The second presenter, who's up in front of the class now, is Cherie Pascal. She's tossing her blond curls and cheerfully talking about how guessing where a moving object ends up depends on something called "representational momentum."

Really? Relevance to anything? Why are people laughing at her jokes?

I know she's smart, though. Grad level research. It's why I should probably be paying more attention, except...

I'm next.

Yes, you are, Jackson. And they're going to kill *you.*

No, I can do this. I'm ready.

You're a string bean coward, loser, nothing. You get up there and...

Shut up! I. Can. Do. This.

Look at their faces. They're thugs! Like the ones who cut up your brother's face back in Renton. Made you watch.

This is absolutely nothing like—

It's exactly *the same. Laughing at you. Attacking you.*

It's not. It's not. It's not.

But my fingers start to quiver, tap-tapping the cue cards rhythmically on my desk to shut out the conversation in my head. I don't need the cards, of course. I never need cards. I have total recall without trying. But having the cards when I walk to the front of the class will make me look *normal*, less of a freak, less likely to get attacked. Maybe.

Oral presentation. Half our grade.

And I need this class.

Cherie Pascal stops speaking. She's done. All the students around me are applauding, even though I bet not half of them followed what she was saying. That will become obvious now when they try to ask question and...

For some reason, Cherie looks at me like she expects *me* to ask something.

My jaw clenches tight and I hold my breath. *Don't look at me! You must know I hate this. DON'T LOOK AT ME!*

I feel a hand on my arm. Jude, my one friend here, sitting at the desk beside me. He whispers, "Doing okay?"

I nod.

But even though it's Jude, I can't look at him. Can't speak. My mouth has dried up. The sterile, cream-colored walls of this University of Illinois classroom have sucked the moisture out of me even as they've retained every sour particle of horny/scared/bored/tired sweat from the college kids around me.

My own beads of sweat pop out all over my face and neck.

This is not good.

My PTSD expresses itself mostly in social anxiety, but never *this* bad.

What's happening?

What's...?

I turn to look at Jude. His round, caring face is squinching in concern.

My breath pushes up higher in my chest.

Cherie finishes and the class applauds. Out of the corner of my eye, I see Professor Tavish nodding her gray-haired head and turning to look at me. They're *all* looking at me. Every student in this class. Because I've never stood up in front of them. I just do my work. Keep my head down. I discuss things with Jude if I talk with anyone. Can't avoid it. He's my roomie.

Do not go up there.

Do not. You'll be trapped. Caught.

This isn't just anxiety, Jackson. It's death!

And all of a sudden, I'm finding it hard to breathe. My heart is racing. My head and skin are so hot I want to scratch my way out of them.

"Jackson?" Jude whispers beside me.

I'm on my feet. Turning. Blinking hard as I walk from the room. *Don't run. Don't trip.*

"Mr. Traine?" Tavish calls me from behind.

Then I'm free of the door and running, tripping, dropping my cue cards so they go fluttering to the polished stone floors. I scrabble to my feet, gasping for air, and leave my cards behind as I run for the stairs at the end of the hall. A fire escape.

"Aaghh. Agh. Agh," I grunt as I run.

I make the fire escape, go through the doors into the dank funnel of concrete and metal railings, and fight the urge to crash down here in a heap.

No. Escape. Run. RUN!

I pound up the stairs. One flight. Two. Three. Four... My heart's pounding so hard now I'm sure my head's going to explode.

I finally make the top where there's an exit to the forbidden rooftop of the University of Illinois Psych building, nine floors above ground level. I twist down the handle and shove. Locked!

No, just stuck.

On my third shove, the door grates open and I burst outside, only to get shoved back against the closing door by an icy November wind. Must have whipped down from Lake Superior in the last hour, roaring over a hundred miles of Illinois flatland to batter the campus with snow and ice. I push my skinny body off the door and stagger into that winter wind with my mouth open in a grimace, letting pellets of snow tear into my cloth coat and whip my long hair around my face, trying to blind me, blast me into a thousand pieces.

I feel an insane urge to push through it to and throw myself onto the wide panel of windows that covers the long plunge of the open atrium.

You didn't catch me! I got away! I'd scream.

I.

Got.

Away!

But I can't even force myself off the wall. My whole body feels like it's going to burst apart. I crumple to my side on the snowy concrete and curl up like a baby, shivering in the cold even though I'm burning up inside. My eyes are streaming. I'm blind with pain and an unidentifiable terror that is always with me, but now out in the open, all around me. Kicking me. Beating me like Dead Eyes did 44 months and 16 days ago in that chop shop after they'd cut up Kenny and dragged him away.

I writhe and shiver on and on until the chimes from Altgeld Hall start their 11:50 chimes two blocks northeast of me.

End of class. End of my GPA. End of my future.

The chimes of the McFarland Bell Tower, the Eye of Sauron, start in from the south quad, clashing, blending, pounding into my head until I'm sure I'm going to puke.

I choke out a gargling scream and try to stuff my fists into my mouth, tasting blood.

Then I hear my name shouted by the wind, over and over—*Jackson! Jackson! Come on! I'm here!*—like it's a real thing, so I have to unscrew my eyes and look...

"Jackson! Good! You see me. Take a deep breath. Come on, buddy. Come on."

It's Jude Spiegelman again. My curly-haired roomie. Only real friend in the world other than my big sister.

He's kneeling over me, doughy hands on my shoulders, shaking me. Patting me. Trying to bring me back. Make me breathe.

Breathe.

Breathe!

Until finally I do. Finally coming down. Gasping. Unclenching. My whole body clenches and unclenches with rough, ugly sobs that scrape my whole insides on their way out.

"It's okay, dude," Jude is saying. "It's okay."

He pulls me up from the ground into his arms, even though I'm almost a foot taller than him. But he's all plushy while I'm the dirty-blond ghost. Losing weight because I can't sleep or eat right. When I close my eye lately, it's just Kenny caught up in drugs, dumped at hospitals, carved up by Cutter.

I'm right there! And here. Every bad place.

I clutch Jude's puffy coat and pull myself into his chest.

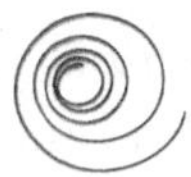

Forty minutes later, Jude's calmed me down and we walk down together to talk with Professor Colleen Tavish.

With still-trembling hands, I hand her my paper so she can read it through slowly, then grill me on it. I find this surprisingly bearable because she doesn't look at me once. She's got thick glasses and ropy gray hair that falls around her face as she leans down to within inches of my paper to read it. It's like I'm looking at another version of myself, someone who's so afraid of personal connection and judgement that they'd rather curl up in a hole and hide than look into your eyes.

And it strikes me that if she's like this, and still got her Ph.D., published leading research on the effects of spousal abuse on cognition and emotional regulation, *and* can teach classes to college kids, then maybe there's a way forward for me as well.

I mean, until now, I've just pushed forward, determined to ignore my increasing PTSD and anxiety. I managed my first two years here with only a few incidents. But that was by operating in an emotional freeze, shutting most of the world out. Jude's been the only person I really speak to. And only because we share a dorm room, half of our classes, and a lot of life interests, if not backgrounds.

Professor Tavish is still reading, so here's Jude's background versus mine.

He comes from a close Jewish family in Chicago that he still visits every weekend. His mom is Eema. His grandpa's Saba. His aunt is Dohda. So much love.

Me, I grew up in Renton, just south of Seattle, with a nanny and two older siblings, Kenny and Kansas. Our parents were never around because they were always traveling, looking after their building supplies franchisees.

When I was seventeen, Kenny started self-medicating his bipolar condition with drugs and got dragged into a street gang called the Demon Monks, I think for his crazy memory as much as anything. I was always trying to pull him out. The last time, the Demon Monks' leader, a guy called "Cutter," made me watch while he carved a D and M into

Kenny's screaming face, one letter per cheek. Then they dragged Kenny away and beat me near senseless, promising to kill Kenny and the rest of my family if I ever talked about any of it.

So I didn't.

Eventually, like my big sister and parents, I accepted Kenny was dead.

I froze it all inside my gut, ran here to UIUC, south of Chicago, and eventually started having random pains that still affect my gait and gut, and make it hard to enjoy simple campus stuff like cruising Green Street, bowling, or watching movies on the quad. Then there's my social anxiety. It preexisted what happened to Kenny, but blew up in a big way in the years following. So whether the trauma caused it or just made it worse, it's all tied together, you know? PTSD is a complicated stew of clammy hands, tight guts, and now, I guess, panic attacks.

I've read about all the treatments that can reduce the intensity of the flashbacks and emotions attached to them. There's CBT, meditation, Rapid Eye Movement therapy, drugs, other stuff.

But here's the thing—and this is critical to understand—memories never fade or change for me. Kansas, Kenny, and I were born with crazy freak memories. When I see/feel/taste/touch/smell something, it sticks in my brain with near-perfect clarity for pretty much forever, as far as I can tell.

Jude calls it a blessing, but—

"What makes you discount the legitimacy of memory suppression?" Tavish growls at me without looking up from my paper.

The lack of eye contact lets my mouth, dry as it is, work up enough moisture to unstick my tongue and speak. "I've put all my citations at the end."

"Name one and what it shows."

"Okay." I think for a second and start with Elizabeth Loftus and her work on false memory syndrome. But because I recognize holes in her arguments, I continue on with the research of LL Kondora, SM Park, KS Pope, WE Hovdestad and CM Kristiansen, J Kitzinger, and a bunch more that I didn't have room to discuss in my paper even though they illustrated the different study approaches done in Europe vs. America, implanted memories, confabulation vs. true amnesia, and the political movements that shaped how the courts have treated "recovered" memories at trial in different time periods, and...

"Mr. Traine."

I stutter to a stop, blinking, seeing Jude giving me a lopsided smile and tapping his watch. Professor Tavish is still looking down at my paper, not at me. But I need to answer. "Uh...excuse me?"

"What did you write on the third line of page four?" Tavish asks.

I blink again. "It starts in the middle of a sentence. '...would be more persuasive if there was empirical evidence of disintegrating associations that...'"

"Yes?" prompts Tavish.

"You want me to continue with the next line?"

"What did you have for lunch on January five, two thousand and one?"

I frown and almost physically feel my eyes dart back and forth, which is a common human trait in someone looking to retrieve an old memory, searching for the visual image. In my case, though, it's because I'm clicking through the age associations. That date, Jan 5, 2001, I'm fourteen years old. Kenny's turning eighteen in another four days. Mom and Dad are out in Wyoming and aren't expected back until a few days after Kenny's birthday. They don't know that Kenny just dropped out of school and is already battling a major heroin addiction. So...four days back from that awful birthday. It's...Friday, forty-five degrees and raining outside the school cafeteria. My friend Jenelle Washington just said something about a guy called Michael Douglas Wilk who went missing on Monday, and I'm about to eat...

"It's alright, Mr. Traine. I was just—"

"Leftover Kraft Dinner. I'd made it on Tuesday with all the broccoli we still had in the fridge added in, plus extra cheese and some garlic powder to make it interesting. I also had a mandarin orange. The second last one we had from the holidays."

There is a long beat of silence. I can hear Professor Tavish breathing. And smell it. She has coffee breath. She says, "Of course, there is no way to verify any of that."

I frown and rattle of what day of the week it was, the weather, the stories and comics I remember reading in the newspaper that my parents had delivered to our house, even though they were rarely there.

Tavish clears her throat. "Yes. Yes." A long beat of silence. "Would you be willing to...take part in a study, Mr. Traine?"

My heart rate, which decelerated to normal from the simple process of me focusing just on my studies and the specific memory challenges, now shoots up through the roof as I realize what I've done, how I've exposed myself to someone who can understand how truly freakish I am.

I will not get caught like Kenny!

Almost like I said it out loud, Professor Tavish raises her head and squints at me through her thick glasses. "Or not," she growls quietly. "No. Of course not." She lowers her head. "You've been studied before. It must be hard, living in so many realities at one time."

Especially bad ones! I want to burst out. But I have to work my tongue around the instantly sticky inside of my mouth to answer. "Yes."

Tavish nods and sighs. She pushes my paper away from me on her desk and sits back in her chair, looking into her lap almost like she wants to take a nap.

Jude speaks. "Professor? Are things alright with Jackson's paper? His grade?"

She jerks her head up again, this time to squint at Jude. "Of course. Stellar work, quite apart from the..." She waves her hand in my direction but avoids looking at me. "If you ever want a referral for your graduate work, Mr. Traine, I'd be honored. You have something powerful that could change our fundamental understandings of memory and time. Do the world a lot of good." She grimaces. "Or give us one more way to tear it apart."

Then she drops her chin to her chest again, and it's clear we're dismissed.

That night, sitting in front of our shared TV and playing *Call of Duty 2*, we finish a Deathmatch multiplayer in which we each carried a decent KDR of 15 and 12 for Jude and me respectively, when Jude puts down his controller and turns to me in his ridiculously battered cloth swivel chair.

"You know who would *kill* to get your memory working for them?" he says.

"Sure. The mob. Or the Chinese triads. I could keep all their contacts and numbers in my head so they'd never have to write them down."

Jude snorts. "Dude, seriously. Someone should make a movie like that."

"Make me a little girl forced to work to protect my family. Have Jason Statham rescue me. I'd watch it!"

"But you know who'd really love your memory? Seriously?"

"Who?"

"The CIA."

"For what? Like spying?"

"I don't know. Or analysis. You know, like taking in endless reams of shit and seeing the connections."

"That's not memory. That's more like...cognitive synthesis or something."

"Or languages. I bet you could learn a dozen languages like that." He snaps his fingers.

"You're missing the big picture, dude."

Jude raises his eyebrows, which makes his very round face look like one of those emoji-things people are using on their phones.

"C'mon. You were up on the roof with me," I say. "You've seen me falling apart for the last couple of months. Remembering everything is *not* a blessing."

"Um, yeah." Jude's face is solemn. Really listening. No judgement. He's what I want to become. "Figured you'd tell me what was going on at some point."

"At some point. But...let's just say I'm going to be lucky just to get through uni, you know?"

Jude smirks. "What's your GPA so far?"

"Doesn't help if I have more of what happened today."

"Counseling, dude. I'll walk you over and sign you in myself. Bet your folks won't even ask what the extra money's for."

"I don't need—"

"Yeah, you do." He's dead serious again. "Like you said. I was up on the roof. I know a panic attack when I see one. Add the nightmares and hiding. Whatever you're remembering, and I'm guessing it's something about your family you won't tell me, and that's cool, you need help, dude. You know you do."

I reluctantly nod, but inside I'm thinking that I will never let someone get so deep into my head they have power over me. I saw what that did with Kenny.

Jude nods, picks up his controller, and selects an offline game—just us against the machine. As he waits for me to follow, he says, "When you get all your shit together, dude? Figure out how to use what you got? There are gonna be a lot of people wanting to work with you."

"On my terms or theirs?"

"Always your choice, right?"

"We'll see."

I click start.

1

Trained for combat

2022

January 1, 2022. Early morning.

I ran loosely around the snow-covered, mostly deserted running track of Garfield High School, Seattle. My spiked running cleats crunched the packed snow and my breath came out in puffs of frost as I stared into the turn.

Bear down. Don't slip.

Ahead of me, standing by the bleachers in a tracksuit and winter coat, was my "coach," Ryan Renn, AKA Smiley. He was the one choosing when I sprinted and how long I got to recover. He was drinking a coffee and grinning at my approach, the bastard. While I'd been out here for an hour now, stretching, warming up, then jogging, running intensely, jogging again...

"Ready for another, Professor?" he called out as I passed.

"If you do it with me this time!" I yelled back.

I figured that gave me at least one more cool down lap.

Maybe.

Smiley didn't have a lot of sympathy for my pain. He didn't care about tapering me off for some competition or trying to keep things fun, just increasing my odds of survival. He was the youngest of four former Rangers, now Lead the Way Security Group, whom my girlfriend Lena had hired to protect and train me.

The idea was, if I kept trying to find my brother Kenny—like I'd done last March when I discovered he was somehow alive but held captive—I'd last longer against whatever forces tried to stop me.

In March, those forces had been the Demon Monks, still led by Cutter. I only survived because I first met Lena, whose work exploring closed timelike curves had triggered an ability in me to time travel ten minutes backward in time when I was sufficiently threatened or traumatized. It wiped out any physical wounds I'd experienced in those ten minutes, but not the mental ones, the *experience*. The rebound of my PTSD symptoms after I got out of the hospital had been...ugly.

It had just about driven Lena away at the time—the screaming nightmares and flashbacks, the paranoid hallucinations of seeing a balding man in glasses and trench coat watching me everywhere I went.

Lena and I had met and fallen in love when I had simple social anxiety. This was another whole level of crazy.

And she was already dealing with her mom having just died of COVID and her father refusing to deal with the estate.

And all my suffering made me decide to renounce my time traveling rather than doing what Lena wanted, which was to tell the Lead the Way team about it so they could help me control the ability. Instead, I told them that human time travel wasn't real, as far as I knew, and whatever Lena had told them about me was a delusion brought on by her research.

Lena exploded in rage.

Alvin Westor, the leader of the LTW team and former boyfriend of Lena, began finding ways to physically terrorize me in my combat training with him to get me to time travel. If he hadn't been such an incredible instructor all the rest of the time, and if all the training I was getting from him, Smiley, and the other two, Big and Doc, hadn't been actually bringing me out of my PTSD cluster faster than ever before, *even with Alvin's terrorizing*, I would have walked.

Instead, I stuck it out.

Alvin proved out his nickname, "Shadow," by actually managing to scare me into two different time jumps—once with a gunshot (blank?) to my face, once by throwing me off a building. But he'd never know he had. All he or anyone saw when I jumped back was my momentary disorientation in my earlier body, then a forceful way of diverting Alvin from doing whatever he'd done the first time around.

"Hey!"

There was a set of thudding sounds and hard breathing as Smiley caught up to me on my right and matched my pace on the track. Grinning, of course.

"Finished your coffee?" I said.

"Yummy in my tummy. Ready for another two hundred?"

"How many more? Alvin's teaching me knife fighting today, so..."

Smiley didn't answer for a moment, and I wondered if he and the others had noted Alvin's sometimes overly aggressive lessons with me. Realized I was asking to not get so tired out from running that I couldn't deal with them.

Knife fighting!

As we hit the back curve, Smiley said, "You want to know how many more sprints?"

"How many?"

"Until you beat me."

He surged ahead, and I automatically kicked it up, my right foot slipping on a piece of hard-packed snow underfoot before my cleats regained traction and let me tear after him.

200 meters.

My brain whirred as I ran.

World record time? 19.19 seconds, Usain Bolt, 2009.

Sixteen record holders earlier, not counting disputed events, it's 20.6 second, Andy Stanfield, 1951.

Just a quick little run.

So run.

I pump-pump-pump-pumped, staying over my toes, leaning just enough around the curve to fight the centrifugal force without having my toes slip out from under me on the packed snow, pacing it to let the lactic acid ease out of my muscles as I hit second 100 meters even as I tried to catch the red stripes of Smiley's track suit ahead of me.

He started slowing. Damn! I was a good fifteen meters back.

I kept going long enough to catch him and match him, calmed my breaths of lung-freezing air, let the lactic acid work out of my muscles as I loped along. In a real race, the runners would be slowing completely to walk it off now, congratulating themselves on their explosive punch and the conditioning that kept them going to the end.

Me, now, I was fighting not to grit my teeth, waiting for Smiley to take off again, leading me into my seventh sprint of this increasingly hellish session. But was going to catch Smiley next time. Because he might be a fucking ex-Ranger, but I was a fucking *psychologist* and *professor* who'd undergone more torture and loss than he'd ever—

He shot forward.
I took off after him.
Pump.
Drive.
Push it.
Do. Not. Tire.
Do. Not.
Catching him.
Catching him...
He slowed.
Damn it!

I couldn't even see the marks he was using for the 200-meter measurement, and I doubted he was 100 percent accurate each time. Of all the Lead-the-Way team, he was the most likely to shave things here and there if it gave him an edge.

But I had more determination, more—

He shot forward again, and I took off after him.

And lost that race as well.

Still, the distances between us when he slowed here getting shorter each time. And by our sixth race, where I'm sure our times were now well over forty seconds and we each were slipping badly on the turns, I pulled ahead before Smiley saw me and could pretend we'd hit 200.

I slowed to a gasping, rasping, lung-freezing trot, then a walk, my face body covered in rapidly freezing sweat, my legs shaking under me, half expecting Smiley to tell me to keep running.

He didn't. I looked back to see he'd dropped to his knees and thin-gloved hands in a pile of churned-up slush, his head hanging and his entire body heaving his middle up and down like his body needed to puke.

I staggered back to him, gave him a few beats to finish the dry heaves, then grabbed his raised hand and helped him to his feet.

He held onto my shoulders as he continued leaning forward, breathing hard and looking ill as he tried to recover himself.

"Goddamn it, professor," he said. "Dee-amn." And a few struggling breaths later, "How old you say you were?"

"Thirty-five."

"I knew that. Whew, you're fierce, homie."

"Motivated."

"Yup." He finally looked up at me and sweaty grin. "Working to win back the lady? Oh, Shadow's gonna have fun with you this morning."

After we both changed into street runners, Smiley drove his Mustang to the gym, tires slipping and sliding on the snowy backstreets. I followed carefully in my little blue Chevvy Bolt. The gym we drove to, La Tarantata, was a hole-in-the-wall boxing mecca for the local gang-bangers in the area. At least that was the impression I'd had the other times we'd come to this place to train. Lots of over-muscled guys with tats. Steamy warm. Nobody wearing masks or worried about social distancing despite the King County ordinances requiring both.

Cutter and his crew would have fit in nicely.

But when I slipped on my double-banded white N95 and walked in, I knew nobody would comment because they knew I was with the group of ex-Rangers in the far corner, whose biggest member, Kajika Bighouse, AKA Big, stood about six-foot-nine and looked like he could pick up any of the wannabe gangsters in here and snap them like twigs.

Ironically, Big was one of the sweetest, quietest, most peace-loving guys I'd ever met. His people were Makah (Salish for "generous with food") Indians. They called themselves *Kwih-dich-chuh-ahtx* which meant "the people who live by the rocks [or cape] and seagulls." Big's specialty on the Lead-the-Way team was communications. He did also happen to be the team's best sniper, which I'd been grateful for last year when he picked off half of Cutter's men with headshots to save Lena and me when I thought all was lost.

As Smiley and I wove our way through the dimly lit guys skipping rope or whapping speed bags, free-standing ones, and hanging heavies, I could pick out the other two members of Lead the Way—Alvin/Shadow and Kai Nishikawa/Doc. With them stood Lena and a shorter woman I didn't recognize.

The two women were the only ones wearing masks.

Even masked up, though, the Lena's Middle Eastern beauty and dusky poise caught me right in the gut and heart. It brought back every bad love song I'd ever heard about seeing your former lover. Not that we were *officially* over. But with all of Lena's trips back and forth to deal with her mother's estate and her anger at me over my refusal to time travel for the LTW team, we'd barely spoken in months. I kept hoping she'd come around. At least let me talk to her about it.

I guessed it was hard for her to even be in the same room with me.

She must have seen me, but she looked more interested in the long folding table beside her that held two upright Spring Water clear plastic barrels with spigots dispensing water than she did in me.

I touched her arm and she half-turned to me just so she could gesture to the woman who stood beside her.

"Jackson, this is Elizabeth Chan, an Amazon rep. Elizabeth, Jackson Traine. Or Doctor Traine. Professor Traine. Take your pick."

Lena's voice was flat, but her words felt like a slap. An Amazon rep? As improbable as it sounded, Lena had insisted it was Bezos' company that had funded her particle accelerator research just north of Seattle, the lab where I'd experienced my first jump back in time. Lena had committed to shutting the lab down after my big sister had told us a bunch of governments were looking to exploit whatever she found. Had Lena restarted it somehow? Was that what she'd been doing all these weeks I hadn't been able to reach her?

Before I could ask, the Amazon rep turned to me and briefly bowed her head. So I turned, forcing myself to actually look at her...and did a double-take.

The non-description "shorter woman" didn't do her justice. Elizabeth Chan's quiet, head-bowed demeanor diverted the casual gaze from the promise of sublime beauty. Mid-to-late twenties, slim, and barely five-five in heels, her large almond eyes had a dark symmetry above the line of her stylishly patterned medical mask. Her hair was as jet-black and smooth as her eyes. Her skin had the pallor of a new moon.

She met my eyes and gave me a shy nod of greeting, then extended a hand. I clasped it, surprised to feel a dry, warm strength. Almost of command.

The contradictions grew when I saw that her other hand had also extended, offering a business card.

"I'm very pleased to meet you," she said, her voice low and Oxford British. Meaning standard English, received pronunciation. Stiffer lips but a clear click on the R.

I looked from her hand, still holding mine, to the proffered business card, to her eyes, and thought I caught a twinkle of laughter there. An enigmatic smile. Only after I took the business card did she release my hand and turn back toward Lena as if I had ceased to exist.

Fascinating.

That breath of discovery changed on a dime when I realized Elizabeth Chan had turned to listen to the quiet conversation Lena was having with Alvin Westor. Maybe about how best to scare the shit out of me one more time to make me perform.

One more time.

Dance, monkey!

With a blaze of frustration, I stuffed Elizabeth Chan's card into my coat pocket and raised my voice to be heard over the sound of some new guy whapping a speed bag nearby. "Are we doing this here or in the back?"

By the back, I meant La Tarantata's second workout room. The one we were in was the main one, with mats and bags in a large half circle around an elevated boxing ring. The room in the back was more of a dojo. They'd covered the floor and parts of the walls with foam matting. Very worn, scuffed, cracked. Fighters trained there for mixed martial arts and there was a lot of rolling around, grunting, and striking the person you had pinned to the ground. By early in my training, I could say I'd been there, done that.

"So?" I repeated, louder when no one acknowledged me.

This time Alvin gave me an economical nod. Like everything about him. Economical and precise. He could strike or shoot someone dead with so few movements you'd wonder afterwards what happened.

And because the thought of that truly scared me, I led the way now to the back room with my chest held high and my knees consciously carrying me smoother than was natural. Like a panther. Like a wannabe martial artist who hoped he wasn't about to get stabbed or carved up.

When I entered the familiar 20 x 20 room, I wasn't surprised to find it empty. Alvin would have booked it, knowing exactly what window of time he could expect Smiley to deliver me to him. Alvin was a planner. It was how he ran the team and how he ran my schedule, fitting in training and protection detail in times Lead the Way wasn't on other assignments, delegating duties to peer security teams when they were. They worked this out with Lena. I took whatever they had to give, not having any real money or dibs on their loyalties myself.

Clearly.

"Shoes? Socks? Bare feet?" I asked, as I boldly stripped off my winter coat and threw it over by a bare wall, leaving me in my sweaty running gear and track pants. Left my shoes on.

I wondered if I was the only one in here who knew just how far Alvin was willing to go to see if Lena's impossible-to-believe story about me being a time traveler was correct. Did even Alvin know?

I remembered meeting Lena's darks side the one time she'd felt she had to make me believe I was going to die. When I'd told her what she'd done, it had almost destroyed her. That helped me forgive her.

Alvin, though, was a trained soldier who'd been in Iraq during the final draw down. I suspected he knew how far he'd go and was good with it. If I accidentally died because of something he did, he'd find a way to make it officially a training accident. He might feel bad, but he'd get over it. Same with Big, Doc, and Smiley.

Now Alvin walked slowly around me, looking me up and down. "You can take off your mask."

The N95 mask. I blushed and removed it, tossed it over by my winter jacket.

This had happened before. It used to be I forgot to put a mask on when I entered a crowd or enclosed space. Now I often forgot to remove it, even when the situation demanded it. Which this kind of training did—an enclosed space without great ventilation; the entry now packed with Lena, Elizabeth Chan, Smiley, Big, and Doc; Smiley, at least, proudly anti-vax because he claimed lived such a healthy life, pumping himself with vitamins, and had already had a mild case of COVID, which gave him natural immunity... Blah, blah, blah.

But since the Omicron variant seemed to mostly just make fully vaxxed people like myself only mildly ill, while I was about to enter a knife fight with a guy who could easily make me bleed out, my COVID-19 observations right now were also blah, blah, blah.

The warm, stiff foam crackled under my feet as I watched Alvin pull two knives out of his knapsack, unsheathe them, and hand one to me, handle first.

I took it, suppressing a shudder at the gentle weight of the weapon. This knife, a one-sided, hunter-style blade with a polished wooden handle, was twin to the knife I'd stolen off Cosmo and used to stab him and the Finn.

Before I'd shot them dead.

All in self-defense, but it still made my stomach turn.

Alvin saw my look. "You've used a knife before? Against a person?"

I nodded.

"You'd never know it from the way you're holding it now," he said and flipped the second blade around in his hand like it was whirling on an outstretched finger or two. Grabbed it. Whirled it again. Grabbed. "This is the outward or 'hammer' position." He held it much like I'd always assumed a knife fighter did. The point was up, sharp edge towards the opponent, me.

I mimicked him, feeling foolish only because there were more people watching this than usual and one of them was Lena.

"And this is the chambered or 'icepick' grip," Alvin said. He did a flippy thing where three fingers flew back, the thumb grabbed, the knife dropped, the other fingers wrapped in around it... Something like that. Now he held the knife with the point down. As he raised it up, I had flashes of the shower scene in Hitchcock's *Psycho*.

"Eee! Eee! Eee! Eee!" I squealed like the violins in the movie.

No one laughed.

Alvin frowned. "Never hold it this way unless you've trained a long time and can do a Kali number eight, backhand from across the body." He demonstrated, whirling into me so the knife was suddenly biting lightly into my right ribs.

I stepped back, my adrenaline pumping. "This is bullshit."

"What?"

"Where are the training knives?"

"Afraid of getting cut?"

"Uh...yeah. I've watched videos. Normal instruction starts with something resin or plastic or even dull metal, so you don't stab yourself or your partner. What the hell is this?" I held up the knife and poked it lightly into my opposing palm. It drew blood.

"Reality," said Alvin.

"Is it?" I stared at him. "You think I don't know what it's like to get cut with a knife?"

"Show me your scars. And not any from falls or your bullet wound. I know you've been shot. I saw it happen. But we've *all* been shot."

I glared back at him. He was recalling when I'd been shot in that last confrontation with Cutter and his guys. He wasn't counting the time *he'd* shot me to make me jump back in time because my jumping back meant it never happened. For him.

For the same reason, he hadn't seen my bloody thighs when Cutter, as just one of his fun times torturing me, stabbed a knife deep into each of them until I couldn't walk without help. No, Alvin hadn't seen that or how I'd kept myself from jumping until I could find Lena. Then I had to jump back a crazy four jumps in a row, almost killing me, but wiping out the stabbing timeline and any of its marks on my body.

No scars on my body, but along with getting the Demon Monks disbanded and Cutter jailed, the main thing I took from that adventure was a collection of mental, ever-present memories of being choked, beaten, stabbed, shot. Hence my post-hospital freakout. But standing here now, staring at Alvin, I decided I'd come to a wall with him.

If he couldn't back away from his near-obsessive desire to push me past my limits, then I was done.

The training I'd gotten from him and his team had really helped give me a sense of personal strength and control that had helped me *handle* all my ever-present memories of trauma. But I would not add any more unless it was absolutely necessary.

And this was not that, was it?

Alvin waited, his usually blank face twitching towards a sneer.

The group near the door shuffled uneasily.

"This what you want, Lena?" I said, looking her way until she met my eyes.

"You know what I want," she murmured.

"What's that? You're talking to me now? What do you want? Tell me!"

"Our agreement."

"Which part? Me sharing my troubles? Me training? Me letting these guys treat me like a baby?"

"You telling me only truth."

"I've done that. What about you?"

"Tell me now. Who you are. What you can do."

"How about you tell *me* first. Where have you been the last four weeks? What have you done? Who are you now? Is there even a we anymore?"

I saw her eyes fill with tears and almost took it back, but my questions weren't just deflection. I wanted to know. So, apparently, did everyone else in this room because they were collectively holding their breath.

"Well?" I pressed.

She sniffed and wiped her nose. "You've changed."

"No shit. That," I shot sideways at Alvin, "is how humans respond to reality. Good and bad. Adapt or fall apart."

"I'm trying to *heal!*" Lena said.

I nodded. "Me too. I just hoped we could do it together."

I handed my knife back to Alvin, handle first, then picked up my winter jacket, shrugged it on. I strapped on my mask like it was a raised middle finger to the unmasked in the room, and walked out of the room and gym into the frozen city.

It wasn't just anger at the way Alvin couldn't stop with the crazy, though. It was Lena's manner, hiding something from me even as she tried to tell me with the introduction of the Amazon rep. Was she continuing her research? And the rep, sticking so tight to Lena, clearly had her own secrets. Her hand grip told me she had far more going on than her demure manner presented.

That thought hit me just as I reached my car and my hand fumbled inside my winter jacket to retrieve her card. All it had on it was ELIZABETH CHAN and a phone number. Nothing about Amazon. No address. Yet another thing out of place here. Why had she even given me this card, holding my hand until I'd had to take it?

Like she wanted to make a personal connection?

Why?

And suddenly my mind was spinning back to the one other solid thing I'd taken out of the Demon Monk's headquarters. A name. During the time Kenny's video-conferenced presence had watched me being tortured by Cutter, he'd managed to tap out a name for me in Morse code.

ZHOU WENLING.

While I'd still been in the hospital, I'd shared the name with my big sister, Kansas, who I believed worked for the NSA, but she hadn't turned up anything yet. Would she if she looked up Elizabeth Chan, Amazon representative? Would the phone number I'd just received help? Could it be that this person shadowing Lena now had actually changed both her first and family name at some point in the past?

Was Elizabeth Chan actually Zhou Wenling?

2

The people who matter

Back in my apartment, in the sweet corner of land between Interlaken Park and Volunteer Park, I found myself standing on the hardwood floor of my living room, trying to breathe away the stress of my confrontation at the gym and how I was going to honor my mental health while still tracking down—

My pulse jumped. Out my main window, standing on the far side of the street, the balding man in glasses and tan trench coat! Staring up at me!

I shook my head and pressed the palms of my hands to my eyes. When I looked up again, he was gone.

Yeah.

Like that.

Most of my PTSD symptoms had lessened with my physical training, but the paranoia seemed to be rebounding.

It would be nightmares and flashbacks next, waking Lena up in the middle of the night with my babbling that the other timelines still existed and we were *dead* in them. Or just she was dead. Or she was a traumatized sex slave and I was a cut up, paraplegic. Or...

Jesus, it was no wonder she'd gotten spooked.

And I'd almost forgotten about the obsessive-compulsive stuff that had spilled out after that.

First, against the advice of both Lena and Kansas, I'd talked to the FBI about Kenny and gotten a cold shoulder.

Second, I'd pushed my young patrol officer friend, Bryan Miller, to comb through all the arrest and court records to see if there were any Demon Monks left, other than Cutter, who survived that I could talk to about Kenny. Two I found but couldn't tell me anything. Two more wouldn't talk to me. Cutter himself, I wasn't going to try. Not yet. Every time I thought of him, I almost crumpled with pain.

Third, I'd wanted to figure out if there were other time travelers, like Kansas had suggested, so I'd ordered the print versions of multiple newspapers—the Seattle Times, the Chicago Tribune, the New York Times, the Washington Post, the LA Times—delivered to my apartment here. Through all of April and May, I'd pored over them repeatedly. If there were other time travelers out there changing reality, I reasoned, I wouldn't be able to identify it online. Online words and videos were too changeable, subject to the whims of whomever published them. If I read a newspaper today, though, and read the same physical pages tomorrow and what was printed had changed overnight, it meant reality itself had changed.

I thought I'd caught a few changes in those early months, both times having to do with some relatively innocuous corporate announcements or political events. But when I tried to point them out to Lena, she was already cutting herself off, I realized now. She'd pointed out that paranoia and obsessive behavior were all part of my PTSD symptom cluster. And visiting criminals, antagonizing the police to turn up *nothing*, was just asking for bad stuff to come back into our lives. I needed to get some professional help.

Then she'd stopped coming over. Or taking my phone calls.

Tracking small changes in print newspapers and tracking nothing leads had no longer seemed important.

"Fucking hell."

My hands were actually shaking.

I'd made such a mess of things.

Happy New Year's Day.

Half an hour later, after a shower, some food, and a careful reading of the one print newspaper I still received, the Seattle Times, I returned to the question of Zhou Wenling possibly masquerading as someone named Elizabeth Chan.

It was wildly racist, of course, to see a Chinese-looking woman and guess she might secretly be the one Chinese name I'd had racing around in my head for nine months like a baby that refused to pop out. Not to mention the improbability of her being attached to Lena, which gave her no obvious connection to Kenny at all.

But she was a nexus, somehow of the three major things I was trying to sort out in my life now—Kenny's whereabouts, my relationship with Lena, and whether I ever would, as Jude once put it so succinctly, "get my shit together."

I had an easy, if not entirely legal, way to settle this.

Kansas.

If I asked her the right way and didn't mess up one of the last long-term relationships I had in my life.

To clarify, she'd basically raised Kenny and I from the time she'd turned thirteen and our parents had decided they didn't need to pay for our nanny, Carmelita, any longer.

When Kansas turned seventeen, she headed east to Harvard on a full scholarship and vanished into what Kenny and I assumed was the bowels of some government spy agency, but when the Demon Monks took Kenny, she still returned home to help look for him.

And later, when I went off to the study at the University of Illinois, she came to watch me receive my Bachelor of Science, majoring in Brain and Cognitive Science. My parents had just not been able to find the time.

On that occasion, Kansas looked...gray. Not her hair. She was only 27 at the time. Her long, strong-jawed *face* looked gray. Her posture. Her manner. The way she spoke had become lower and gravelly, full of portent, like she was used to every word having life and death consequences. Still, when she kissed my cheek in congratulation and patted my arm, my heart melted and I felt like a child again, protected, cared for, and loved.

Then she left to go back to her work, and I went to grad school and into therapy. I wrote research papers and ultimately a thesis on the treatment of PTSD and social anxiety. I followed every recommendation and tailored my Chicago counseling practice and my eventual return here to Seattle to ways that supported gradual habituation and mindful diet and exercise.

Kansas showed up a second time at my doctoral ceremony. She looked healthier that time, thank goodness. With the touch of makeup and her short hair into curls, she reminded me of an early Sigourney Weaver in some movie or other.

She'd confided it was because she'd let herself fall in love and recommended I do the same.

Other than those two visits, though, and one brief appearance one shortly after my Demon Monks adventure of last March—I think she both wanted to hear everything about Kenny and wanted to meet Lena—I had to admit that our relationship had basically become awkward phone calls which Kansas implied could be bugged, monitored, and somehow used against us both. For something.

This Christmas, though, my brilliant sister had surprised me with an ultra-secure VPN'd kind of Facetime/Zoom/Teams knockoff, which she deemed a safe way for me to contact her. Only to tell me the first time I tried to use it that calling just to chat was still *Not Okay*.

She might love me, but she knew, like my parents had made clear to us from day one, love was something doled out in small amounts, carefully, only for good reasons.

Which the question of Elizabeth Chan was.

I rose from my kitchen table, looked out my living room window to confirm there was no balding man in a tan trench coat watching from across the street, and went to my bedroom. I had a desk against the wall on the near side of my bed. I sat down there, turned on my computer, and signed in, used a hack Kansas had taught me to bounce my IP address around the world, entered a ridiculously long and complex URL, went to the address, went through a triple-authentication process for Kansas' video chat and...

I jerked a bit with surprise when a chat window almost immediately to show Kansas' face staring back at me. Eyes somewhat down, actually, since she obviously kept her webcam on the top of her monitor.

"What?" she croaked. She sounded tired. She looked tired. Deep bags hung below her eyes. Her light brown hair looked crinkled and fraying and gray. Her skin was gray, too, though that might have just been the light in her workspace.

All I could see behind her, as always, was a set of shelves that held thick books, binders, stacked folders, and boxes that looked like they'd once contained computer equipment.

"Wenling Zhou," I said. "I mean Zhou Wenling." The Chinese put the family name first. "Have you—?"

"No."

"Not even a—"

"Not even that. I've tracked and done profiles on nine hundred and sixty-eight Zhou Welings. Most are based in China. One's a respected mathematician. One's a noted physician. There are actors, painters, nurses, teachers, children, poor gardeners. No links yet to Kenny, the US military or intelligence services, the Demon Monks, or temporal studies, even philosophically."

"But..."

"I'm keeping track of everything. Logging everything." She looked like she was going to keel over, which made me suddenly wish I hadn't called. This wasn't urgent. It was only my paranoia and anger at Alvin and Lena that had made me call. And feeling useless in this search for Kenny. Without Kansas chasing our one lead, what did I have?

"Kansas, I appreciate everything you're doing," I said carefully. "I know if anyone can find anything from something this slim that Kenny gave me, it's you. I just..."

She waited, looking too tired to make one of her usual sardonic comments on my roundabout conversational style.

"I met a Chinese-looking woman tonight. She was with Lena. Lena introduced her as Elizabeth Chan, an Amazon representative. Speaks with an upper-class British accent. Maybe studied in London?" I gave Kansas the phone number from Elizabeth Chan's business card.

"Logged already. The number, too. Associate of your girlfriend. What do you want to know?"

"Just... She's not..."

"Zhou Wenling? No. Elizabeth Chan was born to wealthy dual-citizen Brits in Hong Kong. Came to America for school and got scouted by Amazon originally as someone with knowledge of East Asia."

My hopes fell, and I grabbed a Kleenex to blow my nose. When I looked into Kansas' face again, she looked stupefied, waiting for me to say something. "Hey," I said.

Her face twitched and her thick eyebrows raised.

"Whatever happened to that person you hooked up with?"

Now her gray face seemed to grow even paler. She sat back in her chair so distinctly I heard it creak and I saw Kansas wore gray polyester pants and a baggy blue sweatshirt with a swirly Washington Mystics logo on the front. WNBA team, I remembered. Terrible early seasons, but went all the way in 2019 before COVID killed everything.

It seemed strange to see Kansas wearing their merch, though. She'd never talked about following sports and she normally wore turtlenecks or business attire, even at home.

"Hey, sis, are you okay?"

She collected herself and gave an odd little laugh. "I'm fine, Jacky. Just tired. Really tired. You need anything more?"

Do I need anything? Like that was all I was to her right now—a burden. On top of who knew how many other weighty burdens she carried.

I gave her a smile and shook my head. "I'm good. Nice seeing your face."

"Lena good? Working things out with her dad?"

"Totally."

"Good. Good." She trailed off into silence.

"Okay, Kansas. Happy New Year."

She nodded and disconnected.

I stood up and paced around the room, feeling that gritty, floating certainty that I'd just missed something important.

Which brought me back to Lena, after all.

She might not be blood, and we might be on the outs right now, but she was the person I *really* wanted to talk to. Besides Lena being the only person other than Kansas who definitively knew about my ability to jump back in time, I loved her. It hadn't been love at first sight when she'd tracked me down to ask about past-life regression therapies I'd done. But there'd been an immediate physical attraction. Then a rapidly grown recognition I had met my perfect opposite number, my complimentary self.

The *complimentary self* was a concept I explained to my patients in therapy as a person who aligned with your values but had strengths in different areas that complimented your own. To some extent, Jude had been a male version of that for me in university. It was why we'd bonded and remained close friends to this day. (Even if I hadn't shared with him about Kenny or my time traveling.)

With Lena, I'd been immediately grabbed by her intellect, so much quicker than mine. Also her boundless self-confidence that I learned was the product both of parental belief and love mixed with their high expectations which she'd exceeded over and over through her schooling and professional life.

Yet even as she roared forwards, sometimes mowing down those in her way, she shared with me a deep belief in reason and learning, truth and empathy, courage and integrity. And she clung to my compassion for others as her guiding star, she'd said, even as she demonstrated that very compassion for me whenever I was desperately fighting my social anxiety or other PTSD symptoms.

So what had really gone wrong?

For some reason—the confrontation at the gym, my paranoia, my abortive conversation with Kansas—it seemed critical that I figure it out. I didn't know how I was ever going to get my mental health sorted out if I couldn't figure out who I should try to hang onto and who I should let go.

First, was there some essential incompatibility?

No! Before she'd lost her mother, all that stuff I'd thought earlier was true. We were each other's complimentary selves. Screw the family backgrounds, skin colors, whatever.

But when she lost her mother, she lost an emotional anchor she'd never known was so grounding.

And she'd lost me as a rational being.

Those were big shoves.

And she'd *still* tried to regularly check in with me, tell me about her dealings with her father, see who my training was going.

Until...what?

Until I started getting stronger? Nine months of becoming physically and emotionally stronger. While Lena struggled with the loss of her mother, arguments with her father, the closure of her particle accelerator research...

Worse even than that, I'd refused to affirm my time jump ability with the Lead the Way team, making her look deluded right when every other source of her power—her mother's support and professional achievements—were being ripped from her. So it hadn't been just my screaming nightmares or obsessive newspaper reading that had driven her away. No, it was my lack of any real understanding of what she needed.

"What a self-absorbed asshole," I said. Meaning me. What I'd done. How I'd behaved. I'd learned how to give to my students in class and clients in counseling sessions, but somehow always assumed I'd be the weak one with Lena, like I was with Kansas, supportive of her choices, but never holding her with the strength she needed. It came from too many years of hiding myself, being barely able to hold it together.

But understanding that was no excuse.

I pulled out my phone and sent Lena a text.

I'm finally seeing how it looks like I betrayed our agreement. Especially with everything else going on. I'm sorry. I love you. I want to make things right. Can we talk?

I sent it and waited for a few moments in the vain hope she'd see it and respond immediately. When there was no sign of that, I pocketed my phone, telling myself that the lack of response meant nothing for the first 24 hours at least. And my gut told me that if I was going to fix things with Lena, I had to be careful not to push too hard.

I got up and went back to my living room, pacing the floor, looking out at the New Year's Day that stayed dry but was getting more overcast by the minute.

I felt melancholy.

More than that. Unsettled.

A year ago, I would have welcomed a day where I didn't have to constantly fight my fear of other people, their judgements, their unpredictability.

A couple months ago, I'd have used this time to quietly could go over in my head (again) everything that Kenny had said to me during the two times I'd seen him on a video call last March. And everything Cutter had said about Kenny or to him. Maybe I'd find that one little detail that would give me a direction to go looking beyond all the dead ends and closed doors I'd tried already. Maybe even something justifying another call to Kansas.

But somewhere in between rebooting my counseling practice, negotiating a new set course I'd teach in the spring at UW, and training my physical body into something resembling an ultramarathon fighting machine, I'd come to accept that maybe I just had to wait for the universe to give me a clue.

Or *maybe* this unsettled feeling was the universe telling me to get off my ass and do something, *anything,* to shake up my perspective. Open a few new doors. Give the universe something to work with.

I gave Ziggy Cheester a call.

It was mid-afternoon when I got out of my car and walked in my fleece and rain jacket up to the front door of the modest four-floor walk-up Ziggy Cheester had directed me to near Pike and 18th. I pulled on my mask and keyed in the security code he'd given me. A voice I could hardly hear over the sounds of raucous conversation in the background heard my name and buzzed open the front door. I pulled it open but hesitated, almost changing my mind.

Ziggy was a Jamaican commercial artist who worked part-time as a police sketch artist, which is how I met both him and Bryan Miller when I was tracking my brother last March. The three of us had been meeting at Ziggy's studio about twice a month since last fall. Always casual, talking music, art, law enforcement gossip, stories about my UW students and, very obliquely, my counselling clientele. The good food and laughs we'd shared had helped me believe I could someday join society as a relaxed participant.

But I'd never come to either Ziggy's or Bryan's home. Now I wondered if I hadn't wildly overstepped the boundaries of our relationship by calling Ziggy up and asking if we could hang out.

The invitation to come here had been instant and genuine, but...it had sure sounded like he had other guests. Family? Friends? Was that something normal people did on New Year's Day? It hadn't been in the Traine house, growing up, but nothing in my house had ever been what you'd call normal.

The building's entry door started to buzz like an elevator did when you held its door open too long, and I jumped backwards out of it, almost letting it close shut. Then I changed my mind at the last second, caught it, and slipped in, found the creaking stairwell, and headed up to the fourth floor.

I could hear what I was sure was Ziggy's party before I even opened the door to that floor. The music was piano, quick steady drums, and lots of brass—stuff that preceded rocksteady and reggae on the island, Ziggy had told me. Ska. More party, less spacey.

And woven with all that music was the sound of loud talking, shrieks, and laughter, including Ziggy's voice bellowing over them all in a way I'd never heard him do even once in our lunch meetings. Of course not. Not with his two white-boy friends.

Which is why I wasn't surprised when the door burst open and Ziggy himself burst out to greet me with his Jamaican accent stronger than usual. "Gud afternoon, Professor Jack-*sahn*. Wah gwan?"

There were suddenly three beautiful young dark-skinned ladies spilling out the door behind him and hanging off the man's arms and neck as they stared at me with wide, excited eyes. They only made Ziggy stumble a little, which was impressive since I knew that Ziggy was sixty-eight years old.

I swallowed, pointed to the ladies, and said, "Girlfriends or nieces?"

That sent them into howls of laughter and calls of, "Oh, Mister Cheeeeester! Oh!"

"G'wan! Weh ya say?" Ziggy shook them off him and pushed them all back towards the crowded room that other black faces were looking out of. To me, he said, "Two nieces. The mouthy one is my granddaughter, yeh? All visiting me here the first time. Big time for family!"

"Well, then, maybe I shouldn't..." I started, but Ziggy had already grabbed me by the arm to drag me in after him.

After I'd thrown my rain jacket by the front door, I was dragged through a bigger rush of introductions and names and laughter and comments than I think I'd ever experienced in my life, even counting my early years in Boy Scouts or the drama club Kenny had made me try.

I was thankful for the way my memory automatically recorded the names and faces of each person introduced to me because I was blushing so fiercely, my heart pounding so hard in the close confines of Ziggy's home, it was hard to focus.

The rush of loud hospitality and instant friendship had made me pull off my mask and stuff it into one of my fleece's pockets, wondering automatically as I did so if I could jump back in time to a pre-COVID-infected state if this turned out to be a super-spreader event. Obviously not, since my jumps only took me back ten minutes at a time with a safe max of two jumps, and I was *not* about to run out of here in the first twenty minutes, but... Such were the times. Such were my thoughts.

On the plus side, I knew Ziggy was vaxed and boosted. Six of his relatives here were visiting from Jamaica and could only be doing so after full vaccinations and tests. I hoped the other ones, who lived in Washington state or had driven up from Oregon and one from California, were vaccinated. Particularly the very old woman who was Ziggy's aunt, and the very fat man who wasn't related but got called "uncle" by all the younger Cheesters.

With all the hugging and dancing and kissing and shoving one another, if there was a single piece of protein-coated Omicron code circulating anywhere in this room, it was going to be replicating everywhere before anyone left.

And that could be a good thing, right? Herd immunity! This gentler variant safely boosting the immune systems of the already vaccinated!

A pretty young woman suddenly climbed over the back of the couch to my left and dropped down in the small space between me and the end of it. Chandice, which she'd told me earlier meant a girl who's very smart and talented. Her high round cheeks were flushed and her eyes sparkled wildly like I imagined Lena's must have when she'd been this age.

"So my uncle says you are the *best* head shrinkuh in the city, yeh?"

"Oh, definitely," I said, matching her volume to be heard over the highly sexual rapping of Doja Cat, an American rapper Ziggy said was hugely popular in Jamaica. I'd been drinking some of Ziggy's punch and suspected my cheeks were as flushed as Chandice's and Doja Cat's by this point.

"*Can* you tell me," she said, weaving her face back and forth close to mine with her eyes wide, "what I'd like to do right now?"

"Um…" I said, transfixed.

"She'd *like*," Ziggy's voice croaked from in front and above us both, "to be getting her pretty-ness out of my couch so her old uncle can sit down."

"No I don't!" she said, but held up her hands anyway, letting her uncle pull her warm body up and away from mine.

Ziggy plopped down in her place and turned to me, grinning broadly so I could see the darkening lower incisor he kept assuring Bryan and me he'd see a dentist about. "The mother of my grandbaby's mama was that age when she catch me just like that. No escape. Nowhere to run."

"Where is she now?"

"Oh, she leave me so fast, I wake up one morning and she be gone. Then one day, years later, I'm still growing my first beard, this other lady shows up with a baby. She says that little girl is mine! Her mother tells her to bring the child to me before she died!"

"And you took her and raised her?"

Ziggy nodded with big loose chin ducks, so his gray-shot beard folded and spread on his chest. He'd been drinking at least as much punch as I had. "You find your family or they find *you*." He poked me hard in my shoulder to make the point.

I stared at him, going through every conversation I'd had with him and Bryan in my mind. I'd told them I had a brother and sister, but little more than that. I opened my mouth to speak…

Ziggy held up a hand and stared at me. "When the balding man comes to me, order me to say who you *are*, who you know, who you be looking to find, I wanna tell him, *Yuh good, tho?* and make him go. But he's a pushy man, professor. Business suit. Glasses. Tan coat. He gonna come back and get everything from me. So you don' tell me nothing more, yeh? No thing."

A hard pit had formed in the bottom of my stomach. "A balding man in glasses and a tan coat? A trench coat? Could you draw for me what he looked like?"

Ziggy gave another loose nod. "Already done. Come. Gwan show you."

A few moments later, we were in Ziggy's bedroom with the door shut against the continuing party in the living room. Ziggy pulled out a large sketchbook from beside his bed and flipped to the last page.

The balding man in glasses, a plain suit, a trench coat, rendered him with the same lifelike flair Ziggy had brought to his part-time gig last March as a police sketch artist, when he'd used my description of the one-time Demon Monk who tried to abduct Lena and me to sketch a face Bryan had recognized as Undercover Detective William Gillespie

Unfortunately, this time there was no excited police officer to give us a name to go with the face. There were just my flashes of having seen exactly this unremarkable middle-aged man. He could have been anyone, from a grumpy neurosurgeon to mid-level ad exec. But something about him said government. Something in the slack, cold eyes behind his glasses. Not merciless like William Gillespie's had been, but just...uncaring. Like they'd seen it all, and were just doing what they were told. A worker drone's deadness. A machine's.

In some ways, that look, which I had no doubt Ziggy captured accurately, unnerved me more than Gillespie's deadly malice or Cutter's sadism had.

"Can I have it?" I asked, not sure why I needed it, but knowing I did.

"You gwan tell me why he's coming for you?"

I looked down, unable to meet the worry in the older man's eyes. "I don't know. Truly," I said. "Maybe something to do with the Demon Monks gang I had that run in with. Maybe people sniffing around Lena's work. I'm going to talk to Bryan about it if it doesn't stop."

That seemed to mollify Ziggy a bit. He handed me the portrait, and I folded it up and jammed it down into my unused fleece pocket to take home with me...

But only after Ziggy and I both went out to share a laughter-and-dish-clanking meal of meal of jerk chicken, a creamy fish stew with a heavenly coconut milk aroma, a steamy pepper pot soup with chopped greens and dumplings, cheap red wine, curry goat on rice, and a dessert of pinched pastry rounds filled with grated coconut and nutmeg.

"Grizadda," Chandice murmured as she pressed her warm torso against my left arm and slipped a taste of the pastry into my lips.

"He got enough sweet already, you!" Ziggy growled at her, making her laugh and thankfully retreat again.

Then my time there was done. Like an alarm had sounded in my head. Like, even with all the good food and alcohol, my quota for new experiences and social submersion had clicked past delight into near panic.

The universe had given me a clue.

It was time to leave.

I got up from my honored place in the spread-out, still-active feast, thanked Ziggy profusely for introducing me to his extended family and hurried, wobbling a little, to his apartment door.

Ziggy followed me quickly and surprised me when I left by gripping my right hand and patting my right shoulder at the same time, leaning close to say, "You are my boonoonoonoos friend."

He teared up when I awkwardly copied the gesture and words, not understanding their exact meaning, but definitely feeling the intent, even through my fever-level anxiety.

"Walk good," Ziggy said and released me into the hallway, the stairs down, and the cold night outside.

3

An invitation is issued

Despite having too many people and too much alcohol swirling in my head, I walked good to my car. Drove good to my parking spot under my apartment building. Climbed the stairs good to my third-floor apartment. Unlocked and entered good. Flicked on the lights good.

And jumped in fright to see two somber men in dark suits waiting for me in my living room. Neither wore a mask. Of course not. The bad guys never wore masks. Where was my mask?

"Holy..." I began and let it die. Was *I* about to die?

"Crap security in your building," said the man on the right, balding but younger than the other guy who'd apparently been following me and interviewing my friends. This man had swarthy skin and his thin hair was oiled-back, his body leaner, and his face sharper, almost hawk-like. He said it thickly, like a Russian mobster, which made my heart pound even harder.

How did they...? Where are their...? I saw two unfamiliar coats thrown over my dining table by my kitchenette. Trench coats. One tan. One black. Did these two carry guns in concealed shoulder holsters like the Finn had? A Glock .45. Easy to draw. Easy to kill with...

"IDs," said the second man in a deep voice, fully American. He had a full head of dark hair but seemed the older of these two, with a freakishly jutting square chin and a posture that made him the one in charge. "Before he shits himself."

The first guy pulled out a wallet from his back pants pocket, stepped forward, and lifted the flap inside the open wallet it to show me a US Government ID with a name—Amit Dadashev. I had trouble scanning the rest because my heart was beating so hard, but I read CIA and what looked like a section identifier in Washington, DC, plus an alpha-numeric office identifier.

"He's got it," said the second man. "All of it. Don't you, Dr. Traine?"

I tried to swallow. My mouth had gone so dry it hurt. My old limbic self had made me break out in sweat that smelled uncomfortably like jerk sauce and cheap wine, but my newer self, trained in practical hand-to-hand combat and firearms now, tried to push the buzz and fear aside to assess, measure how these guys were standing, what they were likely to do.

"Y-your ID?" I directed at the second guy, the leader. He was the one I had to watch.

The man chuckled and stepped forward, too. He pulled out a similar card, displaying it only a couple of seconds before putting it away. His name was Robert Wilson. Same building. Different office identifier. "You can call me Bob," he said.

"Robert Wilson and Amit Dadashev, both HRTA," I said, babbling. Stall. Stall. I had to keep myself clear and figure out which way to go if they jumped me. "Q404 and B220 respectively."

Wilson glanced at his partner. "See?"

Dadashev shrugged. "I could do that."

"Sure you could."

I had to break their pattern, so I snapped, "Shut up! What are you doing here? Breaking into my apartment? You're not fucking CIA. Who are you?"

"We're not fucking CIA," Dadashev said, unruffled. "You heard him. Can I fucking CIA him into submission until he begs to lick the street shit of fucking Seattle off my shoes?"

Wilson shook his head. "I don't think that will be necessary." He turned to me. "Have you ever heard of no-knock warrants and the prevention of domestic terrorism laws, Dr. Traine?"

I was blinking hard at him, my memory rocketing through associations, papers I'd read, books, news broadcasts, investigative journalism pieces, even while I *should* have been backing out my door and running for the stairs. "If you were the FBI, either of those might apply," I said, "though I challenge you to give me the name of the specific act you're thinking of. I'll read it back to you line by line from memory if you can."

The last was a bluff, and I was sure Wilson knew it, but he still grinned back at me and said, "Told you, Amit. Hard to bullshit a smart man who never forgets anything he's ever read or heard. Of course, if certain things are unpublished and unreported..."

"Executive powers," Dadashev growled quietly.

Wilson nodded. "Black bag, unrecorded ops. If we have to do it that way." He walked towards me with such a commanding threat that all my Lead-the-Way training embarrassingly vanished and I backed into the couch opposite the window. I half fell to a sit, my rain jacket whipping open and my fleece under it, like I was a soft fruit getting peeled. Only the thin skin of my cotton tee-shirt protected me now.

Wilson leaned over me for a second, like he might reach down and slap me. Then he suddenly squatted down on his haunches, so his face was lower than mine, broad smile thrusting his square chin up like a handshake. His eyes drifted over me and stopped around my left hip. He reached forward and tugged out the sketch Ziggy had done of their balding colleague in glasses and a trench coat just like theirs. Wilson opened the picture and looked at it. He feigned a lack of recognition, re-folded it, and put it into his suit coat pocket. "You're full of mysteries, doc."

"I'd like that back."

"Too bad we don't get everything we'd like."

My chin was shaking and I could feel my eyes starting to water.

Wilson obviously saw it. He tilted his head and said, "Hey, it's a psych, doc. A joke."

I stared at him, feeling unaccountably ready to burst in to tears.

Wilson shook his head, dropping it a bit sheepishly, like he realized he and his partner had gone too far. "We got a note from your friend, Jude Spiegelman, about you, and we know about your sister's service, so... The crazy part of it is that your landlord? I went to school with him back in the day. I told him what we were doing and he let us in."

He looked at Dadashev and the hawk-like junior partner shrugged and nodded agreeably.

"What you're...doing?"

"Recruiting, man."

I swallowed. I'd just recovered myself enough to realize I was in the perfect position to do a throat strike on him. He was the right distance, his big chin tilted up as he bent forward to look down at me.

"HRTA with the CIA," Wilson said, straightening up. "Stands for Human Resources and Talent Acquisition. We're not the big brains. We chase *down* the big brains! We're people people, you know?"

"Who scare the shit out of your prospects?"

"Yeah, well…"

"Threaten them."

"Hey, it's the CIA! You gotta figure anyone wanting to work for Central Intelligence might have at least a little hankering for excitement, right?"

"Maybe." I nodded. "Maybe someone wanting to do that kind of work."

"Like you."

"Not like me. One thousand times not like me."

"Ah." He slapped his knees and pressed himself up to standing again. "Well. I guess there's a reason they've been trying to kick me and Amit out."

"Speak for yourself," Dadashev growled.

"Anyway, I guess that's it, then. We came, we asked, we leave." Wilson walked to my kitchen table and grabbed one of the trench coats. The black one. When he turned back, he was still smiling broadly, but nothing about it reached his eyes. "Just one thing, though…"

Dadashev had also grabbed his coat and now shrugged it on silently behind Wilson.

"What?" I said, not daring to get up from my couch, like if I did, they'd change their minds and forcibly carry me out.

"Your brother," Wilson said. "Kentucky Traine. You ever wonder where he ended up?"

And there it was. I leaped to my feet so quickly that I had a head rush and nearly fainted. "Where do you have him?"

The two CIA "human resources" men looked at one another—the granite chin and the balding hawk. Wilson looked back at me.

"We followed him, and you, and your sister, from the time you were in first grade. Your sister's aptitudes were obvious. She was easy. Your brother and now you, a little more complicated."

I found myself rocking on my feet, wishing I'd gone for the neck strike and cracked this man's trachea. Once I'd done that, if Dadashev had rushed me, I think I'd have been revved enough for the rest of my training to kick in. I could have taken them. I was pretty sure they weren't carrying guns. Probably saw me as no threat. Nothing to worry about. Nothing much of anything.

"Where is my brother now?" I repeated coldly.

Another traded look between the two men. Again Wilson spoke for them. "That's something we'd like to talk with you about."

"So talk."

"Not here."

"Where?"

Wilson smiled. "I thought you'd never ask." He reached into his suit pocket and came out with an envelope that he held out to me.

I looked at it but didn't take it."

"It doesn't bite. It just has an invitation, a time and address, a supplementary info packet, and transportation arrangements."

"For...?"

"A week from Monday. Six p.m. The George Bush Center for Intelligence in Langley, Virginia. You'll find a return ticket to Washington Dulles, where a driver will be waiting to drive you to and from the meeting. Overnight accommodations in DC proper. A couple nights if you want to explore."

"Five-star accommodations?" I asked.

"We have a deal. It's close to the university."

"You really know how to roll out the welcome mat."

I still hadn't reached for the envelope, so Wilson tossed it onto my kitchen table. "You want to go through the rest of your life not knowing? Think about it."

He and Dadashev left without closing the door behind them.

I realized they'd taken Ziggy's picture of their balding, bespectacled colleague with them.

4

The crazy end of normal

AFTER A DAY OF recovering from a rare (for me) hangover, and from the unsettling visit from the pair of government spies, I drove down Monday morning to my counseling office just southwest of Washington Park.

There was actually sunshine and I could feel the vise of Seattle's cold snap loosening. I was still grateful, though, that my psychometrist/office manager, Megan, would already be in the office. She'd be making sure the lights and heat were on and the coffee and kettle were going for my tea and whatever my first client of the day wanted.

And the invitation to sit for a CIA "interview?"

It reminded me of my third year at Illini, just after my panic attack and semi-private conference with Professor Tavish, when Jude had tried to convince me the CIA would want me for my memory skills. Now I had even more valuable skills to offer. But it was like how I got more in control of my life and drove Lena away—the more power you had, the worse it could be. And with time travel, worse could mean a *lot* worse. For everyone. Did I really want the CIA having access to that?

No way.

But it was an actual lead on Kenny's whereabouts. And though Kansas had left a note on our contact screen that she was unavailable for a few days, I had a good feeling this was going to break the logjam.

The visit from Wilson and Dadashev had also brought another kind of relief. Along with Ziggy's story, it told me all my danger signals weren't just paranoia. I *was* being watched. Just as Kenny and Kansas had been watched.

And it explained why I'd felt so different from my peers growing up. It explained why Kenny had to vanish, and why Kansas hid out behind deep layers of electronic security.

It even maybe explained a little why my relationship with Lena was so fricking hard. Because Lena was brilliant like Kansas, and investigating, of all things, time travel, which made her a target like me.

No wonder we were drawn together like magnets and sparked like cut power lines.

But it was all good.

I could work it out.

I *would* work it out.

Just as I *would* find Kenny.

Until then, as I always counseled my clients, I needed to focus on the things in my control, things I was good at, things that gave me feelings of satisfaction or accomplishment.

For me, that meant meeting a new client today, my first of 2022.

I reached my office building at 8:42 a.m., parked out back in my reserved spot, masked up, and walked in through the rear entrance, past the elevator, to climb the marble stairs into the sanctuary of my second-floor office.

Heavy oak doors with *Traine Counseling* in modest gold lettering at chest height led into a hushed, carpeted entry area with a welcoming glass and polished-oak receptions desk where Megan quietly greeted clients when she wasn't administering psychological tests, taking care of physical office management, or walking the occasional child client to the bathroom down the hall.

Along the left wall, facing the reception desk but mostly hidden from the entry door, were a set of comfortable waiting chairs and a couch for those times when couples or families came in for therapy together.

As I walked in now, fifteen minutes before my first client's appointment time, I saw my new client was already seated there. She was a handsome older woman with a simple steel-gray ponytail, plaid wool shirt over a simple scoop-neck tee, jeans, and well-worn work boots. Blue surgical mask. Not my usual stressed-out business owner, troubled scion of a rich family, or office worker on a health plan.

I murmured, "I'll see you shortly," as I passed her but I wasn't sure if she heard me. She was totally engrossed in what she was reading on her cell phone.

Fifteen minutes later, Megan ushered her in and we began.

At 9:45, with five minutes left in the fifty-minute hour, she inadvertently shared the real reason she was there. To protect my doctor-client confidentiality, I'll call her Cassandra, for reasons that will become apparent.

"Believing all the nonsense about microchips in vaccines, stolen elections, child-trafficking rings in congress," Cassandra said. "Just folks wanting to feel important and in control, like they have secret knowledge, you know?"

"I hear a 'but' coming," I said.

"'Cause you're a good listener."

"What I'm paid for."

We smiled at each other with our eyes and clicked, just like that. I loved all my clients with a deep concern that took me out of my own anxieties to focus on *their* needs, but there were always certain clients, the particularly bright ones with a quirky sense of humor, who I just *got* on a deeper level.

Cassandra was one of these.

"You follow the news?" she asked, clearly qualifying my ability to understand what she was about to share.

"I do."

"Online or print?"

I raised an eyebrow at her. "A bit of both."

"Thought Millennials only consumed bits and bytes."

"I'm obviously older than I look."

She sighed. "You're a baby. Your read the Epoch Times?"

I shook my head.

"The South China Daily Post?"

"These are in English?"

"Both. One's kind of a Falun Gong mouthpiece with good stuff about China if you ignore the right-wing Trump bullshit. The South China Post's out of Hong Kong. Not as good as the Apple Daily which Beijing shut down last year, but good reporting."

"China…" It tweaked something in my memory. One of the changes in reality I'd picked up back when I'd been obsessive about checking.

"They keep changing their news," Cassandra said, like she'd read my mind.

"What do you mean?"

She grimaced. "I train horses. You ever watch a bunch of horses let out to pasture at the same time? Sometimes they mosey out all together, sometimes they scatter. News coming out of China right now? It's scatter, going every which way like they don't want you to know what they're really up to."

"Which is?"

"War. It's coming. Mark my words."

Ah. Everything she'd talked about before this had to do with a general building of dread in her life. "There are definitely political maneuvers and things we don't understand. What does that mean to you? How do you feel about it?"

Cassandra's hands, which had been clenching and unclenching through much of our time together, now squeezed their fingers so hard her knuckles all turned white. "I don't like that people *I don't know* are doing things *I can't see* that may be changing my life *right now.*"

I mentally held her, letting it just be.

Then she breathed out in a big, shuddering whuff into her mask, and looked over at the clock I kept on my desk. "That's our hour. Where are my get-calm-quick tricks?"

"Do you want some?"

She grabbed her ponytail and tugged it out of her hair, shaking out her lovely thick gray around her shoulders. "Let me guess—breathe, change what I'm focusing on, take a walk, call bullshit on the crazy stuff."

"And talk it out with someone who cares."

She looked at me and actually teared up, almost causing me to do the same. "Can I come back here next week?"

"Of course. See Megan on the way out. She'll schedule you."

Cassandra suddenly began taking deep breaths like she was going to sob, but she let it simply drive her to her feet.

I rose as well.

"There's going to be something big happening in the next few days over there," she said. "Watch the news."

"I will."

She nodded, and I escorted her out, making a mental note to find print copies of the newspapers she'd mentioned.

This felt like another little shove from the universe. Things happening in China that were hard to see unless you followed the news? It fit with the item I'd seen change in the physical newspapers back when I'd been obsessed with finding evidence of time tampering.

Or I was grasping at straws until Kansas came back online.

In any case, my influx of new patients meant it took me until Thursday to seek out copies of the Epoch Times and South China Daily Post from Big Little News on E. Pike. I'd come often during my print-obsession days to scan news from all over the world. I wasn't surprised they carried both of the papers I was looking for.

When I left Big Little News with my purchases, I opened my umbrella against the rain and spotted the balding guy in the glasses and tan trench coat. It was my first spotting since Ziggy had confirmed the dude as real.

I flipped Balding Guy the finger. Lost track of him a second later.

I put him out of my mind as I walked back to my car and drove home with my newspaper finds. I pored through them at my dining room table while I ate some leftover stir fry and found myself laughing out loud at some of the wilder Epoch Times stuff. But in both the Epoch Times and the SCDP, I came across stories that reminded me of the story change I'd remembered from last May.

I reached down to the box I kept on the floor against the island that separated my kitchen from my dining/living room. It held the few newspapers I'd kept from that period, the ones I'd noticed changes in when I'd read them the second time through a day later.

To be clear, this had only happened four times, and the changes weren't serious, which made me wonder whether there were sometimes random glitches in space-time, like reality hiccups, things most people would never notice. They *could* never notice them since their brains didn't hold on to alternate time lines when the time lines switched or reset. That was the healthy, normal, human way to live.

For the few people in the world like me, however...

I pulled out the New York Times issue I'd been reminded of. It was dated May 25, 2021. In the international section, I'd circled a paragraph with a red pen. It read:

> Xi Jinping party associate Kuang Dishi has been appointed to head a set of "strong parent" negotiations with Taiwan about the island's scrambling of US-made fighter jets to practice defending their island from an invasion from mainland China.

In the same red pen, I'd drawn an arrow from the end of this paragraph to the top of the page, where I'd noted:

> *They deleted, "The Pan-Green Separatists have urged Taiwan President Tsai Ing-wen to refuse to meet Kuang until the Beijing government acknowledges the 1895 Treaty of Shimonoseki and the 1951 Treaty of San Francisco as starting points for any negotiations." Ad for Hyundai Ioniq 5 was enlarged to fill space.*

Now if this *hadn't* been some kind of random glitch, it meant a time traveler had done something to change the time stream between the first time I'd read the story and the second, both in the same copy of the paper I'd had on my table. The question would be why? Why convince Taiwan's Green Separatists to not do something perfectly in keeping with their mission?

I licked the last of my plate clean like a barbarian and emptied my water glass.

The question of why make the Green Separatists step down became even more interesting when I considered the current issues of the South China Daily Post and the Epoch times that I'd just read. The January 6, 2022 SCDP mentioned Kuang Dishi's negotiator position and said he'd just received death threats from some unnamed party. The January 6, 2022 Epoch Times didn't mention the death threats but talked about Taiwan's growing fear of being taken over by China.

I picked up my copy of the SCDP to circle where it had referred to death threats, just in case tomorrow…

I blinked. Forget tomorrow. The printed news had changed since I'd read it fifteen minutes ago. The paragraph on death threats now read:

A male assistant to Kuang Dishi, a member of China's Politbureau Standing Committee (PSC) and personally appointed by President Xi Kinping, was tragically killed today when he opened a suspicious box addressed to Kuang. The Director-General of Taiwan's National Police Agency says finding the bomber is the police agency's top priority.

Okay. I shoved my dishes further to the side and circled the passage about the mail bomb. Then I put down my pen, and turned back to the Epoch Times. Its front page now had a grainy photograph of a crime scene on the front cover, and above the picture, the title: TAIWAN MILITANTS STRIKE BACK!

The story below went into great detail about the long, slow build of a military resistance in Taiwan that had been set in motion by the deliberately-provocative appointment of Kuang Dishi by President Xi to negotiate Taiwan's capitulation to Chinese rule.

The most disturbing thing was that I had a clear memory now of seeing that photograph and headline on the front of the Epoch Times when I first reached to pick it up from the wire rack in the Big Little News at 5:40 p.m. or so when I'd been there, the rain dripping outside, the sound of people murmuring through their masks as they milled about around me, the steamy smell of them, the swish of their raincoats.

Nor had I lost my memory of the same time, the same day, today, picking up this same issue of the Epoch Times with a headline that had nothing to do with anything in China. The Epoch Times front page headline of that prior memory had to do with the crisis at the US southern border, how Joe Biden was failing, the usual right-wing stuff.

Sometimes the horses scatter, Cassandra's voice repeated in my head.

I looked back to the South China Daily Post and saw the red ink I'd applied, along with the story it had circled, had vanished.

What the—?

In its place was a shortened story about the "strong parent" negotiations and how they would now be delayed as Beijing's chief negotiator, Kuang Dishi, had been involved in a tragic automobile accident in a trip between the airport and the hotel in Taipei where he was going to stay during negotiations. Police were investigating, but no foul play was suspected.

Interestingly, the Epoch Times narrative was largely unchanged other than the front-page photograph now showed a police scene on a highway, and reference to the actions of "Taiwan militants" referred to their arranging an automobile accident versus an exploding package.

After a moment's hesitation, I quickly circled the latest version of these stories in red pen, and noted the earlier versions with that same red pen. Then I placed my hands flat on the table in front of me, let my eyes unfocus, and combed my now multiple memories around the buying and reading of these two newspapers, setting them in order as best I could, recognizing the slippery quality that attached themselves to the memories that had been bumped in a way that didn't happen when *I* was the one jumping my mind back and remaking reality.

It left me vaguely nauseous. Especially since the only memory divergence I could be aware of started from the time I bought these papers. When the timelines had *actually* changed could have been days earlier.

And given that the events had happened on the other side of the world and the only impact here had been some news outlets reporting, if I hadn't been reading those outlets, I'd have noticed nothing at all. And if that was so, which time stream would I be in? One where Kuang was still alive, or this one, where he was dead? And if there *was* more than one existing time stream for Kuang, was there one of me in each time stream that had a different story about Kuang? Or had all earlier versions of Kuang's life, and therefore of the newspaper reporting on him, been erased with the creation of the auto accident timestream.

Was there any way to know?

The weight of it took my breath away, so I was breathing high in my chest, close to panic.

Who was doing this? The idea flashed through my mind that it might be some highly trained, time traveling operative. They try one thing to knock off Kuang and it doesn't work, so they jump back to before the abortive attempt and try something else until they get it right. Here, it apparently only took a few tries, though who knew how far back the time traveler went each time and how much setup he or she had to do.

Or was it a team of time travelers? When Kansas had implied, back in March, that I wasn't the only person who could time travel, I'd thought she was being rational, assuming that if I could time jump, surely there were others. Kenny, at least, since he shared my memory talents. But now I wondered if she actually knew about others. Possibly many others. An army of time travelers, or at least an elite attack unit.

Which begged the question of who was directing them? It certainly could have been some Taiwanese independence group, but it could just as easily have been a group from some other interested nation with a history of recruiting talented people to run secret ops.

And wasn't that why Wilson and Dadashev had visited me a few days ago? Human Resources and Talent Acquisition for the CIA. Just how long might that organization have been using people like me and Kenny to mess with the world?

I felt like I was going to be vomit.

5

The trench coat stalker

I WASHED MY DISHES, checking to make sure the newspapers weren't changing anymore, then I put on my sweats, and reflective rain gear and went for a night run around Volunteer Park to clear my head.

As I passed the lit glass Conservatory, I realized it wasn't just the changing newsprint and the questions it raised about multiple timestreams and government skullduggery that had made me so sick.

Last March, after getting hit with both the ability to time travel and the knowledge that Kenny was still alive, the only thing I'd wanted to do was use my power to find Kenny and bring him home.

I still wanted that, but now I wasn't sure it was even theoretically possible.

The only "home" I even considered bringing him back to was the symbolic one shared by Kansas, Kenny, and me. But if Kenny had been forced to work for a secret government strike group because he could time travel or detect time travelers, then the timestreams he knew, the worlds he'd experienced, might not match up with mine at all. In the same way that Kansas's world of incomprehensible shadows and information flows would also be foreign to both Kenny and me.

We three didn't just have different viewpoints on the facts. We'd literally been experiencing different iterations of the world.

As had I and Lena.

Could you ever be "home" with people who could never see what you saw, hear what you heard, experience or smell or taste or feel what you did? Not *would* not, but *could* not.

That question took the concept of each person being ultimately alone in the universe and ground it in my face.

Hell, maybe I should just give up trying to rescue Kenny and join him in slavery instead.

Needing a quick salve to this bout of existential despair, I called a meeting of the three musketeers—me, Patrol Officer Bryan Miller, and Ziggy Cheester—for lunch the next day at Ziggy's studio in Capitol Hill, right across the street from the Seattle PD's East Precinct. I suspected Ziggy could tell I was emotionally needy when I called him first because he not only agreed immediately, he said he'd make sure Bryan made it and would prepare the same amazing jerk chicken sandwiches on focaccia bread, with onion, garlic, lettuce, pickles, and mayo. He had three kinds of soda to wash it down with.

The artworks leaning up against the walls of his studio, a walled-off-but-open-roofed room inside the factory-like Chelios Design & Print, looked like a series commissioned for a movie company. The pieces portrayed lights cutting through a magical purple-green darkness to reveal some kind of glowing stone in one, a mutant fairy in another, a bloody sword in a third, all done with Ziggy's surreal comic book style.

Made *me* want to see what this movie was about.

We laughed and caught up. I decided that friendship, at least, was a real and tangible good. Even if it threatened to make us all catch COVID from each other.

Then, noting the time and knowing I had to be back for a 1 p.m. client, I asked Bryan whether the CIA could operate domestically. It made him snort the orange soda he was drinking out of his nose.

"Nix, no, no way, can't do it," he said, wiping it up. He was the most cheerily optimistic Boy Scout cop I knew—smooth round cheeks, short chopped hair, clean body, clean language, clean morals—but also, I'd learned, very sharp. He'd actually written his LSATs and been admitted to three law schools, but finances and a commitment to look after his parents had streamed him into law enforcement. For now.

"Let me qualify that," Bryan added. "Their mission is to collect intelligence from foreign nations, and they got into a lot of trouble in, like, the seventies, when they worked with the FBI and NSA to gather intel from US citizens. But they're still allowed to interview US citizens who come back here after living in foreign countries. Just that. It's the FBI and NSA you gotta worry about now."

I ignored the last comment, knowing it was true because of the things Kansas could do. "So if a CIA guy was following me, that would be illegal?"

"Yes," Bryan said cautiously, seeing Ziggy's vigorous nodding to my question. "You got someone following you?"

"Yup."

"And you think he's CIA?"

"Pretty sure. Two guys claiming to be CIA broke into my apartment and waited for me to come home. They knew a lot about me and my family. They said they wanted to recruit me for my crazy memory. I think they sicced this guy on me to make sure I was clean or something before they approached me." I looked at Ziggy apologetically. "They confiscated the picture of him that you drew."

Bryan and Ziggy exchanged looks, and Bryan seemed to be mentally backtracking. "Maybe that's a borderline case?" Bryan said to me. "Vetting a candidate? You want me to ask around about it? See if it's legit?"

I wasn't about to drag Bryan into another part of my Kenny search. The first part had almost gotten him killed. So I shook my head. "Not yet. But...if this guy keeps following me, what happens if I make a citizen's arrest?"

Bryan shook his head. "You'd probably get charged with false imprisonment. Only allowed to make citizen's arrest when you see someone committing petit larceny, like shoplifting. Maybe you could accuse him of stalking, but you'd have to prove repetition and intent."

"Then you call Bry-*ahn* to arrest him," Ziggy blurted.

"Definitely," Bryan said.

I grimaced. "Maybe I'll just politely corner him and ask a few questions."

Despite having Bryan and Ziggy tell me to not start challenging strange CIA men in trench coats, I still left their presence feeling both invigorated and impatient as I masked up and hurried the three blocks back to 14th St. where I'd parked my car. Neither Bryan nor Ziggy knew anything about my time jumping ability and we'd built a friendship anyway. Across ages. Across ethnic and socioeconomic backgrounds. We'd just shared the simpler joys and struggles of our lives—what it was to be human.

Kenny deserved to have that too.

Which brought me back to my simple goal of finding and saving him. Should I be infiltrating the CIA to find him?

No. Kenny could have tapped out "C-I-A" to me when was getting tortured by Cutter with him watching through his remote connection. But Kenny hadn't. He'd typed the name Zhou Wenling. That had to be the way in, and Kansas was going to find it.

I had to just had to be patient and—

Something flashed out of the corner of my eye—a tan trench coat amidst the Friday lunchtime walkers around me. I was at 14th Street so I turned down it and began to run, taking a hard right maybe thirty feet down the block into an underground parking garage. I backed up against its cement north wall, behind an entrance pillar, breathing hard. I ripped off my mask to breathe quieter and tried to blend into the shadows.

Waited. Stilled my breathing.

I watched one, two, three, people, then a group of four walk past on the 14th Street sidewalk.

Then hurried steps.

A second later, there he was, hunched forward in his trench coat, no mask, his balding head and glasses twisting back and forth, looking for his lost prey. From this close, I saw he was about forty-five, shorter than me but carrying a big gut, saggy jowls, and pinched mouth. A mean, fat iguana. Looking for me. Spying on me. Keeping track of me for his overlords.

It was really starting to piss me off.

He'd obviously missed the edge of me that was visible from the street because he now hurried past, oblivious. If I just let him go, he'd vanish in a few seconds and I could still make my one o'clock. In three...two...

Fuck that.

I stepped out behind him and called, "Hey, asshole!"

He obviously recognized his name because he slowed, stopped, and turned. His jowly face was red, shaking, and covered in sweat. I was sure his whole body stank.

For a second, it crossed my mind that if he carried a gun, he might pull it now and fire at me. Even with a handgun, he'd probably hit me. We were only about twenty feet apart.

But that clearly wasn't part of his job, however angry he was at me turning the tables on him, because his bare hands stayed out at his sides. They looked stiff, like he was ordering them to not clench. Like he was worried if he came at me with clenched fists, the awesome strength of his flabby fists and shaking gut might knock me dead. And the look in his eyes said he really wanted me dead.

Eight months ago, that look would have made my eyes water and my body instinctively back away. But since that time, the training Lena had insisted on had strengthened my body, my fighting skills, and, evidently, my intestinal fortitude, because almost without thought I found myself walking toward balding-trench-coat-man with my own fists forming and re-forming, my eyes picking out his best strike points—neck, groin, face, gut, shins, in that order.

"You want to talk to me, pervert?" I called to him as I walked. I chose a name that would tell all the other lunchtime walkers who the bad guy was, even as my over-developed sense of how I looked to others said I looked like the aggressive party.

The same thought seemed to have entered the balding guy's head too because his face and body suddenly went from shaking rage to puzzled fear at my approach.

"Wh-what? Do I know you?" he said in a quavering baritone voice as I reached spitting distance.

A few people had indeed stopped to watch. One young woman had lifted up her phone and looked to be filming us. Great. Especially as the sun had just come out fully for the first time today, so I and my stalker were perfectly lit for the video. Just two unmasked, belligerent goons getting into a fight.

I made myself calm, playing *his* game. "Why have you been following me?"

"I don't know what you mean." His jowls shook as he said it. The guy was good.

"You're totally innocent. Just some random guy."

"Uh...yeah."

"Okay." I turned to the young woman filming us. She'd moved to within about fifteen feet, close enough to record everything but far enough back to run. "Miss? Feel free to record my face. My name is Jackson Traine. I'm a professor at the University of Washington and have a private psychology practice on East Madison, near Washington Park. Now perhaps this 'innocent' gentleman who *hasn't* been following me around would be kind enough to let you tape his face and identity."

The young woman and I both turned toward my stalker to see that he'd turned and was hurrying away. His usual disappearing trick.

But I was so done with that.

"No!" I called out as I hurried after him. "You don't just get to hurry away like that! I'm making a citizen's arrest!" I called out like some Oath Keeper crazy-head and leaped forward to grab the back of his trench coat.

I got a handful of it and yanked hard, making man's body, probably a good thirty pounds heavier than mine, jerk to a stumbling halt.

What he did then was a surprise.

There was a shuffle of his dress shoes that I recognized as a weight change—I'd seen Alvin Westor do it a hundred times when he was teaching me how to kickbox—and this old fat guy's right foot was flying at my head in a roundhouse.

I avoided getting knocked out only because Alvin had pulled that move on me countless times. My upper body automatically leaned back and my right elbow windmilled after the passing leg, catching a tiny piece of it even as his hard shoe heel clipped my nose, sending my blood spraying.

Balding guy still finished his spin on both feet, but a little off balance. If he was surprised that I'd managed any kind of defense, he didn't show it. He was too busy stuffing his glasses into his trench coat pocket, then sloughing that coat for more freedom of movement.

Which was fascinating in itself, the non-spinning, revved-up part of my brain thought. Taking off his coat and planning to obviously fight me here, in the middle of the day, on a fairly busy Capitol Hill street that was only a few blocks from the Seattle Police East Precinct? It didn't exactly scream someone who was trying to hide his identity. I would have bet dollars to donuts that more than one of our gathering crowd of onlookers had whipped out a phone to record this now.

And yes, I'd look like an insane person once those videos hit social media. I could lose my chance to teach anymore at the UW. I could lose counseling clients. But I didn't care. This guy had pushed me too far.

Nor was he backing down. His face was so red I expected to see steam shooting out of his ears.

He ran at me like a bull.

I sidestepped and pivoted left to catch the back of his head as he passed.

Which he'd obviously expected, ducking and pivoting under my swing with his arms wide like a top, before slamming one fist up into my chin. His other hand simultaneously grabbed my nutsack through my jeans and lifted, throwing my brain-fuzzed body in the direction it was already going.

I vaguely heard the grunt of his effort as I flew and hoped he'd put out his back.

Then I smashed into the pavement of the street. A car honked and screeched somewhere. I flashed back to being a teen and having Dead Eyes of the Demon Monks kicking and beating me senseless.

Balding guy had dropped on top of me now like some kind of MMA fighter or, given his proportions, a past-his-prime WWF wrestler. He began slamming his fists into me—right, left, right, left—as I tried to roll and protect my head.

I was losing badly. The guy might look old and flabby, but there was clearly muscle, training, experience, rage, and...

"Assbag!" he growled at me in between thuds. "Scared little retard!"

Get away from this, Jackson! Come on!

But every time I twisted or managed a strike, he shifted and stayed on me, beating my ribs, my belly, then back to my head. Thud. Thud. *Thud.*

"I was supposed to just watch you!" he grunted, slamming a fist hard into my side as he almost fell down face to my face. "Turd!"

"Fuck you!" I shot back, spitting blood at him. I could only see black and red now because he'd closed both my eyes. Pain lanced through my chest and I felt panic kick in. Surely he was going to stop soon. He couldn't kill me out here like this in front of everyone.

"You think I won't kill you, assbag?" he sprayed down at me, like he'd read my thoughts. "Well, you're wrong."

Thud. Thud. Another rib cracked and lanced pain up through my throat and out in a bark of blood.

"Because we know what you can do! We know! So do it, you little creep! Do it! *Do it!*"

Thud thud thud thud. Pummeling my gut.

I'm going to die. Because they...know. But I can't... I won't... I...

I stumbled a little, disoriented, sure I was dying, beaten apart. Then I regained my balance and stopped. Looked around. Realized I could breathe without pain. I was wearing my mask. My groin and face were intact. I was on E. Pine, walking east to...right, to get to my car. On 14th. And... And?

It all rushed back to me and clicked into place.

Right.

You'd think I'd know the drill by now.

I'd just jumped back ten minutes in time from a murderous thug beating me to death. Which meant that at this very moment, that murderous thug, the balding man in glasses, was likely watching me, following me, close enough to be seen if I looked carefully. Because that was part of his frickin' plan, wasn't it? For me to see him just now and then? More often now, probably, since I'd been approached by Wilson and Dadashev and would be expected to understand what it meant to have the balding man following and watching me everywhere I went.

I kept walking without looking back, turning down 14th, wondering whether he'd make a scene if I didn't look around or did and just ignored him.

Had it always been the plan to confront me at some point and see if the balding man could force me to make a jump? Why? Because maybe, despite what the balding man had said, they didn't really know? They suspected. Maybe because of their history with Kenny. Maybe from some other intel. Maybe even from a careful consideration of everything that happened in the Demon Monks' headquarters back in March. I'd had that strange déjà vu session in the basement that now made me think of the memories I had of the times I'd bought the same newspaper editions, each time being a timestream someone else had terminated or multiplied.

So had there been a second time traveler in the Demon Monks HQ? Maybe one secretly working for the CIA?

I stopped dead in my tracks about twenty feet from where I'd cross 14th to pick up my car. If the balding guy wanted to attack me, here was his chance.

Nothing happened other than random people passing.

Which made me think that the balding guy hadn't attacked me because of a plan. He'd attacked because I'd confronted him, thrown him off-balance, made him improvise. He might have actually been trying to beat me into jumping out of desperation so that my whole bit about getting him on camera would be wiped out when I jumped everything back ten minutes.

If he was that easy to throw off his game plan, the dude was as emotionally weak as me. That didn't fit my vision of a CIA operative at all.

But if what he'd said about *knowing* I could time travel was true, that was even more disturbing. Because, for all my suspicions, I couldn't be sure exactly who "they" were or how many of them there were.

All I knew was they knew my secret.

And given that the mysterious "they" could easily be one of the groups Kansas had said were interested in Lena's time travel research, it was important she understand how serious their interest was.

I had to let her know.

6

Set adrift

IF I NEEDED ANY more indications from the universe that Lena and I were somehow made for each other, I received a text from her while I sped to my office to meet my one o'clock client.

Your training session with the boys tomorrow is canceled. Please come by my 3rd floor business park office tonight at 7 pm. Same access code as last March. We need to talk.

Okay, so the tone was more peremptory than friendly. She also surprised me by still having access to the "3rd floor business park office," by which I assumed she meant the medical clinic in Building #4, out in the hills and forests past Redmond, heading for the foothills of the Cascades. But she was thinking of me as I was thinking of her, and she didn't bother repeating an access code she knew was forever in my memory once read.

Yes, I heard the possible five-alarm-relationship-fire in the message, but I'd frankly taken in enough difficult stuff this day already and wanted to believe I was due something better.

I screeched into my parking space and texted back:

My last client's at 6. Make it 8?

Even make-up or break-up sessions have to wait sometimes.

When 6 p.m. rolled around and I ushered my last client out, I was emotionally exhausted and the skin around my upper cheek bones ached where my mask had been pressing tightly for the last five hours. Quite apart from my confrontation with my balding stalker and what it might mean, I realized that even a single jump back in time now was enough to trigger all the PTSD garbage my physical training had mostly managed to sublimate.

It had taken twice my normal emotional reserves to push that down and be fully present for each of my clients this afternoon.

I'd helped them lay down, at least for a while, all their anxieties and questions, their jealousies and anger, their stumbling lost-ness that was such a key element of the human condition. Even Cassandra, whom I was seeing twice a week for the first while, managed to disgorge much of her rising fear over the coming Asian apocalypse and walk away cleansed. Or at least heard.

And I, after giving myself a cursory sponge bath, locked up the office and all the secrets that had been shared therein, and set out for Lena's business park office like a freshly washed young swain en route to see the object of his ardent desire who's been so long absent from him in both body and spirit.

Thick clouds hid the moon and stars, so I plunged into darkness as I left the city and entered the hills.

I let my GPS guide me, though my memory of each final turn leading to the gated entrance and rows of dark buildings jumped out to me with a rush of excitement and nerves. I'd been here only thrice before, but those times had involved many firsts, both good and bad—kissing Lena, watching Lena die, jumping back in time, having Lena try to suffocate me, figuring out how my time traveling worked.

The parking lot lights were on and the gate was open when I drove in. I thought maybe Lena had left the gate open for me, but saw quickly that it wasn't so. In front of Building #4, there were five vehicles parked, and I recognized the four rugged one as belonging to Alvin, Big, Doc, and Smiley. I didn't recognize the fifth, a sleek Lexus sports car that looked so deep red in the low light it could have been dripping blood, but I assumed it was Lena's rental. She was obviously renting from a very upscale place when she deigned to come up to Seattle these days. Family money.

I pulled up and parked beside the Lexus, got out, and found that the old code I had for the building did indeed still grant me access.

I went up to the third floor, entered the wide-open medical clinic that took up most of that floor, and saw the entire Lead the Way team and Lena waiting for me in a standing semi-circle in the main room like this was some kind of intervention. None of them masked. The LTW team never wore masks. It was one of those strange contradictions for Alvin, who seemed so smart and level-headed in everything else.

Then again, Lena wasn't masked. I wasn't masked. Elizabeth Chan, who stood demurely a little to one side and behind Lena like a secretary ready to take notes, wasn't masked.

It was like we all felt in our guts that this was the end of the world somehow, so we might as well take our last breaths freely.

I walked in past the stacked chairs, line of rolling carts and empty hospital beds and came to a stop some five feet from the group.

"Hi guys," I said. Then I waited, saying nothing. Giving them nothing. This was their show.

After a full minute of silence, in which I think they thought I'd break into some kind of apology, plea for understanding, or "aw shucks" dance of confusion, Alvin finally spoke.

"We think your training's over," he said with his usual flat delivery. Flat affect. Hooded eyes. Skinny body with the slightest of slouches that let his hips just forward. He really did look like an upright eel. An upright eel in his usual pseudo-combat fatigues like the rest of his team, their tight gray tee shirts emblazoned with Lead the Way Security on their left upper chests.

Lena, dressed down tonight in some kind of black pantsuit and draping scarves that hid the shape of her body completely, brushed back a stray hair from her face. She didn't have her hair pulled back in a tight ponytail like she did when working. Nor was it loose in wild curls around her face, like when she was laughing or making love. It was just back in a plain hairband. Her makeup was minimal.

She was still stunningly gorgeous, but her expression and serious attire warned me not to respond like a lover or even a man right now.

"It's pretty clear you're no longer taking your training seriously," Lena said.

"You think so?" I said.

"And if you don't care about it, I'm not sure why I should be paying for it, or Shadow's team should be sacrificing themselves on your behalf."

"Ah," I said. "Of course." I didn't mention how she'd tied my commitment to training to our being together, and to our mutual sharing of thoughts, feelings, and personal journeys. Nor that Alvin had, in fact, been providing his training services to me on an "as-available" basis, working around their other paying gigs because they'd provided my training without cost. This because Lena, coming from a wealthy family, had bankrolled their startup when Alvin and the others had left the Ranger corps six years ago.

"Do you feel you got any value from it?" Lena asked coldly.

Given that I regularly expressed my appreciation to each of the guys at every session, save this last one and the couple where Alvin had literally tried to kill me, I knew this was coming from Lena's dark place, not that of Alvin and the others.

Certainly not from Doc, Big, and Smiley, who were all shifting uncomfortably where they stood, like kids watching their parents fight.

Alvin's eyes narrowed the slightest bit, which I knew meant he was trying to assess me right now. For all his coldness and somewhat sociopathic devotion to testing Lena's theory about me, I'd found Alvin to be a remarkably straight shooter. He was highly skilled and had always given his best to our lessons, even when his sub-mission for Lena made him rougher than was called for.

I sighed and gave him a little head nod, hoping it let him know I understood his position and forgave him for it. Which I only realized just then that I did. Because I'd finally understood, here in the public exhibition of Lena's emotional darkness, that Alvin couldn't have done anything but what he had for Lena. Her intensity demanded either devotion or complete rejection. And to reject Lena Cortland would be to reject such a fascinating force of will, a presence destined to achieve great things, that a wise man would rather bear her storms than cut himself off from her power.

"I actually feel," I said, "like the training with you guys has made all the difference in the world for me.

"Big, for the calm that you managed to wash over me even as you were teaching me how to strip, assemble, load, and fire an M16, an M4, an HK MP5, the Sig Sauers, the Glocks, not to mention the grenades, bayonets, and types of wrist restraints, thank you.

"Doc, for patching me up again and again, teaching me the proper way to prepare tea, how to work out the stiffness in my muscles and joints, *doumo arigato.*" I bowed after that one. How could I not?

"Smiley, for letting me beat you in the occasional footrace when I know you can run circles around me any day of the week, for teaching me how to push past my physical boundaries every time we met, for giving me the lightness of heart to find humor in pain, thank you, buddy.

"And Shadow, Alvin, thank you for your instruction not only in the physical arts of self-defense, but in the mental attitude of looking for the intentions of those around you to separate friend from foe and to predict the actions of both. I may never reach your level of perception or planning, but I'd like to think I've absorbed at least some of the attitudes."

I bowed to Alvin as well. Just because. Respect.

I looked at all of them again, one after the other, feeling a sudden certainty that if I ever saw them again, it would be in circumstances that would make my next words critical. "I feel like each one of you men offered a true part of yourselves to me over the past nine months, and I will never forget. I consider you my friends, and if you should ever need me, I will do my damnedest to answer your call."

I put my fist briefly across my heart and was gratified to see the gesture returned, even, in a smooth, subtle way, by Alvin.

Lena was looking almost wildly between the guys and me. Behind her, Elizabeth looked like she was attempting to hide a smile.

"That's it?" Lena said both to me and to the guys. "You're all bro's now for life and the shit that's gone on means nothing?" Her eyes blazed, and she looked directly at me. "You are a liar. An unforgivable liar."

I wanted to nod, because of course she was right. I'd lied to the guys about my power so that Lena had been left sounding crazy and diminished. And though I'd offered to apologize directly to her alone about it and explain why I had to do it to survive, it was obviously too late now. Nor was it something I was going to do with the guys here.

It just wasn't their secret to know.

Hell, it shouldn't have been *any*one's secret to know. The people who somehow did, beyond Lena, were already trying to abduct me for it and maybe use me to mess up the world. I wished I could share *that* with Lena.

"I'm sorry you feel that way," was all I could give her.

Behind her left shoulder, Elizabeth caught my eye, raised her eyebrows, and gave me a slow, smirking shake of her head that told me I'd handled that badly.

She was probably right.

As it was, all I could find it in myself to do as the LTW guys nodded to me and filed out, was stand there and nod back at them, avoiding Lena's eyes. Last to go was Elizabeth Chan, who gave me another pitying smile and head shake as she passed me.

When they'd left and Lena was still there, I turned hopefully toward her, thinking we might talk. If nothing else, I had to tell her about the CIA's interest in me and how that might spill over to her, too.

"I need you to leave," Lena said. "I have to be the last out to lock up."

"No. Please. We really need to talk. There's stuff I have to tell you. About me. About your work."

"You're too late."

"It's not like you ever gave me a chance!"

"Oh, so *now* you're going to fight for us?"

"What the—? Why do think I've been sticking with all this? For you. For us. While you wouldn't let me come with you to Seattle. I could have helped you with your father. With all of it."

"Could you? Really?"

"I would have tried!"

"Too much, too little, too late."

"It's not. It can't be. Look, so many things are changing right now for both of us, but we belong together. We complement each other. You make me believe in the whole concept of soul mates. You—"

"*STO-O-OP!*" It ripped out of her like a primal scream and I finally realized how close to falling apart she was. Her chest was rising and falling hard, her hands were shaking as she raised her right to point at me. "You don't get to talk to me anymore. Not even if you jump back in time over and over. A man who can't stand and say what he is, is nothing."

"But—"

"No. Jackson, I don't think you have any idea how much pain I feel every time I see you. If you actually care for me, you'll get you out of here and out of my life. NOW."

Well...shit.

My ever-helpful brain then suggested that if Lena had nothing to do with me at all, the chances of the CIA going after her work, such as it was, went way down.

Wait! Whose side are you on here?

Both sides, buddy. Read the room. No means no.

I flushed in hot despair, turned, and walked out.

And the worst part of my night hadn't even happened yet.

7

The list

WHEN I DROVE OFF, I looked into my rear-view mirror and saw Elizabeth climb into the driver's side of the Lexus like she was Lena's chauffeur as well as secretary.

I floored it, my heart swimming somewhere down around my ankles.

When I arrived home some forty minutes later, held up by Friday night traffic across the 520 Bridge, I saw Kansas had texted me, telling me to log into our shared face chat.

Finally.

Half-believing she was so all-knowing that she was going to comfort me over the massive rejection I'd just suffered, I hurried into my bedroom without bothering with my apartment lights, logged in, and her face came up at once.

She looked even more haggard than when we'd spoken on New Year's Day. The bags were deeper and darker under her eyes and her hair had definitely gone gray, though she was only forty-two. It looked wild and uncombed on her head and she wore a rumpled sweatshirt that looked slept in.

"Jackie," she croaked and ran a hand shakily through her hair like she couldn't believe it was me.

"Kansas, are you okay? What's happened? Have you been fired?"

She shook her head. "No, no, nothing like that. Still working from home during COVID. I'm on a secure trunk near the campus."

"The NSA buildings."

She looked at me, an odd ghosting going on in her eyes. For all Kenny and my conjectures, Kansas had never once confirmed that she worked out of this infamous intelligence agency based in Fort Meade,

Maryland, north of DC. Unlike the CIA, the NSA was tasked with assimilating intel, both foreign and domestic. Specifically SIGINT, signals intelligence, vs. HUMINT, human intelligence, like the spies the CIA often relied upon. Everything about what Kansas did screamed NSA.

And now, amazingly, she gave me a little jerky nod, like of course that was what she meant and where she worked. "I get everything here, you understand?" Her face twitched as she talked and she seemed unaware of it. "Nothing is blocked. I have full access."

"What did you find, Kansas?"

She looked back over her shoulder at what I assumed was the door to her room or apartment. Maybe she'd heard a sound.

"Kansas?"

She looked back at her screen, the height of her camera catching the twitching of her upper eyelids. "The CIA has you, me, and Kenny on a list," she said.

"Well that explains the two guys who visited me from their human resource and talent acquisition department."

Kansas blinked. "And...?"

"They told me to come to Langley and talk to them. They wanted to discuss Kenny. They implied they had him."

Kansas was blinking harder, processing this. "When?" she said.

"They showed up the same night I talked to you. New Year's Day. They've also had a guy following me around, watching me. I confronted him this afternoon, and he tried to kill me in front of a crowd of gawkers filming it on their cameras."

"What?"

"He kept screaming that he knew what I could do. I figured he thought I'd jump back in time ten minutes and nobody would have seen any of it."

"And..."

"He was right. I jumped." My breath hitched as I said it. These jumps were not okay. Other people deliberately traumatizing me to make me jump was not okay.

Also, because, I was finally getting brave enough to admit, if my jumps just took me back to create a parallel timestream, then all the timestreams of me and Lena getting killed, all the timestreams of me getting beaten, the ones where I beat up or hurt others—they all still went on. The swath of destruction behind me spread wider and wider with each jump.

Kansas was nodding her head and rubbing her nose over and over. "So they know," she muttered. "Which means they have Kenny. I should have known that. I should have!"

"Hey. This is a good thing, right? A clue as to where we can—"

Kansas' head twitched to look back over her shoulder again for a second. "Sh! Don't say anything. Look at this. Don't write it down. The list we're on."

Her finger hit a button on her keyboard and what looked like a captured photo of a physical list showed up on the screen. There were twelve names. An auspicious number. Each had a date and alphanumeric code beside it. The names of Kenny, me, and Kansas were at the bottom. The dates beside Kenny's name dated back two years. The dates beside my name and Kansas' date back to March 2021, around the time I was fighting for my life inside the basement of the Demon Monks' headquarters, shortly after learning I could jump back in time.

But what really freaked me out was the heading above all the names. There was the CIA seal of an eagle head over a shield with a 16-point compass star on it. And directly below it, in all caps, like it was a group or operation name, maybe an order, was the word SCATTER.

A chill ran down my spine.

"Got it?" Kansas said.

I nodded and the screen vanished. Permanently, I suspected. Thinking of what Cassandra had told me, and the changing newspaper stories, I said, "I think I know what they're doing with these people. What they want to do with us. A Chinese party member was killed this week in—"

"Jackson, stop! You don't talk about this. You don't text or write about it. If you—"

But this time, she cut her*self* off and jumped up from her chair. There was a booming sound through the screen speakers, like someone was trying to break into Kansas' room.

The screen went black.

My computer shut off.

I stabbed at its start button. It rebooted, but when I moused my way through the contact protocols, I found the final step, the one that connected with Kansas, was gone.

I stood up and backed away from it, looking around my bedroom, half-expecting someone to come crashing in here, too.

Nobody did.

I walked out into my living room where I hadn't bothered pulling down my blinds and looked out into the Seattle night, Lake Washington glittering with reflected lights in the distance. I had no doubt at all that the balding man was still out there, watching me.

I took a deep, shaky breath.

Letting Kansas solve this for me was obviously no longer an option.

8

Simple detective work

I waited until the next morning before making any decisions. I had to be sure I was thinking clearly. After breakfast, I got my computer working again and tried to reconnect with Kansas.

Nobody answered.

So I went for a run, going through all my options, and decided the most obvious one was best. I was going to use the tickets I'd been given. I'd fly to Langley, Virginia and attend my CIA "interview." Go to them before they came for me. Use the illusion of voluntary compliance to ask about both Kansas and Kenny. If they wanted me to join them willingly, they might even give me straight answers.

I pulled out my phone and texted my decision to Lena.

Yes, she'd said she wanted me out of her life completely and I respected that. Except for two things. First, she'd told me to leave because she saw me as someone who couldn't stand up and say who I was. That was a foolish standard to apply when such a revelation could kill or disable a person, but I was apparently about to meet it by going to Langley.

Second, if I vanished after this meeting like Kenny and now Kansas, there would be at least one person who might understand why and where to start looking, even if she despised me.

After I sent the text, I walked about my apartment, considering exactly how my interview with the CIA might go down. What if they wouldn't answer anything? Did I have anything to pressure them with? It struck me that if I came with some kind of goods on them, some knowledge they didn't expect, I could demand some *quid pro quo* knowledge in return. Maybe they'd even wonder who else I'd told and what kind of insurance I'd given myself.

So what kind of insurance *could* I give myself?

The list, obviously. The designation of the operation: SCATTTER. Maybe I could also detail the CIA's possible connection to the Demon Monks? And the identity of the sloppy, balding surveillance guy in glasses and tan trench coat? Did I have any way to tie those down?

The easiest one to check was the list of twelve names. I sat down at my computer in my bedroom and used the first part of the connection protocols Kansas had helped me set up for our face chats. They masked my computer IP address and made it look like I was connecting to the internet from somewhere in Europe, Asia, Africa, or South America. It was apparently a floating IP. She'd explained its use, not how it worked.

Trusting my location and identity were disguised, I explored assorted news and government public databases, along with more traditional search engines. I found a few hits on the names, but none that described disappearances, explained or otherwise. Not even "Zhou Xiaobo," despite his having the same last name as the mysterious Zhou Wenling. Not Kentucky Traine, either. I suspected even Kansas Traine had vanished like a quiet blip in the massive ocean of humanity, with only I or my parents really caring. Because what did any one person, or 12 people, really matter, right?

SCATTER, as some kind of CIA or government program, also came up blank.

Fine. Then it would have to be the identity of the balding man and/or tying the CIA to the Demon Monks.

I cleaned up and called Ziggy.

Ziggy met me for brunch at a place near his apartment around ten, carrying his art materials as requested. The setting was good for a chat-and-draw. It had an old-time diner feel with round cushions at the counter, crowded booth-style seating, bright lights, and a large crowd enjoying the upscale comfort-food menu, talking loudly, ignoring us.

I ordered a Reuben sandwich with a side of sweet potato fries covered in a Portobello-mushroom gratin. Ziggy went with blackened salmon with shallots, arugula, and lemon aioli. We also shared a stack of griddle cakes with some homemade brown sugar syrup and lemon butter for dessert.

A while into our meal, he pulled out his sketch pad and started drawing the balding guy with glasses again from memory.

"So...you talked to this bad boy?" he said, smacking his lips from another bite of griddle cakes as he finger-rubbed and sketched from his memory.

I'd asked him to leave room for the chest and shoulders because the physicality of the balding guy without his trench coat had been impressive. And I added to Ziggy's recollection with my own.

"I did. Loopier jowls. Thicker brow line. And his nose was definitely crooked like it had been broken before."

As I brought the face out in my memory and through Ziggy's sketch, I realized the man was definitely a brawler. It explained how easily he'd gotten through the shit-load of self-defense training and drills I'd done over the last nine months. But I was younger, fitter, taller. That fight was still an embarrassment.

Another fifteen minutes and Ziggy added some color, catching the pale pinkness of the man perfectly. Ziggy asked if he should add the man's glasses, but on instinct I decided against it. The balding man had taken off his glasses when he'd really started to fight, so it could be the glasses were recent or he didn't need them all the time.

I thanked Ziggy profusely, paid for our meal, and took the sketch from him as we both got up.

"Who you gwan show it to?" Ziggy asked.

"Bryan, probably. But first just people on the street. Shopkeepers. Traffic cops. A public servant in Town Hall. He's been around here. Someone will recognize him."

I got a hit with the thirty-first person I approached in the neighborhood. He was with a group of his friends in a coffee shop on E. Pike, all heavily tattooed like him, and laughed the second he saw Ziggy's work.

"Hey, that's Rick Soder, the Bat!"

"The Bat?"

The guy shrugged. "His nickname. Used to do these amazing arms-out spins when he was avoiding blows. Totally impractical, but showy as fuck. And he had the skills to back it up—kicks, jumps, head butts. I saw him beat Randy Couture in the Light Heavyweight class. Randy-fucking-Couture."

"So this guy, Rick Soder, the Bat, he was a professional fighter?"

"In the UFC and MMA both. He was crazy good. Only retired what? Five years ago? What'd he do? Rob a store?"

"Nothing like that."

"No really. What?"

I sighed. "I think he's working for the CIA now."

The guy's mouth dropped open for a second. Then he looked at me a little sideways and grinned. "That would be cool, right?"

"Wouldn't it?"

Actually, the more I pondered Rick Soder's involvement with the CIA, the more uncomfortable I got. Something didn't seem right. This whole thing with him seemed too...basic? It didn't fit my naïve ideas about how slick the CIA was, but maybe there were levels of employment. Rick Soder was at the muscle enforcer level. Crude. Dangerous.

Which reminded me of my other pre-interview task: getting some evidence of the CIA's connection to the Demon Monks. I knew how I was going to do that, but I wasn't liking it. I was a psychologist, not some frigging hardass detective.

But the more I thought about it, the more I concluded that being a psychologist, and being me, Kenny's brother, might actually give me an edge in doing what I planned to do.

I got my police buddy Bryan on the phone and asked for his help. But when I told him what I wanted, he started stammering.

"Whoah, wait. You want to see *Cutter?*"

Cutter, who'd sliced up my brother's face when I was a teenager. Cutter, who'd later beaten and stabbed me in timeline after timeline at the Demon Monks' HQ until I'd finally escaped and helped the cops and Lead the Way team bring him down.

Cutter had also shot Bryan. Almost killed him. Bryan didn't like the idea of me going near the man again.

But after I explained Cutter might be the only one with a lead to my brother's whereabouts, Bryan broke down and gave me the scoop. Cutter, real name Jonathan Worthal, was being held in the King County Adult Detention building at James and 5th, the southern edge of Downtown Seattle.

"But he's not going to stay there. And getting in to see him? Jeez, I don't know. Lots of COVID case there. And you have to fill out a form. And the prisoner has to, you know, want to see you, so..."

"He'll want to see me," I said.

"Why?"

I remembered the sadistic glee Cutter had taken in everything he'd done to me. It had supposedly been to pressure Kenny to reveal who he was working for, but I knew it was more than that. Something in Cutter's little weasel soul had deeply enjoyed hurting me to get revenge on Kenny. I was betting if he heard I wanted to see him, he'd start drooling like Hannibal Lecter, thinking he could mess with my mind and hurt me that way. Or physically attack me if he could.

To Bryan, I just said, "He'll want to. Can you help me fill out the forms? Now? If I can't see him by tomorrow night, it'll be too late."

Impossible getting through bureaucracy that fast, right? I might have helped it along by calling up another positive police contact I'd made in the middle of all the trauma of last March. He was a physician who'd been posted in the SPD East Precinct the day I'd managed to talk my way in. After I got beaten in the precinct stairwell and tried jumping back in time three times in a row to escape, Dr. Emile Bresden helped me survive my heart seizure and leave the building. After I came out of my post-Demon Monk PTSD relapse, I looked up Emile to thank him in person. The thank you came at a critical time for him and we bonded.

Now Emile was working in the Harborview Medical Center, right across the I5 from the King County Adult Detention building, and was on call with that prison, especially now with all the COVID outbreaks.

Long story short, I called Emile, who took the paperwork I'd prepared with Bryan, and fast-tracked it through the system. I scored a special visitation with Cutter, AKA Jonathan Worthal, Sunday night at 6:30 p.m.

When I got the news, I personally called to thank Bryan and Emile. Then I broke out in a cold sweat, shivering, shaking, and experiencing in vivid sensory recall every cut, punch, stab, bite, and slap of spittle Cutter had given me. It consumed me until I ran into my bathroom and threw up so harshly I thought I might have popped a blood vessel in my throat.

I wore a new N95 mask when I came into the prison, but I swore I could still smell the stink of bodies and desperation like a haze in the air as the guard led me to the visitation room.

The guard opened the door and waited impatiently for me to enter. I was taking almost baby steps. The room was a white box out of my nightmares, with a single table bolted to the floor in the dead center where Cutter...

The door thumped and clanked shut behind me, making me turn back to it, startled.

Only to find my focus jerked right back to the table in the middle of the room again as Cutter, hunched over the table like some kind of demonic cockroach, snickered at me.

I gritted my teeth and broke out in a cold sweat.

He wore a short-sleeve, orange prison shirt over a long dirty jersey, with matching tie-up pants and running shoes below. His hair was still long and greasy. It fell around his bruised, and cut-up face and patchy beard. His exposed teeth had gotten darker again, the recession in the gums more pronounced. The blue surgical mask they'd obviously put on him to follow COVID protocols swung under that beard, hanging from his left ear.

But that wasn't a threat to me, I told myself. *He* wasn't a threat to me.

He held no knife.

He had no power.

This had been ensured by the way his near-skeletal wrists and ankles were chained together and to the table, which was bolted to the floor. The extreme restraints had probably been chosen after whatever altercation gave Cutter his facial cuts and bruises. I presumed they would have confiscated whatever shivs or spikes or rocks he'd hidden on his person before they'd walked him in here.

He raised his upper lip and eyebrows at me now. My move.

Was that the slightest hint of uncertainty in his expression?

I'd told Bryan that Cutter would accept my visitation request, out of boredom, if nothing else. But I also thought a part of him would be calculating whether my visit might be tied to some appeal he was trying to launch. Maybe his lawyer had arranged it and Cutter had to prove he was helpful. Maybe if he could give them something on Kenny and his bosses...

Ridiculous, of course. I certainly had no pull with anyone in the justice system other than a Bryan and Doc Bresden. And the idea that the Seattle PD would believe Cutter's tales enough to start an investigation into a local operation by the CIA was so ludicrous it actually made me grimace.

Cutter must have seen it in my eyes above my mask, because his own gaze wavered like he realized he'd been wrong to hope.

Before he could completely retreat into himself, I pulled myself together enough to slide into the metal chair opposite him. I worked my tongue around in my mouth to get some moisture there and forced myself to look this sadistic monster straight in the eye.

"So," I said. "Jonathan Worthal. It almost makes it sound like you had a mother and father once."

He blinked at me like he didn't understand, and his eyes started drifting away again. Like, even though he'd been in here less than a year, it had already changed his ability to talk with non-felons and people not ready to kill you if you looked at them wrong.

Or maybe I was completely fetishizing the prison experience from too many movies. Maybe Cutter was just depressed that I wasn't here to save him somehow. And if I had nothing to offer him, he had nothing to say to me.

I blurted, "You know, they're still trying to figure out who you were working with."

He raised his eyes back up to mine.

"Who Kenny was working with," I continued. "Who gave him the power to order you and the other gangs around."

Cutter barked an ugly laugh and the look of nasty cunning I remembered returned to his eyes. "He didn't 'order' us," he said with a voice that still slimed out like he wanted to lick your ear then bite it off. He shook his head hard so the hanging mask came off his left ear and dropped to the floor.

"You certainly implied it from the way you were arguing with him, begging for him to just tell you *please* who he was working for. Challenging them to come and get you."

"Business associates. We had stuff to work out."

"But you let them control the communications. You used military codes and protocols when you talked about times and places with them."

"What the fuck, little bro?"

"You think nobody read your texts and emails? You think your face chats weren't recorded?"

I was fishing now, of course. Kansas had tapped into their communications using whatever line bugs she had access to through her work, and she'd told me the Demon Monks seemed to have adopted military communication protocols, but she'd never told me she had any of their specific plans in hand. She hadn't even found what they'd all been trying to do in that big gang summit I'd infiltrated that somehow then got called off *before the time I'd actually entered it.*

Cutter was wickedly canny, or else I was a lousy liar, because he hawked and spat onto the table top in front of me. "You got nothing. The police have shit. Only thing they had on me was shooting that cop. Even that I almost skated on self-defense, a fog of war kind of thing. That was why I threw away my gun right after. Everyone saw that."

I shook my head. Cutter had thrown down his gun once the Lead the Way team had started picking off his men one headshot at a time. Those who had fought back had died. Cutter was just a survivor.

And he was shaking his head at me now, drifting away again. I wondered if he had access to drugs in here.

"Focus, asshole!" I snapped. "Kenny told you nothing about who he was working for or where he was based? Didn't even hint at it? And you still worked with him?"

Cutter's face flushed. "Came with the cut-up face and sweet fucking deal. Way too high tech for any low level. So I guess government or mercs, okay? You think I'd just roll over and play their stupid games for nothing? They gave us companies, dates, deals. We made so much fucking..."

He let it trail off and rolled his head back and around on his neck so I could hear the bones crunching and popping.

When his face came back up, he started yelling. "Guards! Get this fucking dick muncher out of my FACE! Or I'm going to find a way to rip it OFF! YOU HEAR ME?" He kicked his chair out from under him and started jerking and thrashing around, trying to come over the table at me. "*AAAAHHH!*"

But I'd quickly slid off my chair and backed up, far enough away that his spittle and field of chaos couldn't reach me.

A moment later, the room's only door, the one behind me, opened and two guards came in. The burlier of the two ducked behind Cutter and put him in a headlock while the other keyed open his restraints. Then the two of them manhandled this skinny demon, who probably weighed half as much as either one of the two guards, out the door, leaving it open after working their way through it.

I waited a couple beats, listening to the struggles and strangled yells of Cutter, then stuck my head out. The short hallway looked empty. I walked back the way I'd come in and checked myself out.

It was only when I'd left the facility completely and my heart rate had slowed to something approaching normal, that I could go over what Cutter had said, playing the exact words again and again in my head to pick something out of this mess.

There wasn't a lot.

Maybe Cutter's denial of being controlled. That the arrangement had been more that this outside group, through Kenny, had offered "companies, date, deals"—as in leads the computer jocks in the Demon Monk's boiler room had been using?—in exchange for an agreement to "play their stupid games."

That was the crux. The stupid games. Experiments? With Kenny, a man with the power to see time travel changes, acting as the main contact.

It wasn't until I was back in my car and driving back to my apartment in the dark to pack for my trip the next morning that the outline of everything started to gel.

9

Everyone's watching

I checked my texts again when I got home. Almost 48 hours and Lena hadn't responded. It was almost like she'd been serious when she said she wanted me out of her life.

Which was sad, because I would have loved to have shared with her what I thought I'd figured out about what had happened with Kenny and why the people who had him were doubling down with Kansas and me. It not only had implications for me but also for her time travel research. Especially if, as I suspected, she'd decided to keep that research going without telling me.

Against my better judgement, I dialed her number.

One ring. Two. Three. Then, instead of going to the voicemail I'd become all too familiar with in the second half of 2021, a female voice answered. Not Lena's. Very Oxford British.

"Hello, Professor Traine."

"Ms. Chan?"

"Lena's not speaking to you anymore. She handed me her phone just now to tell you so. She'll be blocking your calls from this point forward."

"Seriously? Did she tell you why she's doing that?"

I imagined Elizabeth Chan's shrug. I suspected it was precise. Graceful. "She said you were too emotionally needy. A wonderful person at your best, but willing to lie to a person's face in order to protect your sense of personal safety. She does not trust you."

"The research she promised to stop—she's continuing it, isn't she?"

There was a silence on the phone that said *Touché*. The unusual Amazon rep did not hang up.

"I guess we all try to protect ourselves in different ways," I said.

Still no answer or hang up.

I didn't hang up either. I felt there was some kind of...connection happening here. It was like I could feel Elizabeth touching my arm in the silence, being my ally, asking for a moment.

When she spoke, it wasn't what I expected. "Jude Spiegelman. Your college friend. You should call him."

I took a breath. "Did you do a background check on me, or have you and Lena just been sharing a lot?"

"Both. Since her attempts to shut down our project, I've spent a great deal of time with her."

"You're a fixer."

"That sounds very cold. I helped Dr. Cortland deal with her mother's estate—some legal matters that excluded Lena's father—and showed her how we could safely reestablish her research."

"In the same place? The research."

"With a new crew and more safety protocols."

I snorted.

"Call Jude, Dr. Traine. He'll want you to take your trip."

"Excuse me? How do you—"

She'd hung up on me.

I whipped my socks, underwear, and a couple of clean shirts into my carry-on like I wanted to kill whatever was inside there.

I was worried for Lena, even if she didn't want me to be. But even more, I'm ashamed to admit, I was cycling up so much PTSD paranoia and anxiety that it was like the improved, healthy me I'd become from intense physical training had crumbled. What was left was the real me—anxiety ridden, seeing danger in every direction, having trouble again keeping my current timeline separate from all the ones I'd stepped into that didn't exist anymore. (That I *hoped* didn't exist anymore.)

But it was the paranoia that was worst right now. Because in this timeline, everyone *had* been watching me.

The CIA had followed me and my siblings for who knew how long. Cutter had tracked me down to use as leverage against Kenny. Lena had found me through my published work and seduced me into visiting her lab, her research, her bed. The CIA had sent a talent acquisition team to break into my apartment, and maybe a former MMA boxer to keep tabs on me at the same time.

And now Elizabeth Chan, exotic fixer for the corporate behemoth Amazon, had been vetting me. First it would have been to ensure I was a safe lover for their corporate asset, Dr. Lena Cortland. Then it would be to ensure I wasn't a danger as her ex.

It didn't explain how she knew I had an invitation to Langley, though.

Oh, of course. I'd texted Lena about it.

But the condescending way Elizabeth Chan had told me to call Jude, like I was somehow too emotionally stuck to decide on my own? It was almost enough to make me swear to never call Jude again just to demonstrate I might still have PTSD and anxiety, but it didn't need other people to prop me up. I could manage without Jude, just like I could manage without Lena Cortland, thank you all very much!

I finished packing my computer bag and carry-on, and threw in yet another set of pens for those times I just wanted to write my notes rather than type them.

Anything else?

The day after the CIA talent acquirers had issued their invitation, I'd rescheduled my Monday and Tuesday clients this week, just in case I decided to go. My clients weren't the sort who could handle last-minute schedule changes.

I hadn't actually told Megan I'd be out, though, so I called her now, assuring her she could still go into the office to do any testing she had scheduled. She'd built up an impressive mini-practice in my office testing school-age children for ADD and other functional learning issues, plus employee screens, Myer's-Briggs, depression scales, and situational judgement, etc. Had to keep things rolling along for her even if I was choosing to throw myself back into a crazy maelstrom.

I'd also recorded into an electronic file the list I'd gotten from Kansas, my findings about Rick Soder, the CIA working with the Demon Monks, and my conclusions that the CIA was experimenting on people whom they believed could read the future or change the past.

I put the file into an email with a delayed Send to Lena, Ziggy, Bryan, Alvin, a bunch of journalists, and a few key senators in the intelligence oversight committee in Washington, DC. If I disappeared into a CIA black hole and wasn't back to stop the email's Send in three days, it would be out into the world. Hopefully someone would tug the thread and not just assume it was conspiracy-theory craziness.

And that was it. I was done, packed, prepared, and it was only 9 p.m.

I was antsy as hell.

I pulled out my phone and dialed.

"Yo, dude," Jude answered. Must have seen my caller ID

I explained about my trip to be interviewed for a job with the CIA. I didn't say why they were interested in me, but Jude had no trouble jumping to his own conclusion.

"That's amazing! I told you it would happen, right? That everyone was going to want that memory of yours. And look, what's crazy is I'm there right now. I could be in on it!"

"On what? Where?"

"Langley. S'where they got me working most of the time now."

"Doing..."

"Come on. Seriously? Like you didn't notice all my hints about the government research I'd been doing."

"In Chicago."

Jude laughed into the phone like he was seriously going to bust a gut. "Oh, dude, am I glad I'm going to be there to meet you. What flight are you coming in on?"

I gave him the number.

"Okay, look. They'll have a driver waiting for you when you get there, but I'll call in and see if I can handle the pickup, maybe even be in on the interview. If not, I'll just meet you for a bit before you go in, okay? Give you a bit of a pep talk."

"Oh. My. God." I literally slapped my head. "When did they recruit you? It was during my SPE year, wasn't it? That's why you were 'traveling' so much."

More laughter on the phone. "I always thought you were so incredibly cool with it all. Like the wife and kids who know but don't say anything."

"You're married, too?"

"No way, dude! Though there are some hot women out here. And it's not like I deal with classified stuff anyway. Much. It's mostly just a lot of cool behavioral research. Same stuff we were doing at UIUC." Another laugh. "Oh, dude. This is going to be so much fun."

Despite the continuing sense the sky was falling around my head, Jude had me grinning into the phone. He made it sound like signing up for summer camp. Du-u-u-ude!

"You there?" he asked.

"I am here. Tomorrow at around four, I will be there. I'll look for you when I come in."

10

Spooks and shrinks

IT LOOKED RAINY AND cold outside when I landed in the Washington-Dulles Airport. But I was a sweaty, greasy rag as I trooped with rolling carry-on and laptop bag through crowds of people getting off planes, standing in lines to get on, waiting in chairs with restless children, browsing shops, slurping coffee, and watching me, watching me, watching me, *watching me* as I made my way through them all in my mask and smelly clothes, following the signs to the baggage pickup and ground transportation where my ride, or Jude please God, would be waiting.

Jude's plump, shaggy-curly-haired form jumped out at me the minute I cleared the baggage area. He spotted me at the same time and came running, well, quickly waddling, my way. When he reached me, his arms wrapped around under my open arms in a huge, squeezy hug like the ones I remembered so well from my meltdown times in university.

Those hugs had felt like I imagined mom hugs were supposed to feel. But because Jude had put on a good thirty or forty pounds since then, he'd graduated to full grandma hugs, all fleshy and warm.

When he pulled back, his face over his black, ear-loop mask was flushed red and he had tears in his eyes. As I probably did, too, since we hadn't actually seen each other in person for two years. Then he leaned back to look at me more appraisingly.

"Oy, you have packed on some beefcake there, Jacky-boy."

"High intensity rehab. Read about it. Wrote about it. Finally proved it out right here..." I waved my hands down my sweaty physique that I was suddenly perversely proud of. "...And in here." I pointed a finger at my temple.

"Ah, yes, doctor. I zee. I zee."

"Not shitting you. Fewer symptoms than I've had in years. Though this flight did its very best to knock me back into my hidey hole."

"In that case, Jacky, I am very and extremely proud of your accomplishment, both for making the flight and for fighting your way from the plane to this arrivals area without going into meltdown."

I nodded my thanks with another well of emotion. Because he wasn't kidding. He was giving me a simple, generous recognition of an accomplishment few normal adults would recognize as such. "So are you driving me, or do I get some spook from the agency?"

"Shhh," he said with mock seriousness, then grinned. "I'm your official chauffeur and guide this trip. Let's go."

It was a fairly fast trip, mostly on a six-to-ten-lane highway pelting through rain in a kind of closed-in chute, defined on either side by thick lines of trees or high concrete sound barriers. Presumably the barriers let Virginians living outside them pretend thousands of pounds of fume-belching steel weren't endlessly hurtling past at 60 mph.

Jude was, as always, the consummate conversationalist. We'd agreed, after some discussion about COVID tests and lack of symptoms and exposures, to be part of each other's bubbles, and we removed our masks. This really let him rip. He was almost giddy as he pulled out as much of my private life as I was willing to share, giving me appropriate sympathy for my tough times with Lena, and kudos for my teaching and counseling accomplishments.

Then, when I tired, he took over, talking up a storm about people we'd both known in university that he kept in touch with. And about his move out to Virginia, his choice to live in a red-brick townhouse in Arlington, Virginia rather than in DC, the dating scene for young Jewish professionals like himself, and his recent fascination with some golf game on his phone.

"You've taken up golf?" I asked in surprise.

"Not the sweaty, walk-around kind. It's an *app*." He slowed his speech so that his feeble-minded passenger could catch up. "On my *phone*. I use my *fingers*."

"Speaking of sweat..." I lifted the edges of the light windbreaker jacket I'd put on as we'd walked out to Jude's car at the airport. Hard to miss the stains under my pits. "I was going to wear this polo shirt to the interview..."

"You bring a jacket and tie?" Jude asked now, then held up a finger as he realized we'd reached what would be our one major turn on this entire trip, a long roundabout that took us onto another highway, still wide, but with actually intersections and places where you could see houses and other buildings.

"I did," I said when I was sure he was good again. "Wasn't planning to wear it."

"Wear it. There's places to clean up and change in the building. You'll have time."

His voice and face had gone very serious, so I just nodded.

It was a good reminder that this wasn't summer camp, after all. Not a joke. Not even just a job interview that I could blow off if I wasn't liking the vibe.

No, this was more serious shit than even Jude suspected, and I should probably be reviewing the list of questions and scenarios I'd prepared in my head to keep me focused during my five-hour plane flight.

I tuned out to do so and Jude, recognizing the signs, stayed quiet and just drove.

Twenty-five minutes later, cleaned up and wearing the same suit and tie I'd worn the first time I'd met the dean of the University of Washington when I'd gone in to discuss teaching a course or two for them, I walked out of the immaculately clean washroom in one of the six-story structures of the NHB (New Headquarters Building) vs. the OHB (Original Headquarters Building), all collectively called the George Bush Center for Intelligence, because the first Bush had also been head of the

CIA for a time. I did note that both Jude and the burly gate guard who'd let us drive in after scrutinizing our documents and his logs still referred to it as just Langley. *"Welcome to Langley, Doctor."*

"Good to go?" asked Jude as he caught me looking around.

"Not a lot of signage up here," I said, pulling my N95 mask straps back over my head and adjusting the mask into place.

"Not a lot of visitors."

"But everyone's masked?"

"Outside private offices. I give it two more months."

He led me down a couple of hallways and finally stopped at a nondescript door. When he knocked and opened it, I didn't see endless computer monitors displaying maps and scrolling codes. Nope. Just an office. A large desk, chairs, off-white walls with plaques and a print of a swimming duck, a couple large windows on one wall that looked out across a large parking lot to a winter forest of leafless trees and cloudy gray skies.

What it did have were two familiar jokers I'd expected, but not with joy. Neither man was masked.

"Amit Dadashev and Robert Wilson," I said, intentionally naming the hawk-nosed, darker skinned HRTA officer first because I'd gathered during our first meeting in my apartment that Wilson was the leader. I figured flipping the recognition conventions might to shake up the power dynamics.

It worked. Wilson, who'd been smiling broadly at me when I entered, now stuck out his oversized square chin and gestured toward Jude with it, "Yeah. I see you got your doctor buddy to soften your glide path."

"Is that what this is?" I said.

"Well, why do *you* think you're here?"

"To ask you stuff."

Dadashev contributed a sneer and blew a dismissive puff through his lips.

"You really don't have this welcoming HR stuff down, do you?" I said.

I could feel Jude shifting about uncomfortably where he stood beside me, but I didn't care. I'd feared my social anxiety would come roaring back for this meeting, but now that I was confronting these two again, I wasn't obsessing over their opinions of me. No. All I could think of was how they'd broken into my home, lied about it, and basically threatened that I'd *never* find out about Kenny without them. Not to mention their paid ex-MMA fighter trying to kill me, more of their friends, *presumably*, abducting Kansas, and a whole lot of evidence that I'd been piecing together about how they were trying to not only round up all the time travelers they could, but weaponize them.

"How do you think we should welcome you?" Dadashev said, his Russian accent still dripping with contempt.

"You could offer us chairs to sit on, something to drink, ask me how my flight was. It was sweaty and awful, by the way. The blowers weren't working. We almost had to turn back because someone objected to wearing her mask."

Wilson pushed himself up to standing in front of his desk. It was probably to assert his physical presence, except that I was taller than he was, better educated, and in considerably better physical shape.

So Wilson turned to Jude instead. "Dr. Spiegelman, thank you for bringing Dr. Traine in to see us. You can wait outside. We'll be probably an hour or two. He can text you when we're done."

Jude looked from them to me, clearly trying to keep his face blank, but twitching with so many tells of anxiety that I could have sworn *he* was the one in this room who had the PTSD and missing siblings. He finally just nodded, though, and left.

Dadashev got up, went to the door, and closed it. Locked it.

Oh, shit.

Wilson saw my fear and shook his head. "It's just to stop people from barging in if we're talking about something sensitive. We're not going to keep you here against your will. And again, I'm sorry if we got off to a rough start. You just seem...what? Driven? Determined to piss us off when what we're trying to do is offer you a solid opportunity. Why is that?"

"Why do you think?"

"Again interviewing *us*," Dadashev said.

Wilson glared at Dadashev and the man looked away.

"Let's all sit down," Wilson said.

I nodded and we all sat in chairs in front of the office desk.

Wilson smiled. "Obviously, we know a lot about you already, so why don't we start with your questions. You said you want to ask us 'stuff.'"

"Kansas Traine. Where is she?"

"Your sister? Presumably at her job. Government service. I assume you know where that is since I'm not at liberty to say."

"If she was still there, I'd know. Someone abducted her two days ago. You know anything about that?"

Wilson and Dadashev looked at each other, both apparently nonplussed. Wilson said, "We didn't hear anything."

"Should you have?"

"I...don't know. I guess it would depend on why someone took her, if that's what happened. "

"Not part of your 'acquisitions?'"

"From a fellow agency? Not likely."

"Is it? Who gave you your directive to come after me?"

"'Come after...?' Again," Wilson said, "I think you've somehow gotten the wrong impression, Dr. Traine. The Agency is always on the lookout for remarkable talents. Like I told you when we met, it has followed you and your siblings since you were teenagers. When Dr. Spiegelman informed us you were likely ready to use your gift at last, we were authorized to do some background checks and approach you."

"You're lying."

"Listen..." Dadashev began.

Wilson stopped him with a hand. "About what?"

"Where's my brother?"

"Kentucky Traine. Right. Yes. That, I'm afraid, I did lie about, at least by implication. We don't know where your brother is. When we ran background on you, we saw he'd been drafted into a street gang and then disappeared. We assumed he died, at least until you asked us where he was, like you knew he wasn't."

"He's alive."

"But you don't know where."

"I'm guessing he's with the other nine people like me whom you 'acquired.' Ten, if you have Kansas, too."

Wilson blinked with incomprehension. Either he was a phenomenal actor or he truly didn't know what I was talking about. Which actually clicked into place in my brain. It explained the disconnect I'd felt between their appearance and the continued surveillance by former MMA fighter Rick Soder.

"Need to know," I murmured.

"What?" said Wilson.

I looked him in the eye. "I worked with some organizations when I was studying. Sometimes, with big initiatives, they'll have different people tackle different elements. You might be doing a job without even knowing it just one part of the puzzle."

Dadashev's head was down like he'd actually been paying close attention and was smarter than he looked. "Collecting you."

Now Wilson whirled on him. "What?"

Dadashev shrugged in a way that made me wonder what his background was pre-CIA. "One hand doesn't tell the other hand what it's doing. And we're not even a hand, just fingers."

"Will someone," Wilson fumed and stuck his square chin out further, "tell me what the hell you're talking about?"

Dadashev shut up and looked at me.

I said, "Some part of the CIA is conducting experiments with people like me, my brother, my sister, and nine other individuals who have all been 'acquired' in the last nine years."

Wilson looked between me and Dadashev like we were both crazy. "Experiments like what? On your memory?"

I shook my head. "Why don't you talk to whoever it is you report to and tell them I'm here about SCATTER."

Wilson seemed stumped for a moment. "This isn't why we called you in."

"Or maybe it is," I said. "You just didn't realize it."

"We have questions..."

"I'm sure you do, but they're probably irrelevant. Call your boss. Ask him or her."

"Her, actually."

"Ask her."

"You'll wait here?"

"Couldn't find my way out if I wanted to. And Amit will keep me company."

After working his chin forward and back a few more times, Wilson walked out the door, slamming it tightly behind him.

All that was running through my brain when Wilson left was that he and Dadashev had no clue about my ability to time travel. But when Jude had contacted them, they'd seen I was a person of interest from an early age, presumably for my memory, and they'd done background checks, probably on my school and work history, any run-ins with the law.

So they wouldn't know about the list of twelve names that I, Kenny, and Kansas were on.

But *somebody* in their organization knew.

And I'd just told Wilson to go tell them I was in the building. They might consider this an opportunity not to be missed if they'd been planning to grab me anyway, like they had Kansas.

But unlike her, I was prepared. I had backup and leverage.

Maybe I could get more now.

I looked at Dadashev, who was pacing about the office with a look of troubled concentration on his face, and asked, "Who green-lighted a background check on me?"

He stopped and looked at me like I was part of a puzzle he was struggling with. "There are levels," he said finally, mouthing each word like a chewed piece of meat.

"Like?"

"For you, the Director of Science and Technnology. Your friend's boss."

"Her name?"

"No names. But you're not really a scientist anyway, no offense. So they might have passed the request to Support, Analysis, or even Operations. Again, no names."

"And they might have passed it up the chain if my name was flagged for some reason."

His eyes narrowed. "Why would it be flagged?"

"Why did someone here take my brother and sister?"

"There is no proof of this."

"Rick Soder. Ring any bells?"

"Who is he?"

"Would it bother you to find the CIA is kidnaping American citizens and forcing them to take part in illegal experiments?"

Dadashev frowned. "What are you talking about now?"

"Really?"

I knew, and I'm sure he knew I knew, that the CIA had a well-documented history of experimenting on Americans. From April 1953 to Spring 1963, the CIA had run a program called MK Ultra that used electro-shock therapy, hypnosis, polygraphs, radiation, and a variety of drugs (most notably LSD) on a large population that included forced-or-unwitting soldiers, troubled youths, and prison inmates, to explore brainwashing and other forms of behavior modification.

Exactly how *not* to ethically conduct research.

And the research was still going on here. Jude had told me as much on the way here. I'm sure he believed it was always with willing volunteers.

I didn't.

Dadashev's cell phone buzzed and he pulled it out of his pocket. He hit Answer and held it to his ear. "Yes," he said and looked at me. "Understood."

He clicked off the phone and put it away.

"My partner is bringing down someone who wants to talk with you."

"What a surprise."

Dadashev glowered at me and said nothing more.

The minutes ticked away.

Finally, the door of the office opened again and Wilson stepped in, holding the door open for a suited man who looked to be in his eighties, thin, stooped, and coughing to clear his throat as he entered the room. The white hair on his head was sparse and cut short. The thin skin on his face clung to his one structure like a drum skin except where it sank into deep pouches under his eyes. Those were deep and dark enough to go fishing in. Again, no mask, though his advanced age obviously put him at a higher risk of infection.

The man's deep-set eyes were sharp as they focused on me where I sat, half rising from my seat until the old man gestured for me to stay seated.

In my peripheral vision, I saw Dadashev's jaw actually drop open for a second at the sight of our new guest. Then he snapped it closed as he saw a second man had entered behind the old man. This one was young, about my age, masked like me, but dressed in a dark suit, wore his hair in a blond buzz cut, and carried twice my muscle. He was more football linebacker than CIA analyst. I guessed he was either the old man's nurse or his personal bodyguard. Maybe both.

"Kevin, escort Misters Wilson and Dadashev out." The old man's voice was thin, with a distinct southern accent, but it brooked no dissent. His eyes studied me, not bothering to watch as his aide, Kevin, herded the two HRTA men out the door and into the hall. He returned a moment later, closing and locking the door behind him before he took up a stolid stance behind his master.

"You're Dr. Traine," the old man said to me.

"I am," I said, annoyed at my eyes for suddenly betraying me. They'd decided, at last, that this man was worth fearing, so they'd started to water. My heart rate had sped up, too. It pissed me off. "I don't suppose you'd care to introduce yourself."

"No."

"Of course not."

"But you'll remember my face perfectly, won't you? Search until you find a match. This assumes, of course, that there are publicly accessible pictures of me anywhere. And that you will be at liberty to do such searching."

He kept his eyes focused on mine, ensuring I understood what he was saying. I blinked, trying to clear the liquid from my eyes, hating that he'd see it. I felt my face flushing so hot it tingled.

"You asked about your brother and your sister."

He waited, saying nothing, so I finally nodded.

"And then you mentioned something called 'Scatter.'"

I tried to stare back at him, but couldn't anymore. Swearing silently at myself, I looked down at my hands, now clutching each other in my lap.

"The email you left for delayed delivery? We deleted it, of course. I'd wager nobody but your friend in the hallway outside even knows you're here, do they?"

My heart sank, and I glanced up at the old man's face. I thought I saw just the twitch of a smile in the corners of his thin old lips—a micro-expression. Gritting my teeth, I made myself watch him. I'd remember everything, every word and reaction.

The old man reached into his pocket and drew out a handkerchief. He dabbed his lips with it. "What do you think you'll gain by telling people we're collecting time travelers?"

I went over in my head what I'd written in my now-deleted email. "I didn't. Time travel isn't possible."

Another micro-expression. Annoyance this time. "Alright, 'people who can read the future or change the past.'"

"What I wrote was you're collecting people *whom you believe* can read the future of change in the past." I added just enough disparagement in my voice that I triggered another flash of something that might have been annoyance or even anger. Good. The angrier he got, the more it stabilized me. I could deal with clear enemies better than potential friends.

"You were on the list of twelve. Which one do you think we believe you can do?"

"I have no. Fucking. Clue."

The old man stared hard at me for a full beat and I thought he might snarl or order Kevin to beat me. Instead, his upper lip lifted into a half smile. It revealed a full set of veneers, brilliantly white and completely out of place in a face that otherwise looked like something exhumed from a long-buried coffin.

He stuffed his handkerchief back into his pocket, turned and walked stiffly to the window like he had all the time in the world. He looked out over the parking lot and green space I'd noted when I'd entered this office.

"Did you see the A-12 Oxcart driving in?" he said in his thin voice, almost a whisper.

"The what?"

He looked back at me. "The black jet plane on a pedestal right before you enter the parking lot. You know Lockheed developed that for us. Cutting-edge titanium, special engines, fuel, controls, electronic countermeasures, stealth tech. In 1967, when we were ready to go, it could fly higher, faster, more invisible than any plane out there. Designed to spy on the USSR. And you know what happened?"

I shook my head.

"CORONA satellites happened." He looked back out the window. "They could spy without getting shot down and it was harder for other countries to get mad at them because they couldn't see them. The Oxcart became an ox cart. Obsolete. It flew 29 missions out of Okinawa to help in Vietnam and that was it. Do you find that sad?"

"Do you?"

The old man turned and did his half smile again. "Because I'm obsolete, too. Is that what you think? Or do you think it relates to this Scatter operation?"

I swallowed. "I'm thinking you've reevaluated and you just want to make SCATTER go away, right? It and everyone connected with it. Just let them go."

The old man's lips grew wide enough that the skin on them cracked and he actually laughed, a choking, phlegmy sound that ended in coughing and throat clearing that made him pull out his handkerchief again for a moment.

"Bet you think you're clever coming in here all balls out," he whispered when he'd stowed the hankie again. "Is it a new plan or just a variation?"

"I don't know what you're talking about."

"Guess we'll just have to take you to the basement until you do."

"That's false imprisonment."

"There's nothing false about it, boy." The old man gestured to Kevin and stepped out of the way as the hulking beast stepped forward to grab me with his arms out.

It was so much like the beginning of every second combat exercise Alvin had put me through that my muscle memory took over before my mind even had a chance to assess the situation. I grabbed Kevin's reaching right wrist with both hands, spun to its outside and bent it in an arm bar over my shoulder.

He yelled in pain, up on his toes, feeling like his arm was about to be snapped, which I *was* in the position to do.

"You done?" I said, sure that he wasn't.

When the old man snapped at him, "Kevin!" I released my left hand to drive an elbow back into Kevin's kidneys, then spun and, as he started to collapse, shot my other elbow up to his diving chin.

Crack!

Kevin's eyes went blank, and he dropped to the floor.

I jumped from him to the old man, grabbing the bony hand that he reached it into its jacket pocket. I yanked it out and twisted it so the man grunted and stumbled to his knees.

I fumbled about in his jacket and around his body and waist. No gun. Maybe he'd just been reaching for his handkerchief again.

"We can't let you leave, boy," he grunted at my shoes.

As he said it, something large crashed into the locked door. Then a fusillade of bullets shot out the lock. The door crashed in as Wilson and Dadashev entered with guns out, eyes darting back and forth to take in the entire scene.

I tried to pull the old man up and in between me and the two HRTA men, but the old man pulled away from me and shouted, "Shoot him!"

Shit. Really?

They   aimed   at   me   and   fired   wildly   into   my gut—*Whuh!*—chest—*Ungh!*—neck...

11

Jude's guts and glory

A SWARTHY MAN FROWNED at me. "You have any evidence of this?"

What? I was sprawled in one of the armchairs in front of the desk. I put my hand to my throat. Fine. Chest fine. Gut. *Where...?*

My heart was racing, my head spinning, as I looked around me. I was in an office. Right. The interview. The swarthy man standing there was Amit Dadashev, and I'd just implied the CIA was performing experiments on unwitting American citizens...again.

And then... And then...

Dadashev's phone buzzed in his pocket.

He pulled it out, already looking at me strangely, hit Answer, and put it up to his ear. "Yes," he said and tightened his mouth. His eyes focused on me intently. "Understood."

He put his cell phone away.

Which meant they were coming. I was fully here now. The old man and his bodyguard, Kevin, were on their way.

I swallowed and pushed myself up to standing. "They probably told you they're coming to ask me more questions, but I've changed my mind. I'm not interested in talking to any of you any longer."

Dadashev stepped between me and the office door. "Please, just stay until the others arrive."

I licked my lips inside my mask and shook my head, stepping towards him. "No. I don't think you heard me, I don't want to—"

I whipped my right fist into the side of his face, pivoting all my weight behind it.

His head snapped and he went down, stumbling back against the door. I followed up with a left to his nose and he was down, bloody and writhing, gasping, trying to breathe.

I stared at him for just a second, horrified by my own violence. Then again, this man had been quite ready to shoot me repeatedly in the other timeline.

I kneeled down in front of him and fumbled inside his jacket, found the gun he wore in a shoulder holster. For a human resources interview? I unsnapped the holster and pulled out the gun, sick that I was now very familiar with how these worked. It was a SIG Sauer P226, Alvin Westor's favorite. The SEALs and Rangers had mostly moved on to Glocks 19s, but the Lead-the-Way leader said the ergonomics of the SIG just made it more of a joy to shoot.

The only thing I cared about was that, like the Glocks, there was no external safety to worry about. You just pulled the trigger hard, and it fired. I could handle that.

I held it in front of Dadashev's eyes now as they blinked hard at me. He was still struggling to breathe through his mouth since I'd destroyed his nose.

"If you try to follow right behind me, I'm going to shoot you. If others come after me, I might shoot them, too. Or whoever I'm holding hostage at the time. Got it?"

I wasn't sure if this was a smart or incredibly stupid thing to tell him. Alvin hadn't covered escaping from a CIA headquarters filled with lawmen and women who might want to kill me. But whatever.

I shoved the gun into the back of my suit pants and tightened my belt. Then I grabbed Dadashev by his collar, jerked him away from the door, opened the door, calmly stepped out, and closed it quietly behind me.

Jude, standing outside, gawped at me, stretching his mask.

"Which way did Wilson leave when he came out of here?" I asked him.

Jude pointed down the hall in the direction we'd arrived by.

"Then we're leaving the opposite way."

"What?"

"You can tell them I was crazed and distressed. That I forced you. Whatever works. But I need to you to help me get out of here now. This isn't a joke. This is my life. Help me or I'll just run."

I could see my old friend trying to process it all in his mind, swallowing hard as he weighed the steadiness of my voice and eyes, wondering if I was having some kind of panic attack or hallucination. "What did you say to them?"

"Decide now. Three...two..."

"Let's go," he said and started trotting down the hall in the direction opposite from the one Wilson had taken.

I caught up to him, grabbed his arm, and broke us into a run. "First staircase," I said.

"There," Jude gasped and pointed.

I saw it and ran ahead of him to open the door. I pulled him in as he reached it, then I yanked the door closed behind me. It was a typical fire exit, gray-painted concrete stairs heading up and down, metal handrails, old lighting fixtures that had been updated to garishly inadequate white LEDs.

The SIG had threatened to slide down into the back of my pants as we'd run, so I pulled it up now to reposition it. Jude's eyes went wide, but he said nothing.

As we started thudding down the stairs together, though, he began panting, his face going red. "Just wait. Just wait. Jacky!" He tugged his mask off, desperate.

I grabbed his arm and tugged. We cleared one landing and headed for the next. "Keep going!"

"This...this...building is totally secure," he wheezed. "You can't just duck out and..."

"Not planning to," I said beside him, limiting my steps, but keeping him descending. We passed another floor landing. I wished I could jump down eight at a time, using the handrails to control my descent. But there was no point if I left Jude behind. "I just need to get to a public place with cameras and lots of witnesses," I told him. "A main entrance."

"Okay. Okay, then...stop! We need to go out on the fourth floor, center. That's the most public entrance. We're built into a hill here."

"Fuck! How?"

"We can... We can... Oh. Give me a second." He sat down suddenly on the landing we'd just reached. His chest was going in and out. His face was red and scrunched up in pain. "We go out...this floor. Head to the center block. Take the elevator..."

"Okay. Let's do that."

I pulled off my mask and stuffed it into my jacket pocket so they'd see my face on camera. Then I helped my friend up and we went to the door. Before we went out, I checked him and straightened his clothes and my clothes. To look normal. At least until we got to the exit and someone there stopped us.

"This is insane, right?" Jude said, looking at me.

"I...know. I didn't think this through obviously," I said. "I'll go to jail if I have to, but I'm not going to just disappear like my brother and sister."

"What?"

"Later. Let's—"

There was a loud bang as a door a few floors up crashed open and feet thudded into the staircase. "You two down!" a voice commanded. "You two up!"

The more thudding feet.

"Let's go," I whispered to Jude and we opened the landing door as quietly as we could, slipped out, and pulled it silently closed behind us.

Jude gestured a direction, and we walked like two casual CIA office workers along a more brightly lit hallway than the one we'd left a few floors up. Some twenty feet along, I spotted an elevator another fifteen feet ahead. Jude did too, and we both walked faster. Ahead of us, a couple of women in blue surgical masks reached the elevator and pressed the call button for it.

The elevator arrival bell dinged.

The doors slid open and Jude called, "Hold the elevator, please!"

Then all hell broke loose.

The stairwell door fifteen feet behind us yanked open and Wilson and Dadashev spilled out, their guns drawn. They spotted us and yelled, "FREEZE!" like a bad cop movie. Dadashev took a spread-legged shooting stance while Wilson kept running toward us, aiming as he came.

I turned and pulled the SIG out of my back waistband, but Jude was suddenly in my face, grabbing my gun arm, trying to disarm me. "They'll shoot you!" he yelled. "You aim and they'll—"

Blam!

Wilson's bullet tore through the side of Jude's face, spraying me with bone and flesh and blood as the women in the elevator screamed and I tumbled with Jude, with what was left of Jude, to the polished concrete that was speckled now with—

I was sitting in a faux-leather armchair in...an office. Window there. Two other men in chairs.

Yes.

My head was buzzing like I couldn't hear properly. My heart was beating hard and my whole body was squeezing somehow. Not in physical pain, but in...loss? Something awful had just happened. Something...

It all rushed back to me.

Jude!

No!

I took a deep breath and looked around me. The two men were looking at me. Wilson and Dadashev. Right. I was still in their office. I'd jumped back. Jude was alive. When was this?

"Well?" said Wilson.

"What?" I said.

"You just told us your brother's alive. Do you know where he is?"

I blinked and let my mind race back through the conversation so I knew what I'd told them at this point and what I hadn't. I'd said my sister had been taken and my brother was alive, and neither of them had seemed to know about either fact.

I now knew they had concealed weapons, though. That seemed strange for two guys who seemed to be basically office drones. Which meant maybe they weren't really human resources at all but some kind of field agents playing the roles of office drones. Human Resources. Talent Acquisition.

Yet they hadn't known about SCATTER or time travelers. Old Mr. Southern Whispers had sent them out of the room before we'd discussed these.

Which left, maybe, the possibility that they'd had orders to bring me in and treat me as dangerous, but not necessarily to hold me.

I grinned at them. "You know what, guys? I was fucking with you."

"What?"

"You broke into my *home*. You threatened me. You lied to me. So I took you up on your invitation because it gave me a chance to make my friend happy. Dr. Spiegelman. Now, because I left some landmines behind me that will go off if for some reason I'm detained, and you said I can leave at any time, I'm going."

With that, I pressed myself up out of my armchair and walked to the door.

Dadashev looked like he was going to intercept me but Wilson threw him a look and a shake of the head.

"You walk out that door and you won't be getting a second invitation," Wilson said.

"Thank God," I responded and reached for the knob.

"Not a *nice* invitation," Dadashev added.

I shuddered but opened the door and walked out to where Jude was waiting. Masked. Whole.

It was all I could do not to hug him tightly to me for a second, then run.

No one, as far as I could tell, followed us out, and that night I stayed with Jude in his house in Arlington townhouse, rather than the hotel the CIA had booked for me. I figured it lessened the chances that Wilson and Dadashev or anyone further up the chain in the Company would try to make one last play to bring me onboard.

And Dadashev's threat?

I was pretty sure it was just the empty talk of a man used to scaring people.

Nonetheless, it was one more reason I was glad Jude and I finally had time for a real heart-to-heart talk, something I'd missed from our times hanging out in university and later, on our occasional nights out in Chicago. Right now, it was not only meaningful, it was necessary. Quite apart from Dadashev's parting threat, I was completely shaken up by the time jumps I'd done this day. More than after the ones Alvin AKA Shadow or Rick Soder AKA the Bat, had made me do. Jumping away from getting shot, then Jude getting shot was too much like my time around Cutter, too much of me needing to escape another overwhelming enemy.

Or maybe it was the *same* enemy that I was just starting to get a clearer picture of.

Either way, I needed Jude's calming presence as much now as I had all those times I'd had PTSD meltdowns and panic attacks in university. So we ordered delivery sushi with extra ginger, some edamame and gyoza. When it arrived, we took it into Jude's living room, each took a couch and tray of the divvied-up food, and went to town with our chopsticks.

And talked.

Not about Kenny being alive or me being able to jump back in time, but about the more normal things in my life. Like Lena. Her insistence I get personal defense training and how that had helped me get stronger while she got weaker from her mom dying. How I'd tried to fix it and failed.

His two couches held a jumble of pillows and colorful knit throws that were perfect for this kind of catching up. Jude shared his decision to start going to synagogue again, rediscovering his faith in God even as his eyes had been opened to the incredible complexities of evil in the world.

At some point he finally jumped into dissecting my decision to not join the CIA, labeling me with everything from a fear of commitment to a socialist distrust of authority or simply my hopeless hope that I was going to patch things up with Lena and didn't see how I could make things work with her on the west coast if I was working out here in Langley.

He was pushing pretty hard.

I finally laughed, shaking my head. "None of those. Jesus, you are out of practice."

"Then what? Because sure as anything, something went on in there with those guys that you're not telling me about. You came out so...shaken. I've seen that in you before. Something happened. What?"

I stared at him, suddenly wondering if he knew more than he was letting on.

But if he did, why wouldn't he just say?

Because he knew he was doing wrong? Was he was searching salvation in synagogue attendance? I had a nasty flashback to the undercover cop, James William Gillespie, who'd gotten caught up in the Demon Monks just like Kenny had and had tried to find his soul again by going to a fundamentalist church.

It hadn't worked for Gillespie. Was Jude going down that same rabbit hole?

I looked him square in the eyes. "Tell me how what you're doing with the CIA isn't weaponizing psychology."

"Well, it's not going to be published and peer reviewed, if that's what you're asking," he said, his cheeks quivering.

"Like they never published any of the work from MK Ultra or the Army's research into the most effective torture techniques at Abu Ghraib and Guantanamo."

"That's the past. We don't study torture."

"Anymore."

Jude gave a frustrated shrug. "I wasn't here when that stuff went on."

"But I bet you study cultural differences, right? The kinds of things that might help a foreign national betray their country?"

"That's weirdly specific. We study more general persuasion techniques."

"Including the use of drugs?"

"Where appropriate."

"Oh, dude."

"I know. You hate drugs. They wrecked your brother. But we're not talking addictive substances here, okay? Rarely even psychoactive."

"Using non-psychoactive drugs to increase the psychological state of persuadability? That's quite a trick."

"Ritalin. Psychoactive?"

"Um. Yeah. Methylphenidate's a freakin' stimulant. People use it like amphetamine to study and up the dose for euphoria."

"But when used properly..."

I leaped up from my eating couch, almost spilling my last little plastic container of soy sauce, but I caught it before it bounced off its tray, then turned to Jude. "When you've got a psychiatrist carefully prescribing, testing, adjusting dosages or brand names, that's proper." I clasped my hands together in an unconscious, pleading gesture. "Are you sending agents out to carefully diagnose, administer a drug, observe its effect over time, then adjust?"

"Obviously not."

"Exactly! So what drugs are you working with?"

Now Jude stood up to be on my level. His round face had turned pink. "You know, if you'd joined up, I could probably tell you. As it is, that's classified and you will never frigging know. You'll just be paranoid and angry and..."

He stopped talking and turned away from me, while I backed away from him. When we'd been in school together, we'd shared everything. He knew all about Kenny's addiction and descent into gang life, all about Kansas and my parents, all about my plans and fears. Just as I knew about his brother, his single mom, his goals and fears, and the incredible depth of his soul. He'd always had a deep-rooted belief in the moral nature of humanity and how it was our duty to do what we could to support and encourage that. I think I'd borrowed his belief in humanity all those times in university when my memories of evil threatened to shred my own.

But now this? Particularly since today I'd seen a rot at the core of the CIA. If Jude knew about that, he was either rationalizing or...he didn't know. Both possibilities scared me.

"Dude," I said quietly, turning back to him but not able to actually look at him. "How can you trust that the people using your research are doing anything good with it?"

There was a long beat before he answered, and when he finally did, it was with the gentle, considered tone I knew so well from all the times it had talked me down from my paranoia or other stress reactions back in UIUC.

"I don't trust everyone," he said, stepping closer to me. "I'm not naïve. Lots of politicians and higher-ups in every organization are there for power, money, or ego. I know that. It just means you have to choose carefully. You look at a person's works and their personal mission. If they align and I agree with their mission, then I get onboard."

I looked into his eyes. "You think the leaders in the CIA fit that?"

"I do. Again, not all of them, not all the time, but institutionally? Yes. In my department specifically? Yes."

"And if you knew about people within the organization who were abusing the organizational mission, what would you do?"

"Stop them. Report them. There are systems in place to do that. Safely."

"Okay, then," I said very slowly. "Have you ever reported to or met or heard of a white man who looks old as Methuselah, mostly bald, deep dark bags under his eyes, and talks with Southern whisper, lots of phlegm? Has a big, white, buzz-cutted personal guard named Kevin with him wherever he goes?"

Jude blinked, then seemed to burst with happiness. "Wait. Is that what this is all about? You saw someone here in the building that you know something about?"

"Yes and yes."

"Why didn't you point him out to me?"

I had no answer to that, since the only time, in this timeline, that I hadn't been with Jude in the headquarters was when I was in the interview room with Wilson and Dadashev. I threw it back at him. "You're sure it rings no bells? Not the Director or Deputy Director or head of one of the sections?"

"Not the first two. I haven't met all the heads, but I've seen pictures. None that match your description, which I know is accurate because of that thing in your head."

"My memory."

"That. So you know him from somewhere? You know about bad stuff he's done. But you don't know his identity."

"I can't tell you how I know, but yes."

"Okay." Jude started pacing around the living room. "Then if you saw him here, I'm guessing he's a consultant or visiting from some other agency—the ODNI, NSA, DIA, FBI, NRO, Department of State, Homeland Security... They all come through here sometimes. There's rivalry but cooperation, too."

I thought back to my encounter with the man. Dadashev had been surprised to see him, but both he and Wilson recognized and obeyed him. That might have applied if he was a big player from an outside agency.

I blew out in frustration and grabbed my tray of cardboard sushi containers from the couch I'd been on, grabbed Jude's tray, too, and walked them into Jude's kitchen. When I came back out, I faced him with my hands on my hips. "There have to be visitor logs, right? Can you access those somehow?"

"Um, maybe?" Jude blinked hard, looking down. "There are a lot of people coming through here every day, though. They'd all have clearance. I'm not sure how you'd identify..."

"Seriously? I'm telling you this guy is running an evil program inside the CIA and your response it, 'That's too hard to check?'"

Jude backed up from me, giving himself some space. "Whoa. Now you've moved from seeing some evil old dude to saying he's running a bad program internally here? On your first visit here? You have some inside source on that, or..."

"Or what? I'm suffering PTSD paranoia again? That would be easier to believe, right?"

"Well..."

I bounced up and down on my toes and finally exploded. "Kenny's alive, okay? But he's being held somewhere and I think people are experimenting on him. Kansas was abducted two days ago. I believe by the same people who took Kenny. The bald guy links it all to the CIA!"

Jude's eyes went wide. "Whoah whoah whoah. What... When did you find this all out?"

I shook my head, then decided to answer. "About Kenny being alive last March. The rest of it, pretty recently."

"Since you got the invite to come out here?"

"Around the same time."

"Then what...? You actually never meant to seriously interview. You were just coming out here to look for Kansas? I thought she was working for the NSA."

In for a penny, in for a pound. I gave Jude everything but the time travel. I told him how Cutter had tried to abduct me and ultimately did, how Kenny showed up by remote connection on a TV screen in the Demon Monk headquarters, how I barely made it out of there alive—Jude interrupted me there to say he'd read about my scrape and was waiting for me to tell him. I told him I'd been spied on by some guy claiming to know my "secrets," and that I'd gotten the CIA connection from Cutter and Kansas before she'd been taken.

"So yeah, that's why I came out here. And to see you, of course."

"Dude..."

"Yeah. I don't think Wilson or Dadashev, my two interviewers, knew anything about any of most of this. But the old guy with the whispery Southern accent did. He also said his face wouldn't be in any records anywhere. So...can you check the visitor logs?"

He didn't press me again. He just did what a best friend did who'd heard a tale like that. He nodded and said, "I'll check the logs somehow. I'll tap all my contacts. You want to draw me a picture of the guy that I can show around?"

I snorted. "You obviously don't remember my drawing skills. But you've got a color printer, right?"

Jude nodded.

"Then let me do a Zoom call with a friend of mine. If he's in, I can give you a great sketch."

12

You can't go home again

ZIGGY'S SKETCH THAT NIGHT was so lifelike that when Jude saw it on the computer monitor, and again sliding out of his inkjet printer, he'd visibly tightened up like I had when I'd met the man in person.

The old man's taut face and deep-set eyes had that effect.

Death. The threat of it.

I asked Ziggy to send a copy of the scanned sketch to my email, too, before Jude and I finally called it a night.

The next day at the airport, masked and already feeling the coming claustrophobia of being trapped in a plane for the much longer, broken-up trip back, I found myself hugging Jude tighter and longer than I think I'd ever done. Memories of him getting shot dead were still too fresh.

My parting words to him were, "Be careful."

Three-and-a-half hours later, in the Dallas airport, waiting for my connecting flight to Seattle, I was fighting panic and wishing I'd told Jude, "You know what? Changed my mind. Give me the picture and forget about it. Not important."

The source of the panic? What I'd just listened to in my phone's voice mailbox...

I dialed in for messages almost without thinking the moment I was off the plane with my carry-on and walking out the connector in the Dallas terminal. There were three messages.

Okay. No problem. I clicked to listen to the first one as I stepped out into Terminal C, heading for, what was it? C21? D21?

My mind obviously held that information, but I couldn't focus and almost collided with other exiting passengers as I heard the strained, gulping voice of my office manager/psychometrist, Megan. "Um...Jackson? I don't... I'm not sure how to say this. A man came by the office today at two-thirty, right after I'd finished the Lillyhammer testing. He told me you'd scheduled a fumigation of the office? For cockroaches? He gave me your cell phone number and everything to contact you and check, but you didn't answer. I guess you were on your flight? So I rescheduled the last person I had booked for the day and left the office? Because the man said I couldn't be in there for about an hour while he was, you know, and...well, I figured if I locked up our filing cabinets and shut off our computers, you know. But... Oh, God, Jackson, I'm so sorry..."

The message ended with Megan emotionally overcome.

As I almost was, my breath getting shallow and heartbeat speeding up. I rolled my carry-on and laptop over to a set of mostly unoccupied metal and foam benches and sat down, hunched over my phone, and clicked to hear the next message.

Megan again, more composed.

"When I got back, the door was open, the man was gone, and the office was wrecked. The man, or maybe he'd brought in helpers, had drilled and pried open all the filing cabinets. They took the files, the computers, all the records. They trashed paintings and the furniture. I called the police. They came and took pictures. I'm currently in the East Precinct, where I'm waiting to give them a full statement."

Her voice was shaking again, but I heard her pull herself together to finish with, "Please call me when you get this message."

I pulled the phone away from my ear, my hand shaking, and was about to exit my voice mail and dial, but decided I'd better hear the third message, in case Megan had some kind of follow up I should know about.

It wasn't Megan.

Instead, the very cultured sounds of Elizabeth Chan's voice said, "Dr. Traine, I hear there's been a break-in at your office and your home. You have my sympathies. But you should know this was likely done to send a message. Therefore, they won't be waiting to assault you when you land, but you should still be cautious. And when you're ready to learn what I know about it, call me. You have my number."

Elizabeth Chan's number? Of course I had it. I had no idea what had happened to the business card she handed me when we'd met the one time, but I'd read the number when I'd seen it. Which meant it was stuck in my brain like everything else my senses took in.

Like the odd mismatch between her appearance and her confidence, her background and her job. It. Now her devotion to looking after Lena and her project while keeping tabs on my travels, office, and home. Why?

First things first.

I lifted off my mask and dialed Megan. She answered on the first ring. "Jackson! I am so sorry. It was stupid of me, but the man was so big and...he had your number and...I never imagined anyone in broad daylight would..."

"It's okay, Megan. You're not at fault here."

"But if I... If I'd just..."

"Megan. In your shoes, I would have done the same thing. But it's all right to feel shaken and scared. Some bad people violated our space, yours and mine. They tricked you and hurt you. It hurts me deeply, so I can only imagine how hard it is for you. Are you someplace safe right now?"

Her voice came out as little more than a squeak. "Y-yes. A police h-holding room. They said to wait. And they want to question you when you get back."

I was reminded she was barely twenty-five. Very mature for her age, but still so young. "That's good. They want to make sure you're safe and cared for. If you have a chance, you can ask them if Patrol Officer Bryan Miller is around. He works out of the East Precinct and he's a friend of mine. I'd trust him with my life."

"Okay."

"How are you feeling?"

"Like you said. Hurt. Scared. I wanted to call my dad."

"If he makes you feel safe, do that. And don't worry about the office. I have insurance. I'll take care of it."

"But the files."

"I'll work it out."

"I can... I can come in tomorrow and..."

"Not tomorrow. You take a couple days off while I figure a few things out, okay? You'll still get paid. I'll call you."

She thanked me and hung up.

Which is when I finally let myself fully take in what had happened and started hyperventilating.

To fight the panic, I put my mask back on and did a very aggressive, almost maniacal walk through four of DFW's five terminals, rolling my carry-on and laptop case behind me, before my breathing was back to normal and my head was on straight enough that I figured I could handle going to my onboarding terminal for the second leg of this ridiculously long return flight home.

To a home that had been torn to pieces, it sounded like.

Like they'd wanted to make sure I'd have nothing to come back to and would *have* to give in and join them.

Except fuck that. They might have thought that's what this would do—scare me, shake me up into running back to them, seeking... what? Safety? Answers? A chance to negotiate? Yeah, maybe they thought this was going to put them in a position of strength for a better negotiation with me.

That was not going to happen.

They would never get me.

I'd come after Kenny and Kansas, but the fuckers who took them would *not* take me.

Over the next forty minutes, as I waited for the call to board the second leg of my flight, I did an internet search and called around to find a Seattle restoration company that could handle the rebuild of my office. Latching onto the first person who sounded like he truly understood the scale of what I was asking for, I grilled him and he agreed to come in on Thursday, two days away. I also got the name of a computer-systems restoration firm they worked with for offices and said he'd coordinate with them to fix any wiring that needed to be done as the job progressed.

I thanked him profusely and felt just a little bit more in control when I finally boarded for the delayed, four-hour second leg of being stuck in a masked crowd of tired, sweaty people in the sky.

I got off the plane in Seattle at 10:05 p.m. Seattle time, got the shuttle out to where I'd parked my car, ripped off my mask, and drove to my office. Out of an abundance of caution, I parked a couple blocks away, approached the building carefully, tried to see if anyone was watching it, couldn't, and still tried to change my height and appearance as I snuck in the back door.

I half expected police tape over my office door, but there was none. No evidence to protect? I'd probably ask the police later if they'd dusted for fingerprints, but so many people came in and out of my office, both clients and workers who fixed our computers, our heating and cooling systems, delivered water and, certainly when I'd still been setting things up, furniture and lighting, that the list of visitors could be ridiculously large.

I unlocked the office door, walked in, and turned on the lights.

The sense of violation hit me like a punch in the gut. Chairs had been overturned, paper and office supplies littered the floor, the various art prints that I'd had up on the wall had been ripped down—Klimt's *The Kiss* had been slashed apart so that strips of gold and blue littered the floor; Monet's *Poppy Field near Argenteuil* had been ripped whole from its frame, crumpled, and thrown to the floor amidst the debris from the reception desk.

If Elizabeth Chan was right, it was all gratuitous destruction, meant to send a message. That said what? Be afraid of us? You can't just walk away?

Something else?

My knees felt weak and my stomach queasy as I walked through the damage. Going room to room, the carnage made me want to throw up.

Strangely, the two things that helped me keep my shit together were the very things that distressed Megan the most—the cleaned-out filing cabinets and all the places where the invaders had literally ripped wires out of my walls, popping drywall dust and pieces over everything. I'd had special wire routings done in this old building to network my computers, and tie in the VOIP phone system and photocopier. Now...nothing.

But it was just a money problem. Money and time.

Stealing all my handwritten and computer-entered client records, all the financials and contact information, might have crippled other practices. Not mine. Other than maybe some of the testing Megan had done, everything was scanned, filed, and backed up. Daily. Every note, every record.

So once I bought a new PC, I could sign into my online account, access all my backups, turn over the necessary financial loss records to my insurance company, along with the police report, and I could set about reconstructing what the assholes who'd come in here today had tried to tear apart.

"And you know what, fuckers?" I muttered as I came out into the reception area again and addressed the silent ghosts of the invaders. "Even without backups, I've got it all up here." I poked my forehead.

For a second, just that physical poke threatened to tip me from anger into tears. I fought to keep myself angry instead. I'd need that for when I got back to see what they did to my apartment. In my imagination, if they'd really wanted to get to me, there were things they could have written, stuff they could have smeared on the walls...

I shut off those thoughts before they spiraled.

Just. Go. Check.

So I took a bunch of photos of the different rooms, then left my office, turning out the lights and locking the door before I left. No one jumped me outside. I suspected Elizabeth Chan was right. This had all been about sending a message.

1.2 miles from my office to my apartment building. Seven minutes with almost no traffic. I again parked a couple blocks away and walked, all hunched over and limping, to the building's front door. I entered at 11:55 p.m.

I climbed the stairwell with my carry-on luggage and laptop bag, turned my door key with a tight chest, and gritted my teeth as I turned on the light.

And...

It was okay.

I mean, it was trashed like my office had been. Furniture overturned and broken. Pillows pulled apart. Plates and glasses and my entry mirror smashed, the glass strewn everywhere. Salsa and yogurt poured over the living room's area carpet.

But it had been done professionally, methodically, not personally or creatively. I had no pets to kill and not a lot of personal artworks. Only one or two house plants to destroy. A quick peek into the bathroom showed they hadn't backed up and overflowed my toilet, perhaps to avoid having the neighbors below call the police.

And no one was waiting for me there. It really did just look like they were sending me a message.

Well, message received. You're assholes.

I dropped my bags in a clear space near the door and went to my bedroom.

They'd taken my computer, of course, and grabbed all the handwritten notes, mostly scribbles, that I had on my desk. But the computer, again, was backed up, and there'd been nothing consequential in the handwritten stuff because I didn't keep a diary. I felt a flood of relief when I saw they hadn't bothered taking the few birthday cards I had from Kansas and Kenny and Carmelita, even a couple from my parents.

Then I had a sudden awful thought and ran to my closet. The folding door was already open, yanked off its runners. Half the clothes that had been hung up there had been yanked down, ripped, or thrown around the room.

And in the back on the floor? My Kenny box, where I kept all the physical manifestations of our time together as kids—his home-run baseball that he'd signed and given me, the Boy Scout badges we'd earned together, a recording of him trying to sing "had a bad day"—was gone.

Well...shit.

Okay, that was personal. And a good indication the perpetrators were indeed the same ones who had Kenny now.

I collapsed down to sit in the middle of the floor of my bedroom and looked around, letting the destruction pick at me, still fighting to stay on the right side of that tipping point between anger and despair. Hovering on that edge.

My cell phone buzzed in my pants pocket.

I lay back flat in order to pull it out and because keeping myself angry yet rational was exhausting. I didn't recognize the phone number.

"Dr. Traine?"

Hunh. The female voice speaking proper Oxford British actually sent a shot of pleasure through me. Maybe because she'd cared enough to warn me about what had happened to my office. Also, her voice was soft, and she was my one real connection to Lena now, so I said, "It's me. It's late. Why are you up?"

"You are in your apartment?"

"Spying on me?" I looked vaguely in the direction of my living room window through my bedroom door.

"No. Just calculating the time. Your flight landed at ten-oh-five. It would have taken you approximately forty minutes to collect your car and drive to your office. I guessed you would be naïve enough to examine the mess there for twenty minutes or so before going back to your apartment. That was torn apart as well, I presume."

"Yep. How'd you know?"

"I've had someone following you. When you left Langley, apparently not accepting their offer, I assumed there would be repercussions, so I also hired people to watch your apartment and your office. They had someone watching your apartment, but they've been temporarily immobilized."

My brain was spinning hard now, and not just from the violation of my office and apartment. "Wait. Step back there," I said. "Following me?"

"Yes."

"Rick Soder."

There was a silence on the other end of the line. Then Elizabeth Chan answered like my knowledge wasn't unexpected. "Yes."

"Why? To make sure I wasn't going to get Lena to stop her research?"

"No. That was never going to happen."

I made myself sit up, fighting the head rush. I thought I'd managed to skip jet lag because my trip out east had only been two days. But it was there. Or something was. The stress maybe. Because things were not making sense to me right now. My brain felt fuzzy. I understood what had happened to my office and home. I understood that this woman whom I'd thought was supposed to just be some kind of Amazon rep had had me followed.

I just didn't understand *any* of the reasons why.

"Wait, wait a minute," I said, almost feeling drunk.

"No," she said in my ear. "The time for waiting is done. I waited while you recovered. I waited while you trained your body and mind to be more of a man. I waited while you finally explored the obvious mysteries around what had happened to you in March and went to visit those who caused it."

"Wait... You mean the CIA. You know they were—"

"Enough! I am done waiting for you to figure things out. I am not the only one watching you. You must come to me. Tonight. We must plan how we are going to respond. I will give you instructions."

"You will not!" It came out like a child's defiance, but *some*body had to stand up for me.

There was a beat, then Elizabeth Chan's voice came out, cold and precise. "Pardon me?"

I squirmed my butt on the wooden floor under me, fighting my feeling of dislocation to hold my ground. "You tell me why you're involved," I said, "or I'm not going anywhere."

13

A dark ride

In the long pause, I heard Elizabeth Chan fight to calm her breathing.

I pushed. "Well?"

"I have a brother," she said. "He was taken by the CIA. I believe they still have him and are…experimenting on him."

My determination sputtered. "Wait. You know about…"

"Your brother, Kentucky. Yes. From Lena. From background checks. He was taken like my brother." She paused again, and I pictured her bowing her head slightly to recover her composure. "This is why I have been studying you. Why I don't want them to take you. I need… I *want* you to be my ally. We have a common enemy. Different resources. If we work together…"

"What makes you think you can fight them?"

"Because I have money and knowledge that you do not! Now will you come or keep stumbling in darkness like a little child?"

Well, that snap made me *feel* like a child, sitting there on my trashed apartment's floor, fuzzy-headed and being lectured by a woman I'd met all of twice. But my thinking brain also told me that past the woman's obvious temper and high self-regard, she was offering me an actual way forward in my search for Kenny, and now Kansas. More than I'd have even if Jude put a name to the face of the Southern Whispers nightmare.

I cleared my throat. "How am I supposed to come to you?"

Fifteen minutes later, I'd taken photos for my insurance claim, backed them up to the cloud, took out my phone's SIM card and destroyed the phone itself (per Elizabeth Chan's instructions), grabbed the still-packed carry-on I'd used for my Langely trip but removed my Android tablet, and snuck out the back of my building and north up 15th to turn right on E.Galer.

There was the promised black, SUV-style limousine. Range Rover. Blacked out rear windows.

The short East Asian driver who climbed out to greet me had totally white hair like he was in his seventies, but wore a dark suit, crisp white shirt, and tie. He wordlessly held open the back passenger-side door for me. I swung my carry-on in, followed it, and the driver shut the door behind me.

Moments later, we were heading south, turning onto the I5.

The rear space was...daunting. All tan leather. It had to have an extended wheelbase because the back of it had enough leg room that I could stretch my long legs forward and still not hit the straight, curtained, up-and-down panel that separated the driver and passenger compartments. The center console between the two rear seats had a slanted LED panel that looked like controlled every light, temperature setting, sunroof, window tints (?), sound... I started pressing buttons and a TV screen rose up across the middle of the panel between the front and back seats, with selections for both live and stored selections. Through satellite?

With some fiddling, I found an intercom button on the inside wall that separated the front and rear seats, and pressed it. Adjusted the volume.

"How far are we going?" I asked.

Through the speakers in the center panel the man's voice came back, in a voice superficially as British as Elizabeth Chan's, but with simpler sentence construction and more open L's, O's, and T's. "We are going to Ms. Chan's personal residence about twenty miles past Davenport, sir. Travel time is about four hours and forty minutes. Your seat leans back very much if you want to sleep. There is a small fridge with drinks and snacks. On the video screen, our internet will not be good through the mountains. It should come back when we reach Ellensburg."

"Four and a half hours? We couldn't just fly?" I said it as a joke, but found myself boiling with both shame and anger that I'd simply accepted

Elizabeth Chan saying her "surveillance-free" location was close. What else had she lied about?

"This is safer that flying," said the driver.

"Even in winter?"

"Yes, sir."

"Bulletproof windows and doors?"

"Yes, sir."

Of course. "She doesn't work for Amazon, does she? Ms. Chan."

"That is a question for her."

What a surprise. "Okay. Thank you. What's your name?"

"It is Jian."

"Sorry, that's Jee-ahn?" I repeated back carefully.

"Yes, sir." There was a faint note of pleasure in his voice.

I turned the intercom off. I assumed Jian would find a way to contact me if there was a need to. Or he could just drive me into an underground lair where crazy CIA doctors opened up my skull and wired me into their supercomputer.

Except there was no reason to believe Elizabeth Chan was working with the CIA, even if she was lying about her brother being taken by them. The guy she'd hired, Rick Soder, hadn't been CIA. Hadn't fit. Which meant she was running her own game. Maybe to take them down. Maybe something else.

There was something I was missing.

The brother...

Rick Soder...

Elizabeth Chan...

Whatever it was, it was hitting my fuzzy, jet-lagged brain right now and bouncing off. I was sure it was going to make sense soon.

I reclined my seat to the maximum, turned down the area lights, closed my eyes, and ran self-hypnosis mantras to deal with the dancing demons in my head.

I woke with the changing sound of tires switching from concrete to gravel road, though the smoothness of the ride was unaffected.

I'd left the sunroof open when I'd entered the car and it was still showing an overcast night sky.

I sat up and hit the tilt button for my seat back to follow me. The center LED panel said 4:42 a.m. It meant my internal clock had registered what Jian had said and counted the travel hours to a wake-up jolt.

Outside, there were no lights of any kind other than the dull side glow from the headlights. Then the headlights caught a flash of reflective red that flashed by. Could have been a location indicator or just a mailbox sticker for all I knew.

I found the intercom button.

"Jian? How close are we to our destination?"

"Ten minutes, sir."

Five minutes later, a glow up ahead felt like someone waving in the dark.

All I could think at that moment was how much I needed a hot shower and fresh clothes.

Twenty minutes after being shown directly to a bedroom on the second floor of what appeared to be a massive, chalet-styled house, I emerged from its full en suite bathroom washed and cleaned to change into one of my extra sets of clothing—polo shirt, jeans, running shoes—from my Langley carry-on. Jian had left, obviously, and I heard no other sounds in the house. But the sleep I'd had in the car had taken the edge off my fatigue, and now I was too keyed up to lie down again.

Besides, it was only 5:20 a.m. here but 8:20 in Langley. Jude was up. The CIA was up.

I slipped from the mostly cream-colored bedroom and used the guidance of minimally lit wall sconces to make my way downstairs to the entry foyer. I crossed it to look into a pitch-dark day room. Surprisingly, there was a flickering glow through the room's inner arch on the left. I walked that way, now picking up some quiet classical music—Rachmaninoff?—and entered a kind of great room that had multiple entrances and opened up all the way through the second floor.

To my right was a wall of floor-to-ceiling windows, centered on a softly blazing gas fireplace, with stonework that climbed some thirty-some feet to the ceiling. Beyond the windows, I saw the hint of a patio, but mostly total blackness. No glimmer of dawn yet.

On this side of the windows, maybe fifteen yards ahead and to my left, was the only other source of light, a spread out, twisting, modern art mess of silver tubes and dimmed lights that hung over a long white stone dining table that sat maybe ten feet from the kitchen island and the counters and cooking appliances beyond.

At the long dining table, Elizabeth Chan sat in a thick, deep-red bathrobe. She had a laptop open on the white stone surface before her, multiple files folders spread out around it, both open and closed.

She must have heard me come to a stop because she looked up.

"Professor Traine," she said. So calmly British now that she had me here.

I passed the fireplace to the dining side of the great room, but not closer to the kitchen. Keeping my distance and the table between us. And not just because we were both unmasked. "Ms. Chan. I didn't mean to disturb you. I just…"

"…Wanted to know where you'd been taken."

"Yeah."

She gave me an enigmatic smile and slid from her seat. She pulled her robe tighter around herself, retied it, and walked around the end of the table and straight toward me. Her slippers, I noted, were topped with the same deep-red waffle material as her bathrobe.

I didn't know if it was the strange hour, my own sense of dislocation, or the unexpected beauty of my surroundings, but I could almost *feel* the sway of her hips inside that thick red robe. Then my eyes were caught by her long black hair shimmering with the light from the fireplace behind me. Then her pale neck and chin, flawless. Her lips, pink and perfect. Her eyes, sans makeup, clear and focused on mine as she drew closer. Closer. And…

She brushed past me.

I spun around to see her standing in front of the windows, the fire to her right lighting only the right side of her face and body. She pointed vaguely right. "You'll see the sky lightening over there in about one hour. It will light up the Huckleberry Mountain Range out there," she pointed more centrally, "along with the Spokane River and the Spokane Reservations, filled with indigenous peoples that I'm sure would love to come across that river one day and cut our throats for invading and taking their land."

She turned back to me and smiled. "Which is ironic, of course, since all the white farmers on the prairies out there"—she pointed past either side of my head—"consider me an invader of *their* land. They'd probably love to storm this house one day and cut my throat as gleefully as the indigenous people would like to cut theirs."

I smiled weakly. "Nice to know you brought me to such a place of safety."

"Safety is always relative. You can achieve it by hiding from your enemies, or by giving yourself weapons against them so strong that they fear to touch you."

"Which do you do?"

"Both, of course. The strongest foe is the one you never see coming."

She gave me her enigmatic smile again, which danced in the pulsing light from the fireplace. It was a dance. None of the command or anger she'd shared on the phone last night.

A game.

"Are you my foe?" I asked.

She tilted her head, aggrieved. "I just brought you into my *home*. I told you about my brother. We have a common enemy. Should I have left you to fight them as you had been doing? Uninformed and under-resourced?"

I stared at this woman. She was a foot shorter than me, as much as ten years my junior, and yet she spoke with the imperious attitude of someone used to giving orders. And this house, if it was hers, spoke to her having considerable economic power behind her. "But..."

"You wonder how you can trust me. Because I had you followed. Because I did not stop the men from tearing apart your office or your apartment."

"And when you invited me here, you said it was somewhere close."

"Did I?"

"I don't like games."

She gave a deep sigh and looked down for a second. When she looked back up to me, it was almost like a different person stood before me. Her enigmatic smile, her imperious attitude, were gone. This young woman looked her age, more like Megan had sounded when I'd spoke to her. Mid-twenties and facing things no one should have to face.

But when she spoke, she didn't confirm that she'd misled me. She said, "Let me start by telling you the name I was born with. You know that in China we give our family name first, then the name our parents give us?"

I nodded.

"My family name is Joe." She said it with a very soft "j." "It is spelled Z-H-0-U. My given name is—"

"Wenling," I blurted.

She looked at me curiously, but inclined her head and held out her hand. "It is nice to meet you."

14

Zhou Wenling

THOUGH I GUESSED THE extended hand gesture was meant to be ironic, I reached out to take her hand anyway because my now-pounding heart, the flush of discovery in my face, and my mind teeming with questions, all made me want to feel her flesh.

She let me grasp her hand. She didn't pull back when I put my other hand around the back of her hand, too, wanting to feel her small wrist, the solidity and warmth of her skin. It looked so small inside my curled fingers. So very pale and smooth.

When I looked up and saw her gazing at me intently, I realized I'd held on far too long. I quickly let go.

"How did you know my given name, Wenling?" she asked, giving it a pronunciation that softened the N and extended the *ling* into a more emphasized *lee*-ng.

I paused a second, then said, "My brother told me."

"Kentucky."

"Yes." I found myself backing away from her towards one of the long, white couches around the fireplace, pretending I wanted to feel the leather. I needed some distance. Even in her less imperious state, Wenling had Lena's strength of will and directness with none of the subtlety or humor. It was unnerving.

"How did your brother tell you?" she asked, not moving but still chasing me.

"I...don't think I want to tell you that yet."

"Lena said you thought he was working for or with the Demon Monks gang. But you only saw him on a video connection."

"You talked a lot, you two."

"Yes. Two strong women in a male-dominated world."

"Does she know you're not an Amazon rep?"

Wenling slid back to her enigmatic smile again. A tell, I realized. Stalling, so she could choose her words carefully. "She does not know that," she said at last. "Do you?"

"Let's just say you don't fit the profile of someone Jeff Bezos would hire for the position. And I get the strong feeling it's been a long time since you've answered to anyone but your parents. Assuming you ever answered to them."

As I said it, I realized I was contradicting what Kansas had told me about Elizabeth Chan—that she was an Amazon rep with identifiable parentage and was definitely *not* Zhou Wenling. Which meant either Kansas had been completely misled somehow, or she'd *lied* to me. But why?

Put a pin in it. Focus. There was something I was still missing here.

I brought my attention back to Wenling's reactions to my intuitive guesswork, processing the way her upper lip had flared at the mention of her parents, unconsciously baring her teeth. Disgust or anger? Maybe both.

"Correct," she said now. "But we will not talk about my parents. We will talk of my brother."

Of course. The brother. SCATTER's list of twelve. "Ex-ee-yah-oh-bo," I said, doing my best to pronounce the given name of the only Zhou that had been there.

Wenling gave me another curious look, this time tinged with frustration. "It's pronounced shee-ow-boh," she said slowly, then repeated it. "Xiaobo. How did you know this?"

"The CIA's got a list of SCATTER recruits. Or targets anyway."

She gave me a blank look, but quickly nodded as if she'd known, or that it was important to her that she appear to have known. "Yes. He was taken from me in—"

"2019?" It had been right there beside Xiaobo's name in my head. Like Kentucky had 2017 beside his name. Kansas and my name had no dates.

"—April of 2020."

I nodded. "Okay. So the date's when they identify the ability. They spotted Xiaobo in 2019, but it took a while to reach him."

There was a long silence as she stared at me. I could hear the occasional sputter from the gas fireplace. Finally, Wenling spoke in an icy voice that covered any of the innocent vulnerability with which she'd begun her tale. "Do you have more you would like to tell me, or may I explain to you the mess you have fallen into?"

I sucked in my lips and gestured for her to continue.

She turned to face the darkness outside the huge windows and clasped her hands behind her back like a commander surveying some grand battlefield. "Xiaobo and I were born in a small village in mainland China, but we left home together on the day that Xiaobo learned to travel back in time."

She paused, turned her face to look at my shocked expression, and nodded. "Yes, I know of your ability to do this, obviously. I will get to that."

It clicked over the last piece I hadn't put in place. Rick Soder had known about my ability to travel back in time. Which meant he'd been told by the person who set him to watch me—Wenling.

"Xiaobo was only nine years old," Wenling continued. "I was twenty-one. We found our way to Hong Kong and began carefully using my brother's power to take money from the Happy Valley and Sha Tin horse tracks. I bought us new identities with which I set up investment accounts. Xiaobo picked fast-moving stocks for us, I grew these accounts quickly, and used my reputation to make friends with many bankers and financiers. From them I learned much and used my knowledge to invest every Hong Kong dollar into the markets and private equity, keeping only what we needed for food, shelter, rich attire, bribes, and trading favors. Xiaobo and I also studied English as if our lives depended on it.

"In our fourth year, I called in what favors I could to get our names bumped high on the list for immigration to the United States of America. We did our interviews and immigrated here on EB-5 Green Cards requiring an investment of $500,000, and creating ten permanent full-time jobs in a place the US Government said needed help."

She paused and seemed to be breathing into the darkness, waiting for my recognition of what she had accomplished in those four years.

"That's...impressive," I said. "I didn't know you could bring a sibling over on that kind of Green Card."

"We altered the ages in our papers. Xiaobo became two years younger. For the purpose of our immigration, he became my son."

"Ah. And no one questioned..."

"The Americans in the US Consulate in Hong Kong could not tell. How old do *you* think I am?"

She turned to face me now so that the entire front of her body was lit by the light of the fireplace. Feeling every bit the stupid white American that I was, I quickly changed my earlier guess of her being 25 because she would have been that old when she and her brother left China. Also, her English was far too polished, her ease with American customs far too established, her house here to lived in, for her to have been here for less than five years. "Thirty?" I guessed.

She nodded at me approvingly. "Thirty-one. We have been here six years. In that time, I have created three international businesses, invested in many others, and increased my net worth to just under four billion dollars. Much of that increase has been since the start of the pandemic."

"Why haven't I heard of you before? Why hasn't Lena?"

"There are over seven hundred billionaires in the United States. Also in China. Many of those seek attention, or choose to do things which get attention. Others do not. This house? Does it seem like a billionaire's house to you? Of course not. I have many houses, many assets, and much power, but I do not live a flashy life. This is intentional. It lets me vanish from view when I choose."

What had she said early in our conversation? *The strongest foe is the one you never see coming.* It was like she lived with the sure knowledge she would need to confront a powerful enemy one day.

I whistled. "You think this will help you take on the CIA?"

"One part of the CIA, yes. I have probed that organization a number of times now. It seems clear to me that some people there know about the CIA's interest in time travel while others do not."

"But—"

"May I continue my story?"

I nodded.

"I had no issues with any part of the US government or legal authorities until my brother was taken from me. Then I discovered the police would not make a serious effort to find him. They claimed he was an adult and there was no evidence of a crime. They said interviews with people who knew him suggested maybe he wanted to get away from me and live his own life."

She turned to me and for the first time I saw her totally unable to hide the fierce rage that obviously lived inside her. Her pale face looked sickly green in the flickering light of the fireplace and her chin visibly shook as she said, "They took the words of white, lazy, privileged, drinking friends of my brother over mine. They said I should just wait and he would probably contact me when he was ready. My brother, who I saved from...everything. Who I fled with to Hong Kong. Who I looked after, planned my life around, brought with me to the freedom of American and *made a success with*."

I think even a non-therapist would have picked up that there were some powerful other narratives that hid behind Wenling's words and emotions. I would definitely draw them out at some point. Just not now, as she was almost doubling over in spasms with her rage and...grief?

"You began looking for him on your own?" I prompted.

That brought her back. She straightened, stepped right up to the window and placed her hand on the glass like she could feel, in its coldness, all that she'd done. "I hired private investigators, one after another, until I found one who brought me answers.

"He found that my brother had met with someone from Washington, DC. The man had flattered him, told him he should own a much greater share of our businesses because of all his contributions. He said he *knew* what sort of contributions Xiaobo had been making, and had friends in DC who would pay Xiaobo what he was worth, for doing things that were important, not just about money. This man then paid my brother's drinking buddies to tell stories to the police, and he took my brother with him in a boring brown sedan that drove away into the night."

"From here?" I asked. "From Davenport, Washington?"

Wenling shook her head. "I said I have many houses. I also have different identities. They would not have found us here." Without answering more clearly, she continued. "I sent the investigator to DC with enough money to make as many contacts, bribe as many people as he needed to in order to find my brother. It took him two months before he overheard a whispered conversation in a bar of a man who'd brought in his most recent 'time freak.' When I made it clear that I would use all my resources to shield him from consequences, my detective pursued this lead until he was able to compromise a CIA office worker who shared stories of an operation to collect, train, and exploit the talents of people they called 'chrono-aberrant.'"

I snorted, unable to help myself.

Wenling looked at me, in on the joke. "Like you, Professor Traine."

"Jesus, call me Jackson. If we're going to be allies, I can't do formalities, Wenling." I tried my best to give it the Chinese pronunciation.

In the wrinkling of her brow, I got a glimmer of how hard she'd fought for the respect she now commanded. I surprised myself with a sudden image of me holding her close and breaking through that reserve. I don't know if she caught my blush as she finally nodded. "But in public, you will call me as I am known here—Ms. Chan, yes?"

I nodded back.

Satisfied, she continued with, "My detective found the CIA identified their first chrono-aberrant when a prisoner from the war in Iraq was taken to Abu Ghraib Prison, and somehow gained impossible knowledge about the people torturing him."

"2003," I said. "Salim Noor Al-Rashid. And that would be the place to find one, wouldn't it? Waterboarding."

Wenling raised an eyebrow at me and waited.

"I told you. The CIA has a list of all people they've collected or are planning to collect. There are twelve in total."

"Most are not very useful, apparently," Wenling said. "Some have died. My detective told me a brother and sister tried to escape last year and were killed."

I couldn't help my exhalation at the "last year," which meant it hadn't been Kansas and Kenny. "That must have been Sofia Gomez Gonzalez and Jose Gomez Gonzalez," I said, citing the only two on the list other than my siblings who shared a common last name.

"The only name that my detective confirmed as part of this group with my brother was...Kentucky Traine."

Hearing his name out of her mouth like that, casually labeled as one of the kidnaped or recruited 'chrono-aberrants,' made my blood temperature drop. Because suddenly this whole ridiculous story Wenling had been telling, the torture I'd gone through last March, the insanity of the CIA abducting Kansas and now apparently targeting me, suddenly felt very present and real. Like stones in my gut. Like guys with guns waiting outside in the dark there.

Guys wanting to use me like they were using Kenny.

And Kansas?

Almost without being conscious of it, I found myself walking from the window, around one end of the dining room table, and the kitchen island, looking left to the exit to the main hall and stairway, right to a door that I assumed went into some kind of chef's pantry of exit outside.

"The CIA code name for the operation," Wenling called after me, "is SCATTER. I don't know why they chose that name."

My client Cassandra did, I thought. Scatter. Throw so many changes at the timeline, the world can't keep track.

"I tried to contact the head of SCATTER, but got no response," Wenling said. "I did, however, discover they were planning to insert my brother into a gang in Seattle for some reason. I formed a plan to rescue him."

I stopped where I'd been running my hand along the kitchen counter on the way to check out the chef's pantry. "Your brother joined a Seattle gang," I said.

"Yes."

"The Demon Monks?"

"Yes."

I thought back to my battles with them. I'd assumed it was Kenny who'd seen me when I'd crashed their gang summit and somehow warned them in the past to call the summit off. But maybe that had been Xiaobo.

And during my escape from the basement of the Demon Monks headquarters, I'd had a strangely vivid experience of déjà vu when I'd been running down a hall to find Lena and was sure I was about to come face to face with the Asian kid I'd labeled Pockmark and the gangsters had called Ching.

Again...

"Xiaobo," I said slowly. "He had a bad case of acne when he was younger, didn't he? Left him with a lot of facial acne scars?"

There was silence, then Wenling, from over by the window, said, "Yes."

"I met him. I think he knew something strange was going on with me, but I never suspected *he* was a time traveler." And out of somewhere deep in the back of my creative mind, a couple of different thoughts and possibilities joined together so that I turned toward Wenling now with a horrible suspicion in my gut. "Did you arrange to have me abducted and taken to the Demon Monks' headquarters? Was Detective Gillespie in your pocket, too?"

Wenling snorted. "Now you give me too much foresight. I created...opportunities. I persuaded the University of Washington to offer you a position to bring you back to Seattle. Maybe the CIA would send Xiaobo out to see if you were gifted, like your brother. I also found a brilliant scientist working on time travel and set her up in Seattle. Maybe the CIA would bring Xiaobo to her to study."

I swallowed dryly. "Did you suggest to Lena that she should visit the university and question me about my experiments with past life regression patients?" It's what had led to Lena and me meeting, me visiting her lab and discovering my ability to jump back in time, us falling in love. Me falling in love with her, anyway.

Wenling's laugh at that sounded actually amused, and she walked towards me slowly with her head slightly tilted, as if considering my face. "I had no conscious hand in that. Though maybe I was meant to. Have you heard the Chinese word *yuánfèn*?" It sounded like *oo-en-fen*.

"I haven't studied Chinese. I'm thinking I should start."

She stopped on the far side of the kitchen island from me and leaned on it with her elbows, touching her fingers delicately together before her face. This close, in just the low light from above the kitchen table, I could still see her fingernails were a pale pink, perfectly groomed. Flawless. Like her lips, her skin, her almond-shaped dark eyes. All set off by the deep red of her robe's collar as it hunched up to frame her hands and face, inviting a caress.

"It is a like the English word 'fate,'" she said quietly, "but specifically used for relationships. It can mean two people are supposed to meet, or that they will inevitably meet. Sometimes it is for business or joint ventures, sometimes for romance."

"So you attribute me and Lena meeting to *yuánfèn*?" I emphasized Lena's name as if to remind myself where my loyalties lay despite Lena's rejection of me.

"How could I not? She is researching time travel for me, the sister of a time traveler, and she *creates* a time traveler."

"About that," I said. "Did she tell you? Is that how you knew?"

Wenling gave me her enigmatic smile again, like she was trying to decide whether to disclose a secret. Which in this case was what? That Lena had spilled everything about me to her, from my family history and ability to time travel, to my sexual techniques and size of my penis? Despite knowing better, I felt myself beginning to fume internally, not just against Lena, either, but against Wenling and every woman who'd ever laughed at me, every *person* who'd ever believed they saw my weakness and stupidity and absurd sensitivity and found it hilarious. An old thought loop.

Then Wenling spoke quietly again and broke it. "I learned of your power from an Indian medical doctor, Irene Gopal. I had arranged for her to work with Lena before, checking regularly on the health of all the members of Lena's team and reporting to me anything she learned about how the research was progressing. She knew I would want to know why Lena called her in to do a special medical workup on you."

"She couldn't know how I acquired my ability."

"No. I used what I learned from her to question Lena more fully. We were bonding at this time, as I told you. Her father is a very difficult man."

Unfortunately, I totally got that. If I'd been in Lena's shoes, maybe it would have felt like balancing the scales to reveal my secret to Wenling when I'd refused to disclose it to the LTW team.

I leaned back against the kitchen counter, feeling an incredible weight of my own failure and loss. If I had just told Lena why I had to keep my secret from Alvin's team, maybe she wouldn't have felt betrayed. Maybe she would have let me help her with her grieving. Maybe we'd still be together.

Wenling spoke again, and her voice carried a surprisingly deep empathy. "*Yuánfèn,* I think, might also apply to Lena and I. And to you and I. We three are intimately tied to the mysteries of time travel, by passion or by blood. It is only right that we should have all come together."

I raised my face to meet her eyes. "Do you think that means Lena will remain connected?" *To me,* I wanted to add.

"I am still funding her research. She may be needed."

"As a bargaining chip."

"Her research, perhaps. The exchange of favors can take many forms."

"How much was the particle accelerator?"

She pulled back like she'd been slapped. And maybe I'd meant it like that, to slap her as well as me out of this...thing I was feeling between us.

"The laboratory you set up for Lena to research time travel," I said. "I know the Large Hadron Collider below the Swiss-French border took about ten years and 4.75 billion dollars to build. How much did it cost to build the collider I saw outside of Redmond?"

Wenling grimaced and straightened up. "Asking this is like asking a woman how old she is."

"You asked me to guess how old you were. Then told me. So how much did it cost?"

"A little more than 25 million. It was very purpose specific, and we copied much of the design."

"From the Cornell one. I remember Lena mentioning that."

"Yes." There was a long silence while we stared at each other across the eight feet or so that separated us. Finally, she asked, "Do you feel a little better now?"

"I'm still pissed about...a lot of stuff. But a little better, yes."

Perversely, or maybe reasonably, I understood there was no way in hell Wenling or Lena would ever just walk away from an investment like that. Especially when it was producing results. They just had to readjust security, like Wenling had said, and be ready for government snooping.

Not that Lena, at least, had any clue how far the government might go to steal her research or make sure it never got released to the public.

Wenling nodded, and I could feel her eyes assessing me. It was like she could see everything in me the way Lena had done. But now I wondered whether that was just me projecting. Part of the social anxiety I'd had even before the Kenny stuff and PTSD, was that I'd always felt scrutinized. That other people could see all my issues, my weakest thoughts.

Of course, with Wenling, I'm sure she *was* trying hard to read me. Both my attraction to her, my continuing attachment to Lena, my loyalty to Kenny and how far I'd go to find him. These were things she had to know if we were going to plot together. Any other motivations she had were likely just fantastical thinking on my part.

"It will be light soon," she said. "I'd like to make us breakfast, and when we're done, I'd like to take you for a walk around the property to tell you my plans for our war. I have extra boots and coats for guests. Are you all right with that?"

"Sure," I said.

"Wonderful." She walked around the kitchen island and leaned down beside me to pull open a wide, deep drawer full of pots, lids, and strainers. She pulled out a large pot, filled it three-quarters full of water and put it on what I gathered was an induction stove top on the kitchen island. She turned the heat to max, then turned to me.

"I'll be back in a moment," she said, and left the kitchen and great room. I heard her feet patter up the stairs I'd descended earlier. At about the time the water started boiling, I heard her feet patter back down.

She was now dressed in different slippers, skin-tight jeans, and a loose, white cotton blouse that she'd knotted just above her hips. She'd rolled up and buttoned the sleeves in place. The front quarter of her long, silky hair had also been pulled back from her face and fastened behind her head with some kind of fancy clasp.

She gave me a girlish smile of delight to find me right where she'd left me. With a gesture, she directed me to the other side of the kitchen island and began bustling about, grabbing an odd-looking assortment of food, spices, bowls, a cutting board.

I obviously looked nonplussed because she spun and poked a finger in my direction.

"You admitted," she said, "you should be studying Chinese, so I am making us a Chinese breakfast of congee with cooked pork and a thousand-year-old egg."

She grabbed a frosty-looking Ziploc bag she'd pulled from the freezer and slapped it down in front of me. "This is the Shanghai innovation—frozen rice. As it freezes overnight, the moisture in it expands and breaks the rice into crumbly little bits so it can cook in twenty minutes, not forty-five!"

So saying, she scooped up the bag and dumped what seemed like a tiny amount of the crumbled rice into the pot of boiling water. She half-covered the pot and set a timer.

Then, with a santoku knife of swirly patterned steel, wielded with a speed and precision Alvin would have admired, she chopped what looked like ugly bacon into fine strips. She put that into a small bowl and mixed in corn starch, oyster sauce, and vegetable oil. Setting it aside to marinate, she checked the boiling rice and stirred it with a wooden spoon.

She washed the knife, peeled and chopped a gnarly ginger root into delicate slivers which she put into a second small bowl, washed the knife, and chopped a small bunch of cilantro and a couple stalks of green onion which she put into a third small bowl. Washed the knife.

I realized I was salivating, but I wasn't sure if it was from the piquant smells of ginger, oyster sauce, cilantro, and green onion, or the stirrings I was getting from watching her torso move around inside her cotton top, her hips and slender legs move around below it.

She checked the boiling rice. Stirred it.

She turned to me. "You have not asked me about the thousand-year-old egg."

"I assume that's some kind of joke?"

"They are not a thousand years old. Not even a hundred years old, though they're sometimes called century eggs. They are considered a delicacy by many Chinese. You take duck or chicken eggs and wrap them in a mix of clay, lime, ashes, many different spices, and salt, roll them in rice chaff so they won't stick to other eggs, then store them for several months inside a container lined with garden dirt. The lime and ash create sodium hydroxide that turns the whites to jelly and preserves the egg, but changes it in many ways."

"You make these yourself?"

Wenling laughed. "I would be afraid of doing it wrong. So much time wasted. No, there is a Chinese specialty grocer in Spokane where I send my driver every two weeks."

"And do I get to see one before I eat it?"

She laughed again as she grabbed the small bowl of sliced pork pieces and stirred them into the pot of boiling rice. "Of course. I need to chop them up. The congee is almost ready."

She went to a cupboard beside the fridge and came back with two oversized eggs that each had a mottled, stone-like appearance. Duck, I guessed from their size. Following Wenling's example, I cracked the shell of one and we peeled our eggs together to reveal something that looked like a wobbly amber jelly egg. When Wenling used the santoku to slice each of them in half, the large preserved yolk that was color-banded like tree rings from tan to green to black and finally a soft mud brown in the center.

"They smell a bit like ammonia," I said.

"Some people say they taste like moldy old socks."

"Do you?"

"Those people have poor taste buds or bought bad eggs. These will have the taste of brine and egg and umami. Mixed with the congee and other toppings, it adds comfort and depth inside a base of warmth and happiness. Like me. A perfect host. A good ally. Shall we see?"

With that surprising comparison, she gestured for me to pull back and quickly diced the century eggs. Then she poured the hot congee—it now looked very much like porridge—and its slices of pork into two bowls. She layered the ginger, cilantro, scallions, and century egg cubes on top and brought the bowls to the kitchen island. A second later, she handed me a spoon.

I held it up. "Do the Chinese say something before eating, like grace, or *Bon appétit,* or *Itadakimasu*?"

"Not usually. This is just breakfast."

"With a thousand-year-old egg."

"You're stalling."

"I may be."

"It is what I said—brine, egg, umami, warmth, and spicy freshness. Trust me."

I scooped my spoon deep into my bowl and took a large bite, staring straight into her eyes.

It tasted as good as she looked.

15

Rivers and oceans

FORTY MINUTES LATER, WE were wandering together along the windy banks of the Spokane River. I'd looked at the temperature and turned down the offer of a puffy jacket like the periwinkle blue one Wenling was wearing over an additional sweater she'd put on. I'd pulled on the light gray sweater and windbreaker I'd taken to DC, seeing that the temperatures there and here were close.

I hadn't taken into account the wind chill. I was freezing.

Up the slope from us was Wenling's acreage that we'd walked across while the sun came up. It was mostly lots of frozen scrub grass that crunched underfoot and spread-out fir trees. A real ranch land feel without the horses or cattle. Nearer the river, the trees were denser and more varied, but when we'd found a route down the steep bluffs to the sandy river's edge, there was absolutely nothing to stop the wind. It even went straight through my so-called windbreaker.

The gray riverbank sand had frozen hard enough that at least it didn't blow in our eyes as we walked, but bits still stung my face and the stronger gusts whuffled around my ears like they wanted in. On top of all that, we had to pick our way carefully along the sand because the riverbank sloped evenly down the entire way.

"Looks like the scraped interior of the river itself," I said. I wrapped my arms around my chest to warm myself.

"It *is* part of the river bed," Wenling answered. "The water is very low at this time of year. But I like it this way. It feels very personal. Like I am walking inside the blood vessels of the land."

She stopped and kneeled to stab the bare fingers of her right hand through the frozen crust of what had probably been covered by snow last week. Then the fingers of her right hand. Trying to feel the beating blood of the earth? She looked like a wild thing, lithe and strong, as she had to have been to leave home with her brother, survive, thrive, come to America, and live the American dream.

With a little help from a brother who could jump back in time to tell her what was coming.

"So how do we fight them?" I asked.

"First, do you know what they are doing with my brother?"

"What?"

"I don't know! If I were them, I would make him a spy like they did in Seattle. Put him in a place where things are happening. If things go wrong, he will jump back and sound a warning. They can change direction."

"Possibly."

She must have heard the doubt in my voice because she tore her hands from the sand and stood up, looking at me, her gaze intense, the wind blowing her hair about wildly. "What do you know?"

"Nothing for sure," I said. "I...have some evidence of where I think they have tried to use time travelers, either your brother or one of the others."

"What kind of evidence?"

"Nothing I can show to another person."

"What does that mean? It is evidence or it is not."

I unwrapped my arms and shoved my hands into my pockets now. It didn't help. "When I jump back in time, I'm entering my earlier body then changing what I do going forward. Anyone who sees me after I've jumped back, that's *all* they see. There's no way to know that anything changed."

Wenling frowned. She'd put on makeup before our walk that made her eyes look bigger, her lips redder. I focused on her lips and found that seemed to suck some of the cold out of me as she said, "Yes, of course. But if there is no way for a non-time-traveler to tell when someone time traveled, how have they been able to identify *any* of you?"

I shook my head. "The first one they found must have been something extraordinary. The belief barrier would have been so high. But after that, it would be easier."

"Why?"

"Well, most obviously, they'd now know to look at strings of anomalous events, where a person seemed to get incredibly lucky over and over again. That's one way they catch card counters in casinos. On a bigger scale, that might be how they tag a time traveler who keeps rearranging their life to escape death or improve their lot in life."

Wenling's already pale skin seemed to go even paler and her jaw tightened.

I nodded in sympathy, but I was freezing again, Wenling's red lips or no. My body had started doing intermittent shivers to warm me up. "I need to get out of this wind. Can we go back to your house?"

"You think that is how they found my brother?"

"What?"

"They saw how successful and 'lucky' I was?"

I huffed out a frosty breath. "There have to be hundreds or even hundreds of thousands of people who seem to live charmed lives, but when you look closely, they're just very hard working or smart or intuitive or all three. I think that's what they would have seen if they looked closely at you."

"But they found him," Wenling said quietly.

"Yeah, well, I think at some point they found a second tool to help them identify new time travelers—the kind of memory I and my siblings have."

"Why would that matter?"

I shrugged, wrapping my arms around my body again, not bothering to hide my shivering now. "When a time traveler anywhere near me or affecting my life jumps back, I think I somehow jump back with them. I remember the future they change."

Wenling frowned hard and shook her head angrily. "That is not possible."

"It's true"

She stomped to the upper edge of the riverbank and came back with a fallen branch. She stabbed it into the frozen sand with both hands and walked backward, dragging it to a furrow as long as her body. "This is time moving like a stream in one direction," she said, breathing hard. "If Xiaobo jumps back from here"—she indicated the end of the furrow—"to here,"—she stuck the stick end into the middle of the furrow—"nothing else jumps back with him. There is only him."

"But—" I started.

Wenling shook her head. "So maybe the Xiaobo who jumps back just takes over the earlier body like you say, or, as he appears, there is an instant split in the timestream. Xiaobo One *and his whole world* goes along the original path, while the older, jumped-back Xiaobo Two starts a new path with another *whole world*." She drew a line in the sand, branching off to the left, then running parallel to the first line.

She pointed at the two lines. "Now there is a you in this stream and a you in this stream. The you in the new stream did not see the future that the time traveler came from, so why would you remember it? Perhaps you just imagine that you do."

I stared at her drawings even as I marveled at her easy illustration of the problem. Of course, she'd been living with the reality of time travel for much longer than I had. Ten years longer, in fact. And she was obviously bright. She'd have looked into her brother's power by reading articles or books about time travel, both speculative and scholarly. Infinite universes and all that.

But what she and all those published speculators and scholars had been missing was the actual experience of remembering a future that happened, then didn't. Including a future that vanished from someone other than me changing it.

It didn't fit Wenling's diagram in the sand, unless...

I felt a warmth of discovery flood through me and only realized I was smiling broadly when I saw Wenling starting to turn an angry dark shade, no doubt thinking I was mocking her.

"Please. Wenling. This...this is wonderful. No, wait! You remember I said I think I know what this CIA operation is doing? *How* I know it is definitive proof that I can see when a time traveler changes something in my world." I explained about how I'd witnessed, almost in real time, stories about events being radically rewritten in physical newspapers. "Now maybe Albus Dumbledore could make something like that happen—make a physically printed newspaper change its words to tell a different story... Do you know who Dumbledore is? Fictional wizard in the Harry Potter books?"

She smiled as something warm and wistful flashed across her face. "I read them with Xiaobo. As we learned English. And we saw all the movies before..." Her expression went dark.

"My brother used to read to me when I was a kid, too." I didn't mention what he'd read to me were Michael Crichton technothrillers that I only understood half of. But I think it was the shared time with Kenny, rather than the books themselves, that had the biggest impact.

I suspected it had been the same with Wenling and Xiaobo. Doubly bonding because they were not only reading a story, they were learning a language and culture, a ticket to a better life.

"The point is," I said gently, "wizards and witches and magic are fiction."

"Like time travel?" she said.

"But you have *evidence* for time travel. Your brother. Lena's experiments, including the ones she did on me. And my word, if you believe me."

There was a long pause as she stared at me, pulling her wind-whipped hair back from her eyes and tying it in a ponytail behind her head. "This doesn't explain how you 'remember' something only your future self in a different stream could know."

"No, it doesn't," I said, feeling again the warm revelation that had sparked my earlier smile. I rubbed my hands together. They were still cold, but my excitement seemed to have warmed up my body so I was no longer shivering. "Look, I can't explain the physics of why it would happen. But I can take a stab at the psychology of it. Can I have the stick?"

She handed it to me and I pointed to the lines she'd drawn in the frozen sand. I used my shoe to rub out the second branch she'd drawn. "What if, there is always only one timestream, but it changes? A time traveler jumps back in time to his or her earlier self and changes things,"—I stabbed the stick's point into the middle of the line—"so the future they jumped from ceases to be."

I scuffed out the line above the point I'd made.

Wenling shook her head impatiently. "This does not explain how you would remember it if you have not lived it yet."

I used the stick to bang sand off my shoes. "Have you ever heard Carl Jung's theory of the collective unconscious?"

Wenling frowned and said nothing.

"He posited that a part of our deepest minds that we're not conscious of is inherited, almost like a human birthright. He said this is why we automatically grasp so many primal symbols and archetypes, like the tree of life, the shadow, the tower, the Great Mother, without ever having heard about or encountering these things.

"But what if Jung was wrong about where that instinctual knowledge comes from? What if it comes from time being more like an ocean than a stream? Everyone in this ocean goes in many directions, with streams changing, swerving, sometimes seeming to reverse directions even without affecting other parts of the ocean. That's how broad the human experience is and why some symbols are very different between, say, Asian cultures and European ones.

"But maybe each of us, at some very deep level, has an appreciation of our part of the ocean. We intuitively feel the journey, from start to finish, all at once. And it's that whole arc of life, held all at once in our subconscious, that lets us appreciate certain symbols or significant understandings we come upon as we ride our ocean current. Our conscious mind processes them for the first time, bringing forth a memory connected to other memories both ahead and behind us in our journey, finding meaning there because of all the associations we've made or will make with this experience.

"Then someone steps in and physically lifts up a million gallons from the part of our stream we haven't consciously processed yet and throws it into the air to evaporate? *Phhhtt!* Gone. You ride *this* current now! This is your life stream!

"Ninety-nine percent of the people whose ocean path once included those million vanished gallons had only the vaguest awareness of those gallons to start with, so when they vanish, they don't notice.

"Me? Even as a new version of my life unfolds,"—I drew a new line angling out of the point I'd scrubbed the line back to—"my unconscious mind *that doesn't need to process things to remember them*, taps on my conscious and says, 'Wait a minute? What just happened to all that stuff I knew was coming?' 'What stuff?' my conscious asks. 'This stuff. All of this stuff.' And then I remember everything I lost."

With the point of the stick, I was vigorously circling the rubbed-out portion of my timeline in the sand, and I was surprised to find my heart tight and my eyes wet.

"Only you and your brother have this kind of memory," said Wenling coldly. "Not Xiaobo?"

"Has he ever shown he did?"

"No."

"Well, there you go."

We both just stood in the icy wind for a moment, absorbing that. Then I pressed her on something I'd been dying to ask from the moment she'd confirmed that I was not alone in the world with this power, that Xiaobo was also a time traveler.

"Do you know how far back Xiaobo can time travel? Or how he does it?"

"Always to the beginning of our day. He has not told me how." The last sentence sounded strained, like she actually knew the answer and hated it, or hated that she didn't know.

"What happened to him after the police raided the Demon Monks?"

"He vanished. Back to SCATTER, I assume. Maybe he believes he is doing good for his adopted new country."

She spat at the riverbank, so consumed with hatred that I actually took a step back from her.

She saw my reaction and, with concentration, cast off her darkness. She smiled up at the sun with closed eyes and her whole being seemed warmer and more desirable. Beautiful. But what she didn't realize, I thought, was how captivating I found her strength of will as it drove both intense joy and intense hatred. It was an aphrodisiac of sorts. At least out here where there was enough big sky to soak up the negative and I could appreciate her from a safe distance.

I cleared my throat. "So, the plan to rescue our brothers?"

She nodded and looked back towards her house. "It is...evolving. On our way back, tell me about the news stories that changed."

As we climbed the bluffs, I did. 1) Kuang Dishi visiting Taiwan and getting death threats. 2) Kuang visiting and having his assistant blown up with a bomb clearly meant for Kuang. 3) Kuang himself dying in a car crash between his airport arrival and the hotel where he was booked to stay during the negotiations.

By the time we'd reached the front door of her home, Wenling was nodding and smiling with a canny, scheming look I was sure had served her and Xiaobo well through the years.

She stopped with her hand on the latch. "This is why you did not think they sent Xiaobo out as a spy. He could be anywhere and give an order by phone or text, see what happens, then jump back and give a different one if he had to."

I nodded, shivering again and wishing we could do this inside. "You said he can jump to the beginning of his day, so if he gave it early, he'd have almost twenty-four hours to decide. I get maybe twenty minutes."

"Yes." I saw her brow furrow in concentration, working through how she was going to use me.

Because I had no doubt at all that was the main reason she'd brought me here. She had money, knowledge, and honed political instincts. I had the ability to rewind time in short bursts and, possibly, tell when other time travelers were doing their thing.

"Do you want to talk it through? I may be able to—"

"No need," she said with a quick smile. "I have a planning group."

I shuffled and shivered impatiently. "Care to share?"

"Soon."

She turned the knob, and we went in.

16

Assessing allies

Inside, she made me tea and vanished for a few minutes, only to return with a fancy Huawei smartphone that cost twice what I'd paid for the one I'd destroyed back in my apartment.

"Your burner phone," she said with a bored expression, but watched my eyes with interest.

"I thought the point of a burner was to have a phone so dumb it just did phone calls and texts and then you threw it out."

"No longer. This one gives you functionality, but only within this house."

"Pardon?"

"It was bought with cash from a store in Seattle, but has no SIM card, no cellular plan, no carrier. It operates only on WIFI, using a chained VPN network in this house that bounces the signal through multiple IP addresses. Untraceable, so I'm told."

It sounded like whoever programmed this phone had taken lessons from Kansas. "And I'm to use this for...?"

"You can handle your insurance claims through Skype and tell your family and friends that you are safe but out of touch for a while."

"What if they need to reach me? Is there a phone number?"

"You have a Gmail account, yes?"

I nodded.

"They can send you an email. You can retrieve it and call them back."

I smiled grimly. I wasn't sure this felt right. Of course, she had the right to *lead* this effort, given her greater resources and intel, but this almost felt like I was being led in chains. Or maybe just held in a very comfortable cell.

"What is it?" she said, catching my expression.

"I'm wondering if I should have just gone to the FBI."

"And given them what?"

The code name, SCATTER. Everything Cutter had revealed about the CIA's gang deals. A demonstration of my powers.

"Even if they believed you," Wenling said, "you underestimate how far the CIA will go. My driver took out one person who was watching your apartment last night. This morning, two other CIA showed up to investigate."

"There are laws," I said.

Wenling snorted. "There is power and there is money. This is why you have home insurance." She smiled. "Perhaps from your room?"

I raised my hands in surrender (for *now*) and went upstairs with my new toy. By the time I entered the room I'd slept in only briefly last night, entered, and hopped up onto the stark white duvet that covered the high mattress, I'd connected with my email and Google photos.

Everything was there. It was time to make some calls.

Fifteen minutes later, I'd deleted the *If I don't return* email that I'd programed to send tomorrow. The last thing I needed was for Wilson or Dadashev to insist on a follow up snoop of me that turned *that* up.

Next was the physical mess back in Seattle.

I talked to the Seattle PD, gave a statement, contact info, blah blah. I gave their report to my insurers, along with my pictures and an itemized list (from memory) of everything damaged and the cost of repairs.

I talked with Megan to find she had been thoroughly comforted by Officer Bryan Miller and was happy to go in tomorrow to let in the restoration company.

"But when are you actually *back* back?" she asked at the end of it all.

It brought me up short. I wanted to say a day or two, but realistically...? Everything had been approaching normal with my work. Even having a hopefully reversible split with Lena had been all part of making a healthy life.

But I'd always known it was going to rupture again once I found some solid clues about Kenny.

"I'll update you by Monday," I said.

I'd wandered to the room's south-facing window by then. Outside was the long gravel driveway and endless prairies spotted with fir trees. I could also just see the edge of the garage/coach house where I was pretty sure the Asian driver, Jian, lived, separate and apart from the house, but close enough to be on call. Always ready to answer.

I wondered vaguely whether he'd let me use him as an emergency contact that my friends could call. Assuming Wenling let him have a fully functioning phone.

In frustration, I pulled up Lena's number, realizing that if she'd blocked my old number, she couldn't have blocked this one. I sent her a quick summary of how my timelines had been changed by other people. I included my thoughts on why this could indicate a time traveler who jumped back in time wiped out the timeline he or she jumped from.

It was just an FYI.

For her research.

Sweating, I added my Gmail address to the bottom of the text in case she wanted to respond.

I waited for a few minutes, then a few minutes more, just in case she saw my text and wanted to respond at once.

Nothing. Of course.

Who else? Jude?

I called and got his voice mail. I told him some people had broken into my office and home but I was safe. If he wanted to call me, he could send a message to my Gmail.

Was that it?

No one else in my life?

No one.

There wasn't, really.

Except I was the only one left of their three offspring. And I actually had information about all three of us. That had to mean something.

I dialed my dad's phone first. My expectation, from far too many failed contacts in the past 35 years, was that they'd either let their phone batteries die, or turned them off so they weren't disturbed in whatever important meetings they were—

"Yehhhlo?" said my Irish father's always upbeat greeting, a mashup of Yes and Hello.

"Dad, it's Jackson."

There was a long silence, then, "How do we know it's you?"

It was possible this VPN-chaining thing was altering my voice, but I doubted it. I think it was just that I was so far out of my parents' lives they couldn't remember what I sounded like. Whatever mystery phone number showed up on their call display certainly wouldn't have helped.

I pulled the phone from my ear and pulled up the apps screen to see what came installed. It had both Zoom and Skype.

I put the phone back to my ear. "Have you changed your email lately?"

"Don't be daft. How would people find me?"

"I'm going to hang up and send you Zoom link. Click on it as soon as you get it and we'll talk with video."

Without waiting to hear his idea of my plan, I hung up, pulled up Zoom, and sent him an immediate invite. As I waited for him to receive it and try to sign in—I'd done this only once before with my father and it had taken a while for him to get both the sound and video working—the door to the bedroom I was using opened and Wenling entered.

She'd removed her white sweater, and I was pretty sure the blouse had been re-knotted to just above the top of her skin-tight jeans because I could now see a taut patch of skin that included her bellybutton. A few more shirt buttons had been undone at the top as well. She'd pulled silky sections of hair on either side of her face back and fastened them behind her head. And she'd applied just a touch of extra color to her face—smoke above the eyes, pink to the cheeks, gloss to the lips.

Why?

My father's face suddenly came up on my screen. He probably saw the lower side of my chin as it hung slack in a kind of confusion.

"Jackson?" he snapped.

I looked down, saw his angry-looking face, and raised my phone up before me, keeping it between me and Wenling.

Behind my father's face on my phone, my mother's plumper, smiling one hovered, her frosted highlights bobbing as she waved and said, "Hi, honey!" Almost like a real mother.

"What I'm calling about—"

"We know what yeh're calling about!" said my father. "Yer sister's been kidnapped."

My eyes widened in surprise. "How did you know that?"

"She had an automated warning system, absolutely fierce, to send us a message if she was ever taken out."

I frowned. "Why didn't I receive something from her then?"

"Because yeh knew, didn't yeh?"

"That's not how automated systems work, Dad. If I didn't get anything, I wasn't part of the system."

"Don't talk down to me, boyo. I'm telling yeh what we got and what it said. Said Kentucky was alive. Said you'd likely been snatched, too. Where are yeh, then?"

I let that click over in my brain. "When did you get this?"

There was a moment when he and my mother discussed this in murmurs, then he said, "Saturday. That's right." My mother nodded along.

I mimicked her nodding. "Four days ago. I guess you've been pretty busy with your franchisees."

"Yeh can't imagine, boyo."

"Oh, I can. Did you read anything about what happened to me last March?"

He and my mother conferenced again.

"Never mind," I said before they answered. "Nothing important."

I gathered they could hear the sarcasm in my voice or saw the way my lips must have been twisted because my father's Irish temper roused itself to the earlier indignation he'd apparently forgotten. "Did yeh know," he said with his brows drawing down in a way that once made me cower and probably still would have if he were here in the room with me then, "that Homeland Security called us..."

"I think it was the IRS," my mother broke in.

"Whichever," said my father, voice lilting but like a rolling typhoon, building in power. "They sent a man to us, right to the worksite of our new store in Atlanta, right there in front of our new associates..."

"What did they say?" I asked with a feeling of dread.

"That you were being *difficult*. That Carmelita might be getting *deported*. That we might be getting *audited!*"

"Are your books clean?" I asked.

My father's face went red, but mine was getting equally so. I could feel the pressure building inside me like someone was trying to squeeze it out my eyes, ears, nose, and mouth. I bared my teeth at this man who'd given his seed to make me, then agreed with my mother to mostly forget me.

As they'd done with Kansas.

As they'd done with Kenny.

Before I could snarl some of that out, however, I felt a cool hand on the arm I held the phone with, then the warmth of a body and other arm wrapping around me, with Wenling's face ending up pressed to my left shoulder like some kind of loving girlfriend.

"Hello, Mr. Traine, Mrs. Traine," she purred in perfect Oxford English, maybe with a bit of posh. "It's so good to see you. I've heard so much about both of you."

My father's eyes goggled at me from the phone for a second before he recovered himself and spoke to me only. "Yer sister's message gave us a woman named Lena Cortland as an emergency contact if we couldn't reach either her or you. Said she was almost yer fiancé. Is this her, then?"

"My name is Zhou Wenling," Wenling said, slowing the name as if speaking to someone mentally feeble.

"Yeh're shacked up with a COVID bringer, are yeh?" said my father, again just to me.

I cut the connection and threw the phone onto the bed. My whole body was shaking. Wenling slid off me and took a step back.

"Your parents are bigoted cretins," she said matter-of-factly. It was more, I think, to give me clarity than provide any sort of comfort.

"They...have never been very...present."

"That is maybe better than active abuse. But you are a psychologist. Would their neglect not qualify as a kind of abuse?"

I was finding it very hard to breathe. My face burned. My body leaked cold sweat. Vomit climbed up the back of my throat.

"Well?" Wenling demanded.

"Yes," I said.

"I understand this." She stepped close to me and took both my hands in hers. "I understand you better than Lena Cortland ever could have. I have watched you through the eyes of others for almost a year now. I know more about your past, your love of your brother and sister, your friends and enemies, than she ever cared to find out."

"Because she didn't have me followed and investigated?"

"Because she has always had…everything. And the first time something important is taken from her, a mother too stupid to let herself be vaccinated, she falls apart. She blames you for being needy, then for refusing to do everything she asks. When you do not fit exactly what she needs, you are nothing to her."

It hit a little too close to home, and I pulled my hands from Wenling's and stumbled backward, sitting hard on the high top of the bed. She followed me there, standing directly in front of me, her face now almost level with mine. I dropped my face, ashamed of how talking with my parents could literally make me regress to all the insecurities of my childhood.

So slowly that it felt unreal, she stepped forward toward me, between my knees, until her lower belly pressed against hard against my crotch. The rest of her slim body rose before my eyes, her creamy skin and peach-colored bra framed by a gaping blouse. I could feel her heat. Smell her floral scent.

I raised my flushed face to focus on her face. Her eyes.

"We are to be partners in war," she said quietly and rested her fingertips on my thighs. "Trusting each other. Working together."

I swallowed dryly. "I guess."

"You will tell me what happened with your sister. I will share my body and my bed with you."

"Umm, I'm not sure that…"

"I can feel with my belly that you find me attractive. I find you attractive also."

"That's…not the only consideration."

"What other considerations are there?"

"Promises I made."

"To a woman who has rejected you? When you could have me?"

These last questions were obviously meant to be rhetorical, but when my face bunched up with conflict, Wenling's face dropped into an ugly scowl. She pushed her body away from me and walked to the door of the bedroom.

There she stopped and looked back.

"I've come up with a target that will catch the CIA's attention," she said. "It may need multiple time travels to get it right. If you are still willing."

"I'm... Yes." Though I couldn't recall ever agreeing to that, I really had, just by coming here. It was so obviously my role in our battle. However much it made my stomach flip with revulsion.

Wenling gave a curt nod. "You can help yourself to whatever food you can find in the kitchen for lunch. But we will eat dinner together at six p.m. so I can explain the operation to you. It will happen sometime between then and eight o'clock."

"Tonight?"

"Yes," she said, with the same tone she'd used with my father. Dealing with someone mentally feeble.

Then she was out of the bedroom, grabbing and yanking the door like she wanted to rip the knob off.

She slowed it at the last second, so it clicked closed softly behind her.

Lunch was eerily silent, with Wenling nowhere strikingly absent. But at least the fridge had a good selection of fresh vegetables, hummus, some packages of uncooked sliced meats, and some kind of leftover chicken stir-fry. The pantry had lots of dry food ingredients and cans. The freezer had microwavable frozen meals.

It struck me that even with all her own wealth, Wenling must do her own cooking. She had a chauffeur, but not a personal chef. Privacy reasons?

I made myself a mixed salad with tuna and plain yogurt, hummus on crackers.

The desserts I found afterward were sweet jellies, cruller-type donuts, and three boxes of almond cookies.

I took a couple of almond cookies and an apple back up to my bedroom.

By 2:00, my insurance company had gotten back to me with estimates and papers to sign. I applied digital signatures and sent them back.

Megan had sent a note apologizing for being so stressed. Bryan was looking after her and would be at the office with her tomorrow to make sure everything went smoothly.

Jude left an email asking me to call him at 5:00 my time, which would 8:00 his. I set an alarm on the phone, though there was no way I was going to forget. It was unnervingly close to my dinner time with Wenling, when I'd learn if I was to become some kind of international assassin.

My parents had sent no kind of email follow up. I hadn't expected one. Lena hadn't responded.

I wanted to tell her I was learning about myself and my limits. My training with Lead the Way had made me stronger both physically and emotionally, but it hadn't cured my essential vulnerability to trauma. It was why I'd so assiduously avoided any unnecessary time jumps. I could still crumble like her frozen rice with enough pressure.

But risking all that in the pursuit of Kenny? With the aim of not only rescuing him and Kansas, but also the other people like us who'd been forced into a program that exploited their pain and suffering in order to inflict more pain and suffering on others? That was noble. That was worth risking everything for.

Carefully.

17

Preparing

BEFORE CALLING JUDE, I explored the ground floor of the house. Wenling seemed to have vanished, but I found a laundry room and brought down all the clothes I'd worn in DC other than my suit and shoes, and ran them through a couple cycles.

While those ran, I wandered past a locked door through which I thought I heard Wenling on some kind of conference call. The planning group, I assumed.

Towards the back of the house, I discovered a movie room and, beyond that, a home gym with floor-to-ceiling windows looking out onto trees and sky. Sitting on the gym's floor rubberized floor was a strider machine, free weights, lifting cage, and a bike that looked connected to a large computer screen. Also a mirror wall, a TV wall, and a freestanding heavy bag for a martial arts-style workout.

It certainly explained how Wenling kept fit.

It also reinforced the isolation of the place. She might be in electronic contact with her advisers, but from where I stood now, the house was so eerily silent I could hear the wind blowing outside.

"Jackson," Jude said tightly to me when he saw my face. I'd Skyped him and asked for a face to face over our phones. My friend looked haggard and scared. It reminded me too much of my last call with Kansas and made me wish I'd followed through on my thoughts in the airport to tell him to forget about chasing down the old Southern Whispers guy. Forget I'd ever mentioned him.

But I hadn't and here we were.

"You alone?" he asked.

"For the next forty minutes or so."

"Okay, good." Jude ran his hand through his shaggy hair and took a few deep breaths. In this tiny frame, it was clear all he needed were some little round spectacles to look like something straight out a Jewish comedy. He'd be the desperate Talmudic scholar who just found some important rule the hero can use to win the girl, stay kosher, and star on Jewzy.tv or *Curb Your Enthusiasm*.

"You need a minute?"

Jude shook his head and took a drink from a glass that was on the kitchen table I now recognized from my overnight stay at his place. "So I found the old guy you got your sketch artist to draw for me."

"Name?"

"Andre Poussaint."

"Sounds French." But there had been absolutely nothing in the way he looked or spoke to suggest French heritage.

"Yeah. Creole heritage that kind of blended into the general South. You know why I'd never heard of him, and why I almost plotzed when someone identified him? Because he's a frickin' ghost. Literally a legendary undercover operative who could reputedly look like anyone, sound like anyone. The kind of guy *Mission Impossible* plots were based on. Easily in his 80s now. The person who finally recognized him was sure he was dead."

"But he's not."

"Apparently. Can you tell me where you saw him exactly? Did you actually speak to him about something?"

"First tell me why you're so scared."

Jude licked his lips, then jumped up from the table, carrying his phone with him. His face jounced around in the picture as he went to the kitchen and refilled his water glass. He also pulled a half-eaten tinfoil plate of what looked like strawberry pie from the fridge, and I heard a clink as he set it on the counter. Then a drawer sliding open. Cutlery pulled out. A forkful of pie went into Jude's mouth.

"Jude...?"

"It was the way my contact talked about this guy, okay? Like he could see through walls or something. Kill you with a ballpoint pen. Spoke five languages. Involved in some of the scariest CIA ops ever. If you did something to piss him off, that's bad enough. But if he also finds I'm looking for him...?"

"He doesn't even know I was there," I said calmly. Though I remembered mentioning both my brother's and my sister's abductions in my final timestream at Langley. "At least I never met him. I just spotted him. Obviously not who I thought he was. He must have a doppleganger."

"Who did you think he was?"

I should have been ready for that one. I wasn't. I'm sure it made my answer less than reassuring when I looked down and away before answering, "Someone my sister introduced me to once, years ago."

"And she went into intelligence, right? So it could have been him."

"I guess. You have any idea why he'd still be hanging around the halls of your HQ if he's so old?" *Like running a secret operation that collects and enslaves time travelers to kill foreign nationals?*

"No frickin' clue, dude. My guess? He was just visiting some old pal. Or maybe they called him in to discuss some old operation he was involved in."

Yeah, no. "Probably right. I'm sorry I sent you chasing after a dangerous ghost. Anyone asks, you can say the picture came from the friend of a friend who's researching Cold War stuff for a spy novel."

"Want to give me an author name? Jean-Luc Picarré."

"Ha. You're finally watching *Next Generation*! Best of the *Star Trek* series, right?"

He adopted a clipped imitation of Patrick Stuart and said, "I think we have a spy on the Holodeck, Number One."

"You're living in a real deck of spies, dude. Hopefully the octogenarian one won't give you any problems."

Jude grinned and took another forkful of pie. It seemed to finally calm him down. "Gonna tell me where you're calling from now?"

"Nope!" I said cheerfully. "I am on a bit of a stress vacation, hidden from the world and loving it."

"Stress? Want to talk about it? Was it...because I dragged you out here?"

I laughed. "Not because of you." *A partial lie.* "And I am on vacation from stress, so no talk of it. Right now, in fact, I have to start getting ready for a dinner a beautiful woman is preparing for me."

"Lena?" Jude asked excitedly.

I smiled enigmatically, said, "Later, dude," and ended the call.

Then I checked my email again.

Nothing from Lena.

I gritted my teeth and pathetically sent her another text.

I got off my bed.

Forget her.

Can't. Duh.

Then at least shift your focus.

Wenling. If she was actually preparing dinner for the two of us, I wanted to watch and ooh and aahh at her skill. I think I owed her at least that much for treating me more as a person than just a tool to be used. I guessed it was because we'd both lost a brother. However mercurial and coldly aggressive she could be, that was her one place of true vulnerability. She needed to share it with someone who understood.

And the offer of her body?

Even with the physical heat we'd shared, I honestly wasn't sure where that had come from. But it was probably good that it had been raised and put to rest.

Probably.

18

Long-distance strike

I PULLED ON A gray sweater and went downstairs to find Wenling in full chef attire. For her, this meant that over her tight jeans she now wore a cream-colored hoodie that had tiger print arms and a cut lion cub painted on the front, signed by Stella McCartney.

Wenling didn't acknowledge me as she sliced and chopped, tossed things in her wok and frying pan, so that steam and the sound of spitting oil filled the kitchen. The main fascination point for me this time was the speed and dexterity with which she wielded that santoku knife.

She stopped at one point to rinse it and I blurted, "The swirls and patterns in the metal. Is that Damascus steel?"

Wenling whirled it in one hand. "Four hundred layers around one cutting layer of carbon steel. Fired, hammered, folded, over and over and over, until it can cut through anything."

I noticed the sharpening stone lying out on the kitchen counter. "You have to sharpen it?"

Another whirl of the knife. "We all need sharpening occasionally."

I wasn't sure if it was her or me she was referring to here.

At least the conversation lightened her mood. She even turned on the room's music with a spoken command, and an up-tempo jazz standard by Michael Bublé got her hips swaying as she finished the stir-fry and directed it into a huge crockery bowl, then did the same for the steaming, fluffy rice.

"Please light my candles," she asked as she picked up each bowl with one hand and walked carefully around the kitchen island toward the table.

I grinned at what I assumed was an unintentional double entendre as I went for the matches. I had three of the five candles lit by the time she'd set the bowls down.

Bublé finished as she put silver serving spoons into each, and she said loudly, "You don't have to say you love me!"

I looked at her. "Are you seriously...?"

She smiled sweetly, as a song started up that I recognized as *You Don't Have to Say You Love Me.* The song was a pathetic plea by a rejected lover to just be close, even with no commitments. Really?

Wenling spooned hot rice and stir-fry onto my plate and hers, and breathed it in. "You see, *this* is why we don't say grace before we eat. Some things should be consumed as soon as they're offered!"

"Smells good, but a little spicier than I'm used to."

"All the more reason to try."

"Is it, though?"

Wenling gave a dramatic sigh and head shake. I had to admire the gusto with which she stabbed her chopstick into her food to show how a person's appetite *should* be sated.

I joined in, grunting in satisfaction over the food before asking what the operation was that we were doing this night.

She ignored my question for a few moments until the song ended and she let the ambience go quiet. She finished what she had in her mouth, wiped her mouth and hands with a napkin, and pulled out her phone from under her hoodie and put it on the table beside here, poking some app, typing a query, reading what came up. Then she considered me carefully. "It will be soon," she said.

"What are we waiting on?"

"Since you told me your story this morning about how the CIA's SCATTER program interfered with the Chinese negotiator to Taiwan, I have been discussing what we could do that would make people like you or your brother pay attention."

"A shot across the bow?"

Wenling nodded. "A good metaphor, yes. They must know we see them."

"And...?"

"There is a representative from Huawei named Shen Kong, who is rumored to be a Party Committee Secretary. Do you understand what that is?"

I shook my head.

"The Party Committee Secretary is usually the leader of the Chinese Communist Party organization in a province, city, village, or region of China. There is usually a Governor or Mayor as well, but the party secretary has the real power. There are also Party Committee Secretaries in important state-run companies, too. Huawei claims to be independent, but most people believe it is actually run by the CCP, which makes its Party Committee Secretary not only an important person within the company, but someone who is an arm of the Chinese government itself."

"That is Shen Kong?"

"Yes. He was recently 'promoted' because of the struggles Huawei had had with the United States and many of its allies who have forbidden their government contractors to deal with them."

"Because they're afraid China will spy on them through the tech that Huawei sells them."

Wenling nodded. "Especially with the introduction of 5G technology. Have some wine."

I poured myself a third of a glass for myself and for her. We both took sips. Wenling visibly leaned her head forward and sucked bubbles through her mouthful before swallowing and nodding.

"Shen Kong has been visiting the US off and on for months now to lobby congressmen and women. Conveniently, he just landed at Andrews Air Force Base for one of those visits. But I ensured *this* time he will be surrounded and questioned by American news media. Then he will transfer to ground transportation to travel to the Capitol, a little over fifteen miles away. A half hour drive."

She slid her phone across the table towards me. Two apps were open on its front. The first was a countdown timer on top, set to ten minutes and not yet moving. Below it was a phone app that had three numbers, each with a code name beside it: Horse, Rat, and Snake.

"What am I supposed to do with this?" I asked.

"Guess."

I looked from the phone to Wenling's face. "Three numbers. Three tries. You want to change history twice like SCATTER did in Taiwan, so people like me and my brother might notice."

Wenling smiled. "Yes. And not just any changes. They must be changes like the ones SCATTER did with Kuang Dishi so that they know we know."

"And that we can do the same."

"Yes."

It was cold, terrible, and brilliant. Exactly what I should have expected from her.

Knowing that didn't stop the sudden increase of flood flow in my body, the tension that had started tightening up my neck and forehead, my increased heartrate. Because I now knew that Wenling was going to want me to give some kind of order by phone, then jump back after eight or nine minutes, give a different order, then jump back again to give a third order. Create three distinct timelines. All tonight. Which meant at least two states of emotional trauma so serious my mind would want to leave this body, this timeline, and jump back to an earlier one.

For a noble cause. To stop SCATTER.

Screw nobility.

To save. Kenny and Kansas.

And Xiaobo.

Yes.

Wenling was looking at me now, so calm and confident in my ability and willingness to do this. Was that because it had always been easier for her brother, Xiaobo? It must have been. Because, from her brief history, it was clear he must have been making jumps back in time almost daily for years. I couldn't understand how he could do that and stay sane if his jumps hurt like mine did.

I swallowed dryly. "The horse first? What do you want me to tell him or her to do?"

Wenling breathed out and broke into a genuine smile, showing she hadn't been sure of me after all. Seeing that vulnerability in her again actually helped me. "Yes, horse," she said. "And all you have to do is give the person on the phone one word, 'Xiaobo,' then hang up and start the timer on the phone."

"I call now?"

Wenling turned toward the wall that ran along this side of the room from the kitchen to the big windows and called out, "Open TV. CNN. Volume zero."

A wall panel about five feet above the ground slid up, revealing a screen that had to be at least sixty inches diagonally. It turned on and the CNN logo appeared on the top left for a second before it began playing silently. A blond woman I didn't recognize was talking to the camera with what looked like an airport tarmac where a private jet was deboarding into a gaggle of news media, all waving microphones and cameras at them.

"Do you have your new phone with you?" Wenling asked.

I nodded, pulled it out of my jeans pocket, and passed it to her. She dialed a number and put it to her ear. After a second, it obviously connected, and she spoke softly and quietly in Chinese. Listened. Said something else in Chinese. Opened some app on the phone and said something more as she poked the phone. Then hung up.

She put "my" phone on the table beside the other one and I saw a timer was running. She said, "When it hits twenty, you call. Earlier if Shen Kong starts entering his car."

We watched the timer together, and at forty seconds, I dialed "Horse." Someone answered.

"Xiaobo," I said and hung up. I pressed the button for the time app above the phone app and the numbers started counting down.

"Good," said Wenling.

"What happens now?"

She considered me, then decided she could trust me to continue. "Right now, Shen Kong's translator is telling the American media that a radical anti-Chinese group made up of loosely affiliated Falun Gong, anti-5G conspiracy theorists, and white nationalists are planning to stage a protest tomorrow morning outside the gates of the White House, denouncing China's Huawei's as a tool of a belligerent China which is determined to undermine the power of the United States and democracy in general."

"And this is live?"

"Yes. TV volume four!"

The sound came up on the TV just as the blond commentator obviously heard something in her earpiece. She cocked her head, nodded, and looked directly into the camera lens at her viewers. "In some breaking news, Huawei Operations Director Shen Kong, who just landed in Andrews Air Force Base for meetings tomorrow with members of congress, has been notified of a potentially dangerous protest tomorrow at the Capitol by a group called Western Freedom. We're still waiting confirmation , but Fox News is reporting—"

"Volume zero!" Wenling's command silenced the TV. She said, "When you jump back, it must be to before you gave the order, but not too much before because Shen Kong must be getting off his plane. Can you do that?"

I nodded, though my mouth had gone bone dry.

I stared at the timer counting down and remembered how much had happened in every other jump in the ten minutes preceding them. Usually something that got him fighting, or running, or just getting the hell kicked out of him. Or Lena had been in danger, or getting her throat cut, or...

My heart was pounding now, and I took a few deep breaths. I couldn't let myself get too worked up yet. Still 8.5 minutes to go. Well, maybe six to be on the safe side.

Then I realized that it didn't matter how quickly I jumped back because I wouldn't be changing anything before Shen Kong landed. It was only when I gave my next command that mattered. So I needed to get back now. As fast as I could, because my control over how long it would take me without a direct threat to my life was...tenuous.

I closed my eyes to tell myself I was a failure, a loser, a screw up who could never get things right, who...

Wenling said, "You can time travel now."

I nodded jerkily. It wasn't working! I was too caught up in the pressure to jump and distracted by the *reasons* to jump that I couldn't focus. Yes, I knew I was a failure. I knew that. I knew, but...

I opened my eyes.

Six minutes to go.

My head suddenly beaded up in sweat. I wasn't going to be able to jump. Wenling's plan wouldn't work. She'd see I couldn't do what she needed. She'd kick me to the curb. I'd be taken by SCATTER or simply left alone and clueless.

Not acceptable.

"Insult me," I blurted to Wenling. "Tell me I'm a failure. Tell me I'm not a real man. Don't worry, you won't remember ever doing it if it works."

"Why would I want to do that?"

"Because I may not be able to jump without it."

"What?"

"You heard me."

"You are only telling me this now?" The pitch of her voice was starting to climb. That was good.

I gave a jerky shrug. "Lena didn't tell you that, hunh? I have to fear I'm about to die or be kicked so hard emotionally by myself or others that..."

"You are a nothing man!"

"Yes," I said, drinking in the absolute hate building in her eyes. "And time's running out."

"You are a worthless wanker. A knob head. A maggot. You have a limp penis. That's why you can't accept the offer of my body! You're weaker than a pussy! You're a Flo rag who cannot hold onto a woman, cannot let yourself believe how much that woman hates him! Lena hates you! Because you failed her! Like you failed your brother! Like you are failing me!"

It was sinking in, but too slowly. My defensive shells were blocking her out. Even though I was breathing hard and red faced. I wasn't leaping anywhere. And the clock was clicking down.

"I NEED MORE!" I roared at her and jumped up from the table, began stomping around the room, beating my forehead with my knuckles. "TELL ME I'M USELESS! TELL ME I FAILED MY SISTER, TOO! THE ONE WOMAN IN MY LIFE WHO HAS ALWAYS LOVED AND LOOKED OUT FOR ME AND I FAILED HER!"

"Her name?" Wenling called to me.

"KANSAS! I HAVED FAILED HER! THEY'VE TAKEN HER AND I CAN'T EVEN JUMP TO HELP HER! I'M A LOSER! I'M A LOSER! I'M A—"

I stopped because Wenling had come up behind me, grabbed my shoulder, and spun me around. She was holding a knife in her right hand. Not a santoku knife with its squared-off tip. This was a chef's knife, a good eight inches long and ending in a very sharp and deadly point.

I looked into her eyes and saw a terrifying resolve. "What are you—?"
She stabbed me in my gut.
"Wha—?"
She wrapped her other hand around the one holding the knife and used both hands to thrust upward into me, going for my heart. I could feel it rip through my diaphragm, lung tissue, saw it in my mind as I shuddered and—

I was in my chair at the dining table, sitting across from Wenling, the phone with the animal-labeled quick dial numbers lying flat in front of me.

"Do you have your new phone with you?" Wenling asked.

I shook my head. How did I get back...? Wasn't I just...? The knife... The fucking *knife!*

I leapt out of my chair and stared across at Wenling in horror. I could hardly breathe.

"What is it?" she said.

"You... Oh my God. And I thought Lena was cold."

"Explain," Wenling said, obviously angry about being compared to Lena this way.

"You know what? I'm not going to do that. Because telling you will just make sure you do it again."

"Do what? What will I do... Wait, have you already done one of your time jumps?"

"Bingo! Give the lady a prize for the ability to recognize a chrono-aberration!"

"If you jumped, what was the first—"

"The first instruction? The Horse? To communicate with Shen Kong's security and the White House that there *was* going to be a protest tomorrow morning by a group known as Western Freedom over Shen Kong's meeting with President Biden. Of course, I'm not going to call Horse this time, so that protest will never be warned and will never happen, if, in fact, it was ever going to happen. No, now I'm going to call the Rat, right? Which sounds kind of ominous. You going to tell me what it will do?"

She looked evenly at me. "No. But I must ensure she is in place. Give me your phone."

I handed it over and she dialed a number. Listened. Gave instructions. Then handed the phone to me. "Now you can call."

"Good!" Feeling the reckless flood of adrenaline surging in me from the fact I was alive after being stabbed in the gut twice only moments ago *in the timeline I remembered,* I punched the second quick-dial number beside the word Rat.

Someone answered the first ring, another female, speaking quickly in Chinese. "Ninhao. Wo shi Chu."

I looked at Wenling, who nodded. I said, "Xiaobo," and hung up.

I hit the ten-minute countdown clock and stared at it as it started to count down. My whole body was trembling and sweating. I should have looked at Wenling. I should have asked her what I'd just done. But it was all I could do to not yell at her or go running from the room.

After almost a full minute passed, Wenling said, "Do you want to know what Chu just triggered?"

I looked over at her, not daring to speak.

"It may take another minute." Her eyes flicked to the silent CNN reporting on the TV screen. "Or maybe not. Volume four!"

The same CNN blond news anchor was nodding her head to something being spoken into her ear bud. "Repeat that, please," she said. Then she nodded and looked directly out at her viewers. "Our reporters at the scene of Huawei ambassador Shen Kong's arrival at Andrews Air Force Base report they've seen an explosion on the periphery of Shen's retinue." She tilted her head, obviously reading more of the story on a teleprompter. "We're learning that apparently a welcome *package* that may have been intended for the ambassador was intercepted by one of his aides. We don't know how it got through security or..."

"Volume zero!"

There was a long silence. Wenling took a sip of her wine.

I stared at her, dumbfounded. "I just killed a man, didn't I?"

"In this timeline, yes. But if you can erase your earlier timelines when you travel back and make other choices, he does not have to stay dead."

I swore under my breath and shakily got up from my chair.

"Where are you going?"

"I have to jump, right?" I said. I walked jerkily to the center of the room, looking about blindly. I had to jump back now. I'd just caused someone to be killed. I couldn't let that stand. But I didn't know if I *could* jump back again. Not without... Not...

I looked back at Wenling who was regarding me gravely. Had Lena also told her that the way I normally jumped was when my life was threatened? It hadn't seemed so. Wenling had been shocked the last time (which now never was) that I could just do it on command.

Should I tell her now?

No. No. I wasn't going to let her stab me again. I had to jump on my own. I had to do it now.

"What are you thinking?" Wenling called. "Your face looks strange."

"All part of the process," I said. Then I turned and ran from the room through the entry drawing room, and out of it to the main hall and front door. Would it be locked? Just how free *was* I here?

I grabbed the front door's handle and yanked it down. The door opened! I yanked it towards me and plunged outside as Wenling yelled something after me. I ran. I ran in shoes and jeans and gray sweater out into the pitch-black night.

And stopped, shaking and gasping in my own panic.

I couldn't just run. I had to jump.

The air stank like burnt plastic, bitter and hot, clawing at my throat.

Or maybe it was just me, my imagination turning the night into the seventh circle of Dante's inferno, specifically the innermost ring of it that is made up of blasphemers who do violence to God and nature. Which I did every time I jumped back and rewrote reality. And Wenling did to me.

Pathetic! Do or not do!

Shut up! To do means to kill myself here, physically or psychologically. Die in this *timestream so I can fly back to safety.*

Then doooo it!

I...

Do it, FAILURE! You not only failed Kenny and Kansas and Lena, but you're failing them all over again now by finding Zhou Wenling and screwing up with her, too. Failing. Failure. No wonder you're alone and losing everyone you ever care about, every person who ever wanted your help.

I stumbled on the uneven grass because the accusations in my head were true. One hundred percent vein-burning acid.

Failure.

Fuckup.

Loser.

Gone.

Gone.

GONE!!!

I was sitting at a table with a phone on that table in front of me.

I blinked, my head all fuzzy. It was a dining table. And across from me was Zhou Wenling. I was supposed to call her Elizabeth Chan in public, an Amazon rep. Except she wasn't an Amazon rep. She was a secretive billionaire who'd fought her way out of poverty in China and bought her way to the States. And she'd offered her body to me. I'd refused. She wanted me to fight the CIA with her to get back her brother and my brother.

Got it.

I realized Wenling had been smiling, then talking as I got my brain sorted into its current timeline. She was still talking. "...must be changes like the ones SCATTER did with Kuang Dishi so that they know we know."

I remembered this conversation, of course, and gave the response I'd given the first time around. "And that we can do the same."

"Yes."

And of course, she was right. But this time I understood what she meant by changes "like" the ones SCATTER did with Kuang Dishi. Because so far we'd mirrored them almost to the letter. The political action group protesting Shen Kong's arrival. The letter bomb blowing up one of his aides. Next, we were obviously going to arrange for Shen to be killed on the way from Andrews Air Force Base to his hotel in DC.

Some big rig was already in place to tee-bone the car. Or there was an IUD. Or the car was rigged to explode.

"Are you going to ask me what I need you to do?" Wenling said, smiling, totally confident in her plan, with obviously no qualms about its real-life consequences.

"You want me to dial a number and say your brother's name," I said dully.

Wenling's smile faltered. "How did you know…? Oh." Then quickly, fully engaged: "How many times have you jumped?"

Ha. She even had the lingo now. She was so smart. Our mission needed smart. But not like this.

"Twice," I finally answered her, breathing hard now as if all that had just come before—the shouting at her, getting stabbed, jumping, running away from her and making myself jump anyway—had happened to *this* body, even though *this* body had done none of it. Only this mind. Only this self. This soul. Me.

"And?" she prompted.

"CNN reported what your people did both times. It will be enough for my brother to see the changes and report them. Whoever's running SCATTER will get it."

"Almost," she said, pleased I understood. "Once we finish it. Once we show them what we can do, then they will listen. Wenling turned toward the east wall of the house. "Open TV! CNN. Volume zero."

The wall panel slid open to reveal the CNN woman reporting on the crowd of people descending the stairs from a private aircraft and being surrounded by television journalists. "Do you have your new phone with you?" Wenling asked.

I nodded. "But I'm not going to give it to you. We don't need to kill anyone. We've made our point."

Wenling frowned hard at me, then nodded. She obviously realized I understood everything now. "You are a good man, Jackson. You want to protect the innocent. But you must know that Shen Kong is not innocent. Not at all." Her face twisted into a look of absolute disgust. "You know what he did to become Party Committee Secretary with Huawei? He was a good administrator in Xinjiang. This meant he personally supervised the enslavement, torture, rape, and murder of thousands of Uyghur women and little girls. This is why they chose him.

And why I chose him. This is why I brought the media to surround him. They will tell his whole story at the end."

"I thought..." My head was spinning. "I thought this was just to make a point."

"Yes! Like SCATTER makes a point. Which is why they will know I understand them. That I can predict and stop them!" Her eyes darted to the screen. "But we need to act now."

I wasn't sure I believed her, or even if it was true, it somehow justified ordering this man's death.

Then I realized that Wenling had grown tired of waiting for me to work through the morality of it. She's picked up the phone with the Horse, Rat, and Snake predials on it and punched the one for Snake. When it was answered immediately, she spoke her brother's name, then added a stream of Chinese that was so fast and intense I could barely make out its individual sounds.

She hung up and turned to me.

"Any of the calls could come from me, I think, so long as you told me what to say each time. And now there is no more jumping needed." She gestured to the CNN screen where the silent backdrop video showed a set of dark limousines pulling away from the airplane and gaggle of news media." You are done."

Except we *weren't* done.

Moving faster than I think I had since I'd arrived at Wenling's house—*Was that only last night?*—I jumped toward her and snatched the phone from her hand.

"Don't!" she said.

"It's wrong," I shot back. "You know it is."

I stabbed at the Monkey phone number, then held the phone high out of Wenling's reach should she try to grab it from me.

She looked at me with eyes full of pity.

The phone rang...and rang...and rang...and finally said, in an electronic voice, "The number you are trying to reach is not in service. Please check your number and try again."

That fast. This had obviously been designed as a fast, non-traceable process, right down to a self-deleting phone number, however you did that.

But it still had a regular dial pad on it. I brought that up and dialed 911.

When the emergency operator came on, she demanded to know where I was calling from repeatedly before I could override her and warn her of the threat to Shen Kong's life.

"To whose life is that, sir?"

"Shen Kong. He's a representative from Huawei who's en route from Andrews Air Force Base to the Capitol building in DC, but he's going to be assassinated before he gets there."

"What is your name, sir?"

"That's not relevant."

"And where are you calling from?"

"Are you going to call the police, *anyone,* to intercept him or see that he arrives safely?"

"Please stay on the line, sir. I'm going to have to transfer you to someone who can help you with this."

"No! Don't..."

A transfer tone beeped, and another operator picked up, again female, but with a deeper timbre. "Where are you calling from, sir?"

"Okay, one last time." I repeated the info I had about what I expected might happen and the operator pressed me for details and how I knew the details. Also for my name. And location.

And a surprising question. "Sir, why are you disguising your voice on this telephone call?"

"What?"

"Why are you using vocal distortion on your phone?"

"Vocal distortion..."

I looked up at Wenling, who shrugged sorrowfully. "It was for our protection. I did not hire the operatives directly. We do not want our voices recorded and analyzed."

"Sir?" repeated the 911 operator.

"Oh, fuck," I said. I ended the call and asked Wenling, "How much longer do we have?"

She looked at her watch and the screen. "Perhaps five minutes."

My mind raced a moment more. The Capitol hot line? Was there such a thing? The DC Police? The Maryland Highway Patrol? I could scramble through the internet and maybe find a phone number or two, get transferred around, be asked for my name and location. I could use my Huawei phone, which didn't distort my voice.

Wenling was studying me. "I watched you in the gym when the leader of Lena's mercenaries handed you that knife and later asked you about knife wounds. You have fought with a knife before."

Every moment of it all at once—stabbing Cosmo and the Finn, shooting them, having Alvin ask me about knife wounds. I nodded.

"You've killed someone."

Another nod.

"More than one."

Jesus, she was starting to read me like Lena had read me. It wasn't fair.

"It was necessary then, I'm sure. Like this is necessary now. Come here. Watch with me."

Taking deep breaths, I walked to the other end of the table and sat back against it to better see the silent CNN newscast on TV.

Wenling followed me. She leaned against the end of the table beside me, our arms touching, until I finally handed her the useless phone with Horse, Rat, and Monkey autodials front and center. She took it and swiped them away.

For a good eight minutes we leaned back mutely against the table end, watching the blond news anchor soundlessly detail the spread of Omicron around the world, the CDC's prediction of 62,000 deaths in the United States in the next thirty days, and Ron DeSantis' explanation for letting a million COVID-19 rapid tests expire in the warehouse.

Halfway through DeSantis' soundless gesticulating, the clip of him cut, the blond CNN anchor came back on, and she spoke directly to the camera, directly to her viewers as she had the previous two times we'd messed with the world.

"Volume four!" Wenling commanded.

It caught the news anchor mid-sentence. "...to report a tragic accident tonight on the Suitland Parkway where a limousine carrying Huawei executive Shen Kong was broadsided by an out-of-control, eighteen-wheel tractor-trailer, killing the limo driver and Mr. Shen. The driver of the tractor-trailer has a near spotless record and is, according to police, emotionally devastated. He says the brakes on his..."

"TV off!"

I couldn't look at Wenling. "Two dead. One trucker emotionally scarred for life. This will probably devastate his family, too. The Chinese will assume Shen was murdered."

"There will be no evidence to support that accusation. Do you know why?"

"Don't tell me."

"The driver should not have died. But this is what I think even Americans would call a righteous war. There will be casualties."

I didn't feel righteous. I felt unclean. My stomach roiled. My limbs felt numb and disconnected from my body.

Without a word, I turned from Wenling and walked out of the room as I had before, through the sitting room. But rather than leave through the front door, I stumbled up the stairs to the bedroom I was increasingly thinking of was my free lodgings with Beelzebub, a lower demon who hoped to overthrow the ruler of Hell that was SCATTER.

Tomorrow, I hoped, I'd be able to discuss how, exactly that was going to happen.

Something to make what I'd done have meaning.

I pushed through the door of my room, closed it behind me, and sank back against it without turning on the lights. I felt weak, almost dizzy, from the craziness of everything. I pulled my phone from my pocket and opened my Gmail to check for new messages.

What I saw made my body break out in a cold sweat.

19

The circles of Hell

CORTLAND@PHYSICS.UCLA.EDU, WAS SO FAMILIAR that it was almost like I saw her face instead of the brightly back-lit characters on my phone. The face I saw now neither smiled nor frowned. It was a passport face, still indescribably beautiful, but my creative interpolation of face and characters could no longer manage a sexy or even happy smile, even as it fought hard to keep from presenting my mind with a scowling avatar.

I had the feeling that was about to change from the subject line: *Please move on*.

Feeling my heart drop to my gut, I clicked the mail. And once more, the letters weren't just characters on a screen. It was like Lena was speaking the words straight to my face. The feeling was so intense that, as I read, I wanted to reach out and touch her cheek, beg her to stop.

Jackson,

I'm writing this letter to you because your continued texts to me tell me that you have not fully understood what I said to you. Therefore, I am going to try to spell it out so clearly in this email that you cannot, in good conscience, pretend to yourself or anyone else that there is any room for doubt.

WE ARE DONE.

This means that

1) I do not love you.

2) I no longer even like you.

3) I do not trust you.

4) I do not want to see you in person ever again.

5) I do not want to hear your voice ever again.

6) I do not want you to write to me, text me, or send me anything physical or electronic.

7) If we should happen to be in the same room or in the same place outside for some reason, I do not want you to wave, smile, or even look at me.

8) Please do me the courtesy of never mentioning my name or our past association to anyone. Ever.

You'll note that I'm not speaking of your betrayal or failures as a person. They are what they are. I have no wish to discuss or revisit them. I have moved on and suggest that you do the same.

Alvin has persuaded me to let you know that he and I are back together and adds his personal request that you respect the boundaries I have laid out above.

Dr. Lena Cortland

I couldn't breathe. Or maybe I just didn't want to.

The phone was suddenly too heavy to hold and, as I walked shakily to the bed in the dark shadows of the room, I dropped it so it bounced on the hardwood. I turned a jerky half circle so my back was to the side of the bed and I sat down.

One part of me, the part that was too numb to fully react, was trying to analyze this email, find clues to why it expressed such deep hurt, hatred, and loathing. My "betrayal" and "failures as a person" for instance, begged for clarification and context. Like, I betrayed an unspoken promise to support her telling Alvin about my power? I failed as a person by not being stronger in supporting her need, or softer in asserting my own needs? Or was the "betrayal" somehow a guilty reflection of her own rekindled romance with Alvin?

But even as my therapist's mind churned through that, my emotional self, already reeling from two gut-wrenching time jumps and all their consequences, started to truly get what had just happened. The first woman I'd ever truly loved, who I'd thought had truly loved and understood me, was gone. She was so gone from me she wanted nothing to do with me ever again. Not even a whimper or a wave.

This impossibly smart and empathetic, understanding goddess had just slapped down any hope I'd had of reuniting. Ground it into the dirt under her heel.

With this act, she had consigned me forever to not only never having a wife, but never truly being able to connect with *anyone.* Because if not her, if not the woman who'd gotten close enough to see the real me, then I was essentially unlovable. Even the two people who loved me despite everything, Kenny and Kansas, were gone, likely forever.

I fell back on my bed, feeling my future of being alone forever spin all around me like a great bleak darkness of the abyss. I felt dizzy. Lost. Empty.

The pain welled up inside me like a great, surging scream.

I covered my face to hold it in.

Not here.

Not in Wenling's house.

Never in the house of a woman who accused you of having to "learn" how to be a man.

I gritted my teeth and screwed up my eyes under my hands. I pressed in harder, trying to keep the tears from spilling out.

Be. A. Goddam. Fucking. MAN!

Somewhere during that, I must have heard the click of the door opening, maybe sensed an intrusion of hallways light, but been too overwhelmed to react. But suddenly there was a scuffling sound and the bed surface beside me dipped down like someone was there.

I jerked my hands from my eyes, only to see an uncharacteristically concerned face of perfect symmetry in the shadows above me. It leaned down closer so I could make out the perfect skin, delicate lips, small nose, and almond eyes glittering with tears. Her hands cupped my face as her thumbs smoothed away my own tears. Then the hand ran over my forehead, smoothing back my hair like I remembered my nanny Carmelita doing once when I had been sick with a fever as a child.

"Shhh," Wenling said as she stroked my forehead again.

"I got...," I tried to explain, and found my nose and throat had become clogged with mucus.

"An email," Wenling finished for me. "I picked your phone off the floor and read it. I'm sorry."

I closed my eyes. I had no dignity any more. Lena had stripped that from me. "Not what..."

"I know."

She let the moment breathe as she kept stroking my head. I thought it would let me release all the sobs that had been building in my chest, but it amazingly calmed them. My breathing steadied.

"I am sorry, also," she said, "for making you take part this evening in a something you were not ready for."

I laughed roughly. "Not ready? Like I will be one day?"

"I hope you are *never* ready to do what I felt had to be done."

"But you... What made you so ready to do it?"

There was a long silence, in which I could only imagine what Wenling's face looked like. I still had my eyes closed, wrapped tightly still in my shame and pain, even as she continued to slowly stroke my forehead and hair with one gentle, cool hand.

When she finally spoke again, her voice sounded only a whisper, like she was speaking herself from behind hands hiding her face, metaphorically or not. "Do you want to hear my real story?" she said.

I blinked and opened my eyes. I took in the shape of her in the bedroom shadows, cross-legged on the bed by my head, still wearing her cute tiger hoodie, her eyes waiting. "Yes," I said.

She began.

"You know when I was born? April 5, 1989. You know what happened one day before I was born? The Tiananmen Square Massacre. It was in Beijing, which is up in the northeast corner of China. My family was in a small village in the Guangxi Zhuang Autonomous Region, on the Longiyan River, in Cangwu County. This is in the south, only four major cities away from Hong Kong.

"But when my mother's hero, reformist Politburo member Hu Yaobang died in April and it looked like many of his reforms would be lost, a student-led protest and occupation began in Tiananmen Square. My mother wanted to travel to Beijing to join the protest.

"My father would not let her go. Both because she was over eight months pregnant with me, and because he thought the protesters were fools who would get themselves killed.

"As he predicted, the government declared martial law and the People's Liberation Army moved in, at first peacefully, then letting the illiterate 27th Army of Shanxi Province run down, shoot, and bayonet thousands of people.

"My mother heard this from the village news man who got his first-hand report over a wireless radio. Neighbors told me when I was old enough that she began wailing and went into a difficult labor. There was no time to drive her to a Wuzhou hospital, though I don't believe my father would have paid for that anyway, so my mother gave birth to me on the rough wooden floor of our mud-walled home with a village *jieshengpo* helping her, while my father was off at his job harvesting lumber from the forest.

"The *jieshengpo* told my mother she was so lucky to have a girl, I think to keep her from killing me because I was not a boy. This was during the time of the one-child policy. Neighbors later told me that my father wanted to kill me when he came home to find I didn't have a penis, but by then my mother had fallen in love with me and protected me with screams and fists.

"My father hated her after that. He would stay out and drink away our money. He would beat my mother. When she died after four years of this, he began to beat me instead. I was safe only when attending our village's one-room schoolhouse. Then I turned ten and started growing breasts, so my father whored me out to men in our town and neighboring towns because the lumber mill had shut down and he hated farming.

"He also hated me."

Wenling stopped for a moment and looked at me, rather than the floor. "Yes, he used me for sex as well," she said, as if the question was on my now-bloodless face. "But I think he preferred beating me and having other men fuck me when I wasn't in school. Otherwise, I think he would have pretended I was a virgin and sold me to some rich man in Wuzhou. If I had gotten pregnant during the eighteen months of my whoring, I think he would have sold me and fled somewhere with the money before the buyer found out."

She looked away again and continued.

"I was saved from this when my father met a second woman stupid enough to marry him and Xiaobo was born. I was promoted from part-time whore to part-time nanny and became Xiaobo's mother as much as his big sister. And for a time, my father was almost happy because the mill had reopened in partnership with a neighboring village and he once more had money and respect and a way to fill his time. Xiaobo's stupid mother became a *jieshengpo*, good at helping other woman deliver babies, while never spending time with her own.

"This was the one happy time I remember of my father.

"Then I was twenty-one, out of school and working as a bookkeeper with one of the village's few computers, and the mill shut down again. My father recommenced beating me, his second wife, and his eight-year-old son at every opportunity. I thought every day of escape, but could not leave without Xiaobo, who would not leave his mother.

"Xiaobo became stranger and stranger as the year of beatings went on, rising before everyone and running into the forest to hide. He would sneak back to the kitchen after our father had stomped off to look for work or drink with his out-of-work friends. Sometimes Xiaobo came back too early and our father caught him and beat him until he screamed. Sometimes he made it through a whole day of school and playtime with his friends before our father found him and beat him.

"Finally, on the day of his ninth birthday, our father stumbled in drunk to find Xiaobo drawing in an art pad his teacher had let him take home. He drew a monkey, I think it was. (We had black-crested gibbons in the forests around our village.) Our father grabbed the pad from Xiaobo and tore it into pieces while mumbling and yelling about Barack Obama and nuclear war and the how writer Liu Xiaobo was getting the 2010 Nobel Prize! Why couldn't our Xiaobo do something like that?

"He went to the back door and grabbed a bamboo gardening pole he had never used for beating us before and started whacking Xiaobo with it on his arms, chest, back, legs, avoiding only the face where bruises drew too much attention from nosy others.

"Xiaobo screamed and I came running, so my father turned and began beating me, keeping his strokes to my already-very-scarred back out of habit because my back scars had never scared away men who wanted to buy me for an evening. But I still cried out."

I interrupted. "Your back...?"

She shook her head. "Later. The most important thing to understand about this episode of my father coming home and beating us is that I have no memory of it."

She looked at me and I suddenly understood. "Xiaobo jumped back and changed it!"

Wenling nodded. "Back to the beginning of his day, out in the forest. But this was the first time he had ever jumped, so he was confused and ran back to our house to find me. Too early. My father was still there and grabbed him and beat him..."

"And he jumped again," I guessed.

"So he tells me. After that second jump back in time, he was more careful returning to the house. He waited for our father to leave, then found me, and told me what had happened. Of course, I did not believe him. But Xiaobo was a smart boy. He said he knew this whole day. That my friend Mai would be at our house any moment to walk with me to work. She would show me some bright yellow mushrooms she had found on her way over. There were certain things she would say. A funny gesture she would make.

"Moments later, Mai walked into the house, holding out three bright yellow trumpet mushrooms, *guìhuaer*. Very hard to find. She said the things Xiaobo predicted and made the gestures." Lena imitated them now. They made me think of an overexcited high school girl.

"That convinced you?"

"Almost. Then he told me about our father would come home early from work, drunk, catch Xiaobo drawing a monkey, and pick up the bamboo gardening pole from the back door to use first on Xiaobo, then on me. Xiaobo said if our father did that this time as well, my brother was going to run for the forest and not come back.

"I said if things happened just like Xiaobo said, then I would go with him. We would run away and never come back."

"Is that what happened?"

"Not exactly. Our father went for the bamboo pole and I hit him so hard over the head with our metal wok that he fell down against the back doorframe and slid down, dead. I screamed and made Xiaobo scream. The neighbors finally came to see what had happened. One of them got the village chief and the Party Secretary to come and see what had happened. The neighbors who were there swore they saw our father come in drunk and fall and smash his head against the back doorframe.

"The village chief proclaimed our home belonged to me now, but the Party Secretary said no, it belonged to the state. I said we would take just our personal belongings and leave to join relatives in Wuzhou. Everyone liked that. One of the few people in town other than the chief and Party Secretary who had a vehicle, an old truck, drove us southward to Shang'an and we found another driver there who took us to Wuzhou. From there to Zhaoking, then to Guanzhou, to Shenzen, and finally to Hong Kong. You know what happened from there."

"But how did you get into Hong Kong itself? Don't Mainland Chinese need some kind of Visa?"

Wenling shook her head. "It was not hard. Favors were exchanged. Identities created."

"Elizabeth Chan."

"And William Chan. Yes."

"Whose ages you changed later when you wanted to emigrate to America."

Wenling nodded.

"You survived through all of these travels using Xiaobo's time jumping skills..."

"And my own abilities."

"Bookkeeping?"

"Seducing men with my body. It did not work with you, but some men find me appealing. Even with..."

She let it trail off, the look on her face telling me everything I needed to know about the visual representation of her shame that she would carry with her always. I still needed to see it, though. A final proof of her story.

"You need to see it," Wenling said quietly, again reading my thoughts from my face.

I nodded. "May I turn on a light?"

There was a pause, then Wenling nodded. I rolled up from where I lay on the bed and went to the switch by the headboard that turned on the focused reading light there. The spill was enough to illuminate Wenling, but not harshly. I turned to see if that was okay.

She nodded, and with a movement that looked comfortably familiar, she crossed her right hand over her left at her waist, grabbed the two opposite sides of the bottom of her hoodie, and lifted it up and over her head. The loose white cotton shirt she'd worn since the morning lifted half off with the hoodie, then fell back into place.

Keeping her eyes trained on mine, Wenling slowly unbuttoned the shirt. When all but the last two buttons were undone, the peach-colored bra came into full display. Wenling pushed the shirt off both her shoulders, so it slid down her arms to bunch at her elbows and on the bedspread behind her bum. But she was still ready, I sensed, to quickly shrug it back on at the slightest turn in this interaction.

Rather than clambering onto the bed, I asked, "Can you turn around?"

She did, lifting her knees and turning with such sinuous grace it could have been a dance. But what she displayed directly to me now above the bunched-up shirt, above the waist of her tight jeans, and under the strap of her peach-colored bra, was a roadmap that made me think of a whipped plantation slave or flogged sailor.

Framed by Wenling's pale, smooth neck, shoulders, and arms, was a slender back riven with uneven ridges of rubbery-looking white to pink to dark purple skin, crossing and re-crossing one another to make knots and divots that caused such feelings of wrongness I wanted to reach out and somehow smooth it all away.

"Have you tried...?"

"Micro-needling, laser, chemical peels, fillers, stretchers," she said without turning back to me or pulling up her shirt. "Yes. My back looks much better now than when I arrived in Hong Kong. Back then I sometimes had to wear the opposite of backless dresses to seduce squeamish men. Does it make you feel squeamish?"

I turned that question over in my mind and heart and said, "No. It makes me grieve for what the little girl lost with each one of those marks."

"And gained," Wenling said thickly. "These scars took away my fear."

Or pushed it deep enough to turn into hate inside you, I thought. "A reminder of strength, then?" I suggested.

"Yes." I saw her body quiver a little. She still had not turned to look at me. Her voice dropped again to be barely audible as she said, "But I can hear in your voice that you don't believe it. To you, it shows I am a broken person who can never be fixed. To you, it explains why I can kill as easily as I do business. It is because the beatings that left these marks destroyed the person I should have become."

So smart, yet so ungenerous to herself.

I walked to the bed, reached out a hand, and gently touched her shoulder. It sent an entire chorus of shivers through her, as if the room were freezing cold. I pulled the hand back.

"May I touch your scars?"

She said nothing, so I ran my fingers from her shoulder down her back, over the bumps and marks which were, after all, signs of *healed* skin. A lesson I should probably have been taking about my own mental scars.

My hand stopped at the clasp of her bra strap.

"The offer you made to me earlier today in this room," I said. "Does it still stand?"

There was a long pause, then Wenling nodded her head.

20

An extra ticket

It began slowly, with me unclasping her bra and leaning down to kiss her scars before stroking my fingers delicately up the side of her body to her shoulders and slipping the straps off them.

Then she turned back to face me and waited, letting me take in the full glory of her naked torso, from the uplifted pointing of her small breasts down to the taut flatness of her belly. And when it was clear from the rising swell inside my jean that I truly appreciated her beauty even with her scars, she stood up on the bed, reached to the bottom of my gray sweater and had me lift my arms as she pulled it up and off. My polo shirt followed, so that my upper body was as naked as hers.

We smiled at each other and each unclasped our blue jeans, like we were a coordinated, two-level dance team, each revealing ourselves for the pleasure of the other.

And as we did, I found it triggering vivid memories of sex with Lena, so it was almost like Lena danced alongside her replacement, demanding I compare them.

See! Wenling may be taut, but I am full figured and soft.

Her flesh is a pale nothing. Mine is golden pecan.

She moves with the grace of practice, but my jerky movements are from blind lust!

Until I forcibly kicked Lena from my head and pulled Wenling down to the bedspread with me so that we could roll about exploring each other with our tongues. There was no conversation, no joking or asking for permission, only taking, feeling, following the flow.

For a time, I controlled it, reveling in Wenling's girlish gasps when I stroked her sensitive parts, and the way her body flexed and bent under my hands like a powerful instrument. Then she took control, diving down my chest and belly to stimulate me in ways I'd never even read about before.

I had to fight her off to keep from ending this too soon, and she came up with such a devilish smile that she showed she knew how close she had taken me.

Without a word, I pushed her onto her back, pushed apart her legs and pleasured her as she'd done for me until I hear the high gasping again. Then, in the brief hesitation over my next move, she spoke the only words from either of us in this exchange. "Bedside drawer."

I rolled to it, retrieved a gold-wrapped condom from a box, put it on while Wenling watched me with hooded, intense eyes. Then I entered her with such delicate care that she finally grabbed my bottom and pulled herself up around me in a cry that might have been pleasure, an instinctive bleat of pain, or simply a release back into the flow of our dance that immediately resumed with such building passion that our bodies burned against each other. Like we were going to ignite, burn each other up or explode into a thousand sparks.

And then we did.

Or rather, Wenling did, bucking and shaking under me until the sheer excitement and friction of it dragged me over the edge with my own cry of utter despair...

Hours passed.

Minutes?

Seconds?

We lay together, my larger body covering hers, then rolling off to lie beside her, carefully removing the condom and throwing it to the floor beside the bed.

Breathing.

Feeling her breathing beside me, her nipples rising and falling, the perfection of her profile, face and body, in the light of the bedside lamp something that deserved to be captured in an NFT and sold at some outrageous price to just one buyer who would keep it in his or her electronic vault forever and pull out whenever they needed to be reminded there was such beauty in the world.

I, of course, had no need for such reminders. For me, this vision would always be inside me, captured along with the sweet smell she now had of flowers and musk, the warmth of her right shoulder and leg against my left ones.

And what does it mean?

Shut up and live the moment.

But...

I mean it. Shut up!

Finally, after long enough that my body felt a chill, as I was sure hers must, too, I pulled back just enough to roll to my left, only to find she mirrored my movement almost simultaneously.

We were face to face, chest to breasts, my belly to her groin, the fingertips of her left hand running lightly up and down my spent penis until it started to swell again, even to bob.

I looked deep in to her eyes and she into mine, and still we didn't speak.

A part of me wondered if this was something she had learned from early on, to stay quiet and follow the lead of her lover. Speak only when spoken too, other than expressing delight or admiration. But the more I looked, the more I believed it might be the opposite of that. Something in Wenling's expression was so uncertain and questioning, that it was as if what she had just experienced or was experiencing was so foreign that she didn't know what to say or how to handle it.

Was it an act? Did she think I needed to believe this had been...special?

I didn't think so, but I didn't know.

And before I could test that, she fell back on her physical instincts, stroking me more forcefully and leaning forward to nibble at my lips. To my surprise, she also spoke, murmuring "Wǒ xǐhuan nǐ," before she pushed me onto my back so she could climb on top of me.

She slid herself back and forth over me then, until the chance I might not be capable of a second round became laughable. But when she reached down to direct me inside her, I stopped her and said, "Bedside drawer?"

She shook her head and asked, "If there's an extra ticket, would you go with me?"

"What? Where?"

As if it would be clearer, she murmured in Chinese with the same yearning voice.

I guessed, "Yes?"

Her face deadly serious, she nodded and pulled me inside of her, immediately beginning to ride with a sensual earnestness, a flow of thrusting hips and flexing thighs that made me forget all my questions and doubts, to do more of what my college therapists had said, and Smiley and Alvin in training. *Live the moment. Be here now.*

She made it challenging as she stopped before either of crested and demanded I take her from behind. I knew it was either a final test or final offering of her vulnerability to expose her scars to me like this, but she needn't have worried because, by this time, I was so physically besotted with her that everything about her, each tiny wart and crease, discoloration or scar, was like a daub on a beautiful, all-encompassing meadow in which I gamboled and breathed and stroked to absorb and be a part of. We rolled to our sides, still connected, and I pulled her scarred back hard into my chest as we continued to rut and stroke each other, slow then fast, languorous, then out of control.

Until eventually, the physical bucking and cries of excitement led me again through an unstoppable release, this time with less despair and more letting go.

After this second release, Wenling forbade me from anything but a quick-wipe clean up before we lay together on the sheets, then under the top sheet and coverlet, snuggling and murmuring occasional funny things we had seen in our lives until the murmurs ended in yawns and the silences stretched, and it was clear Wenling was staying with me in this room tonight.

She finally turned away from me in bed, but snuggled her backside close to me for warmth.

I lay reflecting on what I'd fallen into. It was like some twisted, modernized gothic romance, with a rambling mansion out in the middle of nowhere, an unseen butler (in this case, a chauffeur), and a mysterious lord of the manor who hid terrible secrets in his past. Or maybe just the fantasy romances where the heroine falls in love with a billionaire.

Except in either of these scenarios, I was the heroine and Wenling the mysterious billionaire. And I was really only "falling" for Wenling, I thought, because I was on the rebound from Lena and needed Wenling to help me find my brother and sister.

Everything about this sounded pathetic, making the glorious physical pleasures I'd just enjoyed with Wenling more troubling than satisfying. And her question, *If there's an extra ticket, would you go with me?* What the hell did that mean?

I didn't fall asleep until after midnight, with my mind churning through all that Wenling and I had done and what we might be doing next.

A few hours later, my eyes shot open in the darkness.

Something was wrong.

Where was I?

Wenling's house. Right.

But something had...

Oh yes. Sex. Her and I. In this bed. She was right here with...

Except she wasn't.

I listened and heard nothing. Then I did.

The bedside clock said 3:45 a.m.

I slipped from my bed, found my underwear and jeans, pulled them, and padded out of my room.

The sound was coming from downstairs. Wenling. Talking with someone.

I snuck downstairs to listen.

21

Phone call denied

CREEPING DOWN THE HALLWAY towards the back of the house this time, rather than going through the front sitting room, I came to the north entrance of the kitchen and stood just outside the kitchen door, listening to Wenling talking on her cell phone less than five feet away.

"He does not need to hear this," Wenling was saying.

A silence while the person on the other end of the line was clearly trying to persuade her of something.

"No," Wenling said. "His emotional state is...delicate, particularly after his home was ransacked."

A pause.

"Because I have him here. I am looking after him and keeping him safe."

Another pause as my mind raced to figure out who Wenling was talking to. I figured who it had to be at about the same time she said it, scolding like a boss, or the person who has paid for your impossibly expensive research project.

"Lena, again, no. It might lead to a Nobel Prize, but it will also hurt Jackson. Do you understand me? I'm not going to allow that to happen any sooner than it needs to."

My heart had sped up at the mention of Lena's name. Even more at the implication she had something she wanted to tell me. About us? No. Nobel Prize. Her research?

I entered the kitchen. "What does she want to tell me?" I said.

Wenling, standing in a corner of the kitchen counters, wearing only her cute Stella McCartney hoodie, stretched out her hand to hold me back. "No, I will not!" she said into her cell phone and hit the End Call with her thumb.

"What did she find?" I pressed. "Middle of the night. Must be important."

Wenling's cell rang again, and she sent it to voice mail. "It's just research," she said. "Guesswork. Theories."

"About what? Time travel, I assume."

"Of course. It's what she's working on, isn't it?"

"Then why would it hurt me?" *And why would she care?*

Wenling's phone rang, and I went to grab it from her, but she spun from me and shut it off before I could wrestle it from her grasp. She spun in my arms, her back up against the kitchen counter, breathing hard but smiling in triumph.

"Why would it hurt me?" I asked again as I tossed the useless stolen phone onto the counter behind her.

"Everything hurts you."

"What do you mean?" I said, meaning, *How did you know that?*

"It hurts you to jump through time. It hurts you to feel powerless. It hurts you to care for other people. Even sex."

"You think sex hurts me?" I lifted her up so she was sitting on the kitchen counter, her hoodie riding up to reveal she hadn't bothered putting anything on below it, top or bottom.

"I think it confuses you."

Damn her again. When had I become so transparent?

"But you still like it," she said, lifting a bare foot up to my groin and to feel the response that was happening there. That response was accelerated by the exposure her lifted leg provided.

"And do you?" I found myself saying, and actually truly curious about, given her history.

"With you, I think I do. When you give me the proper kind of attention."

The casual spread of her knees made her ask very clear.

Despite everything, I couldn't help but answer.

Later, the two of us sprawled naked, legs entangled, on the rug before the roaring fireplace with the pre-dawn light still nowhere in sight. I said, "I'm going to have to go and see her."

Wenling sighed. "I know. She's running an important test today. I'll have Jian take you to her tomorrow."

"At her lab?"

"No. They'll be watching her lab. I'll arrange a private meeting for the two of you."

"Okay."

She rolled into me, playing with my chest hair as she nuzzled in under my arm. "You're surprised, aren't you?"

Again, like Lena, Wenling had read my thoughts and emotions like an open book. It was disconcerting and made me feel more naked than my lack of clothing. "What would I be surprised about?"

"That I'm not keeping you here against your will. That I'm not insisting we do more time jumps to get the attention of SCATTER. That I trust you to visit an old girlfriend so soon after we've come together."

Way too much to unpack there, all of it kind of true, but disorganized in my head. All I could do was stare up at the ceiling. Then I reached down to pull her leg up, so that she rolled on top of me and I could enjoy the simple physical pleasure of her for a few moments longer.

"Kiss me," she whispered and tilted her chin up under mine.

I did, enjoying the sweet taste of her and her honest need when there was so little else that I understood about her, our relationship, and what-the-hell kind of three-dimensional chess she was playing in her head with me, Lena, and SCATTER.

It wasn't until I was falling asleep that I realized Wenling had co-opted my big reassertion of independence. She'd chosen the time and place of my meeting with Lena. Even how I'd get there. It was a quick jump from handling my balls to keeping them in her desk drawer.

Or trying to.

But when it came down to it, it was still going to be just me and Lena. Because Lena had called about me. To talk to me. Despite what she'd said. I needed to see if there were still any feelings there between us.

If there were, then I'd have to find a way to back down from the physical stuff with Wenling, however wonderful. And handle Alvin. Find a way to make everything work.

And if there weren't?

22

Lena

THE DRIVE BACK WAS both uneventful and surreal, mostly because I was awake for most of it this time, and driving from flat farmland into mountains was so *Lord of the Rings.*

Some four hours later, Jian dropped me off in front of a small Baptist church on the edge of Fall City, an unincorporated rural town, actually, on the southern bank of the Snoqualmie River, maybe an hour east of Seattle, 40 minutes from Lena's particle accelerator laboratory.

"Why here?" I asked Jian before he got back into the limo.

In his quietly dignified way, he looked back and forth along the quiet two-lane road that fronted the church. "Many of the roads here from Redmond are like this. Dr. Cortland would have been able to see whether the tactics she'd been given to evade any watchers were successful."

I studied Jian's placid old face as he spoke, getting ex-military vibes from him. Still sharp-eyed and physically precise.

"What if she didn't shake her watchers?"

"I will do reconnaissance and be close in order to drive you afterwards. If you go with Dr. Cortland, I am to shadow you and coordinate with the private security guarding Dr. Cortland back in Redmond."

"Okay," I said.

Jian climbed back into the limo in his fine suit and tie, and pulled away with a crunch of gravel. While I, in my jeans, button-down dress shirt, and gray sweater—it was actually 50°F and sunny—examined the white board-and-batten church with a shortened steeple up front. It was straight out of rural American, circa 1930. I guessed that Wenling had rented out the entire building for Lena and I. Couldn't be used that much on an early Friday afternoon.

I noted there was exactly one car parked in the small dirt lot beside the church. It was a different rental than the Lexus Lena had been driving the last time I'd seen her. Maybe she'd been worried that would draw too much attention. This was a silver-gray Ford Edge SUV. I wondered if Alvin had chosen the SUV for her and stashed a gun in the compartment between the front seats to keep her safe. Or just brought himself along to do that.

You're stalling.

No shit.

I took a deep breath, fingered the face mask in my pocket, and decided not to wear it. I walked to the front double doors of the church and slipped in.

When my eyes adjusted to the gloom inside, I saw a heated space even smaller than the community church where I'd found Gillespie. It was one big open room with four tall, shuttered windows on either side, scuffed vinyl, a musty smell in the air, folding chairs in racks along the wall.

Lena stood alone in the middle of the empty space, watching me. She'd decided to go maskless, too.

On the other hand, it looked like she'd chosen the most severe, businesslike outfit she could find. Except the smooth, dark blue suit was soft enough to follow the curves of her body. The gray blouse had hints of pink. And even buttoned up to the top, the blouse showed off the creamy milk chocolate of her neck and its little dip into her clavicle. She'd pulled her hair back into a tight bun, but that only highlighted the generous curve of her cheekbones and lips, her strong nose, and her always-arresting dark brown eyes.

The eyes did look serious.

So did her cool voice when she said, "Hello, Jackson."

It was like a harsh slap across my face, and I remembered what Wenling had said. *Everything hurts you.* Maybe this was why she hadn't wanted Lena to talk to me. It wasn't just what Lena might have to say. It was that everything about Lena—her appearance, her voice, how she smelled—were deeply embedded in my neo-cortex, their emotional import in my amygdala. Or that's where they'd be if I had a normal brain. As if was, I just felt like every moment with her infused every part of me at this moment.

"Hello." I didn't want to walk toward her and break the spell.

So she walked towards me. *Click. Click. Click.* Her black, patent leather pumps on the vinyl. She stopped about four feet from me. "I got here about twenty minutes ago. I turned the heat up."

"It's nice."

There was an awkward silence, then we both started talking at the same time. Stopped at the same time. She waved to me. "You first."

"Okay. I just...wanted to say that if you couldn't be with me, I was glad it was Alvin. He's a good guy. A little serious, which I guess fits where you're at right now, but always a good guy. Loyal."

Lena stared blankly at me. "What are you talking about?"

"You and Alvin. Like you said in your very...definitive email."

More confusion now, bordering on anger. "Which one of my 'very definitive' emails did I ever mention Alvin?"

Now it was my turn to be confused. "You only sent one. After I texted you twice a couple days ago."

Lena's face was flushing not. Definitely anger. "You never texted me. Never emailed me or responded to the three texts I sent you on Sunday and Monday. Then I found out someone broke into your office and home..."

"How?"

"Your office assistant, Megan, called me. She said she was worried about you. You'd left work for a couple of days to fly somewhere, then the break-ins happened and you said you were handling it. Except that you'd apparently disappeared off the face of the earth and no one knew how to contact you except via email. So I sent three emails to you, each one increasingly pathetic. You know what I got back? Resounding silence."

"But...that's not..."

"I know. The last thing I said to you in person was I wanted you out of my life, correct?"

I nodded my head.

"Well, I changed my mind about that. That's what my texts were about."

"I never got them."

Her lips pursed and her eyes lowered for a moment as she thought hard. "And not the emails, either, I'm guessing."

"You sent me one..."

"...that was 'very definitive.' Right. Mentioned me being with Alvin. Romantically?"

I nodded, looking away.

She caught that and said, "Can you repeat back to me the entire email, word for word?"

She knew I could, of course. I just wasn't sure I could do it without falling apart as I did, and that would just be silly.

Lena caught that from my face, too, somehow. But rather than using it to attack me like she might have done a week ago, her features actually softened, so she looked like the woman I'd fallen so deeply in love with in what seemed like a different life. "That bad, hunh?" she said.

"Yes."

She took another step closer and started to reach out, but thought better of it. "Jackson, I'm forming a hypothesis here, and I think that email might support or refute it. If I turn away from you, or sit beside you, so I'm not looking at you, could you recite it then?"

I almost laughed. It was straight out of social anxiety 101, though the idea was generally that highly socially anxious or shy people tended to be more comfortable engaging in a mutual task with someone than speaking with them directly.

But the fact she was making an effort to ease my anxiety was more calming than any specific thing she could do. I nodded anyway and pointed to my right side. "Just stand here, maybe?"

Giving a quick huff of relief, Lena nodded and went to stand beside me, facing the same direction I faced. The nearness of her was almost unbearable and made everything that had happened with Wenling seem so superficial, like it hadn't happened.

Except it had. And I knew that was going to come out. Had to come out. Which meant however friendly Lena was feeling toward me right now, it wasn't going to last.

It was probably the inevitability of that state that let me recite the entire 'definitive' email from Lena verbatim. Subject line: *Please move on.*

When I was done, I couldn't help turning my head to see Lena's reaction. Standing this close to her, kissing distance, created an almost vacuum-like sucking at the bottom of my heart. Especially since a part of my brain had, even while I spoke, been processing her earlier words about her changing her mind about wanting me out of her life. Which made what I'd done with Wenling feel like a total act of betrayal, a loss of faith, that made me *deserve* to be tossed out of Lena's life.

But Lena didn't know that yet, so the sudden extreme pallor on her face was from the email itself. Was it one she'd written but not intended to send? Or had she never written it?

"Elizabeth," she said through tight lips.

"What?"

"Elizabeth Chan, my so-called Amazon rep."

"So you know she doesn't work for Amazon."

"Ha. Have you seen her limo and met her chauffeur? Of course you have. He drove you here, didn't he?"

I looked at her, considering. "Just how much do you know about...Elizabeth?"

She caught the pause. "Oh my God. That's not even her real name, is it?"

"What does she have to do with the email?"

"I presume she wrote it, probably with help given some of the phrasing. I didn't. And you didn't get my texts or emails. I didn't get yours. She has a lot of very smart tech people working for her..."

"Like you."

"And you?"

"I'm not that smart. I just have an amazing memory and an ability to jump backward in time."

Lena looked at me closely. Even though we'd been mostly apart for the last few months, she still knew how to read me. "You didn't answer my question. I called her to see if she knew where you were and she told me she was 'looking after you.' What does that mean?"

I looked around a bit. I was suddenly exhausted. "I think I'm going to have to sit down for this next part. I think you should, too."

Walking to the racks of folding metal-and-vinyl-seat chairs to my right, I reached in and pulled two out, set them up facing one another a couple of feet apart. I sat in one and gestured for Lena to sit in the other.

She walked over slowly. "I'm not liking this already," she said.

"You're going to not like it a lot more."

She sighed like she'd expected this and took a seat.

"Wenling knows I can time travel."

Lena colored slightly. "She said she heard it from somewhere. I assume Alvin?"

"It was from Dr. Irene Gopal. She was in 'Elizabeth's' employ."

"Why don't you just tell me her real name?" she said. "I'm already tired of hearing the little quote-unquotes."

"You've become harder," I said.

"We all change. Isn't that what you said?"

"I really am sorry for the loss of your mother. Not just because of how special she was to you, but because I got the feeling, from things you said, that your dad took the loss pretty hard and took that out on you."

Her face really colored this time, and she almost rose from her seat as she spat out, "He didn't even give her a *eulogy!* The man has always been able to speechify at the drop of a hat. Senior partner at Pallister Ross. Went to the Supreme Court twice. Spoke on live TV after Trump did his evil Muslim ban. Could have run for governor of the state. They courted him, you know."

Now she did get out of her chair, too full of memory to sit. "At her funeral..."

She tripped up for a second here and shot me a look, clearly remembering that she'd specifically disinvited me even though it was at a time we were still nominally a couple.

"At her funeral," she plowed on with her chin out, "I had arranged everything because my father just couldn't be bothered. Though he was still quick to criticize every choice I made, from the flowers to the order of service. And then..."

She swept around to look me full in the face, like whatever she was about to say would justify everything she'd done and felt toward her father, herself, me.

"And then, when it was time for him to speak, I announced him and gestured for him to come up to the microphone and he, while I was up in front of all our relatives, family friends, his work colleagues, my mother's colleagues, he just gave this little smile and waved his chance to talk about my mother away like it was nothing."

With her eyes, she held onto that last word like it meant her father had thought her *mother* was nothing. And maybe, by implication, that Lena herself was nothing, just the other dark-skinned woman inconveniently still in his life.

"Did other people speak?" I asked quietly.

"So many," Lena said. "My mother. Was. Special."

"You told me how they were together. I'm sure he knew it more than anyone."

"But he had nothing to say!"

"Or maybe too much."

"But he could talk about anything! That was his skill! Nothing could shut him up! Nothing!"

"Except this."

Lena stared at me, processing that. Then her eyes suddenly flooded with tears. "Do you really believe that?"

"A guess. You know him. You tell me."

She squeezed her eyes shut and pulled a facial tissue from an inside jacket pocket to wipe them. "I can't believe I did that."

"What?"

She opened her eyes, her eyes streaming now. "I screamed at him. When we got home. I screamed that he never deserved her. That she should have found a Muslim man who understood her and appreciated and worshiped her."

"Was that true?"

"Of course not! My mother was not a practicing Muslim and she could never have tolerated the misogyny of that culture. She loved my father. And my father *did* deserve her. More, I get now than..."

She sniffed and dabbed at her eyes again, giving me a long, concentrated look like she was seeing something in me that she'd completely missed before, or perhaps forgotten. It went on long enough that I began shifting uncomfortably.

Finally, she said, "You see, this is why I couldn't have you there with me. I didn't want you to see how dysfunctional I've become."

"That's not why," I said, scrambling to catch her shifting mood. "Not all of it."

"No. Not all of it. The rest...well, we may cover that someday."

"Someday?"

That last finally brought her back to the present, and she sat again in her chair. More eye dabbing and an attempt to wipe the mascara she correctly assumed was running. She sniffed and sat fully upright. "Tell me her real name."

"Zhou Wenling," I said, giving it the full Chinese pronunciation. "Raised in a small village in Mainland China, beaten by her father..." I gave her the whole story, including her under-the-radar billionaire status which some of my quick internet searches had confirmed, and how, in her effort to free her brother from this CIA time travel operation, she'd inadvertently brought the three of us—me, Lena, and Wenling—together.

"It's *yuánfèn*," I said, "the Chinese word for fated meetings or relationships."

Lena had been listening to me intensely throughout this. With my last statement, a light of realization started to dawn in her eyes.

"She brought you to her place near Spokane because she wanted to use your power somehow."

I nodded.

"And you did."

"Yes. Do you want to know what for?"

"Eventually. But first, tell me. Did it wreck you, using your power again?"

I nodded. "It wrecks me every time."

"And did she tell you this tale before or after you were wrecked?"

"Um...after."

"So it wasn't to get you to use your powers."

"It was to comfort me."

"To comfort your sense of dislocation? Your waking nightmares?"

"No. The time travel knocked me down. I went up to my room to be alone, and I got that email from you. That I thought was from you. It sent me over the edge."

"And she came in, conveniently, just after the email arrived, and stroked your head and told you a story about her own trauma."

I frowned, feeling my face coloring. "Yes..."

"I'm guessing there was something else, some clincher, some physical thing she did..."

"She showed me her scars."

"Oh. Did she? Where were they?"

"All over her back."

"She had to take her top off to show you?"

My face was now so red I'm sure I looked as guilty as I felt.

Lena just shook her head with an ugly smile. "That bitch." She stood up and picked up the chair she was sitting on, folded it, and walked it back to stick into the rack it had come from.

She turned back to me. "Well, are you coming? I have something to show you back at the laboratory."

"Wenling says..."

"I don't trust a single thing that bitch says right now. I'm not even sure her scars were real. She plays games. She makes you believe what she needs you to believe. If I were you, I'd just agree and follow me like a good ex-boyfriend, ex being the only kind I seem capable of."

Even as she said it, though, I heard the qualifying "seem" so loudly that I figured I could afford one more beta male dance if it took me to what I realized now was a two-part quest—save Kenny (and Kansas now, too) and win back Lena's love.

To get there, I could absorb whatever Lena had to show me, and go along with whatever Wenling was cooking up now in her little mansion near the banks of the Spokane River. I'd take on the CIA and the whole fricking world if I had to.

I stowed my chair and followed Lena out.

23

Entangled

WENLING HAD REPLACED THE security team guarding the industrial park that housed her secret lab just outside of Redmond. This time the guard at the gate, branded with a stylized "Zero Fail" logo, did a thorough ID check on both Lena and me and our vehicle before we drove in. Just as significantly, they had fortified the entire area with a barbed wire fence, floodlights, and security cameras that covered every conceivable access point outside and in.

"Concentration camp chic," I commented as we drove to Building #4, parked and climbed out.

Lena looked around vaguely and nodded, making me reevaluate my earlier comment that she'd become harder. It wasn't so much a gain of toughness as a loss of what had once been a wonderful sense of humor. Her mother's death and the struggle with her father and me had all been like a punch down from the heavens that hadn't flattened her, but certainly compressed her range of interest in the world.

A few moments later we were exiting the elevator into the sub-basement particle accelerator laboratory that looked much as it had the last time I'd seen it, back when she'd shut it down for the greater good.

Then, as now, it felt like the lower hold of a large battleship—thirty feet from concrete floor to concrete ceiling, walls covered in pipes and cables and vents and metal rigging. And we'd entered from a door ten feet up the wall, onto a gray metal walkway that had a bright red set of rails with a DO NOT CROSS sign to guard you from down into the pit.

Down in the pit before us, covering most of the floor, were dozens of interconnected child-sized white metal pods which I'd learned were power regulators. What they powered mostly was the glassy-smooth metal pipe that ran inside a sheath of five-foot-tall-and-wide interlocked metal cages all connected with wires and bolted to such devices as lynac cryomodule, a misshapen metal construction with dials, switches, and readouts at the far end of the room. It was responsible for accelerating the photon beams in the silver pipe and later stripped them of their energies to siphon them off, eventually, into the beam stop.

It was all so scaled down from giant particle accelerators like the famous 17-mile-in-diameter Large Hadron Collider near Geneva, Switzerland, that you had to question its functionality. But it was actually exploring some of the same things that the LHC was—the deep structure of space and time—and doing it better. As I understood it, it had created, under Lena's leadership, a verifiable kind of time travel having to do with photons. These subatomic building blocks of light, in their dual particle and wave forms were assumed to be identical in having zero mass, but differing in such properties as angular momentum, wavelength, energy, and speed. What Lena discovered was then when they created two photons with near-identical properties at two different times in the collider, a super-attraction between them would lead to the first-created vanishing from its journey around the ring and instead "inhabited" or "replaced" the second almost immediately upon the second's creation. This was all recorded in impossibly small units of time like the smallness of the time travelers being recorded.

Then, I, of course, had been nearly electrocuted by this machine and proven that the super-attraction theory of time travel somehow applied to the human soul or mind essence. Exactly how was still conjecture, of course, since I was the only human time traveler Lena had experimented on. And that, only briefly.

As we now walked the metal grating of the platform for the stairs down in the center pit of the room, I noted there were two new pieces of equipment, painted an ominously shiny blood red, that were lined up in the last stage of the circle before the suitably gray-painted, beam stop. The far side of the room.

There were also more computers monitoring everything, like throwing more computer processing at the data would at least make the mathematics of it all make sense.

Finally, there was more noise and smells than before because Lena had not cleared out her team before bringing me here this time. I smelled someone's Thai Curry meal, another burger and fries, another's poor hygiene.

After making me change into a white lab coat and don a mask, like she did herself, Lena briefly introduced me around. I noted all the names of the six masked scientists or technicians here were different from her earlier team. Except for Dr. Eric Salazar, the youngest of her former team, an authentic genius according to Lena, and hence the only one I'd ever thought to be jealous of. Meeting him last, I understood why Lena had found my jealously amusing. Also why Wenling had decided to allow him to stay on. Salazar, early thirties, had his hair askew like he might have combed it this morning but had since repeatedly played with and twisted it. He presented like someone with Asperger's.

He gripped my hand firmly, but at an odd angle. As he shook it, he looked me up and down thoroughly, but didn't meet my gaze. "You must have a big cock," he said very quickly and intensely.

"Why's that?" I asked.

"Dr. Cortland told Suzanne that she missed having sex with you. Also, she got very sweaty when she told us all you would come by here *today*!" He hammered the last word so hard it was almost a shout in the room, but no one around us paid any attention. His vocal quirks were obviously not uncommon.

"Ah."

"Thank you, Eric," said Lena, pushing at my arm to move on.

"I could smell you," Salazar said at her so fast it was almost one word. "I wasn't sure if it was pheromones or anxiety sweat. The human nose can have *difficulty* distinguishing between them, you know. 0.35153 probability of error."

"Have you run the numbers on the proximal identification tests?"

"No," Salazar said.

"Now would be a good time."

"Okay. I think they're going to line up with the multiple-split hypothesis I proposed. I've already established baselines for a new run."

"Good."

"Have good sex," he said to me before wandering off.

I couldn't help grinning inside my mask as I said to Lena, "Cheerful guy."

She ignored my grin and pointed to where we were going. It was the new blood-red boxes hunched in a line along the accelerator ring, near the beam stop machine.

When we wound our way around all the other metal and cable and people, I noted we were mostly alone at that corner of the room. There were no computers set up here. All the data must have fed back to other locations. Still, Lena made no move to remove her mask, so I kept mine on as well.

"I never discussed with you what happened to the Photon A's in their initial creation path," she said.

"You mean the photons that got produced first and jumped back to take over the ones produced second?"

"Roughly, yes."

"They vanished."

She frowned slightly. "Yes. Did I tell you that?"

"Implied it."

"Well, the implication of them vanishing seemed to be…"

"…that the jumped-from timeline ceases to exist," I cut in. "Paradoxes abound. Which they do anyway, of course, since the human time traveler is now in a younger body but has *knowledge* about things that may now never happen. The best thing about this is that whatever horrible things were happening to the time traveler or the people he was affecting in the time he or she jumped back from, those things no longer happen."

I'd blurted it out so fast I worried I sounded like Dr. Eric Salazar. Except I could guarantee I had none of his scientific or mathematical genius to make up for my warp-speed rambling.

Lena took it in like she'd expected it. "The time traveling photons didn't cease to exist in their original timeline," she said.

I waited for the punchline. It didn't come. "You just confirmed they vanished."

"To the instruments we had at the time, yes."

"But…"

"Eric, Dr. Salazar, was convinced it was just *us* who had changed. Or rather, we were not entirely who we thought we were. That we were products of the modified timeline from the beginning, but our memories were of trying to create time travel and succeeding. At the point where we succeeded, there was a split and a new timeline was created in which we did not succeed."

"Wait!" I touched my forehead. "Schrödinger's Cat. It's alive and dead at the same time?"

"Totally different field. That's an interpretation of quantum physics that says some things only exist in states of probability, e.g., dead or not dead, until they're observed and become one or the other. It's about mathematical certainty and human subjectivity, not actual reality. *This* is about reality. Realities. Because there may be hundreds of thousands of them. Any time a time travel event occurs in any form, we get a new one."

"And you've...proved this?"

"We're very close. The proximal identification tests? They're related to these new add-on devices here. They build on something British physicist David Deutsch thought about—setting up an event that could have two outcomes, but have a measurement that was only triggered by the concurrent existence of both. He tried doing it with one-particle-at-a-time double slit experiments and described what he called 'shadow' photons vs. 'tangible' photons being revealed in his results. Not many were persuaded, but then he didn't have a particle accelerator and time traveling photons to work with."

"And?"

"Well, we've been able to reliably measure the path of a Photon B that's been altered to become a Photon A and have found consistent evidence of altered spin, suggesting quantum entanglement, even though there's no physical evidence of a second photon for it to be entangled with. Dr. Salazar speculated the replaced photon, we'll call it AB, remains attached to the photon B it used to be, on a quantum level, even though photon B is now in a whole other reality, its original timeline."

"The blood red things measure the entanglement?"

"The evidence of it. Yes."

"And you're persuaded, not intrigued by the hypothetical, abstract idea of it, but actually *persuaded*, that this means the old timelines continue."

"In some fashion they do."

I stared at the blood-red measuring devices which, up close, reminded me of giant, bloated mosquitos, full of blood and ready to pop. But it wasn't really them I was seeing. It was, in my peripheral vision, the concerned certainty on Lena's face. And the remembered sound of Wenling insisting, *No, he does* not *need to hear this.* Even if, she'd continued later, it led to a Nobel Prize.

Treating me like a child.

The fact was, I couldn't follow half the physics of what Lena had just tried to explain to me. Quantum entanglement? Altered spin? Double slit experiments? Really? The words made more sense as gross double entendres than anything real.

But Lena believed it meant the futures I jumped out of continued to exist. And Wenling, whose intelligence I was never going to bet against, seemed to believe Lena and her fellow scientists knew what she was talking about.

Which meant, despite what I *wanted* to believe...

I cleared my throat. "So...I'm dead many times. You're dead a few. Jude—there's a reality where he lies on the floor with his brains blown out while I'm taken downstairs to be tortured. And oh, yeah, lots and lots of realities where I'm tortured into a blithering mess. And can no longer walk. And you're beaten and probably sexually abused. And why? Because I went looking for my brother."

I suddenly felt physically ill and had to turn and sit down on the concrete with my back leaning against one of the swollen red machines. They thrummed warmly against my back, adding to my sense of being out of synch here, my body tingling. I suddenly broke out in a foul-smelling sweat and tried to take off my borrowed white lab coat. I couldn't. I was sitting on the tail of it. I gave up in a burst of heat and fatigue. I wiped my wet forehead with the sleeve of my lab coat.

Lena sat down beside me, folding her knees decorously to one side and drawing her own lab coat closed around her to hide her figure. "I'm sorry that I asked you to practice jumping back in time with Alvin."

That brought my head up. "You know he believed you, right? More than me."

"How could he?"

"Maybe not a hundred percent, but enough to try scaring or nearly killing me for eight months. Actually killed me twice. Sort of."

Lena's face went pale. "What?"

"Gunshot to the chest and a shove off a roof. I don't know what his backup was on those. Missing my heart? A crash pad I didn't see?"

Her eyes were wide. "So you jumped."

"Twice. Lots of new scars from all the times I didn't, despite Doc's ministrations. It's why I couldn't face the knife fight training."

She nodded her head. Her eyes looked bleary, but no longer able to cry. "That's when I called you a liar."

"Not exactly. You said I didn't honor our agreement to tell you only the truth. And while that wasn't exactly true, the spirit of it was. When I realized I couldn't do what you wanted me to, I should have told you and told you why. Instead, I let my own struggles get in the way of giving you the connection and support you needed, whether you said you wanted it or not. For that I am more sorry than you can know."

Lena snorted. "Two sorry people and one broken relationship."

If it had been eight months ago, or even four, I would have taken her in my arms at that moment. We could have worked it out. But Lena was right that we were beyond easy fixes now. Her emotional life had imploded. Her professional life might be on an incredible upswing, but to get there she'd had to ditch her earlier sense of innocence and easy entitlement.

And us.

Which meant the wounds went both ways. Along with her cutting me out of her life, this news about the continuation of all my traumatic timelines put a serious wobble in my resolve to go after the CIA and SHATTER.

But only a wobble. Kenny and Kansas needed me.

I leaned forward and managed to push myself up to my feet. Lena did, too. Still not touching me.

"You know what you have to do?" Lena said, her mind still following along with mine somehow, my other self, even though we couldn't truly be together right now.

"Tell me."

"Go back to Wenling."

"The bitch?"

It actually got a brief smile out of her. "If she's as rich as she says, she's your best bet to rescue your brother."

"And my sister. They've taken her, too."

That got a surprised look. "You know who 'they' are now?"

"Yes."

"But you're not going to tell me."

"It's not your fight."

"An arm of the government?"

I stared at her in surprise.

"It makes sense. Your sister said they were interested in my time travel experiments. It's probably because they already knew it was a real phenomenon. They just want me to show them how it works."

I licked my lips. "I am going to talk to Wenling. See what her next move is and whether it's something I can use."

"Just remember, she may want more from you than you think."

"She wants whatever will help her get back her brother."

"She didn't need to seduce you to get that."

I looked down, my face reddening with guilt again, despite it being out in the open. Sort of. "I think she thought she did. She'd seen how jumping affected me. She needed me committed."

"Uh-hunh."

I met her steady gaze. I saw the jealousy and wondered if it meant there was still a way back for the two of us, or that this was what would keep us apart. And did that mean I should lie now or tell the truth?

I chose the truth. "It was good sex. It gave her the assurance she needed about me. Maybe about herself, too. It wasn't anything like what we had, but I didn't think we'd ever have it again, so..."

"You didn't need to tell me that." Lena just stared at me and now I couldn't read her at all.

After an uncomfortable silence, I said. "Thank you for telling me about...all of this." I waved my hand at the red modules and what they signified, but also at Lena and the fact of her and my blocked emails, Wenling's attempts to control the situation. "Once I rescue my brother and sister, I hope we can, I don't know, go out for coffee or something, and maybe talk through, a little more, all the things that happened between us. No secrets. Total honesty."

Lena tilted her head a little to one side. "At some point we may do that, but I think you have the wrong impression about why I sent you the undelivered emails and brought you here. It wasn't to open the door to us getting back together. For reasons I can't discuss right now, that's over. For good. This was something I owed you as a professional courtesy, because I know things about your condition that no one else does."

The chill went straight through me, head to toes. But my mouth kept moving. "Professional courtesy... Asking about whether I slept with Wenling?"

"Political survival as well. I needed to understand my patron. You do too."

"But..."

"Goodbye, Jackson."

She sucked in her lips and bit down hard on them until I finally turned from her and walked away.

24

Lipstick on a pig

I TRIED TO LEAVE the lab with some dignity after what felt like now the third and most definite *real* rejection by Lena.

Even though she still cared for me. That biting of the lips. The tremor in her voice when she'd said "professional courtesy." But something had happened, something "she couldn't discuss right now." A pregnancy? A secret marriage? A promise? A realization? Did it matter? It was getting into movie-of-the-week territory here. I wanted to say that kind of craziness didn't happen to normal people. But I wasn't exactly normal, was I? Nor was Lena. Or Wenling. Nothing about this fucked-up situation was "normal."

I kept my mask on as I took the elevator up to the ground floor and left the building, hoping as I rose that Wenling had assigned Jian, my old, polite, impeccably dressed Asian chauffeur to not only drive, but also babysit me. I'd confirmed my Huawei phone connected only to the Wi-Fi in Wenling's house, so if Jian wasn't here...

He was.

As I walked out of Building #4, I saw him by the limo, wearing a black mask over his nose and mouth as he talked with one of the Zero Fail security guards. Exactly what he'd told me he'd be doing—checking up on the new security.

He spotted me and said something to the Zero Fail guy who faded back to some kind of patrol duty. I suspected that Jian's close association with Wenling meant he outranked every security person on this site.

He turned to me now and gave me an almost imperceptible bow. "Are you staying in Seattle tonight, sir, or going back to Ms. Zhou's home?"

"Has she sent word? Is anything significant happening I have to be there for?"

"There has been no word."

"Then, yes, I'd like to check out my office to see how the restorations are going. And my apartment. Is that okay?"

"The office is safe. But your apartment is being watched. If you stay in town tonight, Ms. Zhou said she pays for any hotel, and also money to replace your wardrobe or other essentials."

"Okay. I need to do the office because I have no way to touch base with my assistant without..."

Jian half-lifted a hand to interrupt me. "Ms. Zhou also believed you need a working burner phone here. She made me get one for you so you don't have to risk buying one in a place that would leave a trace."

He handed me a primitive looking little Nokia phone with a full dial pad and navigation buttons below its tiny screen. I turned it on and saw an icon for a camera, Skype, Opera browser, texting, and a game called Snake. Woo-hoo. I smiled thinly and thanked Jian. *She had me get one for you* meant, *You will only use devices we allow.*

I looked at Jian and smiled. I doubted he'd actually stop me from choosing my own phone, though he'd no doubt report it to his boss. The real question was whether asserting my independence here would impress Wenling or infuriate her and hurt our partnership.

For now, I thought, we'd do things her way.

I smiled at Jian and dialed my office number. Megan picked up on the other end and was delighted to hear my voice. I head sounds of construction going on in the background.

"I sent pictures of the work so far to your Gmail," she said. "These guys are amazing."

"And you're amazing for being there. I'm going to swing by mid-afternoon. Can you ask the crew there to prepare any questions they have for me?"

"You're back then?"

"Just for today. We still need to push all my clients back or transfer them. Probably two weeks to be safe. If there are any you really don't want to handle, leave their names for me and I'll call them when I'm in, okay?"

Megan's agreement on the phone was deflated. "You can't tell me? It's about that trip you took, isn't it? Are you relocating?"

"Yes, yes, and no, I'm not relocating. I'll tell you all about this when it's all over. You still seeing Bryan?"

"Yes." Just that one word, and I knew.

"Good. Stick with him. You're both worth it."

Now she was sniffing. I signed off and said I'd see her later.

Jian had, of course, overheard everything, but his face was perfectly passive, his eyes judgment free.

"So I guess we'll swing by my office around three or four," I said. "Meantime, I'd like to pick up some new clothes. You know Seattle at all?"

"Quite well, sir."

"Okay, then. I'm thinking ideally a bulletproof suit, if they have that kind of thing. Or some concealable body armor and a suit and shirts that fits nicely over it. Also some fresh underwear, socks, and shoes. And maybe...weapons?" Because relying on time travel that just created more and more fucked-up timestreams wasn't the answer.

Jian nodded like my request was all nothing and opened the back door of the limo for me to climb in.

I did.

As he shut the door behind me and I tore off my face mask, I was surprised when my new burner phone rang. But of course, there was at least one person who would have this phone's number.

"I received a notification when you used your new phone," said Wenling in greeting. "How did it go? Are you alright?"

Torn between relief and resentment at hearing her voice, I started to say I was fine, ready to lie through my teeth to this second woman who'd played me, blocked my texts and emails, and sent me back to an old love she knew was going to kick me in my teeth. But as the limo pulled away from Building #4 and quickly out the gate, heading for the city, a last remaining lump of self-respect I carried deep inside me decided that I'd have truth on my side if nothing else.

I sank deeper into my leather seat and said, "It went as bad as you thought it would."

"You told her about us."

"Yes. She wasn't pleased with you. It just seemed to confirm her opinion of me. Did you plan that?"

There was a pause. Then Wenling said softly, "I'd hoped you wouldn't have to go back at all. She already cut you out of her life."

I felt a flicker of rage at her words. "But you still felt you had to block her emails to me, my texts to her, and *make up* a goodbye email from her so brutal it left me weeping on your guest room bed."

Another pause. She obviously figured she had to play this carefully. She was right. I'd made all the windows in the back compartment of the limo shift to dark, so anyone we passed couldn't see my face right now. It was twisted in a combination of self-loathing and building hatred for the woman on my new burner phone who'd helped me into this state.

"Well?" I pushed her.

"I...wanted you," she said. "The more I listened to Lena talk about you over the last year, all the things she'd loved about you and all the things she now couldn't stand, two things became very clear to me. First, she is like a spoiled child who has never learned how to truly love or be responsible for anyone but herself. Second, you are her opposite. You came from a place of want and difficulty, raised yourself up through your own hard work and intellect, yet continued to love and care deeply for others. Especially for your brother and sister. This I understand. And in person, there is also a...magnetism."

I pressed the phone hard to my ear and squinted my eyes tightly shut. The way she purred that last sentence made my penis twitch and my heart ache. Because I knew it was true, the physical attraction between the two of us. But for all my admiration of Wenling's strengths and her devotion to finding her brother, she wasn't...

What?

She wasn't Lena.

Wenling's willingness to kill people she'd never met, for instance. Her lack of hesitation in stabbing me when she figured it would make me time travel. Could I ever actually fall for someone like that? Could she ever fall for me? She said she "wanted" me. But what did that mean?

If there's an extra ticket, she'd asked, *would you go with me?*

What did that mean?

"Are you still there?" Wenling's voice said.

"I'm here. I heard you. I'm just not sure I agree with everything you said. Have you contacted SCATTER?"

"Yes. I'm negotiating a parley. Do you know what that is?"

"Peace talks?"

"Of a sort. They're requesting a more identifiable demonstration of power first."

"Does someone else have to die?"

"No. That was a powerful message, though. It got their attention. They're asking who my time traveler is."

"What have you told them?"

"That it's none of their business. At least not until certain agreements are reached."

"Like what?"

"We'll talk about those when you get back."

"I need some time."

"The demonstration will be the day after tomorrow, Sunday, and the parley likely a few days after. So you can have your time in Seattle. Do what you need to do."

I released a tight breath I hadn't realized I was holding. "Good. I'm going to shop for some body armor and new clothes."

"All right. I'll let Jian know to spare no expense and treat you to any meals and hotel you choose. If he can get you some weapons, that would be good, too."

I gave a coarse chuckle. "I guess our minds are working along the same lines, after all. Though I don't know what you think you can get them to agree to. Do you come to the parlay with guns?"

"There should be no violence. But the strongest foe..."

"...is the one you never see coming. I remember."

"Have fun," she said, holding the last word a little longer than necessary, as if she wanted to add something to it. *Dear? My darling? Sweetie?*

The line clicked and went dead.

As we sat, nearly unmoving in Friday-afternoon traffic backed up behind an accident on the 520 Bridge, Wenling had been pushed out of my mind by an insistent, repeating loop of all things Lena.

There was the first time I'd seen Lena as a mystery visitor in my classroom, the first time I'd heard her voice, heard her laugh, kissed her, seen her frown in concentration, beam in delight. I remembered her crying in remorse over nearly strangling me to death to make me time jump, and I remembered her welcoming me into her again and again, in so many different ways that were all about completion and communion and coming home.

Her Persian skin took on so many shades and textures in different lights—nubbly bark in a sudden cold morning gust of air, silky smooth chocolate in my warm apartment as I inhaled the citrus of her neck and unclipped her bra, bunching and beaded and salty with sweat as we made love or did a long run around Washington Park together.

Every moment was real and perfectly there so that I could almost live it just by closing my eyes. But that wasn't enough. Because the one thing imperfect about perfectly remembered people and moments was that they couldn't change. There was no *future* in a recorded past. No *possibilities.* No chance to hear or feel *I love you* expressed in the endless varieties an ever-thirsty soul required.

Especially when the remembered love was fighting forever with, *Goodbye, Jackson...I think you have the wrong impression...just professional courtesy...So...A man who can't stand for what he is, is nothing...I want you to leave. Now.*

What remained was the simple truth that I had not been enough for the woman who'd been everything for me.

And even if I could now, somehow, meet with the dangerous old Southern Cajun Andre Poussaint, or whoever else was the running the SCATTER program, I had no illusions that I'd be able to overcome them somehow the way that I had with the two-bit gangsters run by Cutter. Especially since I hadn't really overcome Cutter at all. With all my power, I'd just managed to get myself captured, tortured, and free again long enough to call in the cavalry.

Maybe I could repeat that trick with Poussaint? Wenling surely had the resources for a bigger cavalry than the Lead-the-Way foursome. Of course, it might have to be *exponentially* bigger in order to take on a national intelligence agency which routinely worked to take down entire foreign governments.

Would Kenny survive that kind of showdown? Would Kansas? Were they even still alive?

And if they weren't, what did I have left? My true love was gone. My mom and dad barely knew I existed. My best friend worked for the enemy, whether he knew it or not. My office assistant would probably be safer if I never showed up again. And did I really have anything true and honest to share with my students or clients?

I was a dysfunctional fraud on the brink of emotional and spiritual collapse.

So sure, let's get me a nice flak jacket, suit, and some guns in case I somehow get a chance to run in somewhere to save my sibs.

Fuck off, Jackson.

No, you fuck off.

How about we both *just fuck off and...die.*

25

Words of a solider

WE BOUGHT THE BODY armor first, in a nondescript shop in the SODO district where they eschewed face masks even as they sold you equipment to save your life. Even accepting that irony, it was a strange experience having my physical proportions measured to get a remarkably slim, flexible fit that gave me Kevlar protection from my clavicle down to my lower belly. Jian had me move about with it on to ensure I had adequate comfort and freedom of movement.

Next, he took me to a set of nondescript shops that sold menswear, face masks optional. These weren't Marios or Beckett & Robb, but their fabrics and selection, not to mention the prices I hear discussed, were leagues beyond anything I'd ever bought for myself before. And the privacy of the process meant I could try on each piece of clothing over my already-purchased body armor.

I topped them off with a pair of all leather black brogues with custom-fitted insoles that felt almost as comfortable as running shoes, without the grip and cushioning.

Going from there to pistol-shopping in my new suit and armor was a whole new step into surreal consumerism. Outside, the weather was touching on real sun and almost a false spring. But in the hole-in-a-wall gun shop Jian had taken me to, on a quiet side street, with its windows completely blacked out so the only light inside was from the overhead fluorescents, I was getting wicked flashbacks to the gun shop I'd gotten beaten up in last year when I was tracking down gangsters who might know where Kenny was. Here as there, it was less about masks and more about security cameras.

"What type of gun do you want?" Jian asked me as I studied the shelves up behind the single long counter.

"A Sig P226?" I said, coming up with the same gun I'd taken off Dadashev in one timeline of my adventure in the CIA Headquarters. Not that it had helped. "Or a Glock 14?"

"You have shot those?"

"Yes."

"Into a person?"

"The Glock," I said, remembering firing one into the Finn, and then into Cosmo last year when I'd been fighting to escape the Demon Monks and rescue Lena. They'd been first and were still the only two people I had ever killed.

The look on my face as I remembered seemed to tell Jian this. He gave me a stern, level look. Finally, he nodded his head and turned back to the gun store owner and proceeded to haggle with him in Chinese.

At the end of that visit, I walked out with a P226 in a shoulder holster fitted to my body and a backup knife in an angle sheath. Plus an extra clip and lots of ammo. I'd signed no documents. Jian had paid in cash.

We walked to the limo, and I stopped by the closed back door for a few moments, leaning my hands against the car, my heart pounding hard as I tried to smell the ocean air and shut out the sound of traffic on the surrounding streets.

"You are not a fighter," Jian said, stepping up beside me. He'd already stowed everything we'd bought into the limousine's rear trunk.

"No, I'm not."

"But you are going to go with Ms. Zhou to a place where you might have to fight?"

"I...guess? It seems to be the kind of situation I keep finding myself in. And she recommended I get some weapons."

Jian bowed his head and grunted a sound like, "Hyunh." I reflected that for someone more than a foot shorter than me, he carried an impressive amount of personal power.

After a moment of the two of us just standing there, I asked, "You were in the military, weren't you?"

He nodded his head.

"A long time?"

"From the time I was nineteen to when I was forty. Then I became a policeman for many years, until I retired."

"Did you fight in war, then? In the revolution? Or..."

"Yes. And Vietnam, against America. Later against Vietnam. And against the Soviet Union."

"You killed people?"

"Yes. Many people."

"Were you ever scared? Did you ever go in not having any idea what you were going to face?"

"Yes. I was always scared. Many times, before I was in command, I had no idea what we were going to face."

"So what did you do? To prepare."

"Hyunh," Jian grunted again, looking down like the answers were in his feet. And when he spoke, he raised his head but looked up past my shoulder like he was speaking to the wind. "When you cannot know your enemy, you need to know as much as you can about your commanders and what they want from you."

I waited, then said, "That makes sense, I guess."

Jian turned his head to look directly at me, looking up from my chest level with eyes that still drilled into me like he could see all the thoughts in my skull. "You must also know who you are. What you can do. What you want. What you are willing to do to get it."

He waited, seemingly expecting an answer from me about that. I was half tempted to let him know that I'd recently concluded I was essentially a valueless nothing of a human being who didn't deserve to want anything at all. But since I had the impression that might just make him hop into the Land Rover Limousine and drive off without me, I half-smiled and said, "Right now it would be nice to get some dinner, then check into a nice hotel."

Jian held my eyes a beat longer, then dropped his own, nodded, and went to the driver's door, letting me open my own door like a responsible adult ought to be able to do.

I had the feeling he was disappointed in me.

Well, he could just join the ever-growing club.

I suspected it was going to get only worse from here.

But the office check-in was good. The head contractor had a real sense of style. He'd checked pictures of the way our office had been that we'd put in a brochure and gave every indication he'd bring it back even better than before.

Megan, for all that she'd gone through, was actually glowing. The early stages of love will do that to a person.

She seemed to appreciate the responsibility I'd given her, too. With Bryan by her side, she was more than up to handling it.

It actually made me grateful for Wenling, coming back to the position that if I had to face an enemy as treacherous as SCATTER, it was good to have someone sneaky and powerful as a partner.

I needed to honor that.

26

Inside an old movie

THAT NIGHT I MADE Jian join me for a meal at a new restaurant I'd read about and made him talk about his adventures with the People's Liberation Army. He wouldn't say, though, how he'd ended up working for Wenling.

His silence about it shook my momentary confidence in my sneaky, powerful partner. It reminded me how I'd stumbled into the middle of a street gang summit last year by pushing forward with no real idea of what to expect.

I needed to change that. When I got back to Wenling, we were going to have a serious talk about what she knew and how she saw this all shaking out. No more just following along blindly, even if she was, by dint of her resources, akin to my "commanding officer."

Bedding down that night in the Four Seasons, I found myself fighting another negative thought spiral and finally went down to the workout room to break a sweat and push myself hard like Alvin and Smiley had made me do every time I'd trained with them.

After a while, the grunting muscles and pounding heart had settled, and I was able to shower, go upstairs, and fall straight to sleep.

Last thought going down was a part of what *Colonel* Jian had said: *Know as much as you can about your commanders and what they want from you.*

"Excuse me, Jian. Does this line mean anything to you? 'If there's an extra ticket, would you go with me?' I did a web search, and it looks like it comes from a Chinese movie, *In the Mood for Love*."

There was a long enough pause that I wondered if the intercom button I'd pressed on the limo's inside wall that divided driver from passengers was working.

Then he responded, "Yes, sir. A popular Hong Kong movie, *Huā yàng nián huá*."

My heart sped up. "Can you tell me what the line means in the movie?"

Another pause. "It is a complicated movie, sir. I do not think I could explain it properly."

"Do you know if it streams online? Preferably with subtitles?"

"I do not know, sir."

"But your mistress, Ms. Zhou, might?"

"I believe so, sir. She's very fond of movies."

"Thank you, Colonel."

I clicked off the intercom and sat back, smiling grimly. Okay, there was at least one little thing I could figure out about my would-be commander-and-lover. I wasn't sure why, but I had the sense if I understood this question she'd asked me so tentatively, so vulnerably, in the middle of our lovemaking, I'd know at least one true thing about her.

And I thought that I'd better know it before I pulled off whatever proof-of-power stunt she wanted to put me through tomorrow.

That meant tonight was a movie night!

We were back in time for lunch and, after Jian helped me unload my purchases from the car and drove off to the garage and coach house where he lived, I went to the front door and knocked smartly.

Wenling was there a bare heartbeat later, yanking open the door and kissing me before I even had a chance to step in. When she stepped back, dressed in belted, jade-green overalls with a plunging neckline that showed off the tight white tee-shirt underneath, I saw her hair had been pulled back and her beautifully symmetrical face was fresh and clean, with just a little color on the lips and above the eyes. Casually stunning, in other words.

She looked me over with a delighted expression that got even brighter when she saw the things I'd bought in Seattle.

Unsurprisingly, somehow, the first item she went for after we brought everything inside and closed the door was the white plastic bag holding a square, black, molded-plastic carrying case. It could have carried camera equipment or a high-end drill and driver set, but in this case held the Sig P226 in cut out black foam, with its bullet clip in a separate cut out.

She had it out in seconds, holding it up, checking the slide, ramming in the clip and releasing it again, aiming it around the entry hall.

"It feels heavier than a Glock 19," she said, answering my unasked question about whether she'd ever fired any guns herself.

"Heavier trigger pull, too. But really nice on repeated shots once you steady the kickback."

"The Navy SEALs transitioned to the Glock 19. Smaller. Cheaper. Still reliable and accurate."

"We looked at Glocks. I think Colonel Jian got us a good deal on this one."

"'Colonel' Jian?"

"Uh...yeah."

She gave me an odd smile, then cast it aside as she handed me back the Sig and began examining my other purchases.

Like a little girl on Christmas, I thought. Then corrected myself. The main gift giving in China was for birthdays, the Spring Festival, and the Mid-Autumn Festival. Though how someone as rich as Wenling could even get excited over gifts or shopping on this small scale was a little bewildering.

She'd pulled out the two suits I'd bought now, one dark blue and one a lighter, checked gray. Plus dress shoes and socks to go with them.

"I have to see you in this," she said. "Over the body armor!"

"Seriously?"

"I paid for it all, didn't I? I want to see what my money bought. And I think," she said as she looked over the dark blue suit, "that you might just be so irresistible in this that I won't be able to stop myself from stripping it off you again."

"Uh-hunh," I said dubiously, not entirely sure she wasn't making fun of me now. "Can we have lunch first?"

"If you promise to put it on right after lunch. And come outside for some target practice."

"All right. If *you* promise to find and watch a particular movie with me tonight."

That caught her by surprise. "What movie?"

"It's a Hong Kong movie, so I'll need subtitles unless you want to translate it all the way through."

"Now I'm truly curious. The name of the movie?"

I tried to pronounce the Chinese name exactly as I'd heard Jian say it and got a bit of a blank look. So I said, "In English, it's called *In the Mood for Love.*"

"I know," she said at last. Her earlier excited manner was gone. Her face had become a wall.

"Is it something we can stream in or..."

"I have it on Blu-Ray. It can do subtitles."

"That's great! So maybe over dinner, or after dinner?"

"Why do you want to watch this movie?"

"I've heard about it. I wanted to watch it with someone who's lived in Hong Kong so they could explain elements to me."

She thought for a moment. "And after this, we will discuss the demonstration for tomorrow? And you will tell me the best way to make it happen?"

It wasn't a casual request. More like a negotiation. She'd only do the movie if I gave my all to the demonstration. It meant my instinct that this movie was going to give me some serious insights into her was bang on.

If there's an extra ticket, would you go with me?

It made my answer to her request about the demonstration a no-brainer. "Absolutely, we'll do that."

***

What followed was like a fun-house mirror of the last year of my life. First the dress-up in body armor and dark blue suit, including a shoulder holster not unlike the one The Finn had worn, though my P226 was a larger, heavier pistol.

Then target practice, which was a dressed-up version of all the shooting practice I'd done with Big and Alvin at shooting ranges. Except the range here was the multi-acre backyard of Wenling's house, mostly shooting at targets stapled to trees.

And finally, after a perfunctory stir fry meal that Wenling made, refusing to let me near her counters or knives, we cleaned up together and she led me to her media room in the back of the house, beside the gym. It was a room without windows and had a large U-shaped sectional couch, some sections with their own arms that had cupholders and buttons I guessed controlled lights. On the end wall hung an enormous glass screen with a large sound bar sitting on a broad, low, cabinet below that also held a Blu-ray player and PVR device she could presumably record televised content on. Speakers hung in each of the room's corners that I assumed added to the surround-sound experience.

I'd seen this all on my earlier tour of the house, of course, but pretended to see it now for the first time and gave a low whistle over the screen's size.

"Seventy-five inch?" I asked.

"Eighty-five in 8k. It is enough for now." Her mood, which had brightened during my target practice, which she joined in on, had become somber again during dinner so that now her voice was low and quiet. She walked to a tall black lacquer cabinet against the back wall and opened it to reveal hundreds of DVDs and Blu-Ray disks in pristine cases, held neatly upright stack in custom shelves, spines facing out. Jian *had* said she loved movies, but...

"Are these collectibles? Is there a reason you don't just stream them online?"

Wenling had retrieved one slim Blu-ray case from the cabinet and now turned with it, showing me the cover of *In the Mood for Love* even as she closed the door with her other hand. "When I first came to America, I signed up for Netflix to watch only English-speaking movies to improve my language skills and cultural understanding. But these movies could be removed from Netflix at any time. Or the streaming service would fail. Or the internet would have issues. All these problems are in the sites which carry Chinese movies as well."

"So," I said, "you buy them, own them, and they cannot be taken away from you."

"Yes." Her tone showed no apparent recognition of my blatant psychologizing. That could have been because the strain of holding the slim Blu-ray movie in her hand seemed to be taking all of her focus.

She walked to the wall which held the TV screen up on its wall, crouched, put it into the Blu-ray player, which turned on automatically, and walked back to take one of the center seats with arms on either side. This was obviously not going to be a couples-snuggling experience.

I walked forward and took a seat beside her.

She lowered the lights and started the movie.

This is what I saw in *In the Mood for Love*: lots of claustrophobic, run-down apartments, streets, and noodle shops; the color red; quirky, slow-moving cinematography that is often focused on things other than the people who are talking; haunting cello music; two beautiful leads who happened to be great actors; and an achingly melancholic story of hearts betrayed, then yearning, and kept from ever being satisfied because of the moral restraints they let bind them. Plus bad timing that seemed to be there to just to rub in the impossibility of happy endings.

A good movie, if very arty and slow moving. The pacing reminded me of the current Oscar-buzz movie *The Power of the Dog*, totally engrossing for some; too slow and off-putting for others.

Wenling, who had at least half my attention while I watched, was definitely in the "engrossed" column.

I saw her squirm and clutch at her seat every time the two leads, Mr. Chow and Mrs. Chan, so much as brushed past each other in the narrow hallways of their shared apartment building. And when they each discover their spouse was having an affair with the spouse of the other, Wenling's face dropped and she visibly slumped like her heart was as broken as Mrs. Chan's.

When Mr. Chow finally said *in his imagination* to Mrs. Chan, the woman he loved but could never have and so was leaving Hong Kong for Singapore, "If there's an extra ticket, would you go with me?" Wenling literally gnashed her teeth and jumped up from her seat to storm around the entire circumference of the room before returning to her seat without looking at me.

When Mrs. Chan later repeated that exact question in her imagination, presumably to the now-gone Mr. Chan, Wenling again shot out of her chair to do a furious circuit of the room before she came back and sat down.

Then her face, her whole body, seemed to slacken for the last twenty minutes of the movie, the part that was all about the bad timing I referred to. Wenling looked punched down, demolished, and could barely summon the energy to lift the controller to stop the Blu-ray when the credits finished scrolling.

But she did, finally. She raised the lights, stood, walked to the Blu-ray player, retrieved the disk, put it back in its case, and turned off the player. She did not look at me through any of it.

After she turned and walked back to put away the Blu-ray, I was afraid she was about to just walk out the door, so I called after her. "What was it about that movie that affects you so much?"

She froze in the act of returning the disk to its assigned slot in the back cabinet. Then she finished putting it in before turning back to me. Her eyes were bloodshot and wet, which unnerved me. "You really want to know?"

"I do."

She took two steps towards me where I'd turned in my large chair, going onto my knees to look over the back of it comfortably. She stopped. "When I was little, my world was full of magic. But not the wonderful, fun kind. It was the magic of gods who kept the balance in the universe. If you did things one way, all was well. If you did not, you threw things out of balance and invited terrible things."

She paused. "Like what?" I prompted.

"If I didn't eat my leeks, I would marry a man with pockmarks. If I left my shoes on the floor facing my bed, the spirits would see it as an invitation to join me there at night."

"Superstitions."

"Yes, but all around me. From the time I was born. Like control! It only got worse when my mother died. My father would watch everything I did. The gods and spirits, he said, watched everything I did. If I did not do exactly as he said, they would come at night and pull my soul from my body. Sometimes I wished they would."

Remembering the story of how her father had rented her out as a sexual slave, I felt the gorge rise up in my mouth. Somehow, manipulating her through beliefs in unseen spirits was even grosser and more pernicious than just beating her. External scars healed. Internal ones festered.

"Yet one thing I kept hoping," Wenling said, her voice very small, "was that fate, *yuánfèn*, would one day bring me to the man who would save me."

She stared hard at me, challenging me to somehow take the next leap in understanding. I had no idea what she thought I should see.

"I *never* got Mr. Chan!" she cried. "I *never* got Mr. Chow!"

"Which one did you want?"

Wenling screwed up her eyes, put her face down with her hands clenched by her side and screamed so loudly I was concerned for a moment that I'd pushed her too far with this entire inquiry.

"They are both fake! Actors! The colors are fake! The lights! The rain! If they want Ms. Chan to cry, they add glycerin to her eyes! It is all acting! Anyone can do that!"

Then, as if to prove her point, she ducked her head, and when she raised it again to look up at me, her face was sweaty, but calm, her hands relaxed, her entire manner back in its usual poise.

"Wenling, I'm…"

"I think this is done. It is time to describe the demonstration we will do tomorrow."

She did.

27

Proving time travel

We had sex that night. It wasn't lovemaking. I was too aware of her deep yearning for something I couldn't give her and my own yearning for a woman I could no longer have. But it seemed to be part of the joint endeavor we were in and pleasurable on its own terms.

Even if I did find myself taking carefully examining the scars on her back to make sure they weren't, as Lena had suggested, some of Wenling's "acting."

They were real.

Our attachment on that level, at least, was real.

It couldn't remove the stress of our upcoming proof of time travel, though.

We woke up early, had breakfast, I showered and shaved, then Wenling sat me down to go through it all again. As she talked, I kept shaking my head at the awesome, wonderful simplicity of it.

From SCATTER's end, it required only:

a) a sealed SCATTER box,

b) something they'd hidden inside it, and

c) their surveillance of the box until it was retrieved again.

Our contribution would be for me to open that box, examine the contents, then jump back in time with the memory of the contents to before the opening, in which new timeline we'd ensure the box was never opened until SCATTER was ready to confirm our report of what was inside.

Then, assuming SCATTER trusted the secrecy of the box's preparation and established protocols that made it impossible for someone else to scan the box from the outside, or for themselves to miss someone opening it to look inside, there would be no other way for an outsider to know what was in the box other than through the time travel method above.

They could, of course, guess we'd used Harry Potter magic or a Star Trek teleporter beam, but Occam's razor demanded SCATTER go first to techniques they knew actually existed, like time travel. And they'd be right.

Contrast this peek-in-the-box with the proofs I'd done with Lena. Those had required her trusting me as much as I trusted her. I'd jumped back from timelines in which she'd told me secrets about herself I couldn't otherwise have known, and I'd repeated them back to her. It was like telling her what she had in her pockets or what she'd drawn on a piece of paper without showing me. She'd had to believe I hadn't tricked her somehow by studying her life ahead of time, having an accomplice, or pulling some other mentalist shtick. She'd also monitored my body having crazy reactions to a future, traumatized mind, entering it. *And* she'd had the advantage of having proved, to her own satisfaction, the theoretical physics of the process.

But it had all come back to Lena trusting me.

Similarly, with our earlier attempts to get SCATTER's attention, those without Kenny's time travel memory had to trust Kenny that something had actually happened. But if Kenny had been showing signs of rebellion or instability lately...

It was why today's peek-in-a-box demonstration was not just brilliant, but necessary.

Once more Wenling and I stood together in the great room of Wenling's house before her wall of tall windows. I wore jeans, tee-shirt, and sock feet, sweating with anxiety, while Wenling stood coolly to my left, smelling deliciously fruity and fresh, in lime green slacks and a glorious jade green, asymmetrical knit top with matching jade earrings, her hair piled on top of her head with some crazy, bands of twisting polished stones.

Outside, through the windows, the morning sun had just splashed over the snowy peaks of the Rockies and turned the fields of the Columbia Basin between them and us into a light show of glittering frost.

I held Wenling's phone again, with a newly programmed number. I was not, as I'd expected from Wenling's description of the plan last night, going to be opening the box myself. I was just going to be ordering another faceless minion of hers to do so while we watched through what the minion live-streamed to us via their phone.

I'd wondered if the SCATTER surveillance crew might just jump the minion and try to torture our location out of him. But the minute we'd received the location for the box drop, Wenling had immediately sent her own stealth surveillance team to the area. It turned out to be literally minutes from the CIA HQ itself. So SCATTER *could* have overwhelmed any team Wenling sent in, but I was pretty sure the CIA wouldn't want to chance having a deadly firefight break out in the woods near a major artery that fed Washington, DC proper.

Because that's where the box was scheduled to be dropped—in the woods. It was maybe fifty yards off the Turkey Run Trail, midway between the George Washington Memorial Parkway and the Potomac Heritage Trail that ran right by the shores of the Potomac River. Discrete fluorescent flags marked the path to it, visible in the winter forest, but only just.

When Wenling had shared that description, I'd had visions of SCATTER dropping their box and our team never locating it, but Wenling had informed me she'd had reports from both our pickup minion and the surveillance team saying they were settling in place. On the large tablet Wenling now held in the crook of her left arm, we could see the shaky footage of the bare trees and underbrush with pockets of snow clumped here and there despite all the days of above-freezing weather. We heard the rustling and whispered communications between the surveillance team members, who were all dressed in the light grays, greens, and blacks of fall camo.

In Wenling's home in northeastern Washington State, the clock clicked over to 7:50 a.m. and all rustling ceased.

For ten minutes it felt like we were all holding our breath, listening to a trickle of water from somewhere, a few birds chirping, the snap of thawing ice breaking branches.

At exactly 8 a.m., 11 a.m. Eastern Standard Time out in Turkey Run Park, Wenling's tablet feed gave us the sound of crunching boots. The surveillance feed we were getting swung around, trying to locate the sound.

There it was. It looked like some random dude in a puffy, dark blue parka, hiking boots, simple blue wool cap. He carried a box about the size of an orange crate, but smooth, burnished metal all around. It looked very heavy for its size, so I guessed it was lead-lined or something to block a simple scan of the interior. He stopped, looking randomly around him like he knew people and cameras were watching from somewhere, but he wasn't too worried about it.

He set the box down on a patch of dark, dirty moss. He straightened, looked around again, then left the way he'd come.

How many eyes watched him go? Wenling's crew had at least three people if you included the sneak-a-peak minion who now stood up on the side of the clearing a little to the right of the cameraman sending us the feed.

There was no other visible movement.

The minion, wearing the same fall camo gear as his fellows, walked to the box, crouched in front of it, and felt around the top. His fingers fumbled a bit at something on either side of, and there was a quick pop-*pop* and hiss, like gas escaping.

The minion paused, visibly sniffed the air, apparently decided all was fine, and leaned forward as he raised the lid.

"*Scheisse!*"

German, my mind processed. Meaning "shit." Uh-oh.

"Your camera! CAMERA!" he screamed straight at us through the video stream. Then the image jolted as the surveillance guy holding the streaming camera obviously jumped from hiding and sprinted to join the minion. The image jerked and moved so fast the streamed video was a blur until the man holding it finally got planted beside the minion, aimed his camera, and the image resolved into...

A piece of paper. Burning. Crackling. Sparks popping off it.

Specifically, it was a full page of text on the raised bottom of the box, almost right up to where the lid had opened. The paper was burning in from around the edges. It had already consumed pieces of the text as the page shrank quickly. And as we watched, the flame seemed to erupt in spots all over the text, igniting it between them so that in seconds the entire page was burning, shrinking, curling, turning to ash.

As it did, I became aware a high-speed chirping had grown from somewhere deeper in the box. It peaked and...

The feed cut out.

We waited, but nothing came back up.

"They'll call," Wenling said.

We waited some more.

No one called.

"Were they attacked?" I asked, my mind still fixed on the video images burned into my memory.

"I don't know," Wenling said, her brow furrowed. "If so, they must have shot the camera first?"

"No. No, you're right. If they'd wanted to shoot your people, they could have done it earlier. And there were no sounds of shots or any noises other than the fire and high thrumming..."

"You heard that?"

"Yes. Almost like a..." I wanted to say, *like an electric god racing around a particle accelerator*, but it had been nowhere near that big. "An EMP."

"EMB?"

"E. M. P.," I repeated. "Electro Magnetic Pulse. It fries electronic equipment. It would have taken out the camera that was streaming what we saw. But why?"

"Do you know why?"

"I...don't?" I said cautiously, because Wenling had thrown her tablet to the floor and was glaring at me.

"Why don't you? Do you know *anything?*"

"About this?" I started backing away from her. Her face was coloring with what looked like a murderous rage and she was stepping towards me.

"About this. About your brother. About your sister. Do I have to do all the work?"

"I..."

"You know nothing. You come up with little *theories* and play at being a caring, feeling man. But you are no man at all, are you?"

"Okay," I said, finally catching on as she backed me towards the fireplace, her mouth almost spitting and her shoulders hunched, hand half curled into claws. "I get it. I told you in our prep that I in order to jump..."

"You're *supposed* to be leaving me now. You've been hiding behind my skirts. Behind my money. Using me. Fucking me. All for what? Because you cannot do *anything* by yourself."

"Actually," I blurted back, as I backpedaled away from her, "I can. I have."

"You can't. You haven't. Everything you've done for your brother was when you were a boy! Then you ran away. You let him be taken and abused. First drugs from the gangs, then drugs from SCATTER!"

"You don't know they've used drugs," I said as I tripped and half full, scrambling to my feet as she drove in a circle now towards the door to the drawing room. I could peel through there and out the front door again. Escape again. Run away. Maybe even get myself to jump like I did last time?

"SHUT UP!" Wenling screamed at me and lunged at me, spitting, making me dodge to my left, away from the drawing room entrance. Away from my escape.

"I don't think..." I began, wiping the spray of her spittle from my face.

"So DON'T. THINK. YOU DON'T HAVE TIME TO THINK, YOU LOSER. YOU FAILURE. YOU MOTHERFUCKING BROTHER KILLER. SISTER KILLER."

"I never—"

But she didn't even acknowledge it as she screamed at me like she could read my own inner anxiety demon I'd managed to shut up for so long. "THERE'S A REASON LENA REJECTED YOU. BECAUSE YOU'RE WORTHLESS. YOU SHOULD BE DEAD." She lunged forward and punched my chest, making me stumble backwards again. "THEY SHOULD HAVE TAKEN *YOU*, NOT YOUR BROTHER AND SISTER, BUT YOU *RAN AWAY*. YOU'RE A COWARDLY..."

"I'm not. I'm not. My sister..." When had I told her about Kansas? I never told her about Kansas! Except when I talked to my parents and Wenling, she must have heard.

"SISTER FUCKER! FUCKING *FAILURE*. FUCKING SAD USELESS WASTE OF FLESH THAT SHOULD BE DEAD. YOU RAPEY SON-OF-A RACIST PRICK AND BARBIE BITCH! YOU LOSER..."

"*Enough!*"

She shoved me again, and I hit the kitchen island, tripped, and went down, scraping my ribs and falling badly onto my right wrist before Wenling was on top of me, hitting and scratching me and yelling into my face, spittle flying. And while I subconsciously took in all her words and knew they'd become part of me, the main feeling I had was that she truly, really, desperately wanted to grind me into nothing. Maybe because she knew I needed it to jump, but maybe also because I *DESERVED* it. Because that's what fucked up losers did. They sought out affirmations of just how bad they were. How worthless...

Yes.

How useless...

Yes!

How totally deservedly alone and...

I was standing in front of the window with Wenling's phone in my hand. To my left stood a woman. Who? Right. Wenling. Fruity and fresh. Wearing lime pants and a jade green, knit top. Off-balance. Was I going to fall? No. It was her *top* that was asymmetrical.

I was...fine.

I took a couple deep breaths and fought bending down to put my hands on my knees.

I had this.

One jump.

I'd just jumped. It was just...oh, God, this was getting harder every time. Like my nine months of fighting to get my mental health back made it even harder when I ripped off all the emotional scabs that held together my heart and mind.

In the crook of her left arm, Wenling cradled her tablet with the video feed of nothing happening in the still winter forest out near Langley but birds cheeping and the occasional branch cracking. She didn't seem to have noticed my momentary disorientation. Why should she? For her, nothing had happened yet but the boredom of waiting for the guy in the puffy jacket to arrive with the box.

Was she rehearsing her attacks on me in her head? Or maybe she didn't need to. Maybe just seeing me even a little shaken brought out her feral survivor who knew the best way to protect herself was finding the weak throat in your opponent and going straight for it. And whether I was actually an opponent, I was definitely weak.

There was a crunching sound. The guy arriving.

"Oh shit," I muttered and Wenling turned to me, really looked at me.

"You already saw this?"

I nodded.

"Then make the call!"

I nodded again and stabbed the quick dial she'd set up on her phone earlier before passing it to me. A small buzzing sound came from the tablet still cradled on her left forearm. The guy who'd just arrived with the metal box now looked around, *knowing* there was someone in the woods watching him. Someone sloppy enough to not have made sure their cell phone couldn't vibrate against something that would let others hear it.

He didn't run, though. He just set down the box, turned, and walked back the way he'd come.

"Yes?" said a voice in the ear I was now holding Wenling's phone up to.

"Abort mission," I said as we'd planned, in a voice I knew would be too distorted for anyone listening to identify. "Leave now. All of you. You will be contacted later for a debrief."

"You know the package is here..."

"We see it," I said. "Repeat. Abort."

Wenling took the phone from my hand. "This is Tigress. Do not go anywhere near the package. Get your fucking asses out of there without being seen. *Now.*"

"Understood."

Wenling ended the call and watched the video stream shut off as her team presumably booted it out of there. "Idiots," she growled, and the sound of disgust in her voice triggered an entire avalanche of PTSD in me related to what had just happened for me here in this room, but now never would for her. At least for this version of her. This timeline.

In that other, still continuing timeline, I wondered how far I'd let her go before my very, very broken-down will to survive had kicked in and I'd pushed her off me. Would she go for the knife again? Would she just keep screaming and haranguing and trying to kill me as she desperately believed her plan had failed? Because in that timeline, it had.

Or would she eventually stop, try to revive me, win back my favor and enough mental health that we'd try for another go at the demonstration. Or another plan entirely.

Whatever happened in that timeline, I doubted that the Jackson there would ever trust her again.

In this timeline, where her aggressive manipulation had worked...? *Would* I have been able to make the jump without it?

"What now?" I asked.

Wenling looked at the saved image of the metal box in the forest. "We call my contact in thirty minutes. What was in it?"

"A page of text. On fire."

Wenling frowned. "On fire."

"From a chemical reaction, I think, when the lid was opened." I was about to describe the EMP that burned out the camera, but at the last second, decided not to. I wasn't sure why. Maybe because the last time I mentioned it, in the last timestream, Wenling went mental on me, chased me around the room and ended up on top of me, scratching and punching my face. I shrugged my shoulders, "It was...distinctive."

Wenling looked unconvinced. "You should get a drink of something before we call. You look terrible."

I nodded and walked to the fridge. I opened it and considered the wine and beer inside before opting for a glass of water from the sink.

From where she now sat, cross-legged on the floor by the fireplace, still studying the screen capture of the metal box sitting on the forest floor. "If it had only a sheet of paper, why was it so big?"

Because it was mostly an EMP, I thought. I said, "To convey that it could contain anything—and old typewriter, a pair of shoes..."

"What was the text? What did it say?"

"Some kind of philosophical text, I think. The paper had mostly burned by the time the cameraman rushed over to it." That was a bald-faced lie, but I didn't think there was anyone who could contradict it, unless SCATTER had somehow tapped into our video feed and had one of their time travelers with my kind of memory watching, then somehow being dragged back to this timestream.

"You can remember some of the words?"

"All the ones I could see."

"Write them down for me. I don't want you talking during the phone call."

"Okay."

I walked to the kitchen table where Wenling had left her yellow legal pad that she'd been scribbling notes and plans for the day. When she didn't want me to understand, she just wrote in Chinese characters. Which, of course, I stored away and would look up at some later date.

For now, I scrawled part of a long sentence on a fresh sheet, intentionally paraphrasing it the way an imperfect memory might do. I walked it over to Wenling.

In fact, I'd been reviewing in my head all the words on the paper, intuiting somehow the few that had been burned before I'd seen them. Then I realized I could fill in the missing words because the entire piece was from a book I'd read in a Moral Philosophy elective I'd taken in university. The book was Thomas Hobbes' *Leviathan*. The passage that had been burned discussed the warlike, troublesome state of humanity that could only be tamed by allegiance to a strong ruler, ideally a monarch.

Wenling read out loud what I'd written: "Fifth, irrational creatures can't tell the difference between Injury and Damage, so as long as they're not being hit, they're not offended by others, but Man is troublesome." She looked up. "This is philosophy?"

"Pretty sure."

"Hm."

We both fell silent. Wenling continued to study the image of the metal box on her screen, using it to focus, I thought. I wandered around the room, feeling like I was walking along the edge of a precipice. Once more I'd let Wenling batter my mind into needing to jump from a high-stress-and-getting-worse reality to an earlier, simpler one. Which was now this one. Not simple at all, really. It was fraught with a peril, a high-tech, violent gauntlet of it between us and our siblings. Which was where we were going if this demonstration and the last one had done what was needed.

After what seemed like an age, Wenling said, "It's time to call."

She'd taken her phone back from me earlier and now used it to dial another secret number. She put the call on speakerphone so that I could listen in, but as the phone started to ring, she told me, "Don't talk."

I nodded. It was hard enough remembering to breathe.

Someone picked up on the other end and a very confident male voice, precise and clipped, said, "Nobody got into the box."

"We did," said Wenling.

There was a long pause, then, "What did you see inside?"

"A paper."

"Interesting guess."

"I caught fire when the lid was opened."

"How?"

"I don't know. A chemical reaction, I think," Wenling said, echoing my earlier theory.

"Interesting, but again it could be a guess."

Wenling held up the paper I'd given her and read out the passage about irrational creatures and troublesome Man.

There was another long pause and a slight murmuring which suggested the voice on the other end of the line was consulting with someone. It ended with the confident voice saying, "Ha!" in a way that worried me.

Wenling saw my expression and said to the phone, "Is there a problem?"

The man's voice when he came back on was still precise and clipped, but somehow injected with a kind of contained glee as he said, "Not at all. I'm told that much of the passage your time traveler attempted to recall *imprecisely* was burned by the time your camera reached the case to look at the page. However, reconstruction of the passage would have been almost automatic for someone who could recall the seventeenth-century book we took it from, word for word. Your memory is every bit as remarkable as that of your siblings, Dr. Traine. Better, perhaps."

I felt the blood drain from my face. Then it burned as Wenling looked at me, fury twisting her features.

But she didn't hold the look. With great effort, she brought herself back to neutral, smiling grimly. She clicked off the cell phone's speaker and raised the phone to her ear. "You acknowledge what I have in my possession." A beat. "And what I can do with him."

She looked at me and my skin felt like it was trying to crawl off my body.

The rest of the conversation became an odd guessing game based on Wenling's words only. "Of course...He knows all about what you did to Kuang Dishi in Taiwan...He has ways...For a week, maybe. Ten days, or...That would be good...No. Develop it. I'll call you forty-eight hours from now."

She hung up and looked at me again. This time she pressed her phone close to her chest with both hands and her face wore a grim smile. Then her lips trembled. I wasn't sure if it was from fatigue, relief, or some real joy that she might actually have taken a concrete step toward getting her brother back. And my siblings too, right?

Wenling tossed her phone onto the couch beside her and turned to me. "We got him," she said, then stumbled forward into my arms.

I held her stiffly, my heart thudding in my ears.

"No, no, no," she murmured, burrowing into my chest. "Loosen. He already suspected. And what I said—that you are a thing, my possession—that was a game, you understand? Using his language. It's how I've closed so many deals, speaking the language of others."

"Is it?"

She looked up into my face, and the tears in her eyes worked their way through my horror and awful suspicions, through my emotional exhaustion and fear. They melted me. "Yes!" she cried. "You and I are partners in this. He knows that. Beyond the words, he knows I am nothing without you. We will get Xiaobo back. And Kenny. And Kansas. And we will expose SCATTER for the *fuckers* they are."

She began trembling in my arms so violently that I held her tighter so she didn't collapse. As I did, she reached up to my face, grabbed it with both her hands, and pulled my lips down to hers.

Her lips burned and shook against mine, transferring their fire. When her tongue forced its way into my mouth, the transference became a gushing torrent of heat, shooting from my toes through my groin and up.

Caught in its mania, I yanked her in closer to me, then just as suddenly released her to yank her knit top up and over her head. She gasped, and I dropped to my knees before her, yanking down her lime green slacks to reveal the taut fruit inside.

She kicked the slacks off her ankles as I rose, and grabbed at the button of my jeans, twisting it open and working down the zipper. Then she pulled down both the jeans and underwear with her as she copied my maneuver, but not rising up again. Instead, she grabbed a part of me she was becoming all too possessive of. But as possession went from hand to the slick heat and motion of her mouth, I decided to allow it.

Just...*uh*...this...*uh*...once.

28

Necessary allies

Morning sex led to a morning shower. Together. And more morning sex.

By the end of it, I think Wenling believed, not unreasonably, that she'd soothed my horror at being referred to as a useful tool.

She was still reluctant, though, to tell me exactly what had been agreed to in her phone conversation with the Arrogant Prick who'd figured out my identity, presumably by consulting one of his time travelers about what state the paper had been in when its image was captured.

"Are you sure he spoke for SCATTER?" I pressed her. "It wasn't the guy I met in the CIA headquarters."

"He is the one."

But she wouldn't say more until I finally snapped mid-afternoon, saying that if we were true partners, she'd bring me into the planning loop. Not all of the operational details, but certainly the big stroke items like her discussion with the AP.

That got me at least the proposed framework of the parlay she and the AP had worked out. Exact location was TBD, but likely in Washington, DC. The date, TBD, but sometime in the next week. There would be an independent broker of known character who would arbitrate.

"No more specifics?" I pressed.

"That's why we're calling back in forty-eight hours."

"Am I going to be there? Are Xiaobo, Kenny, and Kansas going to be there?"

"To be decided."

I went for a walk.

Chilly day. Overcast sky. Dark, leafless tree swayed back and forth as I wandered among them in the stretch near the bluffs.

I still should have been celebrating. I was going to have a second meeting with SCATTER, presumably with the actual leader, not the violent muscle. (Though it was odd to think of Andre Poussaint as "muscle.")

The lack of any negotiating framework ate at me, though. We'd shown our knowledge of their operations and the ability to basically replicate their operations. What had we gotten in return? An agreement to meet? That was it?

Maybe I should have been trusting in the Wenling's expertise in this area. She'd had to have negotiated many deals with shady characters in both China and here in America to make it to where she was now. She'd also actually gotten a direct line into SCATTER. And she'd shown, time and again, her earnest desire to move ahead with this. She'd given me assurance after assurance, both with her words and her body, *all* of her body.

Yet through all that, Lena's warning kept sounding in my head: *"She plays games. She makes you believe what she needs you to believe."*

That sounded a lot like what Wenling herself had said—that she knew how to speak the language a person needed to hear.

So what was the language *I* needed? Fierce intelligence plus vulnerability? A trembling lip? Someone who desired me so fiercely they'd make passionate love when challenged about something they'd said?

It was actually making me fall for her, even with Lena's ghost hovering in the background.

Which gave me guilt. And disbelief that someone as beautiful, successful, and emotionally scarred as Wenling could actually care for me.

"Dude!" I called out to the out-of-sight river to my left, "you need therapy."

Because that thing she'd said to me in Chinese the first time we'd had sex? Wǒ xǐhuan nǐ. It had taken me a while to track it down using just the phonetics, but it was Mandarin for, *I like you.* Which was apparently pretty close to, *I love you,* in a romantic setting. Given unprompted by a woman who knew I spoke no Chinese.

"Accept it!"

Okay, so, assuming I believed Wenling was doing her best, how could lower my stress about this negotiation? Maybe realize we didn't have to win everything. We just needed our siblings back. Then, if Kansas could find us a congressional oversight committee with clean hands, I'd give them what we knew. Go into witness protection if we had to. Let one arm of the government go after the other. It worked with MK Ultra. Sort of.

It was a plan.

I hitched myself up to a stand and walked back to the house. As I got within about fifty yards, I pulled out my Huawei phone and checked to see if the Wi-Fi connected this far out. It did, barely. If I wanted to make a Skype call, I'd need to go inside. Or...

Detouring to the right of the house on the way back, I walked to the garage/coach house and found the man-door. Rang the bell. As I waited, I checked the Wi-Fi and found it almost as strong as in the main house. A moment later, Colonel Jian answered, wearing an apron. "I am cooking," he said evenly, in answer to my raised eyebrows.

I checked my watch and realized I'd been out longer than I'd thought. It was almost five. Which meant 8 p.m. in Langley.

"Sorry to disturb, Colonel," I said. "Quick question. The bedroom where I'm staying in the main house. Is there a chance it's bugged?"

Jian's eyes met mine with somber interest. "It may be."

"Is this house of yours bugged?"

The corners of his mouth twitched. "It is not."

"Would you mind me making a quick phone call from your place?"

He inclined his head and stepped back to let me in. I entered, and he directed me to his living room/dining room, then hurried past me to the efficiency kitchen on the far side of a small table and that had two chairs. As he proceeded to stir a small pot of sauce and, in a frying pan, flip and stir what looked like celery, egg, and bean sprouts in a pungent, sizzling oil, I pulled out my phone and dialed up Jude for a video call.

He answered on the third ring and his eyes, with even deeper circles under them than the last time, went wide when he saw my face.

"Holy shit, dude!" he yelped. "You're like Mr. Invisible. I left like twenty voice mails, finally got your office girl on the phone."

"Megan?"

"That's her! She told me you were 'out' for a while. Couldn't say where. Not wouldn't. Couldn't. Your home and office got trashed? Your girl thinks you and Lena broke up? Again. Like, what the hell?"

I glanced at Jian at the stove, pretending to cook, but no doubt listening. I'd made a calculated bet coming in here to make my call. Here's where I went all in on it. "There's a program inside the CIA called SCATTER. You know anything about it?"

Even on the small screen of my phone, I could see Jude blanch. He cleared his throat. "That's what had you all upset when you were here? Dude, that program was shut down a couple years ago. Before I came out here. Guy who ran it was supposed to be some kind of genius psychiatrist, but went off the deep end, you know?"

"You're sure it was shut down?"

"That's... You're talking like you think it wasn't."

"Like I know it wasn't."

"Oh, shit." Jude's haggard face jerked up and down as she walked to a couch and sat down. When it steadied again, he was visibly sweating and worried. "Andre Poussaint. Is that why you were asking about him? You think he's...? Is that what you were really here for? What'd you get yourself into, Jackson?"

I looked up and realized that Jian had finished cooking his meal, divided it onto two plates and put the plates on the small table with two sets of chopsticks and two cups, which he was currently filling with hot tea. He caught my eye, stony-faced, and gestured for me to sit. I walked over with my phone, sat, and laid the phone down flat beside my plate of Egg Fu Yung. Jian had sprinkled chopped green onion on top and had a bottle of Kikkoman soy sauce in the center of the table. I had to give him a profound nod of appreciation before I looked back at Jude's face on the phone.

"Who else is there with you?" Jude asked, worried.

"A friend." Colonel Jian was eating by that point and didn't acknowledge this. Which was acknowledgment enough, I thought. "Do you know what SCATTER was doing?"

"Rumors," Jude said evasively. "Kind of paranormal stuff."

"Time travel."

Jude squinched his face like I'd just farted at him. "Dude."

"It's what you heard because it's what they're doing. It's why they took Kenny."

"'Took,' as in forcibly abducted?"

"Yes."

"Because…"

"He can time travel. Or at least tell when someone else has."

"Oh, fuck. Jackson, are you on some new meds?"

I stared down at Jude's face. "I don't do any drugs. You know that. Like you know exactly what it was SCATTER is studying. You're too smart and political not to have researched your peers, what they're working on now, what other programs were going on."

Jude looked almost like he was going to cry as his round face tightened up around his mouth and his eyebrows drew down over his eyes. Finally he said, "Okay. Yeah. It's what SCATTER *was* studying, when it was actually in operation. With a genius psychiatrist heading it, like I said. But everyone says it was shut down two years ago. For abusing research subjects. For wackadoodle science-fictiony claims. I think they put the psychiatrist in jail."

"They didn't. And it's still operating."

"Then it's pretty fucking secret and not being done in any of the psych labs I've seen, okay?" Jude jumped up with his phone but kept it in front of his face. He was sweating heavily and going almost purple. "And for you to… It's like you're accusing me of… Like, why did you even call me?"

I watched him, concerned. He was almost panting now, his chest heaving, and I worried that he was about to have a heart attack. "Jude," I said calmly. "I'm the one with anxiety and panic attacks. You're the chill one. So chill, okay. You're scaring me."

He blinked and wiped something from his mouth. "*I'm* scaring *you*." He suddenly saw the humor in it and his mouth cracked a smile. In a few seconds, he was laughing so hard that tears were streaming down his cheeks.

When he finished, I said, "I wondered if it maybe was started by the CIA, then split off, but Poussaint went *after* me. When I wouldn't tell him how I knew about SCATTER, he threatened to take me to the basement of your workplace and interrogate me there."

Jude looked thoroughly confused. "When? During your interview here? He come in a secret back way or something because—"

"Must have walked right by you when you were waiting," I said, because it was true. Sort of. "I don't know what you were doing. I think the fact I managed to just leave pissed him off. I think he ordered some of his people to toss my apartment and workplace. They stole all my computers. Did you know that?"

"Oh shit, dude." Jude looked honestly stricken. My gut and years of knowing him told me he honestly knew nothing about Poussaint's association with SCATTER, ergo Jude knew nothing about SCATTER, or at least not enough to know who was leading it and what they were doing.

It was all I needed to know.

"I need your help," I said.

"Okay." Jude's attention snapped back to me. "Name it. You got it."

"In a few days, I think I'm going to be coming to Langley or someplace close to it to meet someone from SCATTER and negotiate the release of Kenny and Kansas. But I don't trust they're going to negotiate in good faith. And if they just take me, like they took Kenny and Kansas..."

I couldn't even finish that thought. Because the more I'd learned about SCATTER, the more it seemed to represent the worst fear of where my time travel power could take me. If SCATTER controlled me, they wouldn't just want to traumatize me over and over and over to make me jump. No, they'd be doing it a thousand different ways *and* using the results to kill people and reshape the world order.

Hurt me and pervert me.

I'd always thought of myself as stronger than Kenny, but now I knew that, for all his drug use and mental illness, the way he'd survived Cutter and SCATTER enough to tap me Wenling's name? He was the strong one.

As was Kansas, I was sure.

I was the weak link in the Traine line. If SCATTER got me, I'd lose my mind.

Jude interrupted my mental spiral with, "You want me to provide backup? I know a few serious badass operatives here who've come to me for counseling the last few years."

"No! I don't know who you can trust in the CIA and I don't want to tip anyone off. But just having you nearby to pick me up if I come running... Something like that."

I saw Jude swallow. Being a getaway driver wasn't exactly something he was born to do. Which made his determined nod all the more heartwarming. It was good to have at least one person outside of my siblings I knew I could count on when the chips were down. You just needed people like that on your side. Necessary allies.

"Thank you," I told him. "I'll call again when I know more."

With that, I hung up.

Colonel Jian was staring at me. "I am a better driver."

I nodded. "But you'll be taking care of Zhou Wenling, won't you? What I'm going to ask of you is just some help separating from her if I need to. Even if she doesn't want me to."

He considered this and finally gave a grave nod. Then said, "You think you know what she wants. You do not. You think you know what you want. You do not. Without those, how can you know what you are willing or able to do?"

I stared at him with my brow furrowed. "Does that mean you're going to help me or not?"

He nodded toward the plate in front of me. "Eat. Tell me what you think."

I did. Best damn Egg Foo Yung I'd ever tasted.

29

We can't lose you

Wenling invited me to join her for dinner when I got back, and when I hesitated, she promised to tell me the plan she'd just worked out with her group if I sat and ate.

The meal, a simple braised tilapia with a sweet ginger-soy sauce on a bed of jasmine rice with lightly steamed cauliflower on the side, was good, but the discussion of our upcoming penetration of the enemy's ranks, was...disappointing.

"You are to be used as a threat," she said. "Which means we keep you in reserve, safe and out of sight."

"The enemy you don't see coming?"

"The knife you should never need to use. It is most powerful in its sheath, where your enemy can only imagine how sharply it cuts."

"You get that from Colonel Jian?" I knew it sure as hell wasn't from *The Art of War.*

Wenling shook her head. "I take these from my own experience."

"Literally?"

"After I began spreading stories of my knives castrating rapists while they slept, the men I spent time with treated me more carefully. The principle works in business as well."

"Hunh." I let that sit for a moment, then pressed for more. "Does that mean I won't be coming with you at all, then? I'll be staying here?"

Wenling rolled her eyes. "One must be ready to *show* the knife. Safely."

I thought of Andre Poussaint, his buzz-cut blond bodyguard Kevin, and even the two CIA Human Resources & Talent Acquisition team of Wilson and Dadashev. All four were killers. "Exactly how do you plan to do that?"

"It will depend on the setting, the people, the timing."

"So, I may not have to actually be in the room."

"Do you want to rescue your brother and sister?"

"Of course. That doesn't—"

"Why are you being so afraid? We will do what needs to be done."

Hurt me and pervert me.

It was starting up again, wasn't it? If I just rolled along this way, I'd be back to where I was last March, being tortured and jumping back to do it over and over again. Like Xiaobo must have felt when he'd become a prediction machine for his sister, now a tool of SCATTER. Like this gift inevitably made you a tool for someone else.

A powerful tool, though.

One I still had control over.

SCATTER wanted my power to control the world. Wenling wanted it as leverage against SCATTER. I guessed maybe I could use it as not only Wenling's ace-in-the-hole, but my own.

What do you want?

To…play my game, not theirs?

It would do for now.

"Yes," I said. "We do what needs to be done."

That night I begged off sex, pleading anxiety. Which was true since I always had anxiety, but not the true reason for my avoidance. The truth was, I was afraid my feelings for Wenling were clouding my judgement. Sex with her didn't help.

I took a long shower alone and forced myself to consider Wenling from a clinical perspective.

First, the way she'd survived her childhood had been to accept older men raping her and beating her while she learned to be what they wanted her to be, whether that was submissive or terrifying. It had given her an impressive force of will and a chameleon's sense of her environment. She could read the room, be the room, do what was needed for the room to go where she wanted it to.

Second, she might have *wanted* a white knight and love as a child, but what she'd accepted and adopted were glycerin tears. Use as needed.

Third, she'd groomed herself to physical perfection. She'd clearly practiced sex to become good at it, and she used it like a narcissist to engender obsession, devotion, and admiration, or at least cooperation.

Fourth, she showed no true shame, remorse, love, or attachment.

Except toward her brother? Perhaps.

Toward me? Maybe.

Yet even as I went over all the things she'd done to make this man, Jackson Traine, fall in love with her, the only one that looked unscripted was her muttering, *I like you*, in Chinese, unprompted and never translated or explained.

Except I *had* managed to translate it. Because I heard it, didn't forget the sounds, and had access to the internet. Wenling knew about my memory. I'd described in our walk by the river. It had been that night we had sex and she muttered, Wǒ xǐhuan nǐ, the Mandarin of I like you.

Was this reaching? Maybe. But it felt right. Just as it felt right for me not to have seen all of this behavior pattern earlier. My clinical experience with what the DSM V labeled psychopaths was limited, while the feeling of being heard, understood, and incredibly validated, the psychopath's stock in trade, was intoxicating.

I shut off the shower and began toweling myself off.

What actions did this analysis demand?

We were still heading for a negotiation with SCATTER, which was my best bet to locate and possibly rescue Kenny and Kansas. And Wenling seemed as invested as I was in making it happen. For her own reasons perhaps. Or mixed reasons. A part of me still believed she felt *something* for me.

If it all went sideways? Well, that's why I had Jude and Colonel Jian as backup.

I finally just threw the towel in the sink and went to bed with my tired brain turning those thoughts over and over and over, until sleep finally rose and pulled me under.

I jolted awake in pain. Some animal had just bitten my belly!

When my eyes adjusted, I saw it was worse than that.

Sitting on the edge of my bed was a very old man with a large, drooping nose and rheumy looking eyes behind thick glasses. He was staring at my belly where his left, blue-gloved hand held back the pushed-up clump of my tee-shirt so he could examine the "bite" he'd given me just below my belly button. The teeth, I saw as he raised his raised right hand, had been a wicked looking syringe with a needle that looked thick enough to administer a shot of semen up a cow's behind.

Behind him, an interested Wenling stood watching.

"What did you do?" I said to her, not the man with the syringe. He was only another tool.

"We implanted a transmitter," she said. "It's very small and inserted close enough to your intestines that a casual x-ray might assume it's something you swallowed. It remains in a dormant state nine of every ten hours, during which it's virtually undetectable. Isn't that right, doctor?"

The rheumy-eyed man looked up from my belly and back and forth like he was trying to figure out where the voice had come from. He finally saw Wenling and said, "Yes, yes. Won't set anything off."

Wenling gave me a reassuring smile. "Safety measures, Jackson. We don't want to accidentally lose you. This way we cannot."

I took note of exactly where the transmitter had gone in, so I'd know where to direct whomever I got to dig it out of me. Then I gave both the old man and Wenling a strained smile and said, "I want to sleep."

The two of them left the room.

30

Seduced into danger

48 hours after her initial call with Arrogant Prick, Wenling made contact again. Without telling me.

She came to me afterward in the room she'd set up as a home gym. I'd gone for a morning run and been alternately lifting weights and kicking the freestanding heavy bag to bring back my feelings of bodily control that I'd had when training with Lead the Way in the hopes it would help me get my anxiety under control. It was working.

Sort of.

I was chambering a roundhouse kick when Wenling appeared in the doorway and the surprise made me hop backward, almost stumbling. We'd been operating like two strangers in the house since last night's dinner when my therapist self had concluded she showed strong psychopathic traits. The tracer they'd injected into me had confirmed it.

Now she stood in a skintight pink pantsuit with the front zipper pulled down well below her nipple line, her hair pulled back in a curled ponytail, her makeup emphasizing her eyes and lips. She looked elegant and damn hot. My body, all pumped up from working out, responded, and I had to hunch forward to hide my erection. I grabbed my workout towel and wiped my forehead sweat in annoyance.

"The Capitol, Washington, DC," she said.

"What about it?"

"It's where we're meeting SCATTER."

"In the Capitol building." I shook my head, now annoyed by both by my erection and by her trolling me.

She persisted. "There's at least one senator who's a supporter of the program. We'll be using his office."

"I thought you said the Capitol. The senators have offices in three different buildings—the Dirkson, the Hart, and the Russell—all northeast of the Capitol." I had no idea where I'd read that. Maybe when I'd been researching the CIA.

"Each senator also has a hideaway in the Capitol building where they can go in between votes," Wenling said, visibly pleased she could provide me with general knowledge that I somehow hadn't accumulated. "They entertain constituents there. Sometimes lovers."

"Which category do you fall into?" I was careful to keep my voice dry.

"'We,'" she said. "You will be coming with me."

That finally doused my erection so thoroughly I had no trouble rearing up fully to look at her in shock. "Doesn't that...um...?"

"Put you in danger? Yes, it does. But the security protocols inside the Capitol forbid weapons and everyone in or out is carefully tracked. They won't try to kill or abduct you there."

"And you think it's a good idea to let them see my face?"

"They destroyed your office and home after you foolishly visited the CIA Headquarters. They identified you by name on our phone call. Do you think they don't know what you look like?"

I wrapped my workout towel around my neck like it could protect me. "But they don't know where I am right now. That was part of why I came out here, wasn't it?"

"I need you with me. If things go badly, I need an immediate fall back."

I snorted. "You mean a jump back in time. You've seen what's involved with that. I can't just—"

"If things go badly," she cut me off, "you'll have sufficient motivation."

I met her look and understood in that instant just how uncertain even Wenling was about this meeting, but also how determined. Whatever her reasons, she was going in, and wanted me there to manage the risk.

Fine. I wanted to confront the Arrogant Prick anyway. He was holding my sibs.

"I'll wear my body armor," I said.

"Of course."

"And my gun."

"Firearms aren't permitted in the Capitol."

"Except by the Capitol Police?"

"We leave tomorrow morning. Early. Private jet."

"Okay." I turned from her like I wanted to continue my workout.

"You look good." Her voice came from right behind me.

"Hunh?" I turned to see I was right. Wenling hadn't left. She'd moved in closer, less than a foot away.

"Sweaty. Pumped up. I like you like this. Do you want to come up to my room and fuck? It may be the last time...for a while."

I noted the way she'd paused before the last two words. And whether it was that or the obvious lust in her eyes, and the fact I could now see the bumps of her nipples poking through the pink fabric of her jumpsuit, my erection had sprung painfully back to life in my shorts.

She'd worn that outfit for me, I thought. It was what a psychopath would do. The question I needed to answer was how sane it would be to indulge in her manipulation, pretending it wasn't going to hurt me in the long run.

"Well?" she said, shifting her hips enough to draw my eyes down there. There was no panty line.

"Let's save it," I said.

"Your loss."

When she turned and walked from the room, the twitch and jiggle she put into her booty almost undid me.

The next morning, both of us dressed casually, we drove out with our suit and overnight bags to a small airstrip just south of Spokane that hosted our rented jet.

It reminded me of the limousine Colonel Jian maintained and drove. Once inside, mask removed, I saw the airplane cabin was much bigger, of course, like a plush living room that could seat ten or twelve people comfortably in the leather armchairs or couches, with tables, fine carpets, food and drink, Wi-Fi, and a large screen at either end of the space for entertainment and information.

I was reassured when Colonel Jian, in his dark chauffeur's suit, followed us quietly onboard and took a seat at the far end of the cabin, sitting stonily as if determined to blend into the décor. No matter how much I willed it, he would not meet my gaze. It totally flipped my reassurance as I wondered whether he'd told Wenling about my visit with him, my conversation with Jude.

I'd told Jude where our meeting was going to be and he'd agreed to be in DC today. I hoped I hadn't led him into danger.

Wenling smirked at my discomfiture. "Fang Jian will be driving us when we land in Dulles."

I'd assumed that much. I looked at her for a sign she knew more. Saw nothing.

That was good, right?

During the four-and-a-half-hour flight, Wenling made me watch *Mr. Smith Goes to Washington* with her and discuss how closely I thought the old movie echoed the way the US Senate operated today, and whether I thought I would ever have had the courage of Jimmy Stuart's character if I hadn't had PTSD and social anxiety.

That and the reheated pasta-chicken we ate for lunch left me vaguely nauseous by the time we landed. The jet taxied directly into a small hangar on a side track off the northeast end of the main runways. We climbed out with our overnight bags and walked maybe twenty steps to stow our bags in the trunk of a waiting limousine. Colonel Jian climbed into the front driver's seat while Wenling and I climbed into the back.

The limo had exquisite black leather and trim, but none of the character of Wenling's Land Rover. Like Wenling preferred things both distinctive and best in class, but was willing to settle for the best available. It was how she'd accepted me, after all. Not the best at anything, but with one critical skill. Once she had no need of that, I suspected she'd have no need of me either.

The engine roared to life and rolled us gracefully out of the hanger and onto the same exit and highway Jude had used to take me to the CIA HQ. But for this drive, the sky was dark and rain spattered our windows off and on. Wenling issued no directions to Colonel Jian. Her plans had obviously been discussed and digested earlier.

All she'd told me on the flight was a US senator was hosting a meeting between us and a representative of SCATTER this afternoon in the senator's "hideaway" office in the Capitol Building at four p.m. Beyond that, I assumed she'd tell me what I needed to know when we got close.

Maybe.

You think you know what she wants. You do not.

The sun had burst through the clouds by the time we reached our hotel. Colonel Jian dropped us off in front of it—a red brick hotel with a circular chrome awning over the entrance that said *The George*, with a black-fabric awning bistro right beside it that was presumably part of the same hotel.

No parking to be seen anywhere, but that was Colonel Jian's issue. I hopped out the street-side door and hurried around the back to meet Wenling and grab our overnight bags, looking around with excitement and anxiety. I'd brought along my little Nokia burner but found it didn't even have GPS, so I'd borrowed Wenling's and seen we were just a couple blocks from the Lower Senate Park, a few more to the three Senate office buildings and the Capitol Building itself and the long civics lesson of the National Mall and White house running west from it.

It had always been on my bucket list, but I doubted I'd be seeing much of it this time. Probably wouldn't see anything but the Capitol.

I'd go in, maybe never come out.

At least, not as a free man.

Wenling tugged at my arm impatiently and we ran into the hotel lobby. There we quickly pulled on our masks and, as she got our keys from the front desk, I spotted no fewer than three stylized, almost manga, paintings of our first president. Once we'd ridden the elevator up to our floor, we found our way to what she told me was their one true suite, the "Presidential Suite," no less. It was a mixture of modern and early Colonial. The bathroom was marble everything with a freestanding soaker tub and separate glass-enclosed shower.

I took off my mask. All the rooms smelled like jasmine and oranges. Totally Lena. Like she was watching over me. Warning me about Wenling.

Which is when I consciously took in the king-size bed that was so high, they provided a pull-out foot step to get onto it.

One bed.

Wenling climbed onto it and bounced up and down like a young girl. She grinned at me. "There is a pull-out couch in the other room if you don't want to sleep with me."

If I ever get the chance to sleep here.

"We'll see how I feel after our meeting," I said.

Finally picking up on my mood, Wenling slid off the bed. "Why don't you have a shower to freshen up before we need to dress and leave."

It wasn't a suggestion.

I walked into the bathroom, pulled the door shut behind me, stripped down, and climbed into the shower. When I turned it on, the hot water came out in a wonderful, mind-altering surge that battered my head and shoulders, generously washing my anxiety down my body and into the drain under my feet.

I squirted some of the soap out of the dispenser on the wall and it had more of the jasmine and oranges smell. Still Lena. I slopped it onto my chest, around my neck, under my arms, over my face, and the aroma filled me so it felt like Lena was right there with me, her lush dark body pressing up against me, her arms reaching...

The shower door opened, and I squinted through my soapy eyes to see Wenling's shorter, skinnier, enter.

Before I could clear the soap from my face, her arms had slipped around me from behind and reached down to grab my unexpected erection.

"You were hoping I'd join you, I see."

"I..." I sputtered the last bit of soap from my mouth as she pressed into me and began stroking. "Sure."

And maybe a part of me *had* wanted her there. To relieve the ache, not of my arousal, but of my wanting. To take me away from what I couldn't have. To fortify me against an adventure I wasn't ready for.

I turned around, pushed her up against the glass, then knelt down to spread her legs and arouse her. When she began to squirm uncontrollably, I stood and entered her, hard and quick, thrusting to wipe Lena from my mind.

So there's.

Not.
A.
Thought.
Of.
Herrrrrr.

31

Mr. Traine goes to Washington, nightmare version

AT 3:15, REFRESHED, WE dressed in appropriate business attire, which for Wenling was a tight, black skirt and patterned matching jacket over a cream blouse, with matching purse and pumps, pearl earrings and choker. For me, it included my body armor. We both donned our face masks, left the hotel room, and walked to the elevators. Wenling had told Colonel Jian to bring the limo to outside the lobby doors at 3:20.

The elevator doors dinged and slid open.

With a rushing sound, a masked Colonel Jian appeared behind us and grabbed Wenling's arm so she couldn't walk through the open doors. His face was so tight his lips shook as he said, "You must not go down!"

He kept holding her arm as the elevator's doors closed again and it continued its descent.

Wenling shook him off. "What are you doing?"

"They are waiting to take Mr. Traine outside the elevators downstairs. We must travel a different way."

"Who is waiting? How do you know their plan?"

But even as Colonel Jian prepared to answer, I staggered a bit and my vision went funny. Almost like I actually *had* gotten into the elevator and ridden it down with Wenling, I could see her and me arriving at the lobby level with a slight, cushioned bump. The doors opened. I stepped out. A burly man with a black medical mask who must have been waiting with his back pressed against the wall beside the elevator door, stepped forward and locked a thick arm around my neck, his other hand grabbing my right wrist and dragging it back behind him, twisting and wrenching it up.

Pain. But when I tried to move, the man who held me turned me toward Wenling so I could see that a second masked man stood beside her with a pistol pointed at her head, his right foot holding open the door to the elevator we'd just left.

Nothing to do. No options.

Jump, the Wenling in this vision mouthed at me, but I knew, and she had to know by now, that it wasn't that simple.

"Scream and she dies," said the man with the gun. "Try to get away and she dies and we'll shoot you in the head, close range. No jumping back from that." Then, to Wenling: "Get back in the elevator."

Wenling did as she was told. The man reached in and pressed a number high on the button pad. He stepped out, and the door closed.

Without another word, the two men frog marched me out of the elevator, turned left, and had me out the front door and into a waiting panel van, even as I thought I heard the alarm sounding from the elevator inside. But then I had just enough time to register that the back compartment of the van was empty, with a corrugated, dirty metal floor like some kind of service vehicle, before the men who'd the bodily thrown me in here slammed and locked the back door, making everything pitch black around me.

The engine roared and lurched forward and I stumbled, hit a wall, and sat down hard.

Jump? Should I jump? *Could* I make myself jump before we were God knew where? My ability to control it, to force a jump when I wasn't actually in mortal pain, had grown so rusty that I...

The van swerved and I fell over. Caught myself but hurt my left wrist. I had to hold on.

Jump?

But what if they were taking me to Kenny? To Kansas? Wasn't this why I was here? Because, honestly, had I ever truly believed Wenling would be able to just *talk* SCATTER into letting them go? Even with me as a threat?

Maybe I'd be better to just—

"Jackson? *Jackson.* Hey! Are you sick?"

Hands on my shoulders, shaking me. Wenling's hands.

My focus snapped from the alternate memory to being in the hallway of the Presidential Suite of the George. In this timeline, we had not gone down the elevator. I had not been abducted and thrown into the back of a van. My brain was swirling and my heart thumped in my chest as I tried to process the future in which I'd been abducted and the one here and now where I was going to avoid it.

But for all the fear of how this had happened without *me* causing the jump, a part of me cheered that I wasn't going into defibrillation or having a stroke. It clearly wasn't the absorption of all these extra *hours* that caused me to nearly die after three jumps. It had something to so with the process.

On the other hand, the fact I could be dragged into another timeline, or at least become aware of more than just the timelines I chose... It was terrifying. Could any other time traveler mess with my timestream connection like that? Could I do the same to them?

Wenling shook me again. "What is going on? Did you jump back from the men waiting for us downstairs?"

I looked at her, braced myself, and looked into my memories again. Still in the van. Fast-forward. Still in the van. A long ride. Fast-forward. Arriving at...some place quiet. No, wait. The sound of a plane passing far overhead. Taken from the back of the van, squinting in the sunlight, and being led into a nondescript concrete building. Into an elevator. Down. A long way down. Doors open. A room out of a Cold War nightmare. Banks of computers, screens everywhere, and rooms attached with clear windows. People inside them. Some with monitors. Some hooked up like living computers themselves, electrodes and tubes sprouting from their heads.

And there's one face I recognize even before I truly see it. They're walking me towards him. He's turning towards me in horror as I run eagerly towards him and...

"Jackson!"

I snapped back again as Wenling shook me. I was on the ground, I realized. Must have slumped down as I remembered. I met Wenling's gaze and pulled my thoughts together. "Yes, I jumped. But I didn't cause it. I...hitched a ride on another traveler's jump."

"Xiaobo?"

I shook my head. "I think...my brother."

Colonel Jian cut in. "Yes. He said he was your brother. He called my phone when I was walking to get the car. He said men were waiting for you downstairs and would take you."

"They are," I said and got to my feet. I turned to Wenling. "They have no intention of letting you use me to threaten them. Even if we avoid the two downstairs, they'll just grab me somewhere else."

She pursed her lips together and looked down, swearing very quietly in Cantonese or Mandarin. When she looked up, she already had her phone in her hand. She dialed a number and, after it was clearly answered, barked a quick command in the same language as her cursing. Then she hung up and looked at Colonel Jian. "You have your gun and Jackson's gun?"

He nodded. "In my room."

"Good. We go there. You will both be armed. We will go down the fire escape stairs and get the limousine with your guns ready."

"What if that's not enough?" I asked. "They may already be wondering why we're not downstairs. They may be coming for me."

"Then we should hurry."

She strode back down the hall towards our suite and past it to the next room, where Colonel Jian caught up to her, opened the door and followed her in. As the Colonel helped me don my shoulder holster and Sig P226, chambered with a MEC-GAR clip that held 18 round of 9mm Parabellum cartridges. My body armor had a pocket in the back that the Colonel stuffed with two extra clips.

"You figuring of a major shootout?" I asked.

He held my gaze firmly. "You don't want to run out."

He then started equipping himself while Wenling, I noted, had dialed another number and was tapping her toe. She'd pulled down her mask and held her lips in a grim line. She stopped the toe tap and her entire body drew up straight and stiff as she said into the phone, "If you will not meet us in good faith, we will walk. Right now...No...You have two men by the lobby elevator waiting for us. Would you like me to describe them?...Bollocks...We are now armed. And I have a secondary army which you will not see, following us to our final meeting place. If you interfere with me or my asset, you will see bloodshed that makes last year's January six riots look like sightseeing."

She hung up.

Both Colonel Jian and I stared at her, dumbfounded. Then we both nodded. The Colonel finished his preparations and hurried from the room, heading for the fire escape, knowing now that it, too, might be watched.

We'd have to see how effective Wenling's threats were.

No one accosted us on the stairs, in the parking garage, or driving out and along the six blocks to the front of the Dirkson office building, one of the three that housed the offices of the US Senators, where they did most of their work when not voting or debating bills on the Senate floor in the US Capitol.

Wenling had explained to me en route that we were meeting Republican Senator Antoine Jonquist, of Wyoming who would escort us into the Capitol via the Senate subway. He'd told Wenling that he'd left a marked spot outside the Dirkson for us to park, and it turned out that in this, at least, the Senator had honored his word. It wasn't him Wenling had blasted on the phone, she added. He was a go-between. An enabler. Not part of SCATTER itself.

We pulled on our masks and entered through the pseudo archway that stretched up five stories, pseudo because it was really just protruding block concrete that ran up the side of the square office building with an elaborate concrete triangle sticking out for the two stories about that.

But from such pseudosities come grandeur, right?

We had to leave our guns, holsters, and phones with security (the phones per Jonquist's instructions), but Wenling had already assured us that she had members who were authorized to carry firearms who would be shadowing us as far as Jonquist's hideaway over in the US Capitol itself. And an even larger scatter of staff in both this building and the Capitol who were unarmed backup, using hidden cameras to record everything we and those around us did.

Jonquist's office was on the fourth floor. We found it easily enough and walked into what could have been a large private corporate office anywhere, if one that decorated its walls with far too many pictures of its inhabitant shaking hands with three former US presidents and countless other celebrities, political and not. It also had a peekaboo view to the west of the treed Capitol grounds and even the top of the Capitol dome itself.

Jonquist himself was on the phone when we knocked and a female aide let us in. Jonquist held up a finger at us while he mumbled, "Uh-hunh," and, "Sure, sure." Finally, "You got it," and he hung up and stood to greet us, making no effort to mask up. He was tall, beefy, and balding, with the look of a former football player in his sixties whose muscle had turned to fat, the skin around his jaw slack and thick. It turned into double rolls as he lowered his head to look at us over his glasses.

He took the glasses off, stuffed them into his inner suit jacket pocket, and walked out from behind his desk. He gave me and Colonel Jian a quick glance, then focused in on Wenling.

"So you're the talented big sister," he said in a voice that boomed loudly like he was used to larger spaces or using it to dominate.

"Elizabeth Chan, yes." Wenling did not offer her hand.

"Chan. Riiiight. And these two are your aides? Should say, employees?"

"If you wish. You've met my brother?"

"Xiaobo? Oh, yes. Fine boy. Very committed. Smart. There's one boy who's not a sheep."

I snuck a glance at Wenling's face and saw she'd gone blank and ice cold again. No trace of the enigmatic smile she usually used when she was uncertain of how to formulate a response. To me, this said she saw straight through this man and his games.

"Where did you meet him?"

Something in Wenling's voice finally told the senator that his usual bullshit wasn't going to fly here. His fat lips crooked up. "Well now, that might just be classified. But he impressed me with his intelligence and his candor. Very smart boy."

"You keep calling him smart. What did he say or do that made you think that?"

"Hm. Well. I guess it was the people he's chosen to work with."

"A group of political operatives committing war crimes."

Jonquist gave another fatuous smile. "That seems like a rather extreme characterization."

"I'm sure it does. To you. Are you one of the senators who characterized last year's insurrection as 'legitimate political discourse?'"

"We're going to play word games now?"

"I don't believe you're intelligent enough to do that. Take us to our meeting. You're wasting my time."

Jonquist stepped forward and hunched his considerable bulk over her, which surprised me. The man was clearly not adept at reading other people, or perhaps automatically underestimated Asians and/or women. He certainly underestimated this one.

Wenling's right hand shot forward and grabbed his scrotum through his loose dress pants. Twisted it violently.

The big man's face blanched and his knees half-buckled under him as he staggered backward to his desk. He stared back at her with a face that had broken out in a cold sweat and one of his meaty hands slipped quickly down the front of his pants. Maybe to ensure his junk wasn't torn or bleeding.

He winced and grunted, yanking his hand back out again.

"Avery!" he yelled, and the aide who'd let us into the office and had been standing back in a corner of the room in shock now shook herself and ran forward, eyes wide and frightened. "Get me some goddamned ice!"

Wenling snorted. "You will look like you wet yourself."

The senator glared at her. "Ruined my nuts, I'm gonna sue your ass."

"You would have to prove something of value was lost. Are you finished whining?"

"Sir...?" said his aide. "Do you still want me to get some ice?"

Jonquist forced himself to stand up straight. "No, I don't want any goddamned ice! Go find Pahlniuk and get the reports on mine tailings. Have them on my desk before you leave today. When session starts up again next week, we have to be *ready!*" He faced Wenling. "Meanwhile, I have to take some pissants to a meeting where they can argue for the destruction of America."

32

Time travel ripples

He led us down to the basement and onboard a miniature subway train made up of only three cars in red, white, and blue that Jonquist reluctantly told us was run via fully automated linear induction motors in the tracks. Then he entered the front car, which looked like it could seat six people on the two facing benches, and waved the rest of us to take the car behind it.

Wenling, I, and the Colonel did. Wenling sat me beside her with Colonel Jian facing us in the other bench seat. The doors played a four-note ding-dong, close and the cars restarted with the terrifying sound of a massive electrical current dropping into a deep hole.

After a one-minute ride, we rattled into the Capitol basement and came to a scraping, screeching stop.

Something was wrong.

Jonquist got out of his seat ahead of us and, without waiting for us to join him, headed past potted plants and polished columns toward the set of escalators and stairs.

Something... I had a flash of having leaned forward to talk to Colonel Jian.

Except I hadn't done that now. Wenling had jumped up and out of the open subway car doors to follow Jonquist, and I was just sitting here *looking* at Colonel Jian.

As he looked at me. Waiting. "Dr. Traine?"

He reached out his hand to stop the doors from closing.

I shook myself and jumped up and out the doors, Colonel Jian right on my heels, as the doors went through their ding-dong sequence, rumbled closed, and the subway cars started up again with the terrifying electrical current dropping into a deep hole.

But everything I saw and felt and heard around me was blurry. I saw flashes of myself running *away* from Wenling and Jonquist, not...

"Jackson and Jian!" Wenling called to me from halfway up the escalator, her face flushed and impatient as if she'd only just realized we were not right behind her. "Catch up to us now!"

So I ran, the Colonel right behind me, and every step I took, every leap and bound up the escalator to catch up to Wenling and Jonquist, seemed to erase all the other remembered ones that wanted to take me in a different direction like I was that jumble of horses coming out of my patient Cassandra's paddock and heading off in all different directions.

But it was stupidly fuzzy, more like some kind of walking daydream than the kind of clarity with which every moment of my life was documented and...

"JACKSON!"

I gritted my teeth and focused on Wenling's angry, twitching walk ahead of me in her high-heeled black pumps and tight skirt, Jonquist a little further up, finally waiting for us at a turn off into a long, musty, concrete-over-brick tunnel that was lined with nondescript, numbered doors, and pipes and wires running along the ceiling. Also people—Capitol police, various service and mechanical staff, and junior staffers like Jonquist's Avery. At least two of them seemed to intentionally bump into Wenling and hand her something. Were they some of the people she'd paid off in here?

Focus.

And as we joined Jonquist and walked, turning down one long, musty tunnel after another, the fuzzy daydream I'd had at the subway departure faded.

We finally arrived at a gray metal door that looked twice as thick as those around it, with a keypad and what looked like a safe-lock dial over the handle. A Capitol Police officer wearing a mask and a sidearm stood just outside.

The officer gave Jonquist a respectful nod, but Jonquist barely acknowledge him.

The senator punched a number into the keypad, spun the dial over the handle and heaved the double-thick door open.

We followed him through the deep entrance into what was clearly a formal, electronically equipped meeting room, bare but for the long wood table and chairs that filled up most of the space. This wasn't Jonquist's "hideaway" office, which Wenling had been told we'd be visiting. I guessed it was a SCIF, a Sensitive Compartmented Information Facility where senators went to review highly sensitive documents, electronic or otherwise. The builders had probably repeated the thickness of the door in the walls and ceiling to cut out all auditory and electronic leaking from this room.

Colonel Jian entered as the last person and the door shut behind him with an air-compressing thud. Senator Jonquist, I noted, stepped back past me to stand in front of the door with his arms crossed like an overaged bouncer at a nightclub.

I numbly set a timer running in my brain. God knew I didn't want to, but If I *needed* to jump back to before we entered this room, I had just under ten minutes. Or I could do two jumpbacks in a row from roughly twenty minutes out, and it would stagger me for a moment. Or three jumpbacks from thirty minutes, except it would probably knock me down with a heart attack, stroke, seizure, or inability to breathe. I'd been thinking ever since my "dragged back" time jump this morning about why three self-initiated jumps seemed to be my limit. I had the gut sense it had more to do with accumulating all the psychological (and sometimes physical) trauma I needed to generate a jump rather than the actual amount of time my mind lived in another timeline.

Or maybe, using Lena's latest theory, it was the number of timelines jumped through, with each one leaving a quantumly-entangled copy of myself to fight with at every moment going forwards.

It all made me feel sick thinking about it.

Made me wish I'd never learned to time jump at all.

I pushed that away to focus on the now as the three people who'd already been in the room before us stood up. They were two white males and a South Asian female. One of the males and the South Asian women were in their thirties or forties. The other male, clearly the one in command, was tall, slender and graceful in his movements. His pale, smooth skin swept up his skinny neck past a small chin and mouth to like a champagne flute, ending in a high forehead and higher, swept back hair that was shot with gray. Wrinkles crinkled the skin all around his sparkling blue eyes as he squinted at us. I guessed him to be in his late fifties, and...there was something *wrong* about him.

Wenling spoke directly to him. "Doesn't the use of a SCIF get logged somewhere?""

He smiled at her. "That is why our dear Senator Jonquist, of the Select Committee on Intelligence, is here. Official business. He'll prepare some kind of report or other. It will no doubt make him seem relevant to the Committee and important to the fine people of Wyoming. Now why don't we all sit and..."

Wrong. Wrong. Wrong.

I recognized the Arrogant Asshole's voice as he talked. The odd mix of sharp precision and laid-back certainty. Over the phone, he'd had exposed my intentionally imprecise recollection of the *Leviathan* passage burning in the box in the forest.

Wrong. What he was saying. What he was doing.

I blinked and shook my head.

And suddenly the wrongness got very clear.

It was like he was giving two different speeches at once. This one, but also one where he welcomed us all *before* Wenling spoke, paying special attention to me.

Oh shit. *Breathe.*

The earlier double-vision on the train? That was like that first time with Xiaobo in the Demon Monks basement, here and gone the minute I passed the immediate change and got caught in the present purpose. But earlier today, when Kenny had seen me then jumped back in time to tell Colonel Jian? That was like this. When someone had definitively jumped me back in time without my volition.

But why?

Had I tried to kill someone? Had I fought someone? Had Kenny thrown me back again? What?

And why couldn't I see the whole other timeline? What did that mean? WHAT DID IT MEAN?

Breathe!

My chest thundered inside me. Was I going mad finally, my mind constructing alternate awful realities I could no longer tell from the ones I actually lived? Maybe this was claustrophobia from being in this underground, tightly sealed room. Maybe it was dealing yet again with someone who'd already tricked me once, then tried to have me abducted.

"Why would we believe anything you say?" I bellowed over his voice.

Most of the people in the room flinched, but the high forehead man simply turned to stare at me directly. His blue eyes startled me with their intensity.

And it was no longer wrongness. It was experience vs. memory, sharp as all my memories were.

I saw him now, and I saw my memory of him here, confronting me just like this, before. He'd talked to me. He'd made me feel like a lab rat must feel as it watched a scientist approach it with a syringe or other invasive medical device.

In the current timeline, he nodded to me. "Dr. Traine."

"'Just call me Ew-vuh,' you said. You spelled out your name for us. U-W-E. Uwe. Dr. Uwe Bent."

"Did I?"

"The last time we were here."

"When was that?"

"Same time. Different timeline. But...you knew that, didn't you? How?"

He smiled in confirmation, and I felt the room shrinking around me. Oh, God. Another twist in how it all worked. I'd been dragged back by someone else's jump, but it was only when things the jump changed hit me—Colonel Jian telling me about Kenny's call; this Dr. Uwe Bent, changing what he says and does because someone's told him about what happened in a previous future—that my timeline actually split. At least in my awareness. Only when the ripples of change hit me did I become aware of what happened in my other timeline.

"Again, why don't we all sit down and talk about this?" Bent said.

"Yes, we'll do that," Wenling agreed, her voice low with command.

But I was too busy remembering now to answer either of them. Bent had made us sit the last time. I hadn't talked. I'd just let Wenling adjust her designer suit jacket and carry the negotiation. I'd figured she'd carefully thought through how to leverage the threat of me into getting this man to release her brother and my siblings from the SCATTER program.

Instead, I'd listened in horror as it became clear Wenling was trading me for Xiaobo. That was her plan. Full stop.

You think you know what your commander wants. You don't.

I spun to face Wenling in the now. "You played me. You had me prove my power, not as a threat, but to make me a chip you could barter with."

"What are you...?" She let it tail off and she realized I *knew*. Of course I did. I'd been in this room before. Seen her do it.

As she stepped back from me cautiously, I felt my entire body rush with adrenaline. I wanted to slap her. I wanted to shout and attack everyone around me. Most of all, I wanted to run.

But I'd done that last time, hadn't I?

Memory.

It took some time to get to the moment when Wenling made it clear what she was offering for the return of her brother. But when I finally understood I was to be the sacrifice, I ran for the door and took out its guardian, Jonquist, with a kidney strike and roundhouse kick to his head. Twisting the roundhouse in my dress pants and leather-soled shoes, though, had wrecked my balance, so when Bent's two young colleagues leaped on me with metal truncheons they'd drawn from somewhere, I'd already lost. They broke the bones of both my arms and took aking me so violently to the concrete floor that the pain and sheer despair over how I'd been tricked knocked me loose from my body and I time jumped back to...

...just after entering the SCIF. Damn it.

My arms were healed, but I was still trapped. So I gagged, screamed through my mask, and managed a second jump back to...

...just before we'd disembarked from the subway cars we'd ridden over in from the Dirkson building.

I leaned close enough to Colonel Jian in the scraping squeal of the braking and asked for a diversion.

Yes! Yes! That was what happened!

The second the doors opened, the colonel grabbed Wenling and rushed her towards Senator Jonquist, shouting someone on the walkway behind the train had a gun!

I sprinted up through a knot of people coming down the stairs beside the escalator, turned into a different hallway than Jonquist had taken us through in the earlier timeline, and vanished into the maze of corridors at a fast walk, taking turn after turn until the sounds of pursuit faded.

Then I found myself hitting dead end after dead end—some abandoned stone baths, a storage room—and had to fight a claustrophobic panic as I carefully backtracked, swearing under my breath. I followed a man who looked like a waiter and ended passing a narrow set of stairs leading up.

It took me to a long corridor I knew had to be along an outside wall because I saw daylight through an open office window to my left. And far ahead of me, a wide set of doors. It was all I could do to not break into a run, but I got there, through doors, down a broad set of stairs exiting the northeast side of the building, and I was free.

I hurried across the broad concrete-and-brick mall that also hosted parked cars and black limos, endless business suits in dark colors walking to and from the building like me.

The trees were my target. They had to be lining Constitution Avenue. The maps of the city I'd looked at briefly in The George when we'd arrived unrolled in my brain with a little arrow telling me to walk north, vanish into the city, and regroup.

A young man I brushed past grabbed my arm like he'd been waiting for me.

Zhou Xiaobo, no mask.

He was still the acne-scarred young man I remembered from a year earlier, but harder now.. Meaner. And he'd changed his hairstyle to a spiky, punk kind of thing. Frosted tips.

He grinned. "Hey, professor. Going somewhere?"

Then...

Then I was here. In the SCIF for round two.

I looked up to see Uwe Bent watching me with fascination, holding a hand up to keep the others from interrupting my recall. "Is it all straight now? Integrated?"

He was a scientist observing how his experimental rat performed.

Wenling must have seen that, too, because her earlier worry about me knowing her plans had vanished from her face. She knew she'd brought in what Bent wanted. The hidden security she'd paid to follow us to this room and keep us always in sight obviously made her confident Bent couldn't just take it without payment in kind.

Whether she was right, or Bent had ways to take me without giving up Xiaobo, didn't matter. Either way, I was screwed.

Unless I acted.

With full knowledge of the kind of pain I'd be to escape.

Just like the Demon Monks HQ all over again.

But back then, I'd been so innocent. I worried about the accumulation of mental trauma back then, but it was mostly hypothetical.

Until I got out and the explosion of PTSD virtually destroyed my life. It lost me Lena. It almost lost me my sanity. And the hard work coming back from it? It had only worked because I'd avoided using my power like the plague it was.

The side effect was that every jump I did now hurt twice as much. Both because I'd lost any tolerance of the process and because I fully knew the hell trip it was taking me on.

It was like I saw my keys that had fallen through a thin layer of ice on a mountain lake. They glinted at me from fifteen or twenty feet down. I knew with absolute certainty how diving for them was going to shock me, then rip me apart and maybe kill me.

And I'd been feeling so warm.

Fuck.

With no warning sound, I grabbed one of the wooden chairs from the end of the table and accelerated back toward the SCIF entry door, swinging the chair as I went.

The chair, with all my added momentum behind it, hit Jonquist so hard that even his large mass couldn't absorb it and he stumbled to one side, tripped, and felt.

I spun with my back to the door to meet the expected charges of Thing One and Thing Two, the He and She companions of Dr. Bent, their metal truncheons out and swinging. They cracked against the chair legs and, before they had time to fully adjust, I rammed the chair at the male of the pair, then jumped back to twist the SCIF's door handle and yank.

Locked!

Of course it was.

Then the female Thing hit my right trapezius with a downward blow of her truncheon that felt like a bolt of Zeus. I felt my breastbone crack and something separate in there as my knees collapsed under me and I went down, banging and scraping my face against the door, blood spraying from my nose.

Bent's voice was shouting, "Stop!" from somewhere, but I think the male Thing had already committed to his own berserker attack after knocking aside my ramming chair. He landed on me with a knee and hard-soled shoe, cracking something in my rib cage and swinging for my head.

There are the keys!

My head exploded in pain and my mind jumped hard.

33

The House is adjourned

I WAS IN THE basement corridor, walking.

I stumbled as my mind tried to remember what I was doing, where I was, when I was. Wenling, walking beside me, shot me an annoyed glance, but Colonel Jian strode forward and grabbed my elbow to steady me.

"Thank you," I murmured, recovering myself as Wenling hurried to catch up to where Jonquist had stopped to salute the guard in front of the heavy SCIF door.

"Are you ill?" Jian asked me.

"No. Cover me, please." So saying, I turned and loped as quietly as I could back in the direction we'd come from.

Distracted by the interaction at the SCIF door, neither Wenling nor Jonquist noticed my retreat until I was around the first corner I hit. I heard a vague uproar, but not running steps. Presumably Colonel Jian was telling them I had to find a bathroom or some such.

I hit another T in the hallway, turned left again, and kept moving in a quick march, like some Senator's aide on important business. Maybe even a C-suite exec or lobbyist. You wore an expensive suit and tie and you could be anyone.

A few more turns and I found an elevator that took me up two floors, letting me out into a hallway just off the Rotunda, where one of the general tours was underway. Keeping my brusque manner, I walked through the crowd, fighting the urge to look up and admire the dome high overhead. I bulled on under a set of stone archways into one of the marble-floored hallways on the south side and slowed just enough to casually glance into any of the offices with open doors.

Maybe ten offices in, I found an open door with a room with a couch, chairs, and a desk that looked momentarily deserted. Taking a chance, I slipped in and closed the door behind me. Locked it.

I walked to the heavyset desk.

Loads of folders, papers, books, a computer. A frigging landline phone.

I picked up the phone's handset and heard no dial tone. Pressed nine. Nothing.

Swearing under my breath, I looked around on the offhand chance that whoever had been sloppy or trusting enough to leave their office with the door open and unattended might just have left a procedures manual for...

I stopped and smiled. No procedures manual, but a sticky note on the side of the phone reminded the user how to reach an outside line.

A moment later, Jude's cell phone was ringing on the other end of the line. He answered. The roaring in the background told me he was in a car. When I told him who it was, he snapped, "I've been trying to call you for the last hour. Whose phone are you calling from?"

"I don't know. Some congressman in the Capitol."

"I thought you said you meeting a Senator."

"We did. Things went bad, but I escaped. Now I'm in a congressman's office."

"Ha. Ha. Which one?"

I looked through the papers on the desk, but go the most direct info from a wooden box of branded pens that whoever worked at this desk obviously liked to give out to visitors. When I saw whose office I was in, I almost burst out laughing.

I told Jude, and he snorted. "Seriously?"

"Needed a phone. They made us give up ours back at the Dirkson building."

"Holy shit, you're serious."

"They're chasing me."

"Dude. I feel horrible. Stuck in bridge traffic. Twenty minutes maybe."

"Shit. Okay. Okay." I reviewed in my head the city maps I'd seen at the George this morning. "Approach on Maryland Avenue Southwest or Pennsylvania Avenue Northwest. They both have lots of street parking near the Capitol Reflecting Pool. I'll be near the pool on the west side. Hang out near the middle and I'll find you."

"But, but, whoah…" Jude's voice sounded panicky.

"What?"

"Can't you just…go to the police?"

"Right. Okay. You know what? Forget it. Stupid to drag you into this."

I started to hang up, but Jude shouted into his phone. "No! No, sorry! I'll be there. I said I'd be there. Things look like they're clearing. Fifteen and change."

I couldn't help the sudden sob of relief. I cut it off when the doorknob I'd locked behind me started rattling. "Thanks. Gotta run."

I replaced the phone, took a deep breath, and went to the door. Someone was muttering and jingling on the other side of it, finding their key. My gaze shot around the office.

Hide behind the couch? No. I only had fifteen minutes "and change" to get out of here, around to the west side of the building, and across maybe half a mile of parkland and concrete through crowds and traffic to reach the western edge of the Capitol Reflecting Pool before Jude showed up.

So no hiding.

Also no messing with explaining myself to some Capitol Police Officer if the congressman decided to throw a fit at my trespass.

Which left creative lying. Not my best skill, but one I'd gotten pretty good at after years of explaining why I couldn't look people in the eye or attend any social events, why I spontaneously started sweating or blinking away tears in the middle of intense discussions with someone, why I'd flinch at things and have to fight off panic attacks over things most people barely noticed.

I reached the lock of the door, flicked it unlocked, and pulled the door open.

34

False spring

On the other side of the door's threshold, the stunned face of the congressman I'd seen way too many times on CNN blinked at me and opened his mouth for a characteristic attack.

I held my finger to my lips. "Shhh. Hey, look. Didn't mean to go all secretive in this, but you-know-who—young, pretty, says she catches you looking—made me bring you something of hers that's really 'personal.' I stuck it in one of your bottom drawers so no one else stumbles on it."

"What the hell are you talking about?"

I held up my hands like they were totally clean and pointedly whispered again. "Nothing at all, sir." I turned sideways and slid by him, but shot a meaningful look in at his desk. "Nothing. At. All."

"You stay right there," the man ordered gruffly, his chin sticking out in that pugnacious way he had. But he wasn't going to actually hold me there or cause a ruckus. Not until he checked out what I'd actually left him in his desk. I could almost see his imagination working across his forehead as he thought it through.

He strode quickly toward his desk, and I ran hard for the nearest stairs down.

Last thing I heard before I descended was desk drawers opening and banging shut. Opening and banging shut.

At the bottom, I saw an exit sign, ran for it, and was outside into what I'd forgotten was a bright day.

I squinted my eyes through the sun, picked out my directions, and headed along the side of the building, heading for the Reflecting Pool and, hopefully, my ride out.

The temperature had to be 50°, more spring than midwinter, and even though I'd held back from an all-out run, I was sweating profusely inside my suit by the time I reached the pool's south side and joined the tourists there. I felt like I had a target on my back. Or at least SCATTER goons with binoculars tracking my movements.

No one stopped me, though, as I made my way to roughly the middle of the pool's south edge and faded backwards into the relative camouflage of a leafless elm tree.

No one running in my direction.

No one yelling to find me.

Had I actually escaped?

Like the still water in the Reflecting Pool, the ice had thawed. Spring was here. Time for rebirth. New plans. Second chances.

I checked my watch, conscious it was almost an anachronism in my generation, or at least among my students. A useful one, though, since my phone was back in the Dirkson building's security lockup.

Assuming Jude had given me an accurate, vs. wildly optimistic, estimate of his travel time here. He could show up at any moment. I just had to calm my still-thudding heart and figure out what my next move was once he—

"Hey, professor," said a sly voice from just behind me.

My heart fell into my stomach. I turned around.

Xiaobo stood leering at me.

"How'd you find me this time?"

He cocked his head and tugged at his spiky hair, pushing it around in some kind of clear self-soothing behavior. "Ain't too smart, yo. They're watching you. Second you enter the Capitol, they be on you like a bitch. All the way out here. Leave it me choose the time and place."

"Like you're Bent's key operative."

"*Doctor* Bent, stupid."

"Except he's negotiating with your sister right now to give you back to her."

"Fuck say?"

"In return for me. Maybe cause I'm more reliable?"

"Fuck that!" Xiaobo reached out and grabbed my arm.

35

Wheels within wheels

THE AUTOMATIC SUBWAY CAR that took us from the Dirkson building rattled and bumped us about on its utilitarian seats, Wenling and I facing Colonel Jian, the back of Jonquist's head showing through the large windows of the front subway car ahead of us. Flashing by us on our right were a series of stiff little flags I gathered represented every state in the union. I wasn't actually counting.

Then the automatic train started to slow with a scraping, screeching, electric whine—the ride had taken all of about one minute from the Dirkson to here—and suddenly I was swimming in three different versions of this reality.

In this one, I was seeing, hearing, and feeling the train come to a stop, ready to rise and follow Wenling out of the car.

In another, I was hesitating, experiencing some kind of flashback, so that Wenling finally got up by herself and Colonel Jian had leaned forward with concern. *"Dr. Traine?"*

In the last, I was fully remembering the me in the second me's flashback. I'd just jumped back twice to escape from...from...the SCIF!

Suddenly, all of the two previous visits here and escape attempts broke into my conscious fully formed, the way I *usually* remembered things. And with that, as the subway car doors rumbled open, I had a *satori,* the Japanese Buddhist term for awakening or instant knowing, that seemed to blow open a new understanding of the universe.

If Lena had been there, I would have jumped up in excitement and fear and babbled out everything. Begged her to tell me it was right. Or wrong. Something.

The key was that with multiple time travelers, you could have timeline splits within bigger timeline splits, and to locate yourself, you had to focus on the biggest timeline splits first.

For me that meant focusing on what Xiaobo had done.

From his point of view, I'd been in Timeline One when I rode all the way into the SCIF the first time, jumped back twice (two small splits within Timeline One) to where I had Colonel Jian distract the others so I could escape out of the Senate wing only to meet Xiaobo and get thrown back to...when?

The beginning of Xiaobo's day. That's what Wenling had said—he always jumped back to the beginning of his day. Which presumably carried me back that far, too.

I'd then been in Timeline Two.

Except, apparently, I didn't automatically remember everything when the jump was done to me vs. by me. At least, not until I became of aware of something in Timeline Two that was different from what I'd experienced in Timeline One.

In Timeline Two, I'd hit that point when getting off the Dirkson subway car because in Timeline One, I'd jumped back to that point and started my escape out of the building. In Timeline Two, my subconscious memory of that escape, of that *different reality*, had made me stumble as my subconscious memory had noticed something different.

But I hadn't yet had enough experience with the dragged-back jumps to fully grasp what was happening.

Until Dr. Uwe Bent also behaved differently than in Timeline One. (Presumably because Xiaobo had told him of my escape and how Xiaobo had reset the timeline.) My subconscious noticed the difference and all the memories of Timestream One had flooded back.

I'd escaped again. Xiaobo had found me by the Reflecting Pool and grabbed my arm.

So I was now in Timeline Three, my memory of the other timelines brought back in the same time and place of the Dirkson subway car arrival when I'd 1) simply risen to leave, 2) gasped, and, with heart hammering from a self-instigated jump, ran to escape, 3) stayed sitting, almost-but-not-quite remembering my previous escape attempt here.

"Catch up!" Wenling shouted back at me as she strode after Jongquist across the stone floor.

I finally realized the subway doors were fully open, with Colonel Jian holding them, apparently to make sure I had time to process whatever I was going through.

I jumped to my feet and out the doors, with Colonel Jian right behind me. But rather than run after Wenling, I grabbed Colonel Jian and leaned in close to have my words covered by the *Ding-dong-ding-dong* and rumble of the subway doors closing again.

"I have to separate from the group. Can you cover for me? Give me some lead time before they chase me."

Colonel Jian nodded with his usual serious expression, but this time I could somehow feel in his nod all the weight of his decision to help me. The mystery of that drowned in the still-terrifying sound of a giant electrical current being sucked into a hole as the subway cars revved up again and left the platform.

I slipped sideways to the stairway on the far side of where Jonquist, Wenling, and now Colonel Jian were ascending. Except, as I paused in the shadow of a pillar to watch, Jonquist reached the top of the escalator, stepped to one side, stopped and waited, hands crossed over his chest. He seemed unsurprised that I wasn't coming up the escalator behind them. Nor did he visibly react to whatever Colonel Jian told him.

What the—

A hand soft hand fell on my arm and I turned to see a sweet-faced young woman in a dark suit with a high-necked blouse. "Are you Dr. Traine?"

"Am I... Yes." My brain clicked through every woman her age I'd met, talked with, gone to school with, counseled, taught. It came up blank. "We've never met."

She smiled. "We just did."

I felt something sharp jab my butt and I spun around to see the sweet-face woman had a partner who was significantly less sweet looking. Twenties. Big-boned. Eyes too close together. His hand was inside his suit jacket breast pocket. "Hey, doc," he said.

Surprised my adrenaline had barely spiked, I looked back and forth between them. "What do you want?"

"We're taking you to meet Dr. Bent," said the guy.

"And what if I don't want to meet *Uh*-vay?" I frowned, but it felt fake.

"Now, Dr. Traine," the sweet-faced woman cooed. "Don't be like that." Her voice echoed a bit in my ears. In fact, all the sounds of this subway exit were kind of blending and echoing and taking a kind of visual resonance, like flowing colors.

"Be like what?" I asked. Hunh. My voice sounded kind of floaty too.

"Why don't we just walk this way a bit and we'll talk about it as we go." The woman tugged my elbow.

So I walked with her and her male buddy. It seemed the polite thing to do. And it was kind of nice to have a direction, because all the flowing sounds and colors of things made it really hard to focus.

I stumbled a bit and laughed. Even my legs and feet were having trouble focusing. It gave me a momentary flashback to March of last year when Dead Eyes, Detective Gillespie, put some stuff in my tea that knocked me out. Never did find out what that was.

"Roofies?" I mumbled as I walked.

"Oh no," said the sweet face who'd wrapped both her arms around mine to steady me as we walked. It was a pleasant feeling. Very intimate. "Benzodiazapine drugs last way too long in your system and can leave you totally unresponsive. You probably remember that from your studies."

"Sure sure."

"So we just gave you a bit of ketamine. Different people react differently, but you're reacting great!"

Her mouth and nose rippled as she said it and she gave my arm a squeeze.

I returned a huge, goofy smile. She was really proud of me. It had been so long since a pretty girl was proud of me. Since anyone was proud of me.

Then, honestly, I lost track of whether we were even walking as things slid around in my head.

When I regained full awareness, I think it was my own snoring that woke me. My head jerked up. I tried to reach for my face and couldn't.

I blinked.

I was tied to a chair pulled up at the SCIF's long wooden table. To my left sat Zhou Wenling and Colonel Jian. At the end of the table, Senator Jonquist sat like an impartial judge. Across from me were Things One and Two and from when I'd been here before. Young man and woman like the young man and woman who'd brought me here from the subway platform stairs. Uwe Bent obviously like the boy-girl dynamic, whether in collections or personal protection.

Bent himself was on his feet, walking around with his left arm wrapped around his middle, his right braced on it, right hand covering his receded chin as his fingers moved back and forth on his lower lip.

Self-soothing gestures. He was being challenged by something.

"If you don't, I will expose you," said Wenling beside me. "The program. You. Senator Jonquist."

Bent moved his hand from his mouth, something decided. "Thank you for bringing Dr. Traine to us."

"I have put in place...protections."

"I don't see any. Unless you mean Fang Jian here, former Colonel in the People's Liberation Army. Fought in India and Vietnam, helped suppress all those deadly students in Tiananmen Square." He fixed his gaze on Wenling. "I still have connections in intelligence. Do you think anything you do is a surprise?"

Wenling returned his gaze with such darkness in her eyes I felt a chill run through me. Her words were ice. "You don't know me."

Bent smiled. "Oh, but I do. You fought and clawed your way out of poverty by exchanging favors, by learning how to manipulate people with threats and money. Everything is transactional for you. Everyone can be bought. To prepare for this meeting, you paid off people all through the Capitol, including, I assume, some of the Capitol Police. One of them has no doubt already replaced the guard outside this SCIF. But remember, my dear, that they are outside this room. Whatever happens *inside* this room will be told by whoever emerges from it."

Wenling's upper lip snarled silently, and I saw Jonquist, at the end of the table, blanch and reach for his crotch.

"Cute." Bent waved a hand and spoke to Things One and Two. "Handcuff Dr. Traine then cut him free. Handcuff Ms. Zhou and the

Colonel as well. Prepare for resistance when we leave the room should their forces exceed ours."

While Wenling sat in icy stillness, Things One and Two came for me, pulled my hands further back behind me on the chair, slapped cuffs around my wrists, then began cutting through the rope they'd tied me with.

"What are doing?" I finally blurted, my tongue feeling strange and swollen.

Bent turned to me. "We're taking you all back to one of our labs. We'll eventually let Ms. Zhou and the Colonel depart, maybe after a brief meeting with her brother. You, however, will be with us for an extended stay."

Wenling still hadn't moved, I thought. Then I saw the vague glint of something black and dark down by her hands in her lap, and I finally understood what she was about to do.

As Thing One pulled my chair back from the table so I could stand, I pleaded with Bent as I rose. "You don't want to do this. Really."

"Actually, Dr. Traine, I really—"

Wenling's left hand grabbed the table to give her more force as she whipped her right hand in a slightly rising arc that drove her black-bladed knife deep into my gut.

Even expecting it, I yelled out in pain and staggered back over my falling chair and a confused Thing One. Then I was on the ground and Wenling was on top of me, with Thing Two on top of her, wrestling with her as the weight of both women drove the knife in so deep it felt like it was stabbing my spine, slicing my flesh and internal organs as the struggling weight of women ground it back and forth and all around.

Through my terror at the pain and wave of blackness, I smelled Wenling's flowers and citrus and dank rage as she screamed into my face, "DO YOUR JUMP NOW!"

I complied.

36

Panic never helps

I WAS IN THE chair.

I was tied to the chair.

Was it a chair?

The ceiling above raced with color. The sounds around me blobbed and globbed through my ears and nose and mouth. I. Tasted. Burnt plastic!

My mind. I couldn't hold onto my mind. My thoughts.

I couldn't hang on. I was losing my mind. *Losing my MIND!*

Dissociate! Do it!

Now...

I was on my feet in a hallway. Gray. Concrete over brick. Sliding over brick like thick molasses.

Where? What?

Stomach queasy.

I tasted molasses.

A being of bones and pink flesh had my arm. "Come on, Dr. Traine. Let's keep walking."

Except her words were all slurred.

My walk was slurred.

My thoughts were slurred.

Oh God, I can't focus. Can't...

I'VE BEEN DRUGGED!

Help me!
HELP ME...

Colonel Jian's hard old face was close to mine as he nodded like he'd just agreed to something.

The air shook with the terrifying sound of a massive electrical current dropping into a deep hole.

My heart seized.

I grabbed at it, scrabbling through my shirt and tie like I could rip them open and save myself. Because I also couldn't breathe. My blood had all rushed to my head making my vision red. My muscles started jumping and spasming all over my body and I crashed to the floor.

"I...can't..."

The stone under my cheek was gritty and hard and cold as I swept back and forth over it, unable to control my spasms, unable to speak anymore through the pain and frothing in my mouth.

But I fought to hold onto my consciousness. Last year I'd managed to survive three jumps in a row long enough to text Lena. And later, four jumps in a row, with short breaks in between them to adapt a bit.

I could survive this.

I could...somehow.

Then arms were under me, lifting me. Which had to be Colonel Jian, though how such an old man had the strength, I didn't know.

Not that I could know much of anything at that point. Couldn't see. Could barely think.

The blackness closed in.

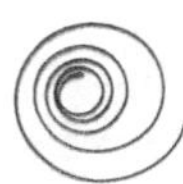

I woke up wearing a surgical mask in some emergency ward.

"The Kaiser Permanente Capitol Hill Medical Center," said a similarly masked woman with a British accent. She sat in a chair by my holding bed.

Pearl earrings and choker, black jacket over a white blouse. Wenling, of course, but for a second my heart had jumped, thinking it was Lena. That I'd been stupid enough to jump three times in a row, almost kill myself, and Lena had come for me. We'd discuss what happened. I'd share my theory that it was the amount of trauma I couldn't integrate with three jumps, not the time. We'd reset our relationship.

"They canceled the meeting," Wenling said, eyes cold.

"I'm fine now. Thanks for asking."

"The doctor was in five minutes before you woke up. He said all your signs were normal and you have no indications of damage. Did you fake the heart attack?"

"No. Lena never told you about these?"

Wenling frowned. "She did not."

"I guess you weren't as close as you thought."

Inside, the fact Lena had kept at least this just between us made me absurdly happy, but I squelched it to deal with more pressing matters. Seeing the thinness of the cloth privacy screen that separated us from the view of staff and other patients, I lowered my voice. "We don't want to meet Bent in a SCIF. Or anywhere no one else can see us."

"Because..." She stopped and her angry eyes open wider in understanding. She lowered her voice, too. "Who is 'Bent?'"

"The guy in charge of SCATTER that you've been talking to. Dr. Uwe Bent." I spelled Uwe for her.

She nodded. "What happened?"

"Which time?"

"How many times?"

"Three so far."

"You are resetting it each time?"

I shook my head. "Your brother. Something bad happens and I jump. I escape. He finds me because Bent has as many people watching us in the Capitol as you do. Xiaobo hits reset and we go through it again."

Wenling was listening intently. "Why did you not tell me before we went to the Capitol?"

"It doesn't work like that. I only 'remember' the earlier timelines once I hit something that's different. Xiaobo jumps and when he lands in the past, it causes ripples of change with everything he does because it's all different, a new timeline. But if he stays far away from me, those ripples don't affect me and I don't realize I've lived a different timeline. You were right about that.

"At least, I *think* that's what happens. Anyway, when I hit something where the ripples hit me, I remember the previous timelines."

She gave a single nod, understanding immediately something that had totally blown my mind and that I still had a hard time working through. It had to be all those years dealing with her brother's jumps. She couldn't be *that* much smarter than me.

Then she hit me with the question I thought I'd danced past. "What bad things happened?"

You sold me out, I wanted to say bluntly. *And you knifed me. Again.*

But I wasn't in a position where I could separate myself from her and still access Bent. And as much as I never wanted to see that monster again, he was the way to Kenny and Kansas. So instead, I said, "Bent has no plans to negotiate. He just wants me. That's what all his backup force in the Capitol building is about. The last timeline, I never even got to the SCIF before they drugged and abducted me."

She looked at me closely, probably wondering how much of her own "negotiating" position I'd seen. Deciding I wasn't planning to run, regardless, she reached down beside her chair, pulled up a plastic bag, and plopped it onto my mid-section.

I reached inside and found both my little Nokia phone and my holstered Sig. The phone, thankfully, still had a charge.

"I need to make a private call," I told Wenling.

"Lena?" she asked.

"No."

Wenling waited a moment for me to tell her who I was calling. Maybe she was also trying to find a reason I should not, or why she should be privy to the call.

When she came up empty, she gave a huff and stormed away from my bed, throwing the privacy curtain recklessly aside as she left the ward.

I looked at the time and saw it was later than I'd called Jude in the last timeline, but I didn't know if that meant he'd be farther or closer to where I was now. When I reached him, it turned out it was about the same. When I mentioned I was trying to avoid another meeting with Dr. Uwe Bent, he sounded like he'd just shat himself. He obviously knew the name of the "genius psychiatrist" who'd run the SCATTER. There was no video chat to actually see that happen, but I could almost smell it.

He said he'd be by to pick me up in twenty minutes. I told him to wait by the front or circle the block because I had to shake someone first.

"Lena?" Jude asked.

"Why in hell would I want to shake Lena?"

"Self-sabotaging behavior."

"Have you not heard a word I said about us breaking up?"

Jude scoffed. "I listen with my heart, padawan."

"Well, get here in less than twelve parsecs, okay?"

"Cutting corners?"

"Dude!" I hissed. "The enemies' gate is down!"

"Leeeeeroyyyy *Jenkins!*"

I laughed, hung up and called to a passing nurse, asking where I could get my clothes and check out. She said my clothes were in a bag under my bed, and she'd send the doctor around.

Two minutes later, I was dressed and debating whether to wait for the doctor or just walk out now before Wenling came back to check on me.

That choice died when a figure in running shoes and scrubs, wearing a mask and cap like he'd just come out of surgery, walked up to my bed and pulled the privacy curtain around us.

He sat on the bed beside me, pulled off his mask, and I saw it was Xiaobo, scowling at me.

"Details, yo."

I dropped my head. "Shit. Of what?"

"How my sister's negotiating to yank me back."

"For me. Yeah. Sure." I closed my eyes for a second, though that was only for show. I never had to reach for memories when I knew the where and when I was remembering. When I opened them, I nodded and whispered, "Here's what your sister said in Timeline One, the SCIF, before I jumped back in time twice and you jumped me outside the northeast entrance. Exact words: 'This is why we showed you what Dr. Traine can do. This is why you agreed to meet.'"

"That don't mean shit," Xiaobo whispered back, which I assumed meant he wanted to hear more.

"Your boss, Dr. Bent, replied, 'Why would I want to give up one of my most eager travelers for someone who doesn't want to work with me?'

"Your sister said, 'Because Xiaobo is inconsistent, isn't he? He gets tired and doesn't want to jump back when you tell him to? And sometimes he does not understand what it is you are asking him to do. He has little education. He has learned his numbers but does not know how to handle people. He has few manners. People do not *like* him. But Dr. Traine is very smart, educated and polished in his manners. He can fit in anywhere. Talk with anyone. And he has the Traine memory so he can tell when things have changed.'

"And Dr. Bent replied, 'All true.'" I stopped and looked Xiaobo straight in the eyes. "It was at that point that I jumped back in time twice to escape."

There was a long silence as I watched Xiaobo. He looked emotionally collapsed, but then he raised his head and laughed nastily in my face. "He's *playing* you, homie. Gonna take you and keep me, yo."

Before I had a chance to respond, he grabbed my arm and...

37

The sales pitch

ALL THOSE STATE FLAGS flashing by on the Dirkson subway wall. Colors and shapes. They distracted me from the annoying sight of Senator Jonquist's head in the lead car ahead of us on this little trip.

I was vaguely aware of Wenling's floral and citrus scent from beside me and Colonel Jian's stolid expression from his seat across from us, as the automatic train started to slow with a scraping, screeching, electric whine.

And all of a sudden, I saw myself getting ready to stand up, and myself leaning forward to speak with Colonel Jian, and myself stuck stiffly in place trying to process everything. All of the previous three timelines were suddenly present, all so clear that I wanted to scream with the sense of multiple-reality disorder. Which *I* didn't get to control. It was being done *to* me. It was a totally other kind of trauma on top of everything else and I'd had enough. Screw social anxiety, social propriety, PTSD, and even basic survival instincts.

I jumped up from my seat even before Wenling and was out the door the second it opened and I ran up beside Jonquist, mirroring his shaggy, former quarterback walk, until he looked at me in annoyance. I yanked off my mask and shoved it into my pants pocket.

"When did you give up your soul?" I asked.

"What?"

"Working with a psychopath like Bent. You know what he's doing, right? Killing people? Regime change? And using kids to do it against their will. Brothers and sisters. Old people. Refugees. He doesn't give a shit. Do you give a shit?"

"I don't know what you're—"

"Oh, shut the fuck up, you fucking politician! Is it votes? Money? Power? Or are you just an ideologically twisted, dumbfuck extremist who's going to 'do what's right' no matter how much it hurts the cannon fodder you throw into it?"

"Listen you little punk..."

"Go ahead, call over a Capitol Police officer. I'll lead them to the SCIF. Sound good?"

Jonquist blanched as badly as he had in the last timeline when Wenling got angry. Probably made worse by the fact Wenling and Colonel Jian had finally caught up to us. We were standing at the bottom of the escalator, impeding the way of busy politicians and staffers who pushed by us, muttering.

Jonquist turned on Wenling. "How the hell do you know we're going to a SCIF? I just set that up this morning."

Out of the corner of my eye, I caught movement from up the far-left flight of stairs. A sweet-face woman in a dark-blue suit and her big-boned partner were moving against the crowd around them to cut to the down elevator just to our left.

I turned and pointed to them, calling over the crowd. "Over here, darling! Make sure you bring enough ketamine for everyone!"

The two paused, looked at each other, and kept coming.

Wenling leaned in close to me. "What is this about? Have you been here before?"

"Oh, yes."

"How many times?"

"This is number four."

"Should we turn back?"

"Definitely not! I'm all in on this. We're going to make it work this time!"

Know your commander and what they want from you.
Check!
Know what you want.
Save my siblings.
Know what you are able to do.
Still figuring that out.
Know what you are willing to do.
Gonna find out.

A Capitol Police Officer was coming down the steps toward us as well, but Jonquist waved him off. "It's under control."

The officer stopped uncertainly and walked to one side of the steps. He tried to be discrete as he pulled up his walkie and spoke into it.

I grinned. "Figure we got about four minutes before this place is swarming with Capitol Police, Senator. Shall we proceed to the SCIF? I'll lead."

So saying, I started up the escalator without looking back. I did have a chuckle at the ketamine duo who were halfway down the neighboring escalator by then. "See you up there," I whispered loudly at them and pointed at the top.

Then I was turning into the first of the long, dank concrete-over-brick tunnels that led to the SCIF where Dr. Uwe Bent was waiting. I hesitated just long enough to turn and confirm that Jonquist, Wenling, Colonel Jian, and the ketamine duo were following behind me. I suspected the Capitol Hill officer was, too, just a little further back. Probably wondering what strange form of insanity was brewing in the Capitol basement among this most unlikely gaggle of suited politicos.

Because I kept up a blistering pace compare to the times Jonquist had been leading, we reached the sealed SCIF door in what seemed like minutes. Jonquist came puffing up to the front and talked with the Capitol Security officer posted there. The guard stepped aside and Jonquist entered the code, spun the dial, and pulled open the thick door.

In we went.

I walked straight up to Bent and stuck out my hand.

A little uncertainly, he took it and we shook.

"Dr. Bent, I'm Dr. Jackson Traine. But you know that already, don't you? You already had my office and apartment trashed, looking to get as much information about me as you could. Maybe shake me up a bit. Make me think you were connected to the CIA. Which you were at one point, until they figured out you were a psychopath."

Bent nodded, amused. "In a manner of speaking."

"DSM-V speaking. Yes. Explains why you and Zhou Wenling get along so well."

The others had filed in behind me by this time. Except for the ketamine twins. I had the feeling they were lower on the SCATTER pecking order, possibly even just muscle for hire on this day in the same way Wenling had hired various Capitol staffers to follow, watch, and protect us. I wondered if they managed the bump they'd one in the last timelines where they'd handed her the knife and whatever else.

"Jackson...," Wenling began in her low voice of command.

I looked at her. "No. Shut up. You had your chance multiple times to do the right thing and you failed. I am not yours to offer to anyone. And Xiaobo doesn't want to leave SCATTER and go home with you. No judgement here on that, but again, see the DSM-V about narcissistic personality disorders to get a clue why."

As Wenling stepped back, momentarily speechless, Thing One and Thing Two both stepped forward with inquiring glances at Bent. They probably wanted to know if they should be drawing out their metal truncheons.

Bent shook his head at them and turned to Jackson again. "What is it you propose to do here, Dr. Traine?"

I looked at him dead in the eye and for just a second, all my old habits of social anxiety flared up and I found myself blinking rapidly, tears starting to form. I looked down and internally shouted at myself to GET A FUCKING PAIR OF BALLS.

Harsh, but what I needed at this particular moment.

The tears were still in my eyes when I looked up and met Bent's gaze again, but I didn't care because the will and drive to get what I needed was pushing me through.

What are you willing to do to get what you want?

At least this much.

"We're going to negotiate," I said.

"All right. What are you offering and what do you want in return?"

I swallowed hard. "I'll leave you with Xiaobo and I won't bring SCATTER down."

"How generous of you."

"In return, you'll release both my brother and my sister."

"You assume I have them."

"If you don't, you have nothing at all to offer me."

Bent smiled and half turned from him. It was almost like the Mona Lisa smile Wenling used when trying to decide on the answer to a difficult question. With Bent, though, it lasted only a second before he nodded. "Of course I have them."

"So?"

"I'm willing to release your sister. For all her memory gifts and intelligence, she has no ability to time travel like you, or sense time travelers, like your brother."

I narrowed my eyes at him. What that sounded like was Bent revealing he didn't know Kenny at all. He had my old take that Kenny was as some kind of seer who could sense time travel events, not travel himself.

I nodded slowly. "Releasing Kansas would be a good start. A show of good faith."

"Excellent! Just as leaving us Xiaobo and agreeing not to 'bring SCATTER down' is a good starting position for you."

I bit my tongue and thought for a moment. The room was silent. The air, tense. Then Wenling cried out like she was being torn apart. "You cannot keep Xiaobo! He is my brother! He belongs with family!"

Bent nodded at Thing One and Thing Two, who stepped to either side of her and 'encouraged' her to sit, ironically, in the same chair she'd negotiated from in the last three timelines.

I crossed my arms over my chest, knowing how it looked but unable to stop myself. "So release Kansas."

Bent raised his eyebrows. "Now? Just like that?"

"Now. Just like that."

Bent smiled. "Okay. Come with me. Everyone else, stay here. Tony, I need the keys to your hideaway." He held out his hand to Jonquist, who grudgingly dug into his pants pocket, pulled out a ring of keys, and separated one of them, which he handed to Bent.

Key held up to me, Bent went to the door of the SCIF, opened it, and led me outside, where the same Capitol Police officer still stood guard, along with the ketamine twins. The Capitol Police officer from the subway platform had apparently decided not to follow us, or had and met resistance at the SCIF.

Bent pointed to the ketamine twins. "You two follow us and stand guard outside the office we're going to.

And we walked.

I understood the choice when we arrived at the nondescript door in another nondescript concrete-over-brick tunnel. It had only been two hallways over and was far more comfortable than the SCIF.

Other than the lack of windows, it reminded me a lot of the second-floor office on the House side that I'd entered to make a phone call two timelines back—comfortable couch and chairs, expensive desk with phone and computer, broadloom carpet, pictures on the walls, knickknacks on the bookshelves and side tables.

"I wasn't about to use the SCIF phones for this," Bent said once we were inside with the door locked behind us. "And cell phones won't work in there."

He pulled out his own phone, dialed a number, waited, and gave a detailed set of instructions to his assistant on the other end, who apparently kept asking for clarifications. Probably because SCATTER never let people go. Something had to be very wrong here.

When he was done, though, Bent turned back to me with a tired smile on his face. "My people who took your computer from your apartment said it contained an interesting, dedicated communications protocol. Beyond NSA level encryption. They wondered if it was how you talked with your sister, but couldn't find the key you'd have to have to enter the shifting passcode. They theorized the key might be an entire page of nonsense text, numbers, and symbols."

"Yes."

"Not realizing, of course, that both you and sister could easily memorize such a page almost at a glance and never forget it."

"Your point?"

"I ordered her released to NSA's protected-persons program. She should be safe in their cold, digitally obsessed arms within the half hour. At which point, I've had my people tell her, you will attempt to contact her from a borrowed computer, using the codes and protocols you two agreed on. I'm told they'll loan your sister a secure room and internet connection and she will know how to somehow receive from whatever address you contacted her at before."

"So we wait."

"Yes." Bent began wandering around Jonquist's office, fingering the man's possessions and looking at various papers and books the senator had left lying around like Bent might be able to discern more of the man's soul. Or it might just have been to distract me, as he was stroking a glass figurine of two lovers entwined when he casually said, "You know the only thing I want from you is you, don't you?"

"Pardon?"

"Leaving Xiaobo with me, not exposing us—they're empty bargaining chips. Xiaobo was never going to leave. We're too well hidden for you to expose us. And we have enough co-opted players in this building today that we can forcibly abduct you at any time."

"You think so."

"I know so." He turned to me, not smiling this time. His bright blue eyes were serious, his high forehead drawn down over them. "Oh, Xiaobo has told us about your previous 'escapes.' It just means that you keep adding to the timelines in which you're working for SCATTER unwillingly. Wouldn't you like to see what happens in one where you volunteer?"

His casual confirmation of Lena's coexistent, quantum-entangled, continuing timelines made me want to gag and sit down. He knew? He knew that every jump I made, I just left another version of myself behind in some horrific circumstance. It was like I'd been masochistically multiplying my traumas across whatever this existence was.

And for what? What did it gain me? If I battled through all the carnage and finally freed Kansas and my brother, only one version of each of us walked out of the wreckage.

Bent had waved a hand and opened his mouth like he was about to take something back, but my obvious horror over his last statement made him pause.

He tilted his head at me, his eyes actually kind. "Come, come. It's not as bad as all that. The number of tormented you's are limited by the number of time travelers you interact with and the number of jumps you do yourself. Also by the choices you make."

I swallowed and pursed my lips tight, hating myself for feeling the flicker of hope I'm sure Bent was trying to offer me.

"Really," Bent said, smiling again, but with encouragement now, not amusement. "Think about what it would mean to join a team that's been exploring the nature of time and our relationship with it for almost fourteen years now."

"Salim Noor al-Rashid."

"He was the first!" Bent's smile grew wider. "How did you—? Oh, through your sister, of course. If she were interested in helping us, her intelligence and experience with analyzing signals intelligence would have been so useful. But threats and coercion rarely produce top results, particularly from the gifted."

"And yet you keep trying."

"Sadly, yes. In the pursuit of a greater understanding of this gift and how it can be used to make the world a better place."

"By kidnapping, threatening, and killing people? Ends justifying means. Really?"

He looked intently at me. "Maybe a better way is something I can learn from you. Even as I teach you how to avoid all the destruction and sorrow you leave in your wake."

I stared.

A gratuitous hit. Rubbing it in.

That was a mistake.

It showed that when he'd seen my guilty horror at the idea of multiple, coexistent timelines, he hadn't jumped on it to help me, but to use s leverage. And if there was one form of evil I despised the most, it was people shoveling lies and pain while they pretended it was truth and goodness.

Even if the offer of teaching me how to jump without leaving pain everywhere was...

I was saved from going down that rabbit hole by the buzzing of Bent's phone. He answered it, listened, and said a quiet, "Thank you." He ended the call and looked at me. "That went faster than I thought. Your sister has been delivered and her new hosts have said she'll have immediate access to a secure room and computer. Shall I help you log into Senator Jonquist's computer on this end?"

Ten minutes later, with Bent considerately out of Jonquist's office and the door closed—it was painfully obvious how Bent was bending over backward to win my trust—I actually connected once again with Kansas as her face appeared on Jonquist's computer screen, my own in a small box at the bottom right so I could see what she saw.

And only because I knew Kansas could see my face did I keep myself from crying and gnashing my teeth. Kansas looked ten years older than herself on a bad day. Her square, bony face looked drawn and gaunt, like she hadn't been eating. Deep, dark circles ringed her eyes like she'd been punched, though I suspected it was from lack of sleep. Where her skin wasn't pulled tight, it sagged loose, gray and coarse. Like her hair, which fell around her face in tangled, lifeless clumps.

She smiled when she saw me, but her tight dry lips cracked and the yellow teeth below them made the smile a rictus of death.

"Jaggie," she croaked. She cleared her throat and tried again. "Jackie. It's good to see you. You got me out."

I had to swallow a few times before I could answer without my voice cracking. "Are you somewhere safe?"

Kansas hesitated. "I think so. I know these people. But Dr. Bent..." She blinked for a moment and I almost imagined her eyes grew moist. "He can make people do things you'd never had thought they'd do. And the people who dropped me here obviously knew the protocols of my NSA section. They knew the people who took me in."

I nodded. "He's trying to get me to come with him willingly. Says he can teach me how to jump without all the trauma. Maybe even with all the drama." I gave a stupid little smile.

I dropped it at Kansas' horrified expression. "No! Jackie, I'm not a psychologist or a priest, but I know evil when I see it. And he's it. Whatever he wants from you, don't give it to him. Don't trust him. Don't let him twist your mind and pretend to know you and what's good for you."

"Okay, I guess..."

"There's no guessing here! This man will mess you up!" She was up from her computer chair now and I had the feeling she didn't even know it. The room revealed around her was a white box. Empty but for Kansas and the computer she'd been talking with me on. Her eyes had gone were wide and fluttering. Her hands waved about and tore at her hair and skin. "He is the *Götterdämmerung!* You know what that is? Ragnarök! The final battle. Don't believe him! Don't go with him! You don't know what he's capable of! You don't KNOW!"

The last word was a screech, and it became clear that her supposedly "secure" room wasn't, because a couple of men burst in through its door and grabbed Kansas by both arms while a third appeared to inject her with a sedative. Ketamine maybe.

After another few moments of struggle, Kansas calmed, then slumped, and the two men who held her by the arms dragged her from the room.

The man who'd injected her stepped close to the computer, saw my face on it, and attempted a reassuring smile that was obviously above his pay grade. "We'll take care of her," he said, shaking his head even as he said it.

And the screen went blank.

Oh shit.

Then the door of Jonquist's office opened behind me.

38

Nothing matters, right?

IT WASN'T EVEN BENT coming back for me but the ketamine twins. They looked ready to repeat their greatest hits as the sweet-faced young woman approached me from one side of the desk and her big-boned partner came at me from the other.

Shit. Shit. Shit.

I scrabbled backwards out of Jonquist's office chair, holding my hands up on either side so they couldn't just sneak a needle in. They were going to have to work for it.

Which turned out to be way too easy. Alvin had covered multiple attackers with me once or twice, but had basically told me that if they knew what they were doing, I was screwed.

I decided Big Bones was the primary threat, so I threw a solid sidekick at him.

He blocked it, but the kicker was that Sweet Face leaped in to grab my head as I kicked, and I felt her stab a needle into my neck.

"Fuck!" I shouted at her as I stumbled and fell, pulling her down with me and with the needle still stuck in deep, burning.

Maybe not ketamine. Maybe they were trying to kill me.

Made no sense.

Bent wanted me.

Needed me.

Yeah? Then why...?

A ham-sized fist slammed across my face as Big Bone saw a chance to get his.

Then my head started to swim. Whatever was in that needle was hitting my brain, the one thing, the only thing, that was *me.* They were drugging *me.* Taking control from *me.* Killing *me.*

Get out of my head, out of my head, get out of my heaaaaaad!

A man...who?...Bent...right...was stroking a glass figurine of two entwined lovers. Could've been me and Lena.

Where...?

I blinked. Jonquist's office. Got it. Okay.

Bent spoke. "You know the only thing I want from you is you, right?"

I wanted to say, *Of course I know that you, disgusting, lying stain on my profession.* But instead, I said. "We've got at least five or ten minutes before I can call my sister?"

Bent looked at me in surprise. "Yes."

"I really need to step outside this room for a minute. I'm sorry. Maybe it's the relief over my sister, or my anxiety. But...the lack of windows. I need some more air. Just whatever's in the hall. Some space."

Bent examined me with concern. "If you're sure. I'll come out and walk with you."

"No! Just a minute. You left those other two out there to guard the door, right? I won't be going far. Just a walk down the hall and back. Please. I'm just..." And my hands were actually shaking. My forehead had broken out in a cold sweat. It was a classic old-fashioned PTSD reaction, an honest one. But it wasn't to the remembered violence of my childhood anymore. It was to the violence that had just been wreaked on me a moment ago, my time. And the violence I suspected was waiting for me just outside the doors now.

And the hopelessness of it all. Of me thinking I could negotiate even Kansas' freedom. Or somehow my own limited autonomy.

I felt like I was going to vomit.

"Please..."

It sounded so pathetic even to my ears that I completely understood Bent's look of disgust as he pointed to the door.

I stumbled to it and opened it. Bent followed me to stand close enough I could feel his breath as he spoke in my ear. "Just down to the end of the tunnel and back." To the ketamine twins who were looking at us both in surprise, he said, "You two, walk with him and make sure he doesn't hurt himself."

They nodded and Bent stepped backward, closing the door behind him with a sigh of air like an exhalation of a crypt door closing.

The ketamine twins watched me with nonplussed amusement as I started stumbling like some half-sentient zombie down the nondescript hallway, towards a T-junction.

Except I remembered exactly which way this hallway went and could put it together in my mind with all the other hallways I'd explored, usually at a run or fast walk as I tried to escape this building. It wasn't that I had an amazing sense of space or had constructed a map in my head, but when I saw a turn or a recognizable door or structure of pipes, I remembered where I'd gone to get there, where I'd have to go to get to an exit route.

And more than that, in the midst of all the pain and anxiety, I had finally had an idea of how to escape this endless loop of escape and capture in the Capitol.

I let myself revel in the trick of looking so pathetic that I'd managed to put about ten feet between me and my minders. They'd hung back, waiting for me to reach the T-junction and turn around.

Instead, I sprinted down the right arm of the tee at an all-out run.

This was when all speed and stamina I'd developed with Lead the Way kicked in.

The ketamine twins had no chance.

I was at the main eastern entrance to the Senate wing of the Capitol, walking slowly now, slouched down and looking around like the dozens of tourists and staffers who were coming down the steps with me, acting as my visual shield, letting me blend in.

I consciously attached myself to a group of six young staffers in dark suits like mine, wearing masks like the black one I'd pulled out of my pocket and fastened around my mouth and nose. They were laughing and talking together as they approached a line of parked cars and I leaned left into the guy beside me like I was part of their group.

I was almost there. Further than I'd gotten at any other time than the Reflecting Pool Escape, and much closer to commercial stores, taxis, police.

A much scruffier young man bumped me from my right and I caught his eyes in my peripherals, feeling my heart sink. It was Xiaobo, of course. I jumped to one side, but he leapt after me, grabbing my arm with a, "We need to talk!"

The timeline didn't end.

Instead, he dragged me forcefully with him south out of the group of staffers and across the wide walkway toward the south end of the Capitol Grounds.

"What are you—?"

"Just walk, yo. We're going for a ride. Just you and me, yah?"

Yes!

The next thing I knew, I was in the passenger seat of a pinkish Porsche with "Taycan" written on the back of it, freaking awesome leather bucket seats that smelled new, and two high-definition video screens stacked up from the center console up the front middle dash. One had a map of the area displayed. One had a drive mode and battery... This was *electric*.

"Seatbelts on, yo."

Yo, I thought with a sudden spurt of fear and put mine on. "Before we go, can—"

My words got sucked away as Xiaobo zoomed us silently backwards through a bunch of scattering pedestrians, then forward in a curve that shot us like a soundless bullet out onto the narrow New Jersey Avenue, wheeling around the cars in our lane like they were standing still, avoiding oncoming cars by a rushing whisper of inches and blaring horns.

At the six-way crossing of New Jersey SE, North Carolina SE, and E Street E, he wheeled us in a wild, squealing, left-hand turn through the red lights and rushing cars, up on the sidewalk by a red brick building that might have been a church, and bouncing back onto the road before sideswiping a concrete lamppost and grinding along a line of parked cars, their side mirrors crunching and exploding, glass tinkling on concrete.

Then we were free again, accelerating like a bullet.

My eyes were stuck on wide. My heart was pumping like it was going to explode. My hands were clutching the leather seats on either side of my hips.

"Bill Murray Bill Murray Bill Murray," I muttered. *Groundhog Day,* driving crazy with a groundhog on his steering wheel because he knows he can't die. He'll just reset. So nothing matters, right? Was I the groundhog in this scenario? Punxsutawney Phil? Was spring coming early if I stuck my head out of this speeding death trap and saw my shadow?

"I hate my fucking sister!" Xiaobo yelled at me as he hung a hard right onto 3rd St. SE, slamming me toward him in the car.

"Okay! Okay! Me too! I got something to tell you!"

"You told me already, yo!"

"No, it's about what you can do to prove *you* have the power!"

Xiaobo punched the speed pedal even harder in response, sideswiping an oncoming car that obviously hadn't seen him coming even though every other car on this narrow two-way was peeling wide for us as we whizzed whizzed through, leaving the sound of honking, screaming, and crashing metal in our wake. And there we blew through another four-way-stop!

I had to work my tongue around to get enough saliva to talk. I couldn't feel my fingers anymore. I think they were buried in*side* the seat leather. "You text me. Early. Before I ever get to the Capitol. Throw off all their plans!"

I wanted to close my eyes as I saw a four-lane cross-road coming up way too fast that actually had traffic lights for the east-west traffic...that were green for them so the lane we rushed toward were filled with cars.

Xiaobo yelled a curse in Chinese and actually applied the brakes, not to stop, but to time his entry then shot across the first two westbound lanes and whipped up hard left, just past, I saw, a raised concrete divider between the two sets of traffic lanes and, on the right, a line of thick metal stanchions that blocked off 3rd at that point.

Had Xiaobo seen both of those? Was he just lucky? A crazy good driver?

Didn't have time to think hard about that as he wheeled around a timed driver, clipping that car's front grill and pulled up hard right again, throwing me toward him.

I took the opportunity to shout my cell phone number in his ear a few times, along with a pneumonic, hoping against hope that he wasn't so far gone in his mania that he couldn't hear me.

Then we were whipping down what had to be 4th, past old red brick buildings and shiny new condos and commercial storefronts, lots of people screaming and more cars crashing, us bouncing a bit when there just wasn't room to get through the madhouse cleanly.

Aaaand...water ahead. Heading for the Potomac? No. I scanned the map in my head and saw we were going to die in the Anacostia.

Xiaobo shot us past a winery to our right and parking lot to our left, across a curb and concreted and grass and fountain strips and wooden boardwalk into another set of stanchions guarding its outside edge.

The stanchions bent and snapped as we hit them, even as they crumpled and yanked down the Taycan's front bumper and hood, and exploded the lights, so that the rear end of the car's inertia was redirected upward. The Taycan, with us inside, flipped and spun like an Olympic dive on coke into the icy gray waters.

Bam! against the waves. Sinking.

If I hadn't been caught by my seatbelt, if I'd hit my head, I think I'd have jumped right then. But instead, part of me had half jumped out of my body in another way, imagining our crash and flight from the outside like the impossible thing it was.

I completely came back into the submerged car now and studied Xiaobo. In the interior lights that had switched on by themselves, I saw his face had taken on a kind of awed wonder over what he'd done. Had he really intended this? Was he truly suicidal? If so, all he had to do was keep himself from jumping back in time and it would all be over.

I didn't think that was going to happen, though, so I repeated my burner phone number and its pneumonic out loud again, staring at Xiaobo until he acknowledged me.

"You text me," I said. "Early." I repeated the number again.

Xiaobo just grinned and tried to lay his head back against the headrest, but we were almost upside down and he couldn't. He started laughing.

The car jolted like it had hit something. The bottom? That soon?

The angle shifted until I realized we hadn't been upside down so much as descending with the car's front down past 180 degrees. With the front now mired in the river's muck, the rear of the Taycan was pushing past our backsides, searching for the bottom.

The entire interior shifted with another jolt as the rolling weight pried the front from the muck and left us finally completely upside down, hanging from our straps. I tried to undo them. Couldn't. I also finally registered that my legs felt strange and wet and saw they were buried in twisted metal. Couldn't draw them out.

"Shit."

I struggle with my door and window. Couldn't make either of them move.

Still...

"We gotta be only what? Twenty feet dow—"

There was a loud pop as the driver's side window, which must have cracked when we first flipped, suddenly imploded in an explosion of small safety-glass balls that splashed against my face as the water rushed in.

Cold.

Yeah. The interior was going to fill in under a minute. We were going to drown if we couldn't get free.

Xiaobo's hanging face was red with the blood rushing into it, his cheeks all distorted. But he had his eyes closed. He was no help.

Would there be a rescue? How long would it take? If I let myself suffocate, could they revive me? How could I even do that?

I started to panic.

Dissociate! I yelled inside myself. *Let go. Let go of this body or die.*

And...

39

The early bird

I CAME OUT OF the shower first and grabbed two towels. I handed one to Wenling.

After a quick swipe or two to my head and body, I leaned my naked butt back against the edge of the sink so I could watch Wenling dry herself. Just because it might be the last time.

She stopped and let the towel hang at her side, framing, not hiding her nudity. "Does this relax you?"

I looked down at my mini-me that I thought had been pretty well exercised. He was starting to bob. "Apparently not."

Wenling gave a slow, satisfied smile. "Good. Then maybe it gives you something to look forward to. After our negotiations."

So saying, she finished toweling off, dropped the towel to the floor, and walked from the bathroom ahead of me with such obvious awareness of her effect on me that I was tempted to run after her, jump her, and insist on a second session on the massive bed the George had provided for us in this Presidential Suite.

But even as I thought it, I remembered the entire reason I'd let Wenling seduce me in the shower was because of how much I'd been missing Lena and aching over the loss of her love. It almost immediately doused my physical desire for Wenling and I finished toweling off and went to get dressed. Sober now.

I only had on my underwear and dress pants when my burner phone dinged at me from the pocket of my blue jeans that I'd carried out of the bathroom and dumped near the bed.

"What's that?" Wenling called from where she was doing her makeup at the large, gold-framed mirror in the living room part of the suite.

"No idea," I called back. But even as I said it, I started feeling the wrongness of the situation. Of the phone dinging. Of Wenling calling to me and me answering back. That felt…off.

Frowning, I dug the phone out of my jeans and saw I had a text message from a phone number I'd never seen before.

One word.

Yo.

Suddenly it was the safety glass of the driver's window bursting into a thousand little beads and washing over me. The wild ride with Xiaobo. The escape from the Senate building. All the escapes. All the different timelines and everything that had happened in them. Everything I'd learned. It was like they'd always been there inside me. It only took a few seconds to get them all lined up in order in my head.

I'd run four timelines in the US Capitol.

This was timeline five.

What now, punk?

"Jackson?" I heard the note of worry in Wenling's voice, though it obviously wasn't enough yet to have her abandon her physical preparations to check on me. "I didn't think you could do very much with that phone."

I quickly erased the text, amazed that Xiaobo had actually sent it. Amazed he'd followed through.

"I don't know," I said. "Maybe I accidentally pressed a timer function earlier. Are you almost ready?"

"Fifteen minutes."

"Okay."

I slipped the phone into my pocket, quickly pulled on my shirt, grabbed my tie, and ran into the bathroom, shutting the door behind me and locking it.

Before I could rethink and start to doubt the plan that had come to me during my last shambling escape from the ketamine twins in the basement of the Capitol, I pulled out my burner phone and dialed Jude.

He answered on the first ring. "Where are you?"

I spoke quietly. "Right now? The George hotel. It's a couple blocks from the Capitol, where we're going to be going soon. Where are you?"

"Just left Langley. Figured I'd drive around the Capitol area and see if I can find a place to park for a couple hours."

"Don't. I have something else I need you to do instead."

"What?"

"I need you to contact Andre Poussaint. You can find him through Amit Dadashev or Robert Wilson, the two guys who I talked to in Human Resources and Acquisition at Langley."

"Wait. Wait. You want—"

"Tell them that in about forty-five minutes to an hour, I'm going to be in a meeting in a SCIF in the basement of the Capitol with Senator Antoine Jonquist of Wyoming, billionaire Zhou Wenling, and Dr. Uwe Bent, current leader of the organization called SCATTER. It is no longer part of the CIA, as you said, but it is very much alive, active. They have Zhou Wenling's brother working for them, my brother and sister, and they're currently trying to recruit me, voluntarily or not."

"You? Why?"

I couldn't take the hurt wheedling in his tone. Like he suspected, but didn't want to say. Like he was hurt I couldn't confide in him after all we'd been through together and all he'd done for me. *Was* doing for me today, with this. "Because they think I can time travel like Kenny."

"Can you?"

I looked up at the ceiling. Down at the floor. The last person I'd willingly shared my secret with had abandoned me over it. The others who knew wanted to exploit me for it. But this was Jude. Jude who'd talked me through panic attacks and been my first and only true friend at university. My truest friend still.

"I can," I said. "But maybe don't mention that to Poussaint, okay? I need him wanting to lock up Bent, not me, too."

I heard a snuffling sound on the other side of the phone. Like maybe the always emotionally balanced Jude Spiegelman was overcome. When he spoke, I could hear it in his voice. "Thank you," he said quietly. "I'll get them."

"No, thank *you*. Last thing? Tell them to bring a lot of firepower. Bent has at least four trained violent operatives in the Capitol basement, but I think maybe a lot more scattered throughout the building to keep watch."

I hung up, stowed my phone, and started tying my tie, sure that at any moment Wenling was going to storm into the bathroom to ask why I wasn't ready.

When I'd finished with the tie, I walked quickly to the bathroom door and put my ear to it. I heard the murmurs of Wenling speaking quietly on the phone, then swearing angrily, then making a sound like she was changing her clothing. Good. I ran back to finish combing my hair and pulling on my socks and shoes. I was just finishing lacing my second shoe when Wenling did finally storm into the bathroom.

She wore a different outfit than she'd worn in all our previous timelines. This was a pantsuit, charcoal gray and nappy, the blouse a thicker cream material, the matching pumps shorter-heeled. She stomped one of those. "Why are you not ready? We have to go."

"Almost there."

I pulled on my second shoe and tied it, donned my expensive suit jacket, and followed Wenling out of the hotel room. I looked at the clock and wondered why Colonel Jian hadn't yet showed up to give us Kenny's warning about my being abducted downstairs.

The reason came to me. In this timeline that Xiaobo had sent me back to, the abduction had never happened because I knew about it from previous timelines and so just avoided it without needing Kenny. Like I was about to do now.

I touched Wenling's arm as she started for the elevator. "No. There are two men downstairs waiting to abduct me. In an earlier timeline, they abduct me, take me to what I assume is a SCATTER operating base, where Kenny sees me and comes back in time to tell Colonel Jian to warn me."

She frowned, working through it, and nodded. "What do we do?"

"Call Colonel Jian to bring the limo to the back of the building just to be safe. We'll go down the stairs and leave out the back. Then call your SCATTER contact and warn him we'll walk if he can't guarantee a safe meeting and negotiation."

I didn't mention the guns and ammunition the colonel and I had loaded up on before leaving last time. They hadn't been needed before, and they'd just become one more messy thing to clean up if, no, *when* I finally made it out of the Capitol.

Wenling connected with Bent on the phone. Her speech to him wasn't exactly the same, but every bit as powerful as the last time I'd heard it. When she was done, we left by the stairs, met Colonel Jian with the limo out behind the George, and drove to the Dirkson without incident.

Beautiful day. The sun was out.

Breathe.

As we entered the Dirkson, I found myself silently praying that Jude was also on the ball and persuasive, because my stomach had already started to churn in anticipation. It was as if I could feel the weight and trauma of each of my previous timelines waiting like an ugly, overpowering mugger at the end of the Dirkson subway ride.

My plan hinged on reading Poussaint's role right. Putting it all together, I figured he'd been brought back into the CIA to search out and extinguish the last traces of SCATTER. The CIA somehow knew it still existed, but hadn't been able to track down its members and stop its operation. So they'd brought in a legendary spy whose experience was ferreting out rogue operatives. He'd thought I was somehow connected to SCATTER when they'd brought me in for my memory abilities and he'd been willing to waterboard me if that had been what it took to find out how I knew about the operation.

And If I could give him Dr. Bent now, maybe he could shut SCATTER down. Which meant I could get Kenny and Kansas back, get myself out of this repeating time trap Bent had caught me in, and not have to keep looking over my shoulder for the rest of my life.

If Poussaint did *not* turn up with the cavalry, I was just going to collapse from the sheer emotional weight of what had come before, regardless of what was going to happen this time.

Knowledge might be powerful, but it was goddamn heavy and frightening, too.

Getting out of the subway inside the Capitol basement, the ghost land of seeing multiple versions of reality became more intense. I was walking through the subway platform, running through it, hiding and getting drugged in it...

I spotted the ketamine twins tailing us as Jonquist led us to the SCIF, and I imagined other SCATTER operatives watching us from every doorway. Did they, too, wonder why Wenling had changed to heavier charcoal clothing?

We entered the SCIF, but before I felt the familiar air compression as the door closed behind Colonel Jian, bringing up the rear, the ketamine twins slipped in through the door and took up standing positions on either side of me. The sweet-faced young woman gave me a smile so engaging I could almost feel Wenling fume from where she stood watching us from three feet away.

Ironic, given how she was mentally preparing to barter me away in return for her brother.

The SCIF door closed and locked and my brain shot belatedly to not having told Jude which SCIF we were in. I could have given him directions. All he had was Jonquist's name. What if the SCIF was somehow booked in someone else's name? How many SCIFs were there in the Capitol? How long would it take Poussaint to convince the Capitol Police to let him enter with his weapons and people? How long before they could find this SCIF? How were they going to break in through what seemed like a very thick door if the guard outside refused to help them?

Mind whirring, I finally let myself finally go beyond the ketamine twins to look at the three people in the room who had stood up on the left side of the long table at our arrival—Things One and Two, and the champagne-fluted face of Dr. Uwe Bent.

Bent's small mouth and sparkling blue eyes looked no different than he had the last time. No extra knowledge that might have come from Xiaobo telling him about the early text in this timeline. The early 'wake up.'

As Wenling stepped forward to take charge of the negotiations, though, Bent ignored her and nodded to me. "Dr. Traine."

"Uwe." I refused to give respect to a man who'd abducted twelve people for the 'crime' of being gifted with the ability to time travel.

Not to mention his willingness to have me abducted, assaulted, drugged, lectured, and forcibly jumped back in time over and over again. He deserved whatever Poussaint did to him.

Wenling's eyes shot back and forth between us. "We have done this before."

Bent inclined his head. "Three times."

I nodded, even though my twisted-up insides released the tiniest bit. Either Xiaobo himself had lost count, or he'd deliberately left out our last adventure, which had been Timeline Four. Did that help me? I wasn't sure. But it was...something.

My clear play here, now that I admitted to what Bent already knew, was to keep quiet about everything else. Because no one but me knew the substance of what had happened in this room or in Jonquist's hideaway office. I hadn't told Xiaobo, so he couldn't have passed it on. And I think only Wenling, at this point, had any inkling how my getting dragged back in time by Xiaobo actually worked in terms of when I remembered things.

Maybe Bent had discovered the mechanism in experiments with his other subjects. He'd certainly tried to persuade me he knew much more about time travel than I did.

But did he really?

He himself had admitted the only people he'd run across with the extraordinary Traine memory were the Traines. Kenny, Kansas, and me. And Kenny was unreliable.

Know what you want.

Save my siblings. Take down SCATTER.

Know what you are able to do.

Still learning, but 1) I now know stuff about time travel that Bent doesn't; 2) I remember more about what's gone on, what's actually been said and shared and threatened and done, than anyone else in this room right now; and 3) I have actual friends who are going to bring the hell of the CIA down on your head, Bent.

Know what you are willing to do.

Almost anything, as long as I can stay sane, and keep my soul together...

I met Bent's gaze and realized he'd been watching me. I think everyone in the room had been watching me space out for a moment there. Bent was smiling. That couldn't be good.

He nodded. "The fact you're not verbally or physically attacking me or anyone else right now means you're hiding something."

"Does it?"

"Everyone has their tells, Dr. Traine. Xiaobo, for instance, gets extra belligerent with me when he's lying. Is this only the fourth time we've gone through this, for example, or the sixteenth?"

He waited. I tried to keep my face blank.

Finally, he waved his hand and walked around the table to get closer to me. He sat back against the edge of it. "Regardless, I assume I've given you the spiel about how, despite your ability to jump back in time, I can forcibly abduct you and make you join me in our work at SCATTER, though I'd much prefer..."

He launched into the spiel he assumed I'd heard before and he was right. I had. There were a few twists in it having to do with some of the other time travelers who'd join them involuntarily and become enthusiastic participants.

Blah blah.

I let a part of my memory store his words for analysis later while I looked around the room, trying to figure out why it felt different from my previous times here. Was it just me riding a knife edge of tension, waiting for Poussaint and his troops to arrive? Or was it the spring-loaded way Thing One and Thing Two's watched me?

Or the fact Bent had brought the ketamine twins into the SCIF this time and positioned them on either side of me? Why had he done that? He couldn't have known how effective they'd been the last time. He couldn't remember the other timelines. The only person who could was Xiaobo, who was never in the Capitol itself, so...

Unless Thing One or Two were...

I looked at them closely, first catching the gaze of the South Asian female, who'd subtly worked herself around the table to stand within an arm's length of Wenling, then the gaze of her white male partner, who'd moved to get closer to Colonel Jian. Neither of the two showed any indication of ghost vision or memories of how things had happened here before.

They could just be good actors, of course, except that everything I'd so far learned of time traveling from myself, my brother, and Xiaobo indicated it pushed the time traveler toward mental instability. Whether it was the trauma that triggered the ability as it did with me, or the identity crises inherent in jumping between different versions of yourself, I was pretty sure I'd catch indications of it in any time traveler I met.

These two didn't have it, any more than the ketamine twins, Bent, Jonquist, Colonel Jian, or Wenling.

So why...?

"Which of course all went to..." Bent let his voice trail off as he looked at his watch and smiled at me. He pushed off the table edge and walked back around to stand at the end, lord of his domain.

"We're well past ten minutes. You jump back to redo the timeline now and Natalya or Pasha will jab some ketamine into you. They're familiar with the indicators of a jump and I've found the surprise of a needle, along with the quick action of the ketamine, makes multiple jumps very difficult."

All blood drained in a cold rush from my head, neck, and torso like cold water rushing down. He was wrong on this point with regards to me, as I'd demonstrated two timelines ago, but that wasn't what chilled me. It was him knowing about my ten-minute limit. And about me doing multiple jumps. Was that common among his other subjects or had he somehow found out from...Wenling? Lena?

More interesting was his wording. "Redo" the timeline. Not "create a new" timeline, but "redo," like there was only one. That didn't match what he'd rubbed in my face back in Jonquist's office...

I reviewed that earlier conversation and this time saw him about to take back the suggestion that timelines continued. He'd only continued because he'd seen how it hurt me.

He didn't know! He was throwing out theories, but he didn't know!

Maybe it was because he needed to believe he was reshaping our world with his work, versus just making multiple messed up copies of it. Otherwise, he'd know that the only people who really benefited from time travel were the time travelers, who could keep creating new time streams until they found one they wanted to stick with. And that only worked if the time travelers were narcissistic, since their actions, like all of mine, left behind significantly more violence, terror, and trauma in the world than before they jumped. For their alternate selves, if no one else.

Bent laughed at me. "I can almost see your struggles with paradox written on your face. Another reason to join us. You have so much to learn from me."

"Do I?"

He tilted his head, slightly unsettled by my tone. "Ah, right. The whole reason you let yourself be brought here after somehow remembering your other timestreams early in the day. How? I'm assuming Xiaobo. Part of his lying to me this morning. Enough of that. He'll be punished."

"No!" Wenling cried out.

She tried to leap at Bent, only to find her arms suddenly pinned behind her and her legs blocked by Thing One, the South Asian woman, who was much stronger and faster than she looked. Even faster and stronger than Wenling, who struggled but finally settled, fuming, biding her time.

As she did, the scuffle between Colonel Jian, who'd tried to leap to her aid, was only now settling. On the ground, Thing Two grunted and sweated to keep the seventy-year-old former PLA officer under him. Bent waited until Thing Two had established control and hauled Colonel Jian back to his feet, the old man's face now scuffed and bloody.

Bent turned back to me.

"As I was about to tell you, Andre Poussaint and his tiny CIA hit squad will not be joining us today. Instead, we have other guests."

At that, he waved his hand and Senator Jonquist banged twice on the inside of the SCIF door. The door opened and three men in Capitol Police uniforms I assumed were fake, brandishing pistols I assumed were real, escorted a small line of people slowly into the room.

Leading them was Kansas, shuffling slowly, looking as bad as I she had when I'd managed to get her "released" in my last timeline. Her square, bony face sagged like a skeleton's, like she hadn't eaten or slept in many days. Dark circles ringed her eyes and her hair fell over them in loose, coarse clumps. But her head came up as she passed Wenling and she jerked to a halt.

"Lizbeth?" she croaked, her tongue cracked and dry.

Wenling looked at her and gave a fleeting smile. "Shades of girlfriends past."

Kansas' mouth sagged open, and she looked around the room. Saw me. Saw Bent. Saw all the strong-arming going on. I could almost see things snap together in her amazing brain, starved and sleep denied or not. Even as I finally put together Kansas' always-unspoken sexual preference and the year she found what she'd thought was love then lost it, only to now realize what it might have been instead—just a way for 'Lizbeth, AKA Wenling, to get information that might lead her to SCATTER.

Kansas nodded at Wenling and tried to gather enough moisture to spit in her face, but finally just shook her head and let herself get shoved onward by the uniformed goon.

Following her, scampering erratically, looking around the room in terror, came my office manager, Megan, of all people.

Then, terribly, Lena entered, looking stricken and tearful.

And finally, his head hanging so low I couldn't see his eyes, trudged Jude.

These were pretty much all the people I cared about most in the world, other than Kenny.

The SCIF door slammed closed. I heard the snicking of locks.

Thing One muscled Wenling past the newcomers and marched her to stand at the far end of the table on the right-hand side. The South Asian woman stayed behind her, still holding her in what looked like a painful arm lock.

The "Capitol Officers" then guided Kansas and the others in to line up beside Wenling along the right side of the table. Except for Jude, who hung back.

Before I could say anything, the ketamine twins, Natalya and Pasha, shoved me to stand in the middle of the left side of the table, facing the women across from me.

Megan looked at me, wide-eyed. "J-Jackson? What's going on? They came to get me a day after we spoke and said you needed me in Washington. You'd paid for the ticket. Everything. Then they locked me in a room...and..."

"It'll be alright," I said. "Just hang in there." I tried to sound calm and reassuring, but my head was buzzing with fight-or-flight adrenaline and questions yelling so loudly that I could hardly look at these people in front of me. These pieces of my heart.

And Jude...?

Bent had spun his backside off the table and was now leaning forward onto it, supported by his splayed fingers in a kind of aggressive version of finger steepling that screamed, *I am in control here.*

His focus was all on me.

"These women were all backups, you understand? The original plan was one of simple persuasion, showing you how joining SCATTER would fill your intellectual thirst to understand your condition, your moral desire to make the world a better place, and your emotional need to have someone teach you how to better manage your power and life."

"You did a crap job," I said.

Bent nodded his head. "Perhaps. Yes. The Senator, the surroundings, the bully tactics. Poor choices in retrospect."

"You think?"

"Though, to be fair, we didn't yet know who, exactly, we were dealing with. We'd only just started accessing your computer records and didn't wholly believe all the wonderful things your friend Dr. Spiegelman told us about you."

"Jude?" It almost stuck in my throat as another set of puzzle pieces started to fall together for me. I looked over at where he stood against a far wall, his head still down, unable to look at me. His pudgy arms, that had held and steadied me through so many emotional rollercoasters in university and beyond, crossed over each other on his soft chest like he could somehow hold in what he'd done.

Bent cleared his throat to draw my attention back to himself. "For me, of course, this is our first meeting. I was disinclined to credit you with the kind of brilliance and determination that Dr. Spiegelman warned me you possessed. I assumed those were of the academic kind, and that your escape from the Demon Monks was mostly due to luck and the assistance of your brother.

"But then you called your university *buddy* almost an hour before you were to come here and I realized that in the same way you managed to charm the pants of two of the smartest women I've ever met, Dr. Lena Cortland and Ms. Zhou Wenling, you might well have charmed Xiaobo to betray me, to somehow contact you when there was no need.

"Hence, we proceeded with plan B. Bring these women here, including your cute little puppy of an office drone. Now we're ready to seriously ask you to join us of your own free will. Fun, yes?"

"Fun how?"

"It's a game. I'm going to ask you again to join the SCATTER team voluntarily, with no reservations, and every time you say no, I will shoot one of them."

As he reached into a rear waist holster to bring up what looked like Glock, Jude's head finally shot up. "That wasn't the plan! You can't! There's no greater good in—"

Bent aimed his gun straight at Jude's head and Jude shut up.

Fighting both an urge to trigger a series of jumpbacks that could reset this nightmare and an urge to leap across the corner of the table to grab Bent by his long, scrawny neck, I asked "How did you get Lena here?"

Bent raised his eyebrows. "You mean did we abduct her like we did your brother and sister? No. Jude just asked. Told her you needed her. Love makes people very easy to manipulate."

"Love?" I turned my face back to catch Lena looking at me, her eyes filled with tears of confirmation. Which somehow changed...everything.

"Jackson, don't!" Kansas cried out from beside Wenling. "You cannot give in to this man! You have no idea what he'd capable of! What he's planning!"

Wenling used the distraction to kick at Thing One's shins and twist herself free. Then she threw herself onto the table, rolling across the middle of it so fast she was on the floor to my left before Bent had fully processed it.

His gun came up, aiming to the right of my head, then my left, as I felt Wenling ducking right and left behind me. A second later, her hands grabbed the back of my suit jacket, shoved me forward toward Bent, and literally ran up my legs and back to throw herself at him with an ungodly screech, jacketed elbows high like two swords about to slash down on either side of Bent's neck.

He shot her while she was still going up. *BOOM! BOOM!*

Smoke from the muzzle met red puffs from the chest of her blouse.

She thumped face down on the table top.

Lay still.

40

Choices

In the silence after the bang and thump of Wenling's body, a wild commotion broke out near SCIF door.

Colonel Jian's face had contorted in grief and he was moaning and shouting in Chinese, his voice so blurred with emotion that I could hardly distinguish the individual sounds.

But rather than let the old man run to Wenling, Bent signaled Thing Two, and the big-boned man clubbed the back of Colonel Jian's head so hard the old man fell forward and lay still.

Like Wenling lay still.

Blood oozed out around her chest, dark brownish-red and viscous, making a small lake on the table top.

In the renewed silence, Bent released the clip from his Glock—*ssslick!*—examined it, and shoved it back in. *Kuh-snik!* "Get rid of the body," he snapped.

Thing One, who'd failed to restrain Wenling, now jumped onto the table, ran across it, scooped the up the bloody corpse as if it weighed nothing, and ran with it to where, having knocked again for the SCIF door to be unlocked, Jonquist held it open for her.

When she'd exited into what I assumed was now a protected hallway, given all the sights of abuse and murder it was hosting, the SCIF door closed again.

Bent called for attention. "Heyup!"

He aimed the barrel of the gun at Megan's face.

Her skin went white and she shut her eyes, her lips have open and trembling.

"So what do you say, Jackson Traine? That's one down. Will you voluntarily join SCATTER and participate in our experiments, following my directions with positive intent and an open mind? Or do we make it two?"

I stared at him. My entire body felt empty, a battered husk. I was just a consciousness floating above it, taking in the man's high forehead and blue eyes that had not a whit of human compassion within them. I knew why he'd chosen Megan first. He deemed her the furthest from the center of my heart. He figured I might need at least one more dead body to persuade me and he thought he could kill Megan to shake me up, but not push me so far as to mentally freeze of go berserk on him.

Kansas would be next. Not because I loved her less than my own life, but because I was sure Bent had heard my reaction to him saying Lena loved me. *Boom!* He figured he could blow away Kansas and I'd still do anything at all to save Lena.

God, yes!

He wasn't wrong.

But he was also totally wrong.

Because a conviction had been growing in me from the moment I'd heard Andre Poussaint was not coming. It had grown when I'd realized Bent had gone after everyone I cared about. And that Jude, my closest friend, was already corrupted by SCATTER and had betrayed me.

The conviction was simply that we didn't always get to choose what we were willing to do to obtain our deepest desires and needs. Our desires and needs set the price, and it was up to us how we answered.

Pursue your goals or give up.

Save Kenny and Kansas, Lena and Megan, all the people Bent had abused and would abuse in his experiments, the people he would kill...or don't.

What are you willing to do?

Same answer as last year. Whatever it takes. But...smarter.

Even if it takes your sanity and destroys you?

I won't let it. Because I'm realizing that maybe my memory and jumpbacks are not a curse. They let all of my previous lives from all my timeline live in me, even if they also struggle or die and entangle each other. They're part of my ocean, and I can see a place out there where I rescue my loved ones, put SCATTER down, and survive!

"I'm going to count down from five, Jackson."

Such a precise, almost bored voice. But he was enjoying this, too, I thought. A little taste of sadistic pleasure. It was no coincidence he'd chosen all women to use as collateral in this war of wills.

"Five...

"Four...

"Three..."

"I'm in," I said.

Bent didn't lower his arm. "With a full commitment and an open mind?"

"Yes."

The arm came down, and I again saw the brief hesitation. Like he saw something inside me he couldn't quite interpret.

He nevertheless turned to all his henchmen and woman in the room. "Take the women outside. Kansas Traine to base. The other two to quarantine. Jude, go find some cleaning supplies for the table. Jackson, you'll be coming with me personally."

I held up a hand. "No!"

Bent cocked his head at me. "Backtracking already?"

I ignored him for a moment as I sent reassuring glances to Kansas' tortured eyes, then to Megan, and finally to Lena, who nodded to me in a way that said...everything.

"Dr. Traine!"

I turned back to Bent. "You want me, you got me, Uwe. But not if you play mad doctor with these women. I know you want Lena to continue her work in her laboratory. I know you care nothing at all about Megan. And I know from a different timeline that you've already tested Kansas and found she has no time travel power, nor will she help you in any other way. So let her go. Let them all go. Then leave them all alone. I'll find out if you don't."

Bent stared. He raised his hands in front of him and wiggled his fingers like a magician. "Woo woo. Magic man."

I simply stared back, seeing more of him than I suspected he'd ever seen of himself.

Bent smiled. Shook his head. Laughed. "You're a tough little nut for someone who, I'm told, could hardly say two words in front of a class of students a year ago."

At this point, I expected my eyes to finally start watering as my social anxiety kicked in, my reflexive fear of being judged, my paranoia, my nightmares brought on by trauma and, more recently, time dysphoria.

But my eyes stayed dry because I *saw* Uwe Bent and what he wanted to do with me. How much he needed me, just as Zhou Wenling had needed me. Less than they said they did. More than they understood.

And they stayed dry because I knew I was going to survive my time with SCATTER even if it meant going as crazy as Kenny and making *that* part of my ocean. I think I owed my big brother that much. Just as I owed these women.

Bent finally tightened his mouth and nodded. "Alright. They're free to go now. Natalya and Pasha,"—he pointed to the ketamine twins—"you will escort these ladies, along with Dr. Spiegelman and Senator Jonquist, back to the senator's office in the Dirkson building. There the good senator will arrange for their swift, generously funded return to their different homes."

As the Ketamine twins rounded everyone up like cattle, Lena tried to step toward me.

Bent held up a hand before the ketamine twin I gathered was named Natalya, could physically strike her. "Ladies, I assume you all understand that speaking about SCATTER or myself or any part of this affair will revoke your immunity from our attention. *We* will know. No magic required."

I smiled at Kansas, Megan, and Lena one last time.

They were driven from the SCIF.

Bent turned to me and smiled like he'd just had the best bowel movement of his life. "This," he said, relishing each word, "is going to be so much fun."

Epilogue

In a final attempt to appear in control, Bent led me from the SCIF without looking back.

I lingered, grinning coldly at his departing back, not moving. Finally, Thing Two, the South Asian female who was the last person in the SCIF with me, shoved me so hard with her metal truncheon that I stumbled and tripped forward. My forehead smacked down on the table where Wenling had died, and Thing Two shoved me with her boot so my face slid through the still-congealing pool of my former partner's blood.

I pushed myself to my feet and staggered around to face Thing Two, but her truncheon was still out, and my plan wasn't to fight. Not now. Not yet. Not with at least three pieces of my heart on their ways home. Maybe even four if I looked forward to a spot in the ocean where I forgave Jude.

"Move it," the lady thug growled.

I started out after Bent, wiping Wenling's gore from my cheeks, eyes, and mouth. Unconsciously, I licked away the blood that smeared my lips.

I caught myself, expecting to gag.

Instead, I frowned in surprise and walked faster.

Wenling's "blood" tasted like corn syrup.

Afterword

Hi, Terry Hayman here.

Thanks so much for reading *Scatter*, book #2 of Jackson Traine's story. Jackson and a growing cast of characters are going to finish this story arc with book #3, *Fuse,* , and I hope you'll come along for that ride.

In the meantime, if you enjoyed *Scatter*, please leave a review and tell me what you thought. You can scan the QR code below to find a link that will take you to where you bought it. Your review has the power to influence so many other people to read this book. It's the stuff of life for indie authors like me and will be greatly appreciated.

Stay well. Stay happy. I look forward to sharing more of Jackson's story with you soon.

Also by Terry Hayman

Novels
Jumpback
Chasing the Minotaur
Jessica Falls
Shelter
Bone Dance

Short Story Collections
Being Human: 5 heartfelt tales of fantasy and science fiction set on earth
Off-World: 5 tales of adventure set on other planets
Dark Paths: 5 short stories exploring the darker sides of human nature
Life Knots: 5 stories of ordinary people fighting their destinies
Messed Up: 5 stories of crime and consequences
Used by Magic: 5 stories of people caught up by powers unseen
Shorties: A collection of sublimely quick story punches to the head, heart, and gut
Vamp: 5 stories of bloodsuckers, romantic and otherwise

About the Author

Terry Hayman, former lawyer and son of a beloved psychologist, is the author of many novels and over a hundred short stories under various names. You can learn more about his work and subscribe to his newsletter at www.terryhayman.com.

Next up – Fuse

Jackson Traine: Book Three

FUSE WILL CONCLUDE THE opening trilogy of Jackson Traine's adventures in a powerful way that will once again change everything we thought we knew about time travel.

Stay tuned!

PS. For regular updates, some free stories, and the chance to win great giveaways, sign up for Terry's newsletter at www.terryhayman.com.